D1392572

Books by Gary Meehan

TRUE FIRE

TRUE DARK

TRUE POWER

GARY MEEHAN

Quercus

First published in Great Britain in 2015 by

Quercus Publishing Ltd
Carmelite House
50 Victoria Embankment
London EC4Y 0DZ

An Hachette UK company

Copyright © 2015 Gary Meehan

The moral right of Gary Meehan to be identified as the author of this
work has been asserted in accordance with the Copyright, Designs and
Patents Act, 1988.

All rights reserved. No part of this publication may be reproduced or
transmitted in any form or by any means, electronic or mechanical,
including photocopy, recording, or any information storage and retrieval
system, without permission in writing from the publisher.

A CIP catalogue record for this book is available from the British Library

PB 978 1 78206 917 1
EBOOK 978 1 84866 846 1

This book is a work of fiction. Names, characters, businesses,
organizations, places and events are either the product of the author's
imagination or used fictitiously. Any resemblance to actual persons, living
or dead, events or locales is entirely coincidental.

10 9 8 7 6 5 4 3 2 1

Typeset by Nigel Hazle
Printed and bound in Great Britain by Clays Ltd, St Ives plc

For Lyndsay and Peter

one

Cate wouldn't sleep after her night-time feed and was determined no one else in the Lord Defender's mansion would either. Megan perched on the edge of the bed, watching helplessly as Synne paced with her daughter, rocking and shushing Cate in an effort to calm her. This had been going on for days. Megan had feared something was wrong, but Rekka's doctor had examined Cate and proclaimed her fit and well. Just noisy.

There was a muffled *harrumph* beside her. Afreyda emerged from under the covers and began to pull on a jerkin.

'Where're you going?' asked Megan.

'To the barracks,' said Afreyda. 'Willas has a bunk for me there. I need some sleep if I am to train tomorrow.'

'She'll drop off soon.'

'Maybe.'

Afreyda continued dressing, covering her dark, toned body with leather and furs. Megan found herself watching, but hurriedly turned away when Afreyda caught her. She concentrated instead on Cate and the increasingly exasperated Synne, but she feared her gaze was no more welcome there.

Afreyda grabbed a bag. 'Are you using this?'

The grubby sack Aldred had given them for safe keeping in Staziker. Megan shook her head. Afreyda tipped the sack up; a motley collection of shapeless shirts fell out. Afreyda kicked them under the bed and shoved a few of her own things in it.

'When will you be back?' asked Megan.

'I do not know,' said Afreyda. 'It might be best if I stay at the barracks for a while. Give you some room.'

'You don't have to.'

Afreyda nodded, gave Cate a quick peck on the forehead, then left. Megan watched the impression she'd left in the mattress slowly disappear, then turned to Synne.

'Let me take her,' she said, holding her arms out.

Synne shrank back and tightened her grip on Cate a notch. 'It's my job.'

'I know, but . . .' Megan had asked – begged – Synne, Cate's foster mother, to come with them to the Snow Cities, to nurse the baby Megan couldn't. 'It's my job too.' To comfort her child, to keep her warm and fed, to protect her from the fanatics who would set her up as a Saviour and a war lord.

'You need some rest,' continued Megan. Even in the

moonlight, she could see the bags under Synne's eyes, the disarray her heavy blonde locks were in. 'I'll walk with her a while, take her somewhere quiet.'

The appeal of sleep overruled Synne's scepticism. She slipped Cate into her mother's arms. 'She likes it when you talk to her,' she said. 'Softly. Don't hector.'

'I don't——' started Megan. Cate screwed up her face; Megan dropped her voice. 'All right, softly does it.'

Megan bid goodnight to Synne, who was already collapsing on to the bed, and padded barefoot out into the darkened corridors of the mansion, her route marked by the occasional puddle of lamplight. They had it luckier than most of the refugees they'd brought over the Kartik Mountains into Hil, who spent their nights shivering on floors begrudgingly offered, or in tents whose canvas walls blocked out only a small fraction of the howling winds. Winter was coming to the Snow Cities; each night was colder than the last. Megan feared that, despite the efforts of the refugees and the Hilites, the shelters they were constructing wouldn't be finished in time or, even if they were, the makeshift cabins wouldn't offer enough protection. And then there was the food situation to worry about.

Cate's cries brought her mind to more immediate matters. 'You want me to talk to you?' Megan said to the baby in her arms. 'What about? A story? Would you like that?' Cate fell silent for a moment and regarded her

3

mother with wide eyes, as if unsure what this strange lady was offering. 'How about the first story we all hear? About a man called Edwyn, who lived in a place called Statham, a long, long way away, a long, long time ago?'

Cate raised no objections, so Megan continued, adjusting her hold slightly to relieve the pressure on her arm. 'He was a humble man was Edwyn, or so he would have it –' Cate giggled; Megan wondered if this was a theological comment or wind – 'who lived the best life he could, always helping others, thinking not of himself, even though the rest of Werlavia thought of nothing more than fighting and greed and cruelty. One day two visitors appeared to him. They said they were messengers of God, come to save the people of Werlavia. These messengers – these Saviours – instructed Edwyn in the laws of God and told him to go forth to every corner of Werlavia and teach His people. And he did, uniting the lands of the warring counts into the Realm, with him as its king and priests to teach the Faith.

'Werlavia knew three hundred years of peace, apart from in Andaluvia, where the Sandstriders live, and the Snow Cities, but it's best not to go into that considering who's putting us up at the moment. But then some people came along who said, "We don't need the priests to understand the Faith. We can communicate with God directly." The king and the priests denounced them as witches and there was a big war. The witches were

4

defeated but the king was killed – in circumstances we've all agreed not to look at too closely – and so the priests took over the Realm.

'However forty years later the witches came back and they said they had a prophecy the Saviours would return. The priests were too cowardly to fight them and so it was left to one woman to lead us and she loved us so much she made me her daughter and you her granddaughter and . . . and . . .' Tears pricked Megan's eyes as memories flooded her mind, of that terrible day Eleanor had sacrificed herself to allow the rest of them to escape the witches. The loss had left an aching void she'd never be able to fill.

Lantern light spilled around the corner. A Hilite guard started when he saw them and reached for his weapon, but he relaxed when he recognized Megan.

'*Ti máda*,' he said, bowing his head slightly. It was one of the few phrases of Hilite Megan had picked up. *Ti máda* – my lady. Shame prickled Megan. The title was Eleanor's not hers. What had she done to deserve it, other than survive?

The guard leaned in to examine Cate. Before Megan could stop him he played a rough finger across her daughter's soft cheek. Every muscle tensed. Thoughts of flight were interrupted only by calculations whether to kick out first. Then Cate's giggles told her this was nothing more than someone delighted to see a baby.

'Sorry,' she said. The guard regarded her blankly.

Only a few Hilites could speak Stathian, which was still more than the number of the Faithful who could speak Hilite. The only one Megan knew of was Damon, and he was far away, dead or imprisoned or Saviours knew what. More shame there. Whatever had happened to him, she'd let happen.

Taking her leave, Megan continued to wander the mansion. She found herself outside the Lord Defender's study – it was somewhere to sit – but stopped as she heard voices coming from the other side of the door. A man and a woman. Fordel's considered tones and Rekka's haughty ones.

'. . . waiting's helping?' Rekka was saying.

'There's no point in moving too early,' said Fordel. 'Let their desperation ferment awhile.'

'And what if she proves uncooperative? She doesn't seem particularly enamoured with the idea.'

'We're lucky she brought a ready-made replacement with her, aren't we?'

Megan's throat tightened. They were talking about her – her and Cate. Eleanor's titles weren't the only thing she had inherited from the countess: she had also received Eleanor's claim to the throne of the Realm. It was a tenuous claim, but the priests had dealt with anyone with a stronger one. And what was Megan's would become Cate's on her death.

Too late Megan recognized the sound of footsteps

6

approaching from inside the study. She froze as the door was flung open. Fordel stood there, his face hardening. He was the city's chief bureaucrat and its effective ruler, though if you asked him he'd insist all he did was keep an eye on the kitchen staff and write the occasional letter. Despite the lateness of the hour, he seemed as fresh as ever, grey hair and beard neatly trimmed. Did he need sleep or did he just subsist entirely on paperwork?

'Yes?' he said.

Megan's brain failed her. 'I was . . . er . . . um . . .'

'Indeed.' He looked back into the room. 'You have a visitor.'

Fordel glided past. Megan tried to force her legs into a retreat but they wouldn't move.

'Hurry up,' said Rekka. 'There's a draught. We have enough of that in the great hall. I don't know what the roofers are doing. Growing new thatch from seed, I suspect.'

Obedience kicked in. Megan entered the study to find Rekka sat at the desk, copper hair spilling out on to the fur wrapped around her shoulders, skin almost as pale as the pelts. Her mother, Eleanor's aunt, had been married off to a previous Lord Defender of Hil – an act of diplomacy negated by the first war against the witches – while Rekka had wed one of his successors; Lord Defender might be an elected position, but the candidate pool was a little limited. Megan's adoption meant Rekka was now her cousin. As family members went, she was preferable to her sister, Gwyneth. Just.

'I'm sorry,' said Megan. 'I didn't mean to disturb you.'

'*You* didn't,' said Rekka, her gaze directed at Cate.

'She's a bit . . . you know what it's like.'

'Not really. That's what servants are for.' Rekka shivered and drew her fur tighter. 'Give the fire a poke, would you? It's getting cold.'

Megan was halfway across the study before she realized the implication of Rekka's words. She sighed. The Countess of Ainsworth relegated to a minion's role. In a way it felt more natural, something she knew how to cope with.

To free a hand so she could grab the poker, Megan had to swivel so she could support Cate on her hip. It seemed so easy when Synne did it, but Megan felt she was going to drop her daughter any second now. She gave the embers a quick prod, then dropped on to one of the couches that ran at right angles to the fireplace.

Rekka seemed in no rush to indulge in conversation, or share the wine she was sipping, so Megan rocked Cate and stared into the flames; when she shut her eyes and tried to block out everything but the heat, she saw their after-image on her eyelids. Fordel and Rekka's conversation replayed in her mind. Their plan to put her on the throne was crazy, and liable to get Megan laughed at or killed; only the fact the idea was so ludicrous it could never happen gave her comfort. But what would happen once Rekka and Fordel realized that? Would Megan be turfed out, forced to raise her child alone in the frozen north? She held Cate a little closer.

There was something else about the conversation: she'd been able to understand it. 'How come you and Fordel were speaking in Stathian?'

Rekka shrugged. 'We've been doing that since we were children. Keeps things private.'

'And what would you need to keep private?'

'Oh, you know, affairs of state.'

'Of state, huh?'

'What are you implying?' said Rekka, her eyes narrowing. 'That Fordel and I . . . ? I'm not exactly his type.'

'No, no,' said Megan, glad the glow of the fire hid the glow of her cheeks. 'I just meant . . .' What exactly? That they'd been plotting against her? Best not go there. 'I thought the Kalvert women were everybody's type.'

'Only if you like women.'

'Ah . . . and that's . . . and you . . . ?'

Rekka shrugged. 'There's no law against it. Well, not since we rid ourselves of the Faith all those centuries ago.'

'Why are you so down on it?' asked Megan. 'The Faith. Your own mother followed it. She even brought her own priest.' Not that he'd survived for long.

Rekka selected a book from the shelves and came over

to the fire, furs swishing in her wake. 'All those rules and laws and strictures?' She tossed the book on to the couch beside Megan. 'Does anybody obey every word written in there? Do you?'

The evidence Megan didn't had finally fallen asleep in her arms. 'We try.'

'You *try*?' said Rekka. 'If you really believed, you'd *do* because you'd be too terrified of the consequences otherwise.'

'And I suppose your devotion to your god is absolutely pure?'

'Oh, Megan, the gods care no more for our devotion than we care for that of ants.'

'Gods? Plural?'

Rekka settled opposite Megan and snuggled into her furs. The way the flames picked out her features and made her hair shimmer reminded Megan of nights huddled around a campfire with Eleanor. Her heart broke a little more.

'You think there's only one god, that he created everything by himself?' said Rekka. 'To get a world this screwed up, you need a committee. Anyone who's cast themselves on to the open seas, thrown themselves into battle, felt a baby quicken in her womb, knows how little regard the gods have for them. All they have is their will and their wits.'

'Why did the gods create us only to ignore us?'

'Why did you create Cate?'

'It was . . .'

'. . . an accident?'

'But I care for her more than anything in the world.'

'Would you still feel the same about her if you had a million children?'

Megan reached for the Book of Faith Rekka had thrown beside her. She flipped it over, hoping to find some counter-argument, only to drop it like a kettle heated too long when she saw the star-broken circle – the symbol of the witches – etched on to its cover.

'Sorry,' said Rekka, with all the sincerity of a rattlesnake. 'It's so easy to get the Book of the True mixed up with the Book of Faith. I mean, they're almost identical.'

'It's the "almost" that's important,' muttered Megan. She poked at the book. It slid across the couch and dropped to the floor. She felt a little better now she couldn't see it.

'I understand,' said Rekka. 'You have to maintain the pretence of belief if you're going to be queen. The people like piety in their leaders even if they have none themselves.'

Megan slipped her arm back around Cate. 'I *do* believe,' she said. 'And I'm not going to be queen. No one is.'

'It is best to refuse crowns, initially,' said Rekka. 'Makes you seem less power-mad.'

'If the people wanted a monarch, they had forty years to approach Eleanor or her father.'

11

'They didn't need one then. Now, with all the priests dead or skulking in Janik and the witches about to take New Statham and no one having a clue how to win this war, someone needs to step up.'

'But why me?' demanded Megan, her voice rising high enough to disturb the sleeping Cate. She rocked her back to quiescence. If only her own worries could be soothed so easily.

'Because you survived everything the witches threw against you,' said Rekka. 'Because you're the one they fear. Because it's your sister we're fighting.'

Gwyneth. Just like with Eleanor, it hurt when Megan thought about her sister, but for entirely different reasons. She wondered what would have happened if the witches had found some other twins to foist the prophecy upon, whether she and Gwyneth would still be home in Thicketford, comforting each other as tales of the faraway war made it down to their village.

'The witches don't fear me,' she mumbled.

'Oh, they do,' said Rekka. 'They're calling you "The Apostate" – do you know that? They're scared they've got it wrong, that you're the one God favours, that they're following the wrong sister.'

'You want me to be Queen of the True as well? Saviours, why don't you go the whole hog and proclaim me Diannon Empress?'

12

There was silence for a minute, broken only by the cracks and pops of burning logs, before Rekka spoke up. 'Talking of the Diannons, I was at the docks this afternoon. I saw your friend. She was speaking to Konáll.'

'Who? Why?'

'I was looking for Tóki. He'd gone missing again. Last time he ended up on a fishing boat and we didn't see him for two weeks.' Rekka considered. 'It was a very peaceful two weeks.'

'No, why was Afreyda speaking to this Konáll?' said Megan.

'Why should I know?' said Rekka, with the smirk of one who knew exactly why. 'Where did you find her anyway?'

Megan's hand drifted to the ragged tip of her ear; her thoughts to a fight long ago in Eastport. 'I stole her from my sister,' she said.

'Any idea why she's trying to get to Kil M'sta?' asked Rekka.

Kil M'sta: the Sandstrider capital, at the other end of the continent on Werlavia's southern coast. 'What? No. Why?'

'Konáll's the skipper of a ship sailing for there in a couple of days' time –' the firelight caught Rekka's eyes as she tilted her head slightly, making them gleam – 'and given the Sandstriders are allied with the witches . . .'

'You think she's trying to get back to Gwyneth?'

'And taking a prize with her,' said Rekka. 'The Saviour the witches have been searching for this past year.'

Cate.

two

Anxiety stole any chance Megan had of sleeping that night. She couldn't believe Afreyda would take Cate, but she had learned from bitter experience that people were capable of anything, that closeness was never a guarantee against betrayal. Damon had given them up to the witches; Gwyneth had given herself to them. Even Eleanor had been planning to kill Megan at one point. You could never know what someone was thinking, what desperation could drive them to.

As soon as it was light, Megan hurried to the barracks in search of Afreyda. She was already gone, up to the Kartiks for training in mountain warfare with Willas. Megan opted for the next best thing and went in search of Konáll, to see if he could confirm or add to Rekka's story. While she didn't think her adopted cousin would lie to her outright, Megan wouldn't put it past her to edit events for her own amusement.

The fishing fleet had returned overnight, bringing

with it much-needed stocks of seafood and the less-needed stench of such seafood. Megan wove around the waterfront, struggling to keep her feet on decks made slick with fish guts. She should have thought to ask Rekka what ship this Konáll captained and where it had docked. Her first few enquiries brought blank looks and she feared Konáll had already sailed for Andaluvia, that the claims of mountain training were a ruse to buy Afreyda time, until she realized none of the Hilite sailors could understand her Stathian. She resorted to over-enunciating Konáll's name in a loud voice and exaggerating a shrug. Someone took pity on her and pointed her to a sturdy merchantman moored near the Lord Defender's mansion. Megan grunted. Back where she had started.

She made her way to the ship, stepping over a phalanx of crabs that had escaped from their pot and were making a spirited, if protracted, bid for freedom. As she attempted to board, a hairy sailor popped up over the bulwark. Megan jumped back. The gangplank bounced beneath her, as if preparing to throw her off.

She stuck her arms out to regain her balance. 'I'm looking for Konáll,' she said. The sailor jabbered back in Hilite. 'I was told he's the captain of this ship. Captain? *Ko . . . náll.*'

'You no Konáll,' said the sailor.

'No, I'm loo—'

'Konáll *man.*'

'Yes.'

'You woman.'

'Can't deny it.'

'You have no . . .' The sailor mimed the missing appendage.

'For which I'm eternally grateful,' said Megan. 'Do you know where Konáll is? He was talking to my friend, Afreyda. Woman with dark skin?'

'Two beers.'

'What?'

'Please?'

'This conversation's reached its limit, hasn't it?' Megan held up a palm and gave the sailor a rueful smile. 'Thanks, anyway.'

'No beer?'

'Afraid not.'

None the wiser, Megan made her way back to the mansion, taking the long way round so she could brood. Had she said something to Afreyda, something to drive her away? Megan's emotions had been raw after Eleanor's death. Subconscious feelings might have made themselves known without her knowing. They might have scared Afreyda, encouraged her to keep her distance to avoid an awkward conversation.

'Mother, have you reconsidered?'

Megan started, shook her head to bring her back to reality. Clover was sat cross-legged in her usual spot: fifty paces from the Lord Defender's mansion, as close as the order Fordel had issued would allow her.

'Reconsidered what?'

Clover scrambled to her feet. 'To allow me to serve the Saviour.'

Allow one of you *near her?* 'Her name's Cate.'

'I meant no disrespect,' said Clover, cringing.

And that was the problem; there wasn't a scintilla of disrespect. Clover shared the rest of the True's reverence for the child they thought was one of the Saviours. But, unlike the rest of the witches, who wanted Megan dead, her reverence extended to Megan herself. Megan had only herself to blame for the adoration. By sparing the former spy's life, she had issued a debt she'd rather not collect.

'Look,' said Megan, 'why don't you go rejoin the wi— the True?'

'I don't understand.'

'I can arrange safe passage. The True army's outside New Statham. You can meet up with them there.'

Clover's eyes widened as she realized what Megan was saying. 'I cannot leave the Saviour.'

'We'll be fine.' Technically Clover was still Megan's prisoner, but what harm could releasing her do? Anything she could tell the witches, Damon already had.

'I cannot leave you and the Saviour among these . . . unbelievers. They will use you for their own ends.'

'And who started that?' snapped Megan. She made to

18

barge past Clover, but Clover had already scurried out of the way. 'Leave or stay, I don't care. But stay away from me and my daughter.'

'I will be here when you need me.'

Megan snorted and marched into the mansion.

Afreyda didn't return until the following morning. Megan caught up with her on the training ground, where Willas was drilling his men. Afreyda was in a light shift, the sweat gleaming on her bare arms despite the cold. She was twice as graceful as any of the lumbering soldiers, slashing and lunging and pirouetting like a dancer, her attention totally given to the sword in her hands.

Willas called the drill to an end. The men dispersed. Megan intercepted Afreyda as she headed for the barracks. 'You looked good out there.'

'Thank you,' said Afreyda, panting from her exercise.

'You'd better be careful,' said Megan. 'Willas'll be wanting to conscript you. Unless . . . Unless you had other plans.'

'Other plans?'

'Like, if there's somewhere you'd rather be.'

Afreyda looked apprehensive. She took Megan by the hand and marched her around the back of the barracks, where lines of frost still clung to the wall. The muffled sounds of soldiers, boisterous but unintelligible, leaked through gaps in the rough timbers. Someone was having a good time at least.

'I was going to talk to you.'

No denial then. Megan's stomach knotted. 'Before or after you left?' she said, her voice beginning to choke.

'I left?'

'You're not trying to find a way out of here?'

'Yes, but . . .'

'Back to *her*?'

Afreyda's brow knotted. 'Who is "her"?'

'Gwyneth.'

'What? No!' Afreyda reached out for Megan, who knocked away her arm and stepped back. 'I am looking to get back home.'

Home. The Diannon Empire. A continent and an ocean away. Of course. Why wouldn't Afreyda want to return there? Megan felt shame for having suspected treachery – and hated Rekka for planting the seeds of suspicion – but that was nothing to the despair that threatened to overwhelm her. She was losing her last friend, the person who'd kept her going after Eleanor's death, who reminded her there was more to life than duty and survival. At least Afreyda would be safe from the war, but that almost didn't matter to Megan if she would never be with her again.

Unable to contain herself, Megan spun on her heel. She stalked the length of the barracks, gravel crunching beneath her boots. She sighed and wrapped her arms around herself, ostensibly for warmth but in reality for the illusion someone was holding her. The silver waters of the inlet could be seen through the buildings scattered out in front of her, waters Afreyda would soon be sailing.

There were hesitant footsteps behind her. Afreyda's hand brushed her shoulder. Megan jerked away for form's sake.

'I do not want to go on my own,' said Afreyda. 'I want us all to go. You, me, Cate, Synne. We could go to Timi Na. It is at the southern tip of the empire. I have a . . . friend there.'

'How do you expect us to get across the Savage Ocean?'

'There are ways, if you know the routes and the winds and don't just blindly try the shortest route like merchants from the Realm.'

Megan turned to face Afreyda. 'Won't the Emperor arrest you if you break your exile?'

'We would be far away from the capital, safe from him and the witches and the priests . . . and the Hilites.'

The thought made Megan giddy. To be free of all this: the unrelenting pressure, the ever-present danger. But her reaction to Afreyda's idea betrayed its impracticality. It was nothing more than a delicious fantasy.

'I can't,' she said. 'I can't abandon the Faithful.'

Afreyda took Megan's hands in hers, her black skin contrasting with Megan's olive, and stroked them, the calluses from her training scratching Megan in a not unpleasant way. 'You led them to safety,' she said. 'What more can you do for them? Do you want to stay because you actually want to be queen?'

'No, of course not.'

Shouting drifted in on the breeze: barked orders somewhere in the distance. 'Look what politics and power games did to my father,' said Afreyda. It was her family's failed rebellion against the Diannon Emperor that had led to their exile to Werlavia. 'Do not get involved.'

'I said—'

'Just because Eleanor wanted it does not mean you have to.'

Megan jerked away from Afreyda, possibly harder than she'd intended. 'Eleanor only wanted it because she thought it was the best thing for the Faithful.'

'That is not what you said at the time.'

'Yeah, well . . .' Sometimes it had been hard to separate Eleanor's ambition from her duty. It felt too much of a betrayal to admit that though, even to Afreyda. 'What do I know?'

Afreyda shivered and rubbed her bare arms, the cold finally overtaking her metabolism. 'I must go. Willas wants me to talk to his men about how to fight guns.'

'You?'

'I was top of my class at the Imperial Officers' Academy,' said Afreyda, bristling.

22

'I know that,' said Megan, 'but how are they going to understand you?'

'Willas will translate.'

Now it was Afreyda's turn to spin and march off. Megan sighed and leaned against the barracks. That hadn't gone quite how she expected, but at least Afreyda wasn't leaving. Whether they'd speak again was another matter.

She wandered back around to the training ground. Willas was there, exhorting two boys who were raking the sand level. Scars were still fresh on his bare arms, scars he'd suffered distracting the witches while Megan made her escape from Staziker. Back then Megan had tried to thank him, but her stuttered words had merely caused mutual embarrassment at their inadequacy, and Willas had mumbled something about duty and gone off to berate his men.

'I thought Afreyda was with you,' said Megan.

Willas shook his head. 'Everything all right between you two?'

'Yes . . . no . . . I don't know.' Megan ran her fingers through her hair. 'She wants us to go hide in the empire.'

'Might be best if you were far away.'

'From the witches?'

'From Rekka and Fordel,' said Willas, scratching his beard. 'I don't know what they've got planned, but I do know they won't be the ones facing the consequences.'

The distant shouts she'd heard earlier were louder

here, close enough Megan could discern they were in Stathian, not Hilite. She exchanged quizzical glances with Willas and they hurried through the streets up to the mountain road. A vast column of people and supplies stretched back all the way to the tunnels. There weren't just civilians, there were soldiers too: a good few hundred of them, keeping the people in line, preventing them from disintegrating into a pillaging mob. Commanding them was Aldred, a farmer turned lieutenant in the army of the Faithful. He had been Eleanor's – what? – lover, Megan guessed. She had hardly spoken to him since the funeral. Megan recognized the pain in his eyes too much to press her company upon him.

Willas marched up to greet Aldred. 'Where did you find all these people?'

'Coming out of Gerland,' said Aldred. 'The priests have sealed Janik.'

After the witches had routed the Faithful at Kewley – when Megan and Eleanor had been forced to abandon Damon and Afreyda – the remnants of the army had retreated to Janik. Given the witches' imminent capture of New Statham, the hillside city was the last sanctuary in the Realm for hundreds of miles around. And if that sanctuary was now denied them . . .

Yelps of protest gave way to muttered apologies. The crowd parted to make way for a priest. It was Father Galan, High Priest of Eastport, and one of the few of the Faith who knew why the witches wanted Cate. He'd tried to have Megan executed while she was still pregnant; she had prevented Gwyneth having him beheaded. In retrospect, it was an unbalanced exchange.

Father Galan straightened his patched-up robes and stepped up to Willas. 'I need to speak to whoever's in charge.'

'Don't worry,' said Willas. 'They'll find you soon enough.'

'We need to discuss the refugee situation.'

Willas stared up the line and blew out his cheeks. 'It'll be a tight fit, but Tiptun and Downín said they'd take some.'

'You think this is all we have?' said Father Galan.

'There's more in the tunnels?'

'More in the Realm. Twenty thousand more.'

They convened in the great hall to discuss the looming crisis: the electors of Hil, led by Lord Defender Vegar, Rekka, and Fordel; a committee of refugees, headed by Father Galan; Father Broose, who had fled from the Realm with Megan and Eleanor and had attracted the devotion of an odd band of Hilites who followed the Faith. Megan herself stood beside Willas, off to the side, half hidden by a pillar. She had asked him where Afreyda was; he'd looked embarrassed and mumbled something about her volunteering for guard duty.

There was no attempt at debate between the two parties – the language barrier saw to that. Instead there was raw argument: no point, no counterpoint, just outpourings of emotion. The unremitting shouting made Megan's head throb. She leaned back on the pillar and massaged her temples, trying to expel the cacophony, and made to say something to Willas. He wasn't paying any attention. There was a wistful expression on his face. Megan followed the line of his gaze: to the high table and Rekka.

Seeing Megan's stare, Willas buried his face in his beer. 'Childish crush,' he said, the noise in the hall reducing his voice to a mutter, 'nothing more.'

'I didn't mean to pry.'

'We had this . . . gang, I think you'd call it, when we were kids. Me, her, Fordel. We spoke Stathian to exclude the others. We thought we were so . . . I don't know . . . important. She was my first kiss. Didn't go any further. She was in love with Fordel.'

'And who was he in love with?' said Megan. 'You?' She'd meant it as a joke – or a half-joke at least – but Willas's look told her she was more accurate than she'd intended. 'Sorry.'

Willas shrugged. 'Like I said, childhood crush.' He was trivializing it, more for his benefit than Megan's, minimizing a pain that still lingered. 'She passed me on to her sister.'

'Sister?' Rekka had never mentioned a sister. No one had.

'My wife. She died. Childbirth. Twenty years ago now.'

'Oh, I'm sorry,' said Megan. 'The baby?'

Willas shook his head.

Megan was spared any more awkwardness when Vegar slammed his fist on the table and bellowed. People shut up. You tended to do that when a bearded hulk of muscle with a mace the size of a small child shouted at you. The Lord Defender went on for some length, his tirade fuelled by the flagon of ale a servant constantly refilled, until Rekka patted his arm.

She turned to the Faithful. 'What my husband is saying, is that we simply don't have food for another twenty thousand. We'd all be starving within the week. Plus the queues for the bathroom would be terrible.'

'What did he really say?' Megan asked Willas.

'The gist was, "Screw you, you brought it on yourself." Only with a lot more swearing. And some comments about the Saviours that might cause a religious war if we weren't already having one.'

'We have to find food!' called out one of the refugees. Many of his fellows took on this sentiment and the words echoed around the vast space.

Rekka waited until the noise had died down before turning to Fordel. 'You hear that? We *have* to find food. What have you been doing all this time?'

27

'Exercising a deliberate policy of not finding food, it would seem,' said Fordel.

Rekka repeated their exchange in Hilite for her husband and the other electors. They responded with jeers and gestures that needed no translation, apart from one that, when Megan asked Willas to explain, made the veteran soldier blush.

Father Broose clambered to his feet. 'If I may?'

'Who the hell are you?' asked Father Galan.

'I am the High Priest of Aedran.'

'I wasn't aware Aedran had a High Priest.'

'It has little of anything any more, thanks to your warmongering.'

Father Broose held up a copy of the Book of Faith. Megan shook her head and looked up to the ceiling, where stars glittered through the gaps left by the workmen engaged to repair the roof. Bringing up religion wasn't going to help.

'"And thus, Edwyn and his Army were lost in the deserts of Andaluvia, and Dryness clawed at their throats but he urged them to Obey the teaching of the Saviours. Some turned their back on him, and Perished in the sands, but those who kept the Faith were Rewarded by an Oasis and their Thirst was Quenched."' His followers nodded their approval and made the Sign of the Circle.

'Sorry,' said Rekka, 'I don't speak stupid. You might have to explain that to me.'

Father Broose trembled, struggling to contain his temper. 'Those who put their faith in God will be rewarded.'

'Fine. He can reward them on their side of the Kartiks.'

'Not exactly hot on this diplomacy stuff, is she?' said Megan.

'You didn't know her when she was a little girl,' said Willas. 'I've got more scars from her than I ever got in combat.'

Father Broose jabbed an accusatory finger at Rekka. She raised her eyebrows in mock primness. 'You cannot deny the Faith lands secured for them by the Unifier in the name of God and the Saviours!'

Father Galan motioned for Father Broose to sit. The old priest obeyed with ill grace. 'Perhaps we could reach a compromise, bring through those most in need? The young, the old, the sick?'

'You want to bring diseased people into a packed city,' said Rekka, pulling a face.

A translation rippled through the Hilites, provoking concerned murmurs. They stepped away from the refugees, some subtly, some making a great show of it.

Fordel spread his palms apologetically. 'We'll provide for those here,' he said to Father Galan, 'but the rest will have to take their chances in the Realm. I hear there are plenty of abandoned towns and villages for them to shelter in.'

'And when the witches come for them?' asked Father Galan.

'It's not them they're coming for.'

Fordel's eyes flicked over to Megan. Father Galan followed the direction of his gaze. Megan shuffled nervously and felt for a knife. The solid grip reassured her.

'Indeed,' said Father Galan.

Fordel motioned to Willas. 'Send a detachment, captain. Secure the tunnel gates. And double the guard on the Arrowstorm Pass.'

Willas didn't react. Fordel scowled and whispered in Vegar's ear. The Lord Defender barked an order. Willas pushed himself off the pillar and straightened.

'The men'll be overjoyed,' he muttered to Megan.

She touched his arm. 'Will you . . . ?'

'Don't worry,' said Willas. 'I'll keep Afreyda stationed in the city.'

Rekka led Fordel and Vegar out of the hall, signifying the meeting was over. The crowd dispersed. Father Galan glanced in Megan's direction. She was in no hurry to speak to him, but he crooked a finger at her and swept outside. The first Pledge of Faith: *I pledge obedience to God and His priests.* Megan had no choice but to follow.

They circled outside the hall, dodging the equipment left behind by the roofers. 'I hear congratulations are in order.'

'Congratulations, father?'

'You *are* the new Countess of Ainsworth,' said Father Galan.

'Congratulations?' snapped Megan. 'Do you know how it happened?'

Father Galan held up his palms. 'I apologize, my child. Your predecessor was a . . . remarkable woman.'

He took a step further into the shadows and placed a hand on the small of Megan's back, intending to bring her with him. He flinched when he made contact with the knife she had stashed there.

Megan pulled away from him. 'Was there something else, father?'

'The child?'

Now it was Megan's turn to flinch. 'Don't even think—'

'She's here?' asked Father Galan. Megan said nothing. A pointless denial, but it allowed an illusion of safety for a few seconds. 'Do the witches know?' Megan turned around and stared up into the mountains. 'They'll be coming here.'

Megan swallowed the lump in her throat. 'Fordel says we've got until spring.'

'Fordel!' Father Galan snorted. 'What exactly are the two of you plotting?'

'I'm not plotting anything,' said Megan, careful to leave Fordel out of her denial.

'Are you seeking to revive Endalay's claim to the

31

throne? Don't give in to the temptation, my child. It will destroy you. The priests will destroy you.'

The arguments were all too familiar – Megan had used them herself against Eleanor – but she also remembered the countess's counter-arguments. 'What if it's the only way to unite the Realm and the Snow Cities against the witches?'

'You think *you* are the only one who can save us?' said Father Galan. 'Who does that remind you of?'

Megan shuddered at the comparison to Gwyneth. If she did try to become queen it would only be to protect the Faithful, not out of personal ambition. But, then, hadn't her sister claimed the same?

three

Damon rinsed the kerchief out in the trough of gritty water before retying it over his face. It didn't help much. The air was thick with dust from the slowly disintegrating walls of New Statham and the only way he could have had more stone in his body would have been to eat the damned things. The city was proving stubborn, even for the guns of the True. Its outer walls didn't meet at the entrance but overlapped, forming a curved corridor along which any arrival had to pass, vulnerable to archers on both sides. This structure protected the gates from a direct assault, meaning the True had to attack the walls themselves – cliff-faces of limestone thirty-odd feet thick and fifty-odd feet high. They had eventually hit on the idea of a sustained attack on the same spot, though given the inaccuracy of their weapons this was more intention than actuality. Still, it was only a matter of time. There was only so much battering any one thing could take.

The witches hadn't known what to make of Damon

since their return from the Kartiks. Friend or foe? Believer or blasphemer? Damon didn't know himself. He had left a part of himself up there in the mountains and had been in a dazed, half-alive state ever since. Eleanor was gone, and no matter how much he tried to downplay his role in her death he knew he was responsible.

Damon needed a drink. He made his way through the camp, picking his way along the muddy streets formed between canvas walls, heading for the command tent. Rivulets trickled underfoot, some more yellow than others, waves rippling through them each time a gun fired. Damon had got used to the noise; he'd begun to use it to mark off time. What was it like in the capital, knowing each boom brought you closer to your end?

The guard at the tent gave him a quizzical look but let him past. Damon was one of the True. They were all fighting for the same cause, all equal before God and the Saviours, no need for priests to rule them. Damon could go where he wanted. Except away.

It was a little clearer inside, but particles still hung in the air making everything hazy, as if Damon was already seeing through drunken eyes. The wine was at the far end, past the table where the captains argued: Osgar, the general and supreme commander of the witches, withered but strong, like a ravaged oak; Tobrytan, stiff and fanatical despite Megan's capture of his daughter; Sener, practical and rational, only his father, the general, saving him from

34

punishment for what might otherwise be considered heretical views.

Damon sidled around to the wine table and poured himself a cup. It was sour. *Figures*, he thought.

'Look at them,' said a female voice. *Megan?* 'Bickering like schoolboys over the rules of some game they've just made up.'

Damon turned. Gwyneth stood behind him, her black hair in need of a brush, her once-pure gown smeared with dirt. She had a goblet of wine clutched to her chest. Like the sound of guns, it was such a common occurrence Damon only half noticed it now.

For some reason, Gwyneth seemed to like having him around. Damon wasn't sure if she saw him as a proxy for Megan, someone she could gloat and vent at, or merely someone her own age, a respite from the war-obsessed old men. It must be awfully lonely, being the Mother of the Saviour – no one was exactly queuing to invite her to parties. She'd brought it on herself of course, but Damon wondered what he would've done in her place, if he'd known what the True had planned. Megan had fought, but she'd had Eleanor. Who would have helped Gwyneth, who would have even listened to her? The priests had refused to believe the True still existed until they had bombarded Eastport. She had chosen to accept her fate absolutely, put all doubt aside.

'We should be heading north,' said Gwyneth. 'I don't know why we're still here.'

Because New Statham still had a sizeable garrison and, after the witches had blown up the leaders of the Faith in the palace at Eastport, it was the only hope of any immediate organized resistance. Break the capital and the Realm would be open to the True. Plus, if the witches did decide to head north to the Snow Cities, the rear of its army would be exposed. The witches might have the guns, but they didn't have the men to absorb the casualties a guerrilla force might exact.

'Why don't you put a stop to all their nonsense?' said Damon.

'The city will not fall until we have secured the Saviours.'

'I can see how a couple of babies would give you the tactical advantage.'

'It would inspire the True,' said Gwyneth. 'Cow the New Stathians. Demonstrate what we're doing is God's will. Better than . . .' She made a gesture with her hand, forgetting the goblet. Wine splashed on to Damon. He grimaced. 'Better than this pointless waste of ammunition. We might as well smash our heads against the walls.'

'You could always suggest it.'

'Perhaps you could volunteer? Show us how it's done?'

Beat his brains out on cold stone? Damon couldn't deny he deserved it. 'It's not only force can conquer a city,' he said.

'Really?'

'You could always try knocking politely.' Gwyneth gave him the same exasperated look he'd received so many times from Megan. 'Edwyn did it at Janik. Of course, he had secret converts to the Faith inside the city to let him in.'

'There are no True in New Statham,' said Gwyneth.

'For amnesty and a thousand sovereigns, I'm sure you'll soon find some.'

'Bribery?'

'More commissions, consultancy fees and miscellaneous expenses paid to intermediate facilitators.'

Gwyneth curled her lip. 'You cannot pay someone to be True.'

Oh, you can, thought Damon. *We're all corruptible; we're all desperately looking for the easy way out. Offer it to us and we'll snatch it before you can say 'betrayal'.* 'How about the auxiliaries you recruited in Ainsworth?' said Damon. 'You think they're all absolutely loyal?'

'They know the penalty if they're not.'

You couldn't pay someone to believe, but you could frighten them. The Book of Faith had a whole chapter devoted to the suffering that would be meted out to those who rejected the teachings of the Saviours and forsook God. Especially moneylenders, Damon recalled from his time in the seminary; Edwyn must have fallen behind on his mortgage repayments.

'A bit of gold could prevent an awful lot of death and

destruction,' he said. Gwyneth gave him a blank look. Damon shuddered. This was not a girl who thought those things were worth preventing. 'It can speed things up. Then you can go after Meg— Then you can ride north.'

A draught of cold air heralded a newcomer: a soldier with burn marks down the left side of his face. Someone had got too close to an exploding gun. He hurried up to the captains' table and saluted.

'We've breached the wall,' he said.

The outer *wall*, thought Damon. New Statham had three, each thicker than the last.

'Can we get the guns through?' asked Tobrytan.

'Not yet, sir.'

'Men?'

'Thin men, sir.'

'Take those who will fit and secure the outer city,' said Tobrytan.

'You're going to send the men into Saviours-knows-what without artillery support?' said Sener.

Gwyneth cast a glance at Damon, then stepped forward. 'No, he's not,' she said. 'The blasphemers have seen what we can do. It is time to offer them a choice.'

It felt less like a triumphal parade, more like a funeral procession. The world was eerily quiet now the guns had stopped, just the relentless crunch of boots and hoofs as the True marched through New Statham. Sullen citizens gazed at them from the edges of windows or the shadows of alleys, cheeks sunken by hunger, dirty faces streaked by tears. The accusation in their eyes seemed to be reserved for Damon; it was as if they knew not only of his defection to the True but of his betrayal of Eleanor in the Kartiks.

The trek through the city was taking forever. The main road wound its way between the three rings of walls as if they were a labyrinth, rather than cutting straight through to the heart of the city. It was another of the defensive measures Edwyn the Third had insisted upon, tripling the distance to the palace, giving the city's guards more opportunities to attack any invaders and more time for the king to escape. As the city had never actually been attacked until now, it merely gave its citizens something to grumble about.

The vanguard of the witches' army moved from the outer city into the middle city. Edwyn had used the spaces between the walls as parks where he could hunt in safety, but in the centuries since his death they had developed into cities of their own, populated by rickety buildings four or five storeys high, that seemed as if they'd collapse if looked at with anything stronger than peripheral vision. They passed the shack Damon had stayed in when he had arrived in New Statham after escaping the seminary, packed in, a dozen to a room. There he had learned to survive on the streets using any means necessary: pickpocketing, burglary, fencing, forgery, smuggling, prostitution, rigged games of chance. He had also learned there was no honour among thieves, and so had his comrades when one night Damon had relieved them of their ill-gotten gains and skipped south to Hickton.

After an interminable trudge they arrived in Saviours' Square. The palace loomed above them like a displaced mountain, its towers straining for the sky as if its architect thought the best way to reach heaven was by stairs. No building in the Realm could match its scope or grandeur, mainly because Edwyn had bankrupted the treasury to pay for it and none of his successors could afford to compete.

The city's guard was standing in parade formation, their numbers not as great as the True had been led to believe: fattened by rumour or thinned by comrades? Had those reluctant to accept the witches' terms been cut down by those whose loyalty to the Faith was a little less absolute? Civilians lined the edge of the square, curious despite the situation. No priests though. Damon hadn't seen a single one since they had entered New Statham.

The True parted to display the guns they had dragged along with them – huge chunks of dirty iron, still smoking and stinking of sulphur as if they had been chiselled from the bowels of hell. An order sounded. There was a cacophony of weapons – swords, pikes, knives, maces, bows – hitting paving stones. A second signal had the soldiers of New Statham ripping off their surcoats, which were emblazoned with the sign of the circle, and casting them aside, exposing plate armour and stiffened leather.

An officer stepped forward. There were only lieutenant's pips on his shoulders. What had happened to the captain?

'We have your word? No further harm will come to the city?'

Osgar leaned on the huge battleaxe which he used only as a walking stick these days and looked over to Gwyneth. He grimaced. The general hadn't been keen on the plan – Damon suspected it didn't involve enough slaughter for his tastes – and had only agreed to it to humour the Mother. When the city had signalled its willingness to surrender – or at least certain inhabitants with idiosyncratic definitions of solidarity and access to sharp implements had signalled their willingness to surrender – he had been as surprised as anyone.

'True will not harm True,' Osgar wheezed.

The lieutenant's eyes narrowed. 'That's not what we agreed.'

Gwyneth bustled forward. A hiss shot around the guards, prompting True soldiers to step around her, forming a bodyguard. They'd heard about her in the city then, but what exactly? Damon doubted it could be as bad as the reality.

'We come to renew the message of the Saviours,' she said, raising her voice, 'free from the pollution of the priests.' Osgar looked unimpressed but made no effort to silence her; the True were loath to contradict one another in front of outsiders. 'Those who recommit to God will be allowed to continue their lives in peace.'

'You never said we would have to . . . have to join you.'

'Why wouldn't you want to?' said Gwyneth. 'You freed yourself of the priests, didn't you?'

The lieutenant swallowed. 'We have them under arrest.'

'Is that local slang for "hanging from the city walls by their entrails"?' said Gwyneth. 'Sorry. Southern girl. Not from round here.'

'We have no authority to execute anyone.'

'The second Pledge of Faith gives you that authority.' *I pledge to uphold the Faith and destroy its enemies.* Gwyneth flicked her hand. 'Never mind. Is there anything else you wish to discuss?'

'There was . . .' The lieutenant glanced back at his men. 'But it can wait until later.'

'Don't be silly,' said Gwyneth. She whispered into the ear of one of her bodyguards, who peeled away and went over to one of the carts the True had brought with them. 'We can deal with it now.'

'I don't want to put you out,' said the lieutenant, twitching. He looked like he wanted to run. 'I'm sure you need to . . . to rest after all the . . . all the invading you've done.'

Gwyneth gave him a sly smile. 'Oh, it's *no* trouble.'

The bodyguard returned, heaving a small chest way too heavy for its size. Gwyneth pointed at the lieutenant and the bodyguard deposited the chest at his feet. There was an unmistakable *chink*. For the benefit of those who did mistake it though, the bodyguard kicked open the chest. A heap of gold coins glittered in the sunlight.

A wave of astonishment and anger burst forth from the city guards. A couple lunged for the lieutenant and got in a few blows before the True beat them back. Damon guessed the lieutenant hadn't told them giving up the city wasn't solely to save the population from the horrors of siege and pillaging.

Gwyneth looked to the lieutenant as he dabbed his bleeding nose. 'I guess you'll be reconsidering the benefits of being True,' she said.

four

The footsteps of Damon, Gwyneth and the True captains echoed like applause. There was a mustiness to the air: less like entering a room than opening a tomb. The throne room had been unused since the spring, when the War Council had gathered to plan the retaking of Ainsworth, and detritus from that meeting still littered the floorboards: maps showing routes that had been marched and hastily retraced; parchments containing battle orders that were never followed; discarded food that had decomposed to evil-looking blobs.

As they marched across the room, light streaming through stained glass cast lurid colours on their skin. The windows depicted the Unifier's conquest of Werlavia, which the conquered seemed very happy about despite their wounds, dismemberments and beheadings – the glaziers had got very good at red. Damon wondered how the True's victories would be written, whether the desperation and dread would be commemorated.

'You probably want to get the cleaners in,' he said. 'I know this firm. They hardly ever nick anything.' The captains turned to him, a collective what-the-hell-are-you-doing-here? on their faces. Damon wasn't sure they'd accept 'morbid curiosity' as an answer.

Gwyneth ascended the steps that led to the Unifier's throne. It had been unoccupied for four decades, its scarred wood offering another history of the Realm: the mismatched back leg that had to be replaced after the throne had been damaged on its journey up from Statham; the pockmarks that demonstrated just how bad Edwyn the Fourth was at darts; the dark patches said to be the blood of Aldwyn the First, assassinated after his lords had a violent reaction to his proposal for yet another suicidal attempt to invade the Snow Cities. Gwyneth dusted its seat with her sleeve and sat down.

'Prepare the troops,' she said. The acoustics amplified her voice, making it dominate even the vastness of the throne room. 'We march for Hil tomorrow.'

'No, we do not, Mother,' snapped Osgar.

'You're questioning my orders?'

'He is kind of in charge,' said Damon. Everyone glared at him again. 'Not helpful?'

'The men are in no fit state to march hundreds of miles and tackle mountains only the Unifier was able to sur—' Osgar broke off in a coughing fit – 'to surmount.'

Sener hurried up to his father to check he was all

right. The general waved him off with an irritated flick of his hand. 'We cannot fight the Hilites and the winter at the same time.' The general coughed again. 'We need to consolidate our hold on the city, resupply, rearm. We will attack in the spring.'

'The *spring*?' spat Gwyneth. 'She could be anywhere by then.'

'If God wants us to have the Saviour,' said Sener, 'he will lead us to him.' He had always been ambivalent about Joanne's prophecy.

Gwyneth turned to Tobrytan. 'And you agree?' Tobrytan shrugged. 'You're happy about my si— the Apostate holed up in the Snow Cities laughing at us while she does God knows what to your daughter? What was her name – Clover?'

Damon doubted Tobrytan was happy about anything, ever. 'I do what God commands,' the captain said.

'And you think God doesn't want us to secure the Saviours?'

'The decision has been made,' wheezed Osgar. He turned his back on Gwyneth and began to hobble out of the throne room. 'And get out of that chair. You look ridiculous.'

That night, Damon found an out-of-the-way corner of the palace to hide away in. It looked like a servant's quarters: a bed a toddler would have found cramped; whitewashed walls mottled with mould; a dirty window obscured by condensation; a pitcher of water that had long since been colonized by algae. Most of the palace staff had marched with the army on its ill-fated attempt to retake Ainsworth – you couldn't expect priests to look after themselves during such a long journey – and the rest had scarpered once they knew the True were making this their base.

He curled up on the bed – stretching out wasn't an option – and pulled the grubby sheet over himself, more for the illusion of comfort than any actual warmth. He craved sleep but he was scared to. He'd see her again, her final breaths rejecting him, her body tumbling into nothingness. Had Eleanor killed herself to spare him or spite him? Was there a chance of redemption or should he pray the True were right in their beliefs and he had done nothing less than God's work?

There was a scuffling outside his room. Damon curled up tighter, a small boy huddling against the monsters. There was whispering, then the creak of hinges. Damon wriggled back until the wall blocked his way. Candlelight briefly haloed the silhouette of an approaching figure before the door squealed shut.

His eyes adjusted back to the gloom, confirming the identity of the newcomer. Gwyneth. Damon relaxed his locked-up muscles and sat up.

'Up for a midnight feast, are we?' he said. 'A pillow fight? Have to warn you, I fight dirty.' In the seminary, the boys had stuffed their pillows with books, slates and the occasional brick.

Gwyneth leaned in close. She had changed and bathed, found a scent of roses and vanilla – a perfume left behind by some priest's mistress, Damon guessed. To his surprise, she slipped a hand under the sheet and touched him in a way that made him feel better than he had any right to.

'Did she do this for you?'

'Meg—?' Damon cleared his throat. 'Megan? We weren't . . . It wasn't like that.'

There was a glimpse of a smile, lit up by the moonlight that had the misfortune to struggle through the window. 'No, it wouldn't be.'

'It'd be like doing it . . . you know . . . with your sister.'

'Yes, my sister.'

'No,' said Damon, 'your sister, rather than *your* sister. The generic as opposed to the specific. You not remember your Stathian classes?'

'Brother Brogan was very boring. I used to catch up on my sleep during his class.'

'I suppose you were up all night a-plotting,' said Damon. He rambled to distract from what Gwyneth's hand was doing. 'Of course, if we still spoke Werlay everything would be clearer. It's got a much wider set of pronouns. Mind you, one of them does mean "the man who stole my pig in the dead of night", so it is open to accusations of over-specialization.'

'Do you always talk so much?'

'It's my substitute for –' he squealed – 'action.'

'Do you like my action?'

Damon tensed. 'It's certainly better than a lot of the things I've endured.'

'Will you do something for me?'

'You should have said. I would have gone first. I tend to be a bit of a sleeper.'

'I want you to kill the general.'

Damon smacked Gwyneth's hand away and scrambled off the bed. 'You want me to kill . . . ? Are you mad?' He remembered who he was talking to. 'Well, of course you are, but, I mean . . .'

The accusation flew over Gwyneth's head, which was helpful since Damon was keen for his own to stay attached.

'He will lead us to our defeat. We cannot stop until we have the Saviour.'

'Why?'

'We have been tasked by God.'

'Did He set an actual time limit?' asked Damon.

'Osgar's an old man with all the imagination of a lettuce.' Gwyneth tucked her gown under her and sat on the bed. 'We could have been dug in here for weeks or months thanks to his rigid thinking. You come along and we take the city within a day.'

'It wasn't a particularly original idea,' said Damon.

'And I'm not sure . . . single-mindedness is a reason to kill someone.'

'You saw how Osgar treated me,' said Gwyneth. 'Who does he think he is? My grandfather?' *Not considering what you did to your last one.* 'He's a sick old man who'll be lucky to see out the winter. You know he hates you, don't you?'

'Not as unique a feeling as you'd think,' said Damon. 'I can live with it.'

'He's just looking for an excuse to have you executed.'

'I can live with that too. Well, you know, probably not literally . . .'

'Do you want me to give him one?' asked Gwyneth.

'That probably *would* kill him . . . Oh, you mean an excuse.'

'To execute you.'

'You know, in the grand scheme of things, I'd prefer it if you didn't,' said Damon. *There are people far more deserving of signing my death warrant.* 'Why don't you ask Tobrytan?'

'He's too in love with following orders.'

Gwyneth slunk out of the bed and headed for the door. Was that it? Had he talked himself out of it?

'You'll do it?'

Maybe not. 'I'm not really a killing kind of guy.'

'You'll do it.'

'Don't you have bodyguards and whatnot to do your dirty work?'

'*You'll* do it.'

five

The steam rising off the surface of the pool made it look as if it was on fire. Synne was over at the shallow end, supporting Cate as they floated on the water. Megan watched her daughter's little limbs kicking in a frenzied imitation of a swimmer, laughing every time she made a splash. It was a heart-warming scene of mother and child at play, but heart-wrenching if you were the displaced mother.

Hot springs were dotted all along the foothills of the Kartiks. This particular one was for the use of the Lord Defender and his family. Steep rocks formed irregular walls, turning the pool into a private bath, albeit one open to the sky. This time of day, Vegar and Rekka's children would usually be here, splashing and playing and making enough noise to have the dead organizing petitions of complaint, but they had been packed off to Downín on an 'educational exercise', which Megan suspected was code for 'to give their mother some rest'.

Megan slipped out of her clothes. She made herself wait a few moments, until the chill mountain air raised goose pimples all over her exposed flesh, then plunged into the pool. The warm water caressed her weary body, dissolving her worries and soothing away the pain. Megan submerged, shook her hair out, then kicked her way over to Synne and Cate.

Screams greeted her surfacing. Synne grabbed the bawling Cate and backed off towards the side. Megan started to go after them, then stopped, realizing this would only agitate them more.

'It's only me,' she said, pushing the wet hair from her face. 'It's only me.'

Synne relaxed, but not entirely. She rocked Cate, calming her down. 'You shouldn't have done that.'

'I'm sorry,' said Megan. 'I thought you knew I was there.'

Synne shook her head. Cate was still pouting, her cheeks red. Megan held out her arms. 'Here, let me.'

'You?'

'I am her . . . Please?'

Synne waded across to Megan and placed Cate in her outstretched arms. 'It's all right, sweetheart,' Megan said softly. 'It was just Mummy playing.'

She shifted Cate on to her left arm and tapped the surface of the pool, sending droplets flying. 'See?' Cate giggled. Megan hit the surface again, harder this time. Too hard. Water splashed into Cate's eyes and she started to cry.

'Saviours, I can't do anything right, can I?' muttered Megan. She looked down at her tearful daughter. 'Sorry for taking your name in vain.'

'She's getting tired,' said Synne. 'I'll take her back to the room, get her down.'

'I only just got here.'

'But we didn't.'

Megan couldn't argue with the sleeping patterns of a six-month-old. She had a few moments with Cate while Synne got out of the pool and dressed, then had to hand her over. She could have gone with them, ignore her redundancy, but pride prevented her. It was easier to pretend she was delegating, that she really was a countess and had servants to take care of the trivialities, that it didn't wrench her insides every time she saw her daughter taken away. She stayed in the pool, letting the water numb her, drifting off into nothingness.

Scuffling from the other end of the pool woke Megan. Evening was falling, and the cooling air had thickened the mist rising from the water, meaning she could see nothing bar ghosts. A shape advanced through the fog, solidifying into the form of Fordel. He was completely naked. He stretched and, eyes closed, took several deep breaths. Had he seen her? Megan made to back off and clamber out of the pool, but she too was naked. Her clothes were at the other end of the pool – along with her knives. She sank into the water instead.

'I'm sorry,' said Fordel, eyes still closed. 'I thought you wouldn't be bothered.'

Megan turned around, embarrassed by her embarrassment. 'I'm not.'

Fordel stood there until he started to shiver, then plunged into the pool.

'You do that too?' said Megan. 'Make yourself cold so the hot water feels all that much better?'

'It opens the pores.'

'That what it is?'

'If you want to –' Fordel motioned to the rock ledge that circumnavigated the edge of the pool – 'there's no need to be shy in front of me.'

'Yes,' said Megan, 'I'd heard. About . . . you know . . .'

Fordel started to scrub himself, massaging his close-cropped hair and beard. He stared down at his ink-stained fingers and rubbed them on the back of his hands. It had no effect. 'I always forget to bring soap,' he muttered.

'Do people mind?' asked Megan.

'The ink?' said Fordel. 'You want to see what some of my compatriots have their hands in. Well, you don't actually. You'll never have the fish pie again.'

'Not that,' said Megan, wishing she hadn't started

down this particular route. 'About you? About you liking –' Fordel cocked his head – '. . . boys.'

'Boys? What am I – twelve?'

'Men then.'

'Maybe they do, maybe they don't,' said Fordel. He flashed a wolfish grin. 'It's not wise to antagonize the person who controls the tax auditors.'

'And is there someone . . . ? Do you have a . . . ?'

'Ími,' said Fordel. 'He's the official mathematician.'

'Hil has an official mathematician?'

'The Realm doesn't?' said Fordel. 'And you call us uncivilized.'

'What do you do when you're . . . ?'

'In bed?' asked Fordel. Megan squirmed and nodded. 'Paperwork, mostly. We're very diligent.' He finished his scrubbing and lay back in the water. 'Don't get obsessed by dangly bits and holey bits and what goes where. Man and woman, man and man –' he gave Megan a pointed look – 'woman and woman, it's all the same thing. You're with someone you love and you want to be with them in every way possible. Though when you get to my age the possible ways are fewer in number.'

He started to drift off to the other end of the pool. Megan could have hung back, taken the opportunity to leave, but she gave a little kick and floated alongside him. 'How did you . . . ? How did he . . . ? How did you know?'

'Know what?'

'That the two of you liked each other. Even though you're both . . .'

'Same way anybody does,' said Fordel. 'You take a chance and hope your heart doesn't get broken.' He rolled over in the water. 'If you did take a chance, I'm sure she'd listen.'

'I don't know what you mean,' said Megan, her heart thumping.

'Of course not.'

Fordel hauled himself out of the pool and stood at the edge, rivulets streaming down his body and collecting at his feet. 'We've had word from Janik,' he said, towelling himself off. 'They're organizing elections for a new Supreme Priest. We should consider making our move before you have a rival.'

'You really think I can rival the Supreme Priest?' said Megan. Even hearing herself mentioned in the same sentence as him was mind-blowing. 'That's—'

'What have the priests to offer the Realm?'

'They saved us from the witches before.'

'A lifetime ago.'

'What have I to offer the Realm?'

Fordel flashed his lupine grin and started to dress. This wasn't about what Megan could offer the Realm, it was about her offering the Realm to Fordel and Rekka. They wanted another Vegar, a figurehead they could manipulate, only instead of controlling a single city, they wanted the entire continent.

'I don't want to be queen,' she said. 'I'm only interested in defeating the witches. We should be working with the priests not against them.'

'Very diplomatic. I think you're going to be a natural.'

'It's the truth.'

'Of course,' said Fordel.

He took a step towards the exit. '*Sila ta.*' It was another of the few Hilite phrases Megan had learned, or at least partially learned. It meant either 'see you later' or 'we fight at dawn', depending on which syllable was emphasized. As she could never remember which was the less-belligerent variant, she had been reluctant to try it in conversation.

She watched Fordel disappear between the rocks then hauled herself out of the pool and hurriedly dressed. Squeezing out through the same gap, she emerged on to stairs cut into the mountain, steep and rough and irregular as a priest's gratitude. She took each one slowly, side on, bringing her feet together before cautiously feeling for the next step, worried her ankle would twist under her and she'd plummet all the way down to Hil. How Synne managed this while carrying Cate was another secret of motherhood Megan feared she'd never grasp.

Angry voices from below made her pause, as much for respite from her perilous descent as from curiosity. She pressed herself into the rock wall by the side of the steps. The distance and the twilight made it hard to see what was going on or make out what was being said. Fordel was talking – arguing? – with a man in priestly robes. Not Father Galan or Father Broose. Hard to tell, but it looked like one of the latter's followers. Had Father Broose been ordaining acolytes? That was a right reserved for the Supreme Priest. It wouldn't be the first time Father Broose had accorded privilege upon himself.

Fordel looked up in Megan's direction. She instinctively drew back. Soldiers stormed up to Fordel and the priest. There was a confrontation. A fist struck out. Fordel crumpled. Megan let out an involuntary gasp. Heads snapped up in her direction. Someone pointed. Two of the men barrelled up the steps towards her.

Megan stared down, unable to move. These were soldiers of the Faith. She had fought with them, fled with them – admittedly more the latter than the former. They could mean her no harm, surely? But Megan had more than enough experience of armed men coming at her. She turned and scrambled back up the steps.

Her foot slipped and flew out from under her. The steps rushed towards her face. She got her hands up just in time, gripped on to the rock, cried out as the stone rasped the skin off her palms. She pulled herself up, or tried to at least. A hand grabbed her ankle. She tried to pull away. The grip tightened. She kicked out with her free leg. There was an impact, a crack, a yell of pain followed by one of alarm. The lead soldier released her leg and fell backwards, on to his comrade behind him. They tumbled down the steps. Megan hastened upwards.

Panting, she found herself back at the spring. She hurried through the ever-thickening fog, circumnavigating the pool in search of another way out. There wasn't one, but the place was open to the sky; perhaps she could clamber over the rocks and make her way down the mountain. Megan rushed around, looking for the easiest point to climb. The rocks ranged from a little over her head to twice her height. She found a spot that wasn't too vertical and prepared to climb.

She froze. Two figures in the mist. Huffing and puffing and vituperative comments condemning Megan in terms normally reserved for her sister. She crouched and huddled next to an outcropping.

'. . . bitch go?' said one man.

'She's not getting out of here,' said the other. 'You go that way, I'll take this.'

'You want us to split up?'

'You scared of a girl?'

'After the fight the other one put up? They say this one's worse.'

The other one? Afreyda? Agitation clawed at Megan. Was she all right? What about Cate? Saviours, what about

Cate? If they – and at present she didn't know who 'they' were – were coming for Megan, they would go after her daughter too. Megan had to get to her, protect her, take her to safety. That meant going through the men who'd come for her.

She peered around the rocks hiding her. The hazy shape of a soldier shimmered in the fog. Megan tensed, took deep breaths of the clammy air. She thought about what she was going to do to her compatriots, the people she claimed to be fighting for. Did 'me or them' justify her actions? Maybe if she gave herself up they could resolve everything peacefully. Maybe, but she couldn't risk it.

A stomping of boots cut off the time for contemplation. Megan spun out of her hiding place, sweeping her leg around as fast as she could. Pain exploded in her calf as she hit the soldier's shins. Megan ignored it, let her momentum carry her around as the soldier flew through the air. She stuck out a knife. There was no need to thrust. The soldier broke his fall on the blade, skewering himself through the throat.

Megan tried to ease the body to the ground, but the weight was too much. Armour clanged upon stone, a racket even the sodden air couldn't dampen. Wordless shouts pierced the fog. Megan's head snapped from side to side. She couldn't tell which way it was coming from. Only one thing for it. She threw herself in the pool.

She kicked off the side, shooting away as fast as possible,

unsure how visible she was beneath the surface. A rock crashed into the water in front of her, bubbles streaming in its wake as it plummeted. Megan cut to the side, hoping that would confuse her attacker.

The bottom of the pool inclined upwards. She'd reached the shallow end. Megan planted her feet and pushed up. Her head spun as air rushed into her lungs. She held herself steady, watched through a curtain of matted hair as the remaining soldier raced around the pool, his form shifting from phantom to man as he approached. It was one on one. Eleanor had warned her she'd never win a straight fight, not against a much stronger opponent. But there was more to strength than size.

She advanced until the surface of the pool was just above her knees. Water streamed down her body. Steam billowed off her in great clouds. The soldier took a step forward. He had his comrade's sword as well as his own, one in each hand. He twirled them both. Clumsy, but Megan had no wish to get in their way. She held back, out of reach.

The soldier considered his options. If he was going to strike her, he'd have to enter the pool. Megan swept her hair back, waited for his decision. He poked a tentative boot into the pool. Water crept up the leather, darkening it. Megan slowly stretched back a leg, checking the footing behind her. Doubt showed on the soldier's face.

'Come on in,' said Megan. 'The water's lovely.'

61

The mockery did its job. The soldier plunged into the pool and slashed at Megan. She stepped back, evading the blades that sliced the space she'd just vacated. The soldier lunged, slipped, dropped his swords, fell over in the water. Megan threw herself after him, knife first. An arm whirled out of the water and smacked into her. There was an almighty splash as she slammed into the pool. Water roared in Megan's ears. Hands clawed at her. She fumbled for another knife. Fingers squeezed her face as if trying to claw it off. Megan wrenched the blade out and thrust. The water robbed her strike of its momentum, and that was before the soldier's armour deflected it.

The fingers crawled up her face and pressed into her eyeballs. Twin columns of pain spiked into her head. Megan forced herself not to panic. She ran the tip of her knife across the man's armour until she felt flesh yield underneath it, then rammed it in. Clouds of scarlet bloomed in the water. The pressure on her released.

More soldiers would come to check on their comrades. No time to waste. Megan waded out of the pool and hauled herself up the rocks. Her wet hands slipped on the stone. She went to rub them dry on her clothes. They were saturated; everything was saturated. Her body caught up with what this meant. Her teeth chattered from cold.

Movement was her best defence. She thought about using the steps, but the other soldiers would be waiting there. Best to keep to her original plan: climb down the mountain, letting the rocks and the dusk cover her. As carefully as her palpitating heart would let her, Megan climbed the wall surrounding the pool and straddled the ridge at the top. All that remained of the day was a pinkish hue edging the horizon. The first stars were starting to come out. Down in Hil, pinpricks of light dotted the city. It looked peaceful. Everything looked peaceful if you were far enough away. Maybe that's why God never felt the need to intervene.

She made her way down in a sitting shuffle, like a toddler learning to navigate stairs. There wasn't enough light to risk standing up; besides, keeping low reduced her visibility to the soldiers at the bottom of the mountain. She gauged her position, judging where the steps were relative to her route and shifted right.

The slope levelled out. Megan pushed herself up into a run, dashing through a narrow band of trees until she reached an area that had recently been felled to provide wood for much-needed shelters. She bent over and rested her hands on a stump. The breath she sucked in chilled her insides.

No time to stop: she had to get to Cate. Megan moved on, crouching and trying to ignore the shivers that racked her body. She reached the outskirts of Hil. Still quiet. That was wrong in itself. There should be workers making their way home, the clatter of pans as dinner was made, the roar of drinkers celebrating the survival of another day. What the hell was going on? Something was wrong; something was terribly wrong. Had the witches made it into the city? *Saviours, no. Saviours, please, no.*

Flitting from cover to cover, Megan made her way to the Lord Defender's mansion. Soldiers patrolled the city, grim-faced men wearing the sign of the circle. Maybe the witches weren't responsible for this, whatever 'this' was. She thought about stepping up to one, demanding to know what was happening, but instinct warned her against it and instead she hid whenever she heard the stomp of their boots, shivering in the dark, clenching her jaw shut to prevent her rattling teeth giving her away. Once, when she rested her hand against a wall to steady herself, it came back sticky. Blood. She wiped it off on her wet clothes.

More soldiers swarmed around the mansion – Megan would have to sneak in. She crept around to the back. Rekka was definitely the type of woman to have secret passages, but she was also the type of woman to *keep* them secret. There didn't seem any obvious way in, though the gloom would have made it hard to spot any entrance not painted brilliant white and lit like a pagan shrine.

A hand slid around her mouth. Megan would have jumped high enough to clear the mansion had she not been held down. 'There's a cellar door around the western side, Mother,' a voice whispered in her ear. 'I don't think the soldiers know about it.'

Megan recognized Clover's voice. She let out a muffled grunt of indignation and relaxed a bit. The hand was withdrawn. 'You've been spying?'

'I *am* a spy,' said Clover.

'It's a hobby as well as a vocation?'

'I was worried about the Saviour,' said Clover. 'You've come for her?'

Megan nodded. 'Have you seen her?'

'The soldiers drove me away before I had the chance.'

Megan noticed one of Clover's eyes was half closed. She reached out, touched swollen flesh. Clover winced and drew back.

'I'm sorry,' said Megan.

'It wasn't your doing.'

Maybe for once it wasn't. 'What's going on here?'

'I don't know. Soldiers suddenly appeared everywhere. They arrested people, declared a curfew. The Faithful have taken the city.' Clover shook her head. 'The True would not turn on their allies. We keep our word.'

'Pity it's not a very nice word.'

A look – shame? embarrassment? – passed across Clover's face. 'The cellar is this way,' she mumbled.

She led Megan around the edge of the mansion's gardens, pausing every few yards as a patrol stomped by. They reached the west side and crawled under a bush, each of whose tiny needles wanted a scrap of Megan's flesh. Clover pointed out across the lawn.

'There, Mother,' she whispered. 'That indentation in the grass? See it?'

'Barely,' Megan whispered back. 'We'll have to hope it's open.'

'It is open.'

'How do you . . . ?'

'I have used it before,' said Clover. 'I wanted to see the Saviour.'

Megan shuddered. 'That's not disturbing.'

'Lady Rekka's servants drove me off before I could.'

That was something at least. Even though Clover would never hurt Cate, there was something skin-crawling about the idea of her worshipping Megan's daughter. Something else too: a spike of jealous anger at the witch's appropriation of her child.

Megan swallowed the emotion and concentrated on the immediate task. The cellar door was about twenty yards away. She wasn't going to get to it without being spotted by one of the patrols.

'I'm going to need you to create a distraction,' she said.

'Whatever you need, Mother.'

'Haven't I told you not to call me that?'

'Sorry.'

'Draw the guards off,' said Megan. 'Then get away from here as fast as possible.'

'Where to?'

'I'll leave that as an exercise.'

One pair of soldiers disappeared around the corner of the mansion, leaving only two guards on the side of the building where Megan and Clover were hiding. The men passed their position.

'Now!'

Clover rolled out from under the bush and skipped towards the house, her footsteps just loud enough to draw attention. The two soldiers whirled round and yelled. Clover veered away. They gave chase.

Megan scurried across the lawn. The trapdoor to the cellar had been covered in turf – were it not for the slight dip you wouldn't know it was there. She felt around the edge. The fit was too tight to get her fingers in. She groped around in the grass and found a thin rope. She pulled. The door rose like a crocodile's jaw.

'Hey!'

Megan's head snapped up. Two more soldiers, thundering towards her. She threw herself down the trap and promptly slipped on the rickety stairs. Sharp edges punched her all the way down her spine to her ankles. No time to nurse the pain. She twisted, leaped and grabbed the rope. Soldiers' silhouettes darkened the steps. Megan yanked. The cellar door slammed shut.

Muffled voices sounded above her head. 'How do we get this thing open?'

'Stick your sword in the gap. Lever it up.'

There were grunts of exertion, then a nerve-shredding shriek as metal snapped. 'Cheap piece of shit!'

'Hey, what's this?'

The rope started to slither out of Megan's hand. She pulled back, yanked out a knife and sawed away frantically. Out of sight above her head, the soldiers pulled harder. She resisted, putting all her weight against the rope, continuing to cut away.

The rope split. Up above, there was a thud followed by swearing. Megan scrambled down the rest of the steps and, fast as she dared, made her way through the pitch black of the cellar. Crates and barrels rapped her shins; low-hanging beams clocked her in the head. If she could see at all, she'd be seeing double.

She bumped into some stone steps and clambered up them on all fours. Momentum carried her through a door and into a kitchen. Silence greeted her entrance, but her mind played back the last few moments. It hadn't been silent before, something she realized just as a group of middle-aged soldiers looked up from their beer and dice.

'Um . . .'

'Why are you all wet?' asked one of the soldiers. The others looked at him, their expressions not sure this was the most relevant question.

Megan inched towards the exit. 'Um . . .' As answers went, its ubiquity made up for its vagueness.

'Hey, aren't you . . . ?'

Megan's inching turned to mile-ing. She was out the door even as the soldiers were throwing chairs back and reaching for their weapons.

Floorboards squeaking beneath her soles, Megan charged down the corridor. Clomping up ahead forced a change of direction. She dived into the nearest room and found herself in the bedroom of one of Rekka's children: a boy, if the detritus of wooden swords, toy boats and alarmingly stained underwear strewn across the floor was any indicator. Megan scurried across the room and squeezed under the bed.

The door was kicked open. Megan held her breath, as much to avoid breathing in boy stench as to avoid giving herself away. There was a grunt, then the sound of receding boots. Megan breathed a sigh of relief, then made the mistake of breathing in. She clasped her hands over her mouth and fought the gag reflex.

When she had recovered, Megan wriggled out from under the bed and considered her options. If the soldiers knew who she was, they'd know where she'd be heading. But if she didn't go there, what was the point in all this?

She crept out into the corridor and got her bearings. Not too far away: just up the next floor and along a bit. She headed for the stairs but promptly scurried back at the sound of marching, hiding behind a door as a squad trooped past.

'Where're we going *now*?' a weary Rekka demanded.

'Great hall,' replied a soldier.

'Couldn't you at least have let me put a wrap on? Do you know how draughty that place gets, especially after the state the builders left it in.'

'Least of your problems.'

Their voices faded into the distance. More footsteps shuddered through the mansion. Megan got the impression – or hoped – they were heading for the exit. Everyone gathering in the great hall for the after-coup party? She waited until silence returned before scurrying upstairs. The first floor was deserted. She hurried along to her own room and eased open the door.

The room had been turned upside down. The bed was on its side, the contents of the wardrobe flung across the floor. Cate's cot was tipped over and empty. There was no sign of Cate or Synne.

Aldred, however, was there! ripping the drawers out of the chest.

six

'Where is it?'

'Where's what?'

Aldred drew his sword and advanced on her. 'Tell me. Now.'

Megan drew back, bewildered. Instinctively she reached for a knife. What the hell was going on? What was Aldred doing?

'Don't,' said Aldred, flicking his sword at her descending hand.

'You wouldn't really . . .'

'Where's the bag I gave you in Staziker?'

That? Why did he want that? He'd shoved it into her arms the day the witches had come for Cate, but it had contained nothing more than old clothes. What was so special about it?

'Tell me!'

There was a frightened intensity to Aldred's expression that made Megan's skin tighten. This was the man Eleanor had fallen in love with, who had fought with them, and now he was threatening her? 'Afreyda . . . Afreyda took it.'

'Where?'

'The barracks.'

Aldred's guard dropped. 'The barracks?' he mumbled to himself. 'There might still be time.'

Megan looked again at the room, or rather its remains. It was as if someone had eviscerated it. 'Where's Cate?' she asked.

'What?'

'My daughter. Where is she?'

'Don't know, don't care.' He sheathed his sword and tried to push past Megan.

She blocked his way. 'I answered your question,' she said, this time actually drawing her own blade. 'You answer mine.'

Before Megan could react, Aldred grabbed her knife hand and rammed it against the door frame, forcing the weapon out of her grip. Megan cried out in pain, then in alarm as he grabbed her by the throat. Her legs were hardly able to keep up as he marched her backwards into the corridor. They tangled up in each other. She tripped, bringing Aldred down with her. He landed on her with an impact that forced the air from her lungs.

'Do you really think your brat's worth this?' he spat. 'If it wasn't for her, she'd be alive.'

Megan gasped for breath. Eleanor? This was all about Eleanor? She could almost understand the rage: she had directed enough of it at herself. 'Eleanor . . . Eleanor thought so.'

Aldred grimaced and snorted. He clambered off Megan, looked down at her as if she was some tramp who'd drunk herself into a stupor on the streets, then headed for the stairs. Megan rolled over and scrambled for her dropped knife.

'I won't let you hurt Afreyda,' she called out after Aldred.

'Not much chance of that,' he said. 'They've taken her to the great hall. She's going to be tried for murder.'

Megan rushed after Aldred, but by the time she reached the front doors of the mansion he'd disappeared. There was still a guard on patrol. She ducked back into the house, waited until he had passed, then scurried across the lawn and into the darkened streets.

Where was Cate? What had happened to her? Scenarios played out in Megan's mind, some that left Cate safe, some . . . not so safe. There were any number of places between the Lord Defender's mansion and the hot springs; Synne could have sought sanctuary in one of them when trouble erupted. Megan could check them all, given time, but she was likely to draw unwanted attention to herself. The soldiers had been coming after her and Afreyda –

did they know about Cate too? Her importance to the witches?

There was a commotion in the street. Megan's instinct to hide was well-oiled by now. A squad of soldiers hustled a group of Hilite electors – old and middle-aged men for the most part – past her position. One of the Hilites snapped and rammed his elbow into one of the soldiers' faces. The rest of the soldiers pounced on him, reducing him to a pulp with their fists, boots and sword hilts. They left him a bleeding, groaning lump on the ground and pushed on towards the great hall.

Megan slid in behind them. If the soldiers had Cate, they might let slip where they were keeping her; if not, Cate was safe for the time being and it was Afreyda who needed her help. When they reached the great hall, however, Megan didn't have a clue how she was going to provide that help. The place was swarming with soldiers – at least a hundred of them.

Smoke curling through the gaps in the thatch gave her an idea. The builders' ladders had been kicked away and lay scattered on the ground, as if they were part of some giant child's game, but there was more than one way up. Megan slunk around to the back of the hall. It was quiet here – no patrols; there was no way in, just solid wood and small windows of smoky glass set high in the walls. Megan spotted what she was looking for: a series of spikes hammered into the timbers; emergency access to the roof. She looked up and swallowed. It wasn't that high – three, maybe four, storeys. A fall might not even kill her. Unlikely to leave her in one piece though.

She threw herself up the makeshift ladder, initial enthusiasm giving way under the tyranny of gravity. *Keep going*, she told herself. If she paused she'd only think about the iron digging into her fingers, the strain on her muscles, the icy wind freezing her sodden skin, which got icier with every foot she climbed.

A gull squawked at her as she clambered on to the roof, protesting the invasion of its realm. Megan shooed it away and made her way across the steep thatch. Despite her efforts to keep her footsteps as light as possible, scraps of dried grass broke away and fluttered off in the breeze. She prayed no one below would notice.

Megan reached one of the holes in the roof and peered in. Through the clouds that wafted past her from the fires below, she could see nothing beyond the criss-crossing beams apart from a sea of heads, both helmeted and bare. Soldiers, refugees, Hilites. Megan needed to get closer. She considered the beams. They were thick and looked strong enough to hold her weight, and this high up it'd be dark and smoky enough to cover her.

She slithered inside and wrapped herself around the tarred timbers. Down below – a lot more down below than she liked – three priests were congregating around the high table. Father Broose and his acolytes. Where was Father Galan? Was he part of all this?

There was a shout from the floor. Before Megan knew it there was a *crack*, and a crossbow bolt was quivering in the strut next to her head. She clung to the beam as if it were her grandfather. The commotion increased. More bolts were fired. The last one was met by a pathetic squawk and a cheer.

'Got you, you bastard. You won't nick my bread again, will you?'

Megan's hug of terror became one of relief as the shot gull hit the floor. The beam remained unconcerned in either case.

Father Broose rapped on the table. The hall fell silent. 'Today marks a turning point in the history of the Faith. By returning this city to the Realm we have—'

'Oh, please,' said Rekka, her scorn cutting through the room. Megan shuffled along so she could see her. She stood amidst a phalanx of guards, hair shining like copper in the firelight, body stiff and imperious. 'There is no Realm. The True control New Statham, the Sandstriders have Ainsworth, the north has emptied itself, and what remains of your army cowers in Janik waiting to be annihilated. You have no leaders, no ideas and, after this display, no hope.'

'We have God and the Saviours.'

Rekka sneered something in Hilite that made her

compatriots laugh. Father Broose went puce just from her tone. He barked an order. A soldier smashed his boot into the back of Rekka's knee. She cried out and crumpled to the floor. The Hilites shouted out their discontent and edged forward. Flame caught on steel as the soldiers brandished their weapons. The Hilites stepped back.

Father Broose rounded the table and advanced on Rekka. 'Those of you who wish it will be readmitted to the Faith. Those who do not . . .'

'Will be murdered?' said Rekka. She tried to stand but her leg gave out from under her.

'Those who reject the Faith can cross the Kartiks. It is a fate to which you were willing to condemn others. Meanwhile, this place will be a sanctuary for true believers.'

'Sanctuary? The witches are coming, whoever controls the city.'

'They won't come if we give them reason not to.'

'And what reason would that be?' asked Rekka.

'We know about the child.'

Fear scraped across Megan's skin like a thousand razor blades. 'Child?' said Rekka.

'Don't play innocent with me.'

'Vegar always likes it; especially when I—'

'Where is she?' snapped Father Broose.

'How should I know?' said Rekka. 'With her mother, I assume. I'd be careful about tangling with *her* if I was you.'

That was something, at least. Father Broose didn't have Cate. Megan offered up a heartfelt prayer of thanks.

'I suggest you persuade your husband of the correct course of action.' Father Broose considered for a moment. 'Once he has recovered.'

'If he's—'

'He was given the opportunity to surrender peacefully. Talking of which . . .'

He motioned to someone blocked off from Megan's view by more beams. There was a familiar cry of indignation and Afreyda was shoved forward until she stood next to Rekka. Fury burned within Megan at her mistreatment.

'You slaughtered two men of the Faith,' said Father Broose.

'They attacked me,' said Afreyda, her voice calm and matter-of-fact.

'They were sent to arrest you.'

'I did not want to be arrested.'

'You show no repentance for what you did?'

Now a little emotion did creep into Afreyda's tone. '*I am not the one who should repent.*'

'I believe all Diannon citizens have the right to resist arrest,' Rekka said to Father Broose. 'Some weird custom. She doesn't understand. Go easy on her.'

'That is not true,' said Afreyda.

'I was trying to help you,' hissed Rekka.

'Oh.' Afreyda turned to Father Broose. 'I obey the laws of the legitimate authority. You are not the legitimate authority.'

'Do not question me —' even from her high position, Megan could see saliva splutter from Father Broose's lips — 'heathen!'

'Heathen?'

'It's Stathian for someone who thinks for herself,' said Rekka.

Father Broose jabbed a finger at Afreyda. 'For the crime of murder you are hereby sentenced to death.'

Megan gasped. It took all her self-restraint not to drop from the ceiling like an avenging raptor and plunge a knife into Father Broose's heart. She stopped herself in time. That would only get them all killed. She had to bide her time, wait for her opportunity, even if every fibre of her being cried out in outrage and terror.

Father Broose turned to one of his priests. 'I take it you have a gallows here.'

'Down by the far docks, but it's not been used for years.'

'Executions are the tools of tyrants,' said Rekka.

'God's rule is not tyranny,' said Father Broose.

'Tell that to those who don't believe in Him.'

Father Broose gave a weary wave of his hand and returned to the table. 'Take them away.' His head drooped. The harshness dissipated from his voice. 'Meanwhile, let us pray. It has been a hard night for all of us. God, born of the eternal universe . . .'

Megan's momentum slid her off the roof far faster than she was expecting. The horizon spun and found itself in alarming positions. The ground began to accelerate towards her. She stuck an arm out, grabbed the spike at the top of the wall and dangled in mid-air. She swung a leg, looking to find something to support her feet. She found it by ramming her shin into it. Her eyes filled with tears, which at least meant she couldn't see the hard earth spinning below.

Fast as her trembling limbs would allow her, Megan climbed down the spike ladder, dropping to the ground earlier than was strictly necessary. She crouched and squeezed soil between her fingers, promising never to be so far away from it again, then hurried around to the front of the hall. Two sets of guards were heading away: one in the direction of the barracks, one towards the docks. She scurried after the latter.

They made their way past empty jetties and neglected piers. Megan flitted between barrels and empty crates that stank of fish. Only a couple of boats remained, stragglers at a party long since over. Most of the fleet had sailed after disgorging its catch, off to trawl the seas for more food to fill the bellies of the city's swollen population.

The opportunities for cover were becoming less

and less frequent. Megan was reduced to edging along a warehouse wall and simply hoping none of Afreyda's escorts looked too closely or, preferably, at all. She reached the limit of the building. Nothing but bare deck from her position to the gallows. It stood on the edge of the very last pier, as if shunned by civilization, the dim glow from the soldiers' lantern picking out its simple but chilling form.

There were four soldiers. Too far away to sneak up on, and as Afreyda had her hands tied behind her back she wasn't going to be much use. Charging them would be suicidal, but what choice did Megan have?

Voices floated down the waterfront, faint but clear. 'Right then, lads. String her up.'

'Problem there, sarge. No rope.'

'What do you mean, no rope?'

'Do you want me to jump up and hold on by my hands?' asked Afreyda.

'Shut up, love. It was one of my mates you skewered.' The sergeant dithered for a moment, then pointed at one of his men. 'Odi, go get some rope.'

'Where from, sarge?'

'This is a port, isn't it?'

'Yeah . . .'

'And what do you find in ports?'

'Ships, sarge.'

'Oh for Saviours' sake.'

'And sailors, sarge,' said another of the soldiers.

'And aubergines,' said the fourth.

'What?'

'I'm from Levenport, sarge. Number-one trading centre for aubergines in the Realm.'

'And we needed to know that because . . . ?'

'My dad grows 'em.'

'He's not a hangman in his spare time, is he?'

'No . . .'

'Then he's not sodding relevant, is he?' snapped the sergeant. 'If no one gets me some bloody rope in the next minute I'm going to start cutting heads off.'

'The High Priest didn't give us permission to . . . Oh, you don't mean hers.'

One of the soldiers broke away from the group and headed back towards Megan. She pressed against the wall and slunk down, trying to merge into the warehouse. The soldier – Odi, Megan assumed – spotted her anyway. He strode over to her.

'What you doing here?'

Megan held a hand up to him, keeping the other one tucked behind her back. 'Spare a shilling, sir?'

'Don't you know there's a curfew?'

'Thought there'd be less competition,' said Megan. 'Half a shilling?'

'Get out—'

Odi made to backhand her. Megan whipped her non-begging arm forward and sank a knife deep into his thigh.

She twisted, hearing the muscle fibres tear in the silence of the night, before Odi's pain receptors caught up with his mouth and he shrieked.

Megan leaped to her feet, throwing her weight at the soldier. He staggered and fell. Megan followed him, slipping in the huge puddle of blood that had already spurted out of Odi's wound. He aimed a half-hearted kick at her. She rolled out of the way, wrenched her knife out of his leg – which caused another ear-splitting shriek – and charged at the gallows.

The soldiers drifted towards her as she ran, their body language suggesting uncertainty. It didn't stop them drawing their swords though. Silver moonlight slashed across steel. Megan was going too fast to stop. The only choice was to commit herself absolutely.

'Afreyda!' she yelled. 'I'm coming for you.'

'I see!'

'No, literally!'

Megan hurled her knife at the soldiers. They flinched. Afreyda took advantage of their momentary distraction to barge them aside. Megan leaped at her, caught a flash of alarm in Afreyda's eyes, then the two of them were flying off the pier and tumbling through the air.

seven

As they plummeted through the icy water, Megan fought the instinct to release Afreyda and strike for the surface. Afreyda couldn't swim and her panic made her squirm in Megan's embrace. There was no way to reassure her, encourage her. All Megan could do was hold on tight and pray Afreyda trusted her.

She twisted, her occupied hands and the burden they held meaning she had to kick twice as hard to stop from sinking. The blackness made it impossible to see, the pressure on her lungs made it hard to think about anything other than sucking air back into them. Afreyda went limp in her arms. Had she given herself over to Megan or to a less earthly power?

They bumped against something. Megan risked unwrapping an arm from Afreyda to feel what it was. The slimy stone of the seawall. She pushed up, slowly as she could. She had to minimize the splash, hide their surfacing from the soldiers.

More darkness greeted them as they broke the water. They were under the pier at the point where it joined land. The sudden availability of air made Megan spasm. She fought it, rationing her breaths. Afreyda began to buck in her grasp. Megan clamped a hand on her mouth.

'Slowly,' she whispered.

Afreyda nodded. Megan released her hand a little. Afreyda's breath warmed her chilled skin.

A sliver of light flitted above their heads: the soldiers' lantern through the gaps between the slats. It briefly illuminated one of the pillars holding the pier up. Almost within arm's reach. She gave a little kick. They drifted towards it.

Megan wrapped an arm around the pillar, jamming Afreyda between her and it. Boots rattled the planks above them.

'Thought I heard something, sarge.'

'Yeah, well, I wouldn't look too closely if I was you.'

'What d'you mean?'

'You know who that girl was?'

'No.'

'The witches call her the Apostate.'

'What's one of those, sarge?'

'I don't know, but do you want to mess with someone the witches went out of their way to name?'

'What do we tell the High Priest?'

'The Diannon girl threw herself in the water before

we could hang her. She drowned. She could hardly swim with her hands tied, could she?'

'S'pose not, sarge.' There was an anguished shout in the distance. 'What do we tell him about Odi?'

'He missed while trying to sheath his sword,' said the sergeant. 'We'd better go see to him before he bleeds to death.'

Footsteps receded. There was a pause and curses of agony as they retrieved their comrade, then they picked up again, slower than before, and faded into silence. Megan looked around. There was a ladder halfway along the pier. She unclamped from the pillar and headed for it, swimming on her back, Afreyda pushing on to her with all the buoyancy of a brick.

'You could at least kick,' hissed Megan. Afreyda did so. They started to spin. 'In the same direction as me.'

They reached the ladder and clambered up to the pier. Afreyda bent over on all fours, coughing and spluttering and showing general disapproval of all the water that had entered her lungs. Megan crawled over and slapped her between the shoulders. She pulled a knife out of her sodden boot and began to saw through Afreyda's bonds.

'Are you all right?' Megan asked.

'Why did you . . . ?'

'It seemed like a good idea at the time,' said Megan.

'Could you not have just threatened them? They are obviously scared of you.'

'I didn't know that then.'

Afreyda rolled on to her back, rubbing her now-free wrists. Her clothes clung to her, revealing her every curve. Megan felt something twinge inside her. No time for that now.

She helped Afreyda to her feet. 'We have to get indoors, out of these wet things –' her subconscious sniggered – 'before we freeze to death. Then we have to find Cate.'

'Willas has her.'

'Willas has her? Why not . . . ?'

Afreyda bristled at the omitted 'you'. 'I distracted the soldiers while he got her away. I stand out a bit more than he does.'

'Where did he take her?'

'Up in the mountains. There are caves there.'

'She's safe?'

'For the moment.'

For the moment. Megan's instinct was to run to her, but that would mean crossing the city and risk attracting the attention of Father Broose's soldiers. Better Cate stayed with Willas. Megan had responsibilities in the city.

Squelching and shivering they made their way back into town. Megan pointed at one of the houses. Lights shimmered in its windows; faint coils of smoke crept out of its chimney and curled into the sky like lazy dancers moving to steps only they knew.

'Here,' said Megan. She rapped softly against the door. 'Know any Hilite?'

'Only *tiviki dámant plesántes*,' said Afreyda. 'It is what Willas uses to dismiss us at training.'

Megan rapped again. 'Possibly not much use.'

'True. I think *plesántes* is a rude word.'

'How rude?' said Megan. Afreyda whispered in her ear. 'That *is* rude. And probably impossible.'

'I know someone who could do it,' said Afreyda. 'Mind you, she was quite—'

The door opened a crack, revealing one wide eyeball and a forest of facial hair. Megan did her best to look pathetic and helpless. 'Could you help us, please?' she said.

'You Faith.'

'Yes . . .'

'*Tiviki dámant plesántes.*'

Afreyda's limited Hilite *had* come in handy. Who knew? 'We're not your enemy,' said Megan. 'The soldiers tried to kill us too.'

Afreyda tapped her chest. 'The Faith . . .' She mimed being hanged, which made up in melodrama what it lacked in realism.

'Can we . . . ?' Megan pointed at her and Afreyda and then inside. 'We can pay.' She pulled out a pouch of coins Rekka had doled out to her to help during her stay in Hil. She had no idea how much was there: whether it was a king's ransom or a child's pocket money.

The householder took the pouch and counted its contents. His expression softened a little. He opened the door a little more, looked up and down the deserted street and invited them in.

The heat hit Megan like a tidal wave, making her skin prickle. She resisted the urge to dive for the fire and shoulder away a woman who was tending to a pot of bubbling stew. She offered the woman a timid wave and another to the two small children who were sat at the table gawping at her and Afreyda.

The woman stared back warily. The man limped over to her – his ankle was strapped and he needed a stick to support himself. He handed over the pouch and had a brief conversation. The woman beckoned Megan and Afreyda over and pushed two steaming bowls of stew into their hands.

Megan forced the food down so fast it blistered the top of her mouth. 'Thanks for this,' she said between mouthfuls. 'Do you have any . . . ?' She pulled at her saturated tunic.

The woman got the message or at least appeared to. She barked orders at the man Megan assumed was her husband. He returned a few moments later with a pile of clothes. Megan and Afreyda sorted through them, selecting anything that remotely fitted. Melancholy swept through Megan. How many times had she done this with Eleanor?

Megan made to undress, then realized the householder was staring at them, waiting for the show to start. She cleared her throat. He grinned. His wife scowled and dragged him out of the room.

Clothes hit the floor with a splat. Megan warmed her cold, wet skin at the fire and snuck a glance across to Afreyda, who was doing the same thing. Afreyda's athletic perfection only made Megan aware of her own shortcomings: the nasty scar across her thigh; the bruises, scrapes, stretch marks and broken veins that mottled her skin; the ragged ear – not that Afreyda could complain about that. Even if what Megan was thinking was possible, what did she have to offer?

'This doesn't make sense,' said Afreyda.

'I think you wrap it around you like this.'

'Not the clothes, this . . . I do not know . . . this takeover. Father Broose cannot hope to hold the city.'

'They're scared,' said Megan.

'And stupid.'

'Don't knock stupidity. It's saved you on more than one occasion.'

'This stupidity will not save them,' said Afreyda. 'It will kill them. Willas has hundreds of men in the tunnels.'

'Might not be enough,' said Megan.

'That is not all. He got messengers away to the other Snow Cities.'

Megan stared into the fire as she calculated what that meant. 'That gives us . . . what? A couple of weeks before they march on us?'

90

Afreyda shook her head. 'The Tiptunites have a company less than a day away from Hil. We were meant to be training with them.'

'How many men?'

'About a thousand.'

'Saviours . . .'

'The Faith cannot hold the city against an attack from this side of the mountains,' said Afreyda. 'The Hilites and the Tiptunites will outnumber them at least three to one. And that is before the other cities mobilize.'

'It's going to be a massacre.'

Megan could envision the ignored pleas for mercy, the hacked-down bodies, the blood seeping across the streets like an infection. It didn't require much imagination; she'd witnessed it often enough. She had brought the Faithful here without thinking what it would mean for them – she had been too obsessed with Cate and her own desires. She should have tried harder with Fordel, persuaded him to make some concessions to the refugees, instead of letting him back them into a corner.

'Someone has to persuade them to surrender,' she said.

'The Hilites?'

'The Faithful. Father Broose and his acolytes.'

'Will he listen?' said Afreyda.

'Not to a simple peasant girl, no,' said Megan. 'But maybe to someone with a little more authority.'

eight

A call out in the street woke Megan. She opened her eyes to find dawn's first rays dappling the straw-covered floor, the fire burned down to a few dull embers, and Afreyda wrapped in her arms. Reluctantly she untangled herself and went to see what was happening. The smoky glass of the windows reduced the activity outside to flitting blurs.

'What is it?' asked Afreyda, her voice thick from sleep.

'I don't know,' said Megan. 'I can't see properly and they're speaking Hilite.'

'Perhaps it is all over?'

'Perhaps.'

Megan risked opening the door a notch. One of Father Broose's priests stood in the street, declaiming to the world. He was protected by four soldiers of the Faith who shivered as the odd snowflake drifted on to their grubby uniforms.

Megan eased the door shut again. 'Perhaps not.'

The householder strode out of one of the interior

rooms, dressed in a nightshirt that was a little too short to be considered polite.

'Do you know what's going on?' Megan pointed outside and gave an exaggerated shrug. The man walked his fingers then mimed hammering and sawing. 'I think the curfew's been lifted so people can go out to work.'

'I am glad you are here to translate,' said Afreyda.

If people were allowed back out, that was good. It would occupy the soldiers and mean Megan and Afreyda wouldn't have to sneak about so much. It also increased the risk someone would recognize them of course.

The householder disappeared out into the backyard. There was a gush and splash of running liquid, then he returned with a foaming jug. He wiggled it at Megan.

'That is beer, right?' she said. The man poured himself a cup and downed it. 'All right.' She pushed an empty cup over. 'I think I'm going to need it.'

Afreyda got up and began to stretch. 'You understand the plan?' said Megan.

'Yes,' said Afreyda, 'but I do not like it.' She reached down to her toes, legs straight, palms flat on the floor. 'You should not do this on your own.'

'I need you to get Cate. If it all goes wrong, run.'

'And if it all goes right?'

'I'm tempted to say run even faster.'

Afreyda rose. 'We should *both* get Cate,' she said, 'then make for Tiptun. Father Broose made his choice.

He should face the consequences.' Maybe he should, but Megan couldn't condemn the Faithful without even trying.

There was an explosion of noise as the children burst into the room, their words unintelligible but their demands obvious to any parent – breakfast, playthings, attention. Amidst all the politics and terror and violence, life went on. People needed food, shelter, someone to love.

Megan and Afreyda shared the kids' porridge then it was time to leave. They made an awkward goodbye. Megan, unsure how to thank the family, curtsied; the householder, in turn, gave her a paternal ruffle of the hair. It was good to be reminded people could be kind. Especially if you paid them.

With the fleet at sea and memories of the curfew still lingering, the streets around the docks were quiet. Afreyda tucked her hands in her sleeves and pulled her hood down low. 'Can you tell it is me?' she asked.

'No one carries off mangy fur quite like you.'

'Can you see my skin?'

'No, you're fine.'

Afreyda turned to go. No, Megan couldn't let her go like this. She remembered what Eleanor had said to her once. When you thought there was a chance you might never see someone again, you had to tell them how you felt, you had to be with them. For however short a time.

'Wait!'

Afreyda spun back round. 'What?'

94

'I . . .' Megan's courage evaporated as soon as it was called upon. She had fought witches and confronted priests and swum rivers and marched from one end of Werlavia to the other, but nothing was so scary as her own feelings and the dread of rejection. 'Give Cate a kiss from me.'

'She will not know it is from you.'

'*I* will,' said Megan.

Afreyda gave Megan a solemn nod before rearranging her hood and hurrying down the street. Megan took a few deep breaths to steady her beating heart and, raising her own hood, headed the other way, into the heart of the city. The people milling around were wary – the soldiers gripping their weapons tight, the civilians keeping their heads down as they scurried to their destinations. There was a yell. Megan looked down an alley to see a soldier being dragged away. The unmistakable crunch of breaking bones followed soon after.

Megan entered the great hall. There was an odour of sour beer and body odour the holes in the ceiling couldn't quite clear. It had been used as sleeping quarters the night before, and sergeants and corporals were still kicking awake a few stragglers hoping for a lie-in. Megan picked her way through to the high table. A soldier was slumped across it. She pulled his chair – the Lord Defender's chair – out from under him. The drop to the floor jolted him awake.

'Hey! What the . . . ?'

Megan sat down and lowered her hood. She tried to imagine how Eleanor would do this – apart from being more beautiful and poised and with far better hair. 'What's your name?' she said, haughty as possible.

'Er . . .'

'You can't remember?'

'Hang on,' said the soldier, bleary-eyed. 'It'll come to me.' He frowned and massaged his forehead. 'Andswarian.'

'Well, Andswarian, I want to speak to Father Broose.'

The soldier rubbed the sleep from his eyes. 'Hey, aren't you . . . ?'

'Megan of the house of Endalay, Countess of Ainsworth, Baroness of Laxton and Herth, First Lady of Kirkland, Overlord of the Spice Isles and Defender of the Southern Lands.' Andswarian gawped. 'Just tell him "Megan". He'll infer the rest.'

The other soldiers began to realize something was going on. They drifted towards her.

Megan leaned back and rested her feet on the table. 'What does a girl have to do to get arrested around here?'

Father Broose strode into the great hall, indignation incarnate. 'You dare come here?'

'You dare offer my daughter to the witches?' said Megan. 'Do you know what I usually do to people who try that?'

96

Father Broose took a step back, a little put out. 'Why is she sitting?' he snapped at Andswarian.

'Er, well, she wasn't doing any harm, father.'

The men hadn't known what to do with Megan while they'd been waiting for the priest. None of them were professional soldiers. A few months ago they would have been farmers, smiths, craftsmen. How should they treat a girl who had given herself up?

'You'd best stand, love,' said Andswarian.

Megan swung her feet down and stood up, trying to pretend it was the most natural thing in the world, that fear wasn't coursing through her veins. She swept down to Father Broose.

'You killed two soldiers of the Faith,' said Father Broose.

'I'm sorry about that.'

'You know the punishment for murder?'

'Yes.'

'You seem unconcerned,' said Father Broose. 'Do you expect me to show clemency because of our shared past?'

That shared past involved getting him out of Kewley before the witches got to him. 'I expect you to follow the law as laid down in the Book of Faith, father.'

'I will.' He cleared his throat. 'I hereby sen—'

Megan leaned in. 'Just one thing, father. I am a citizen of Ainsworth. Only the monarch or the lord of my home county can pass judgment on me.'

'The lord . . . ? You're asking to try yourself?'

'I'll settle for Father Galan,' said Megan. Father Broose's eyes narrowed. 'The High Priest of Eastport, capital of Ains—'

'I know where Eastport is,' said Father Broose.

'Sorry, father. You northerners do get confused with southern geography.'

'Why do you want Father Galan?'

'Don't worry,' said Megan, 'he's unlikely to let me off. He's tried to have me killed at least once.'

'Then why . . . ?'

'If I'm going to die, it's going to be properly. You don't want the Faithful and the Hilites to think you're some murderous tyrant, do you?'

'It is the law, father,' said one of Father Broose's priests.

Father Broose turned to him, an incredulous look on his face. 'You think to lecture *me*?'

The priest shuffled awkwardly. 'No, father. Just remind, that's all. It's been . . . you know . . . Things get forgotten. Chapter seven, paragraph eight, where Edwyn lays out . . .'

Father Broose's glare froze the words in the priest's mouth. 'Thank you, Brother Hlér.'

The crowd murmured in agitation. 'Very well.' Father Broose motioned to a squad of soldiers. 'Go fetch Father Galan.' His voice darkened. 'Make sure he knows what's expected of him.'

'While you're at it . . .' said Megan.

Father Broose sighed. 'What?'

'I believe I'm allowed someone to speak in my favour.'

'Chapter seven, paragraph nine,' said Brother Hlér in the smallest voice possible.

'Unless you can summon one of the Saviours,' Father Broose said to Megan, 'it's not going to help you.'

'I'd like Fordel.'

'That jumped-up pervert?'

'He is alive, isn't he?' said Megan.

'Alive and lecturing us on prison administration,' said Father Broose with a grimace.

'I'm sure you can spare him. Indulge a countess. The job doesn't come with that many perks.'

Father Broose gave a tired wave to another squad. As they left, Megan spun on her heel and returned to the high table. She wanted a drink, but she feared the cup would shake itself out of her grip. Instead she gripped the edge of the table, hoping the pressure would squash her nerves. How had Eleanor done this? How had Gwyneth? It was a performance, a self-confidence trick, and if she got her lines wrong she'd face more than catcalls from an angry audience.

The hall was filling up: soldiers and civilians, both Hilites and refugees from the Realm. Word had got around something interesting was happening. The bigger the audience the better, but Megan couldn't ease her increasing anxiety. She took deep breaths while trying not to appear as if she was doing so.

Father Galan was escorted into the hall, followed moments later by Fordel. Both men were bruised and bloodied, but whereas the High Priest simmered with impotent rage, the Secretary maintained a look of bemusement.

'This is monstrous, Broose,' spluttered Father Galan. 'You'll—'

'I need you to pronounce sentence on this citizen of your county,' said Father Broose. 'Nothing more.'

'Isn't it traditional to hear the evidence first?' asked Fordel.

'She admitted her crime.'

'Not to me she didn't,' said Father Galan.

'Very well.' Fordel jabbed a finger at Megan. 'Girl, say your piece.'

Here goes. Megan straightened, wishing she had Eleanor's height. 'I am Megan of the houses of Endalay and Kalvert, Countess of Ainsworth *and legitimate descendant of Bardanes the Avenger, King of Werlavia.* I hereby claim the throne of the Unifier, all the rights and privileges granted to him by the Saviours, the lands of the Realm and the allegiance of the Faith.'

nine

The great hall fell silent, so quiet you could almost hear the snowflakes drifting in from the gaps in the ceiling. People glanced at each other, expressions of doubt, confusion and incredulity etched on to their faces. Megan hadn't been expecting cheers of approval, but *some* element of support would have been nice.

'Are you serious?' said Father Broose.

'Are you serious, *Your Majesty*?' Megan corrected.

'I've never heard such a pile of nonsense.'

Megan looked to Father Galan. She could see the calculation in his eyes as he debated which side to come down on. *Come on*, she silently urged. *Play your part.* 'Gaderian Endalay's daughter did marry the son of King Bardanes . . .' he said.

'That was nearly two hundred years ago!'

'And the Saviours appeared to the Unifier nearly four hundred years ago. We don't dismiss *that*, do we?'

'There is no throne for her to claim,' said Father

101

Broose. 'It was abolished after the war. I should know, I was on the council that abolished it.'

Father Galan smiled slyly. Megan got the impression he was starting to enjoy himself. 'If you were, you would know the council had no powers to abolish an institution explicitly granted by the Saviours. The council merely abolished the aristocracy. The throne was left in abeyance until a . . . suitable candidate could be found.' Namely, one who survived the priests' attempts at slander, exile and assassination.

'And you think you have one? This . . . this . . . ? How can she claim to be legitimate? The Endalay woman wasn't married.'

'All adopted children are legitimate,' said Fordel. 'It's a quirk of the law. They also carry the same rights of inheritance as natural-born children.'

'And what do you know of our law?' demanded Father Broose.

'It's much the same as ours. We got lumbered with it after the Unifier paid us his visit.'

Father Broose paced the hall, wringing his hands as if he could squeeze another argument out of them. 'This is all a legal fiction you've concocted to justify your grab for power.'

Of course it was. Every claim for power rested on fictions: that it was granted by God, blood, precedent. In the end, though, you had one person trying to persuade a hell of a lot of other people they should be listened to above all others, that they knew what was best. Megan might not know what was best, but she did know what was better.

She turned her attention to the crowd and raised her voice. 'A Tiptunite army will be upon us before nightfall. Those of us they don't slaughter will be exiled back to the Realm and left to the mercy of the witches, and we all know they have no mercy.' Mention of the witches prompted murmurings of anxiety from the massed ranks. 'The Hilites gave us sanctuary when they had no reason to, and to turn on them like this is near unforgivable. But only near. I can negotiate with them – sort this mess out. I might not be the best queen you could have, but I'm the only one. And I'm the last chance you have of staying alive.'

'We have come too far,' said Father Broose. 'The Hilites . . .'

'They'll welcome an amnesty. They don't want to see any more death either. Do you, Fordel?'

'It does lead to lots of ill-tempered probate actions.' Fordel spread his hands magnanimously. 'We would welcome a peace accord with the Faith, led by a restored monarchy. One that respected our rights and independence.'

'And what of the tens of thousands beyond the mountains you left to the mercy of the witches?' asked Father Broose.

Megan had known this was coming and she didn't have an answer for it. The crowd stared at her, waiting. She swallowed, tried to think of some non-committal platitude.

'I . . .'

Fordel held up a hand. 'If it pleases Your Majesty,' he said, 'I've been reviewing things with the leaders of the other cities. We think we might be able to accommodate the additional refugees.'

This threw Megan, though the crowd muttered what she hoped was approval. 'You have? Why didn't you tell me?'

'It was an administrative matter,' said Fordel. 'Nothing to bother you with.' The fate of thousands an 'administrative matter' – there was a bureaucrat's answer for you. 'We'll be happy to discuss the details with representatives of the Faith.'

Father Broose jabbed a gnarled finger at Megan. 'I am not going to disobey the Pledges to gain what is already ours. *I* pledged to uphold the Faith and destroy its enemies.'

'Not following the Faith doesn't make people our enemies.'

Someone in the crowd shouted, 'Yeah!' Megan took it as a token of support. She stepped to within arm's reach of Father Broose and slipped a hand inside her sleeve. Her fingers brushed the handle of her back-up plan, warmed by her fiery body. She hoped it wouldn't come to that, but the calculation was frighteningly easy. Thousands of lives in exchange for one.

'It's time to make a decision, father. Either recognize my claim or order your soldiers to move against me.' She leaned in and lowered her voice. 'Only make sure they're yours before you do.'

The men lining the room nudged one another, exchanged muttered comments. Which way would they go? Did they understand what was going on? Did they care? Were they waiting for someone else to make the decision or were they going to realize the power lay in them and the arms they carried?

Father Broose stalked to the high table. He sat down and folded his arms. 'Pah,' he said. 'Have your fantasy. Do with me what you will.'

'I'm not going to do anything with you,' said Megan.

'Your Hilite cronies then.'

'The amnesty applies to all.' Megan took a deep breath and looked around the ranks of soldiers. Father Broose might have given in, but would they? 'Where's your commanding officer?'

The men looked among themselves. 'Not here,' one eventually said.

'*Any* officer?'

'They're always the first to bugger off.'

'All right, then –' Megan counted the stripes –

'sergeant. Order all the men in the city to stand down and release any Hilite prisoners.'

'Um . . .'

'Fordel will go with you. Make sure there are no . . . misunderstandings.'

'I'll have to insist the soldiers of the Faith disarm themselves,' said Fordel. 'Temporarily of course. As a sign of good, er, faith.'

'You should have insisted on that before all this happened,' said Father Galan.

Yes, thought Megan, *you should have, Fordel. Why didn't you?* 'Sergeant?'

'This amnesty sounds more like a surrender.'

'We're guests here,' said Megan. 'Would you go into your neighbour's house waving your sword?' The sergeant made to speak. 'No, don't answer that.' She foresaw him trotting out decades' worth of border disputes, noise complaints and wars over whose latrines emptied out on to whose land.

'As hosts we'll make sure there's plenty of food and drink available,' said Fordel.

The sergeant nodded in appreciation, then looked to Father Galan. The High Priest gave a slight nod. 'All right.' He motioned to Fordel. 'After you.' The two men marched out of the hall.

Megan turned to a squad of soldiers. 'Would you take Father –' Father Galan's cough didn't quite

106

disguise the word 'brother' – 'Broose here somewhere safe?'

'Safe as in "safe from harm" or safe as in "safe from people seeing him come to harm"?'

'The first.'

'Your call, ma'am.'

The soldiers led the dejected Father Broose away. Megan spun slowly on her heel, taking in all the people staring at her, waiting to see what would happen next. She didn't have a clue what it would be, other than it was time to find her daughter.

Cate was in the Lord Defender's mansion, gurgling away to herself in her restored cot. Megan scooped her up. The gurgling stopped. Cate didn't start bawling, but the expression on her face did seem to say, 'You again?'

'How are you, sweetheart?' said Megan.

'I'm fine.'

For an alarming moment, Megan thought her daughter of a few months had learned to talk, which suggested she *was* the Saviour and raised all kinds of questions, until she recognized Synne's voice. She turned round. Synne was trying to restore some order to the room.

'I'm . . . I'm sorry. I thought . . .'

'That I wasn't important?' said Synne. 'Did you worry about me at all?'

If you're fighting for the people, Megan's inner critic

107

scolded, *it would be nice if you thought about them sometimes.*

'Of course I did. How are you?'

'I said I was fine.'

'Wasn't sure if that was just, you know, ventriloquism.'

'What?'

'Nothing,' said Megan. 'Have you seen Afreyda?'

Synne scowled. 'She is at the infirmary.'

The world stopped. Possibilities and consequences rushed through Megan's brain. 'The infirmary! Why didn't you tell me?'

'You would have had to notice me first.'

Megan looked down at Cate, reluctantly settling in her grasp, then over to Synne, who sighed and held her arms out.

Megan burst into the infirmary and hurried along the rows of beds, where soldiers and Hilites nursed broken bones, split heads and simmering grievances. Men nudged each other as she passed, muttering comments unheard or not understood. She paid them no heed. Despite Synne's assurances, she had to know Afreyda was going to be all right.

Afreyda was sat at the far end of the stuffy cabin, having a gash in her arm sewn up by Willas. Megan wanted to throw her arms around her but held back and offered nothing more than a supportive smile. In return, Afreyda gave her a wave with her good arm.

Megan leaned in to examine her wound. Clean but nasty. 'Does it hurt?'

'Yes.' Afreyda winced. 'Especially if you prod it.'

'Sorry.'

Willas passed Afreyda a bottle of clear liquid Megan suspected wasn't water. Afreyda uncorked it and downed a hefty slug. Her head lolled. She passed out.

'You're meant to rub it in,' said Willas, peering over her sprawled form. 'Keep the cut from getting infected.' Afreyda failed to respond. Failed to do anything in fact.

Willas turned to Megan. 'So, queen, huh?'

Megan nodded distractedly. She pointed at Afreyda. 'Shouldn't we . . . ?'

'She'll be all right in a minute.'

'How do you know if you're meant to rub the stuff in?'

'Let's just say she's not the first to make that mistake,' said Willas. 'Or even consider it a mistake.'

Spasms racked Afreyda's body then she went rigid. Her eyes snapped open. 'What . . . ?' she croaked.

'How're you feeling?' asked Megan.

'I am not.'

Megan looked to Willas. 'Is that normal?'

'Possibly . . .'

'Something tells me you're not a real doctor.'

'I only do the basics,' said Willas. 'Stitches, setting broken bones, hangover cures . . .'

Megan sat on the edge of the bed and stroked Afreyda's hair. She seemed peaceful enough. 'What happened out there?'

'A few scuffles. Nothing serious.'

'Nothing serious?' Megan pointed at Afreyda's arm. 'What caused that? A dirty look?'

'No one's a corpse who shouldn't be,' said Willas. 'Though I don't hold out much hope for your weird little stalker over there.'

'My . . . ?'

Megan looked across to the bed opposite, where a sheet was drawn up to the chin of a still figure. Scarlet bloomed across the linen, beginning to brown at the edges. She crept over, knowing what to expect but praying she was wrong, that it had nothing to do with her.

As Megan's shadow fell over her face, Clover's eyes fluttered. Megan let out a little gasp. 'She's not . . .'

Willas frowned and shook his head. He pointed to a wooden bowl beside Clover's bed. A crossbow bolt sat in it, its point and shaft smeared with blood as if a child had made a half-hearted attempt to paint it.

Clover's eyelids fluttered. 'Mother?' she said, her voice struggling to rise above a whisper.

'Hey,' said Megan, equally softly.

'Is the . . . ? Is the Saviour safe?'

'Yes.' *She always was. What happened to you was completely pointless. I should have sent you away, but instead I used you.*

110

'Can I . . . ?' Clover coughed. Blood dribbled from the corner of her mouth and down her chin. 'Can I see her?'

'I . . .'

Clover tried to push herself up. She barely managed a couple of inches before she slumped back down again. 'Please, Mother.'

Megan had spent so long denying the witches' fantasy it seemed hypocritical to indulge it now, but could she deny the last wish of a dying girl? Seeing Cate would give her some comfort, even if it was the comfort of a lie.

'I'll go get her,' she said. 'If she gets cranky because I woke her up, it's your fault.'

Clover managed a faint smile. Megan hastened back to the mansion, plucked Cate from the arms of a bemused Synne, and ran back to the infirmary as fast as she thought Cate could tolerate.

It was too late. Clover was gone; her head slumped to the side, death already leaching the colour from her skin. Megan buried her face into the warmth of her daughter's body and murmured the all-too-familiar words of the funeral prayer.

The celebration of the peace that night was an ill-tempered affair. Hilites and Faithful split into two distinct clumps, glaring at each other across the no-man's-land between them, soured rather than cheered by the beer that flowed. Missiles arced between them – cups; food scraps; once, rather enterprisingly, a whole bench — until Fordel deployed a contingent of newly returned border guards to keep order.

Megan was on her own. Afreyda was still sleeping off the drink Willas had given her; Cate was back at the mansion with Synne. Initially stilted conversations with the refugees became more raucous and one-sided as the evening wore on. Congratulations became pre-emptive blame. Tentative questions about the food situation, how long the cabins would take to complete and when those south of the Kartiks would be let through became shrill demands she personally achieve everything. The refugees accepted she had by some trick averted potential disaster, but it was just that: potential. It was an abstract concept, hard to grasp and, anyway, in the past. Their gratitude evaporated under the pressure of more concrete concerns. If Megan couldn't deal with them, what was the point in her being queen?

The muggy heat in the great hall coupled with the alcohol made Megan tired and irritable, slowed her brain down. Her attempts at regal concern dissolved into schoolgirl snappishness. Someone jostled her — probably by accident. She found herself reaching for a knife, only the wide eyes of those around her staying her hand. She muttered an apology and stumbled out of the hall.

Out in the streets the cold air pinched her cheeks, sobering her or at least giving the illusion of doing so. She wove through the fringes of the party, refusing requests to celebrate she suspected might not be mutually enjoyable. No one pushed too hard. Her reputation preceded her, protected her. For the moment at least.

Megan hadn't realized where she'd been heading until she found herself there: Eleanor's grave. It had been on the edge of town when originally dug; now half-completed cabins stood sentinel. She sat on the icy ground and brushed off the headstone dust that had drifted in from the building site.

'Is this why you were so eager to sacrifice yourself?' she said. 'So you wouldn't have all this grief?' There was no reply, but even the silence of the night seemed wiser than Megan. 'You could have warned me what you were planning. Given me a chance to prepare myself. Or tell you to sod right off.'

She sighed, ran her fingers through her hair. 'I'm not you. I'm not sure if I can keep doing this. I've been lucky so far, but how long can I stay lucky? I've not had to think beyond the next day. Now I've got thousands of people looking to me, demanding everything, and I've no idea where to even start to start.'

'Haranguing the dead?'

Megan twisted her head. It was Fordel. 'It's the only way I can win an argument with her,' she said. 'Did you follow me?'

'I was concerned. Don't want to lose a queen before the day's out. It would look careless.'

'Funny how things worked out how you wanted them.'

'We're all victims of events.'

'Some of us are keen to make ourselves victims,' said Megan.

'I don't know what you mean.'

'Willas just happened to be in position to get Cate to safety? Rekka's children just happened to be hundreds of miles away in Downín? The city guard just happened to surrender without putting up a fight? There just happened to be a thousand Tiptunite soldiers on the doorstep?'

'When you put it like that . . .'

'Father Broose's acolytes – they're working for you, aren't they? What did you offer them?'

'They *are* Hilites,' said Fordel. 'They know where their loyalties lie. But in the spirit of religious reconciliation, the bar on followers of the Faith being electors of Hil is being lifted.'

Bribing them with their own rights: an easy bargain. 'What if I hadn't been able to get the Faithful to step down?' asked Megan.

Fordel looked at her knowingly. Megan's veins couldn't have run colder if she had opened them up to the night air. 'That was never part of the plan, was it?' she said. 'You didn't expect me to survive and claim the throne, did you?'

Moonlight gleamed off Fordel's eyes. 'It was an unexpected bonus.'

'You wanted the priests dead, me a martyr and

Cate queen. Saviours, you're as bad as the witches. You manipulated everyone: me, the refugees, the people of Hil, Vegar—'

'I did not manipulate the Lord Defender,' said Fordel.

'Really?'

'I let his wife do it. She's had much more experience.'

Fordel wandered around Eleanor's grave. 'What do you think is better for Hil, for the rest of the Snow Cities? A religious zealot or someone who recognizes other people have a right to exist? We need each other. And with the priests taken care of, there's nothing to stop us.'

ten

The old man had soiled himself all three ways and was only standing because he was being held up by two burly menservants. Beside the trio, a man in the rich clothes of a merchant was rubbing his hands. Damon felt despair wash over him. The merchant was trying to wash away the guilt, he realized. Or maybe Damon was projecting his own.

Gwyneth looked up from the Unifier's throne, which she had taken to treating as her own personal armchair. 'We're not taking in unwanted grandparents,' she said. 'Drop him in the Rustway with the rest of the trash.'

The merchant smiled unctuously. 'If it pleases my lady, I've brought you a priest to, well . . .'

The soldiers in the throne room snapped to attention, though what threat the old man posed Damon couldn't say.

'This is a priest?'

The old man shook his head frantically. 'No, no, no. I'm just a . . . I'm just a pilgrim eager to learn the teachings of the Saviours.'

Gwyneth looked around. Tobrytan and the other officers were off officer-ing. Her gaze fell on Damon. 'Question him.'

'Me?'

'Determine if he's a priest.'

'How do I—?'

'Do it,' said Gwyneth, 'or I'll have you strangled with each other's intestines.' Damon wondered what types of books she'd been reading to get those kinds of ideas, then remembered some of the grimmer parts of the Book of Faith, the bits they *didn't* get the kids to act out on Saviours' Day.

He approached the old man, as close as olfactory considerations would allow. Could he condemn this pathetic thing to the witches? He'd seen what they'd done to the priests they'd captured. Pre-mortem cremation was the favourite. But how could he prove a negative?

Damon examined the man, looking for clues. He had a shiny pate, which could be simply ageing – the priests had introduced the tonsure to excuse male-pattern baldness. No sign of the priests' usual obesity, but a few months of rations did wonders for the figure. The clothes, underneath the stains, were rough wool. Easy enough to come by for a few pennies. Nothing conclusive.

Damon gave him a small wave. 'Hello,' he said. 'Drink?'

'Some water –' hacking coughs gripped the man – 'some water would be most kind.'

Damon threw his hands up in the air. 'He's innocent,' he said to Gwyneth. 'No priest would ask for water.'

'I'm not convinced.'

Damon grimaced and turned back to the man. 'You said you were a pilgrim. What did you do before that?'

'Silversmith, sir.'

'Silver, huh?'

Damon looked around. He plucked Gwyneth's ever-present goblet from her hands, chucked the dregs of wine on to the flagstones to an indignant cry from Gwyneth and handed it to the would-be silversmith. 'Tell me what the hallmarks mean.' *Please.*

'Certainly.' The man examined the base. 'Eight hundred fine silver. Made in Janik in the year 270. Not a very good piece. One of hundreds knocked out for Edwyn the Fourth's many parties, I'm guessing.'

Thank the Saviours for that, thought Damon. The soldiers around the throne room relaxed. He and the man shared a mutual nod of relief. Damon made to take the goblet back. He then noticed the man's fingers. Stained with decades' worth of ink. He hadn't spent his life smithing silver – he'd spent it writing. And there'd only be one reason he would be keen to hide that.

Damon swallowed his suspicion. 'No priest knows about practical matters,' he said to Gwyneth, trying to affect a casual shrug. The old man had probably picked up the knowledge from a father or an uncle in the trade. 'Let him go. He's harmless.'

'Release him,' Gwyneth said to the merchant's men-servants.

The old man dropped to his knees, either voluntarily or involuntarily. 'Thank you, my lady, oh thank you.'

Gwyneth preened a little. 'Can I go now?' Damon asked her.

Her eyes flicked to the witches lining the room. She cocked her head. One strode forward. Damon's mouth started to form an objection. An axe swung through the air. Hot blood splattered on to Damon's face. The old man's torso toppled forward. His head rolled away, his expression still one of gratitude.

'What?' said Damon. 'He wasn't . . . I'd . . .'

'I realized I didn't care,' said Gwyneth. She beckoned Damon to her. 'Now do what I told you to do,' she whispered into his ear, 'or I'll realize I don't care about you.'

The miniature crossbow was exquisite. Varnished hickory stock, gold-plated limb, silver trigger, the targeting sight a pearl with a notch carefully filed into it. Its reduced size limited its range, of course, but at this distance its target wouldn't stand a chance. Unfortunately for Damon, its target was his head.

'I've come to buy, honest,' said Damon through his held-up hands, thinking there was no surer way to flag your untrustworthiness than appending your sentences with 'honest'.

'I don't serve witches here,' said the apothecary at the other end of the crossbow.

Damon glanced down at the uniform the witches had provided him with. 'It's not what it looks like,' he said. 'Honest.'

'Get out!'

'I have money.'

'Show me.'

Damon slowly lowered his hands to his belt. He fished out the pouch Gwyneth had provided and tipped its contents on a nearby table. Sovereigns gleamed in the light of the scores of candles lining the perimeter of the shop. The apothecary's eyes gleamed in turn. Damon pushed one of the gold coins towards him.

'How about we call that a pre-service tip?'

The apothecary's crossbow vanished along with his hostility. He crossed the room and pocketed the sovereign with a speed and dexterity that appealed to Damon's sense of professionalism.

'What does sir require? Something for the lady in your life?'

'You could say that.'

'Got her into trouble?'

'More the other way round,' muttered Damon. 'I'm looking for – I don't know what you'd call it – an anti-ageing product.'

'Anti-ageing? As in . . . ?'

'Stop it altogether. Yes.'

The apothecary kept his face straight, but his eyes couldn't help flicking to the pile of gold on the table. Damon scooped them back into the pouch one by one, pausing each time to give the apothecary time to count them. He cocked his head. The apothecary pursed his lips then disappeared through a beaded curtain.

Damon followed him into a dimly lit back room. Tapestries stitched with occult-looking symbols hung on the walls. A skull grinned from the top shelf of a bookcase, looking decidedly cheerful for someone who had died and had the flesh boiled from his bones. Coils of incense wafted through the air with the artificial sweetness favoured by those who wished to mask a hobby that involved evisceration.

He noticed the light source. 'Black candles? Really?'

'Too much?'

'At least you don't have a stuffed . . . oh, you do.' A crow stared at Damon with glassy eyes, its malignancy forever perpetuated.

'My customers find it reassuring,' said the apothecary. 'Now, what kind of solution are we looking for, sir?'

'The kind of solution that makes everything look completely natural.'

The apothecary pursed his lips. 'That could be hard. Young women don't suddenly drop dead, sir. As a rule.'

'It's not for *her*. It's *for* her.'

'Ah. I understood it was your girlfriend you were looking to . . . preserve.'

'She's not my . . .' Saviours, after the events of a few nights previous, maybe she thought she was. Damon tried to swallow but found his throat too scared to move. The last man she'd been involved with had been brutally killed. This was not a woman who broke off relationships with an 'it's not you, it's me'.

'It's for a man,' said Damon. 'An old man.'

'That makes things a lot easier, sir.'

The apothecary selected a key from a ring and unlocked a drawer. He took out a jar of crushed herbs and measured a small quantity into a scale pan, which he then poured into a pouch made of dried skin. Damon thought it best not to ask what kind of skin.

'That should accomplish what you're looking for,' said the apothecary, handing the pouch over.

'And it'll look natural?'

'As if his heart had given out.'

Damon noticed a door behind the apothecary. A back exit? For a moment he thought about asking if he could use it – evade the escort waiting for him outside. But that still left the middle and outer cities to sneak out of and if the True caught him, well . . . They had hung, drawn and quartered a city guard who had tried to instigate a rebellion, a punishment not seen since before Unification. Damon preferred his internal organs to stay, well, internal.

He handed over payment for the herbs. 'Would sir be wanting a receipt?' asked the apothecary.

'I'm not entirely convinced we should be leaving a paper trail,' said Damon.

'As you wish, sir. Some customers need one. For tax purposes.'

'Poison's deductible?'

'No –' the apothecary grinned in what was definitely not an advertisement for his dentist – 'but health care is.'

According to Gwyneth, the general kept wine by his bed to help him sleep at night. All Damon had to do was tip the herbs into the cup and let bastardry take its course. Whichever way you looked at it, it was cold-blooded murder. While his ethical objections to such an act weren't as strong as they should be, he still feared the consequences, for his body if not for his soul. But what choice did he have but to do what Gwyneth commanded and hope she didn't drop him in it?

Osgar's room was in the old royal apartments, a couple of floors below Gwyneth's. It was empty for the moment: no general, no wine. He must still be plotting with Gwyneth and his captains. How could she look him in the eye, knowing she had ordered his death? Damon would have been at least a little embarrassed. But then, how long had Gwyneth known what she was going to do to Megan and their grandfather? Straightforward assassination was nothing more than a household chore to her now.

Damon looked for somewhere to hide. The room was bare but for the essential furniture. Judging from the discoloration in the paint and the gaps in the dust, it had been stripped recently – the general's ostentatious austerity. Damon crept outside. A tapestry hung from ceiling to floor, depicting the priests' victory over the True or, rather, the priests' victory over a demon army three times their number. He wondered why the True had left it there. Perhaps they didn't recognize themselves among the vanquished.

He squeezed in behind it. The mustiness made him want to sneeze. He jammed his knuckles in his nostrils and pulled his sleeve over his mouth. It helped a little. He found himself dozing. The hour was late and the constant stress was tiring him out. Here, cloaked by the heavy fabric, it was easy to forget everything, surrender to the darkness.

The scuffing of leather upon stone jolted him awake. He peeked out. A soldier carrying a pitcher and a goblet. Osgar's midnight nostrum. The soldier disappeared into the general's room and reappeared moments later, empty-handed. Damon watched him troop away. Osgar himself would be along soon. It was now or never. He slipped out from behind the tapestry, contemplated the stairs the soldier had taken. Away from this. Into Gwyneth's wrath.

He trudged into the general's room.

Damon sat down on the edge of Osgar's bed, weighing the pouch of herbs in his palm, nerving himself to pour them into the pitcher of wine standing on the bedside table. A few seconds, that's all it'd take, and then he could be out of there. He thought about praying, asking God for guidance, but when had God ever answered? *Sod it.* He tipped the pouch into the wine and made to leave.

Approaching footsteps, the rasp of Osgar's voice as he ordered unseen men to let no one disturb him, the crash of boots snapping to attention. Damon looked around at the barren room in despair. Only one thing for it. He threw himself to the floor and crawled under the bed. Some assassin he was, reduced to a child's tactic.

Candlelight shimmered across the floorboards. Springs creaked and pushed into Damon's back. He waited for the telltale tinkle of liquid. It didn't come. Of all the nights to turn teetotal. He wondered if the apothecary would give him a discount for repeat business.

There was the burnt whiff of extinguished candle. More creaking and scratching as the general made himself comfortable. A broken spring clawed Damon in the shoulder, the shoulder where the True had forcibly tattooed the star-broken circle. He gritted his teeth and endured the pain in silence. There was no other choice but to wait out the night.

Necessity kept him awake. He couldn't afford to fall asleep and let his snoring or even heavy breathing give him away. Instead he lay there, staring into darkness, thinking about everything he'd ever done, everything he'd had done to him. Saviours, what a pathetic existence. Surviving from day to day, pledging allegiance to whoever was most likely to kill him if he didn't. Maybe once the war was over the True would let him go and he could . . . and he could do what? Repeat all this somewhere else?

There was a commotion out in the corridor. Changing the guard? Above Damon, Osgar shifted but didn't wake. Someone entered, closed the door behind him. Boots crossed the room, as silent and indistinct as a phantom's in the blackness.

The bed jerked. 'Tob—?'

The general's query was reduced to muffled squeals. The bed rocked from side to side. Springs clawed Damon. There were repeated slaps against the mattress. And then all was calm.

Damon lay as still as possible, holding his breath, willing his heart to stop its conspicuous thudding. Something scurried across the floorboards beside him. Wiry fur brushed his cheek followed by the flicks of a sinewy cord. A rat.

The intruder paced around the bed. His intonation of the funeral prayer confirmed his identity: Tobrytan. He'd killed Osgar, but why? Had Gwyneth got to him too?

The rat's tail continued to swish at Damon's face. He tried to nudge it away with his head. This only served to pique the rat's interest. The tail was replaced by the fleshy point of a nose. Damon's nerves fluttered, muscles contracted, cramp stabbed the soles of his feet. He just had to hold on a few more seconds, surely. Tobrytan was almost finished. Damon mentally recited the last few words along with him.

'. . . out of death comes life.'

Tiny teeth nibbled at Damon's lips. He snapped, batted the rat away with his fist. It screeched in protest.

'What?'

Damon's hand froze in mid-swipe. Metal slashed against flint. There was a spark, then the warm glow of a candle. A few seconds later, Damon was staring into Tobrytan's grim face.

'You know,' said Damon, 'I don't think I'm cut out for rat wrangling.'

'Get out from under there.'

Tobrytan stood back up. Damon considered staying where he was, but Tobrytan was perfectly capable of thrusting his sword through the mattress. He wriggled out and got to his feet. Osgar was sprawled out on the bed, his pillow haphazardly shoved under his head. That's how Tobrytan had done it: he'd smothered the old man.

'Should I ask?' said Damon.

'He had lost sight of what was important,' said Tobrytan. 'We must secure the Saviour. At any price.'

Easy to say when you weren't the one paying that price. 'You want to march on Hil?'

'God commands it.'

'And the fact your daughter is held prisoner there . . . ?'

'What are you doing here?'

Damon brushed the dust from his clothes. 'Oh, you know,' he said, trying to sound insouciant. Tobrytan's hand moved to his sword. 'You think that's going to help? It'll make things look very suspicious.'

'I caught you standing over the general's body and brutally hacked you down while trying to escape.'

'You *do* have a sense of humour.'

Tobrytan grinned. It was the most unsettling thing Damon had ever witnessed. 'Will anyone believe anything else?'

'Will anyone believe a weakling like me could overpower Osgar?' said Damon. 'He might be old, but he was strong.'

Doubt flickered across the captain's face. Damon wandered around to the bedside table and picked up the pitcher. 'I think it's safe to assume I have no interest in grassing you up,' he continued, 'so why don't we walk away and practise our shocked faces for when we learn Osgar has died?' He poured a cup of wine and held it out to Tobrytan. 'Let's drink on it.'

Tobrytan hesitated before accepting the cup. He raised it to his lips then paused.

'Go on,' said Damon. 'It won't kill you.'

Tobrytan cocked his head. He proffered the cup to Damon. 'You first.'

'Me? I never touch the stuff.'

'I insist.'

'You have seniority. You should—'

'*I insist.*' Tobrytan thrust the cup into Damon's hands.

Black specks floated around in the wine. The dose had been for an old man: maybe Damon would survive it, especially if he vomited it up as soon as possible. On the other hand, it could make death a more drawn-out, a more agonizing, process.

Steel flashed in front of his face. Tobrytan's sword. 'What are you waiting for?'

'The cheese plate?'

'Drink.'

'I've been thinking, I should really give up booze. It only ever gets me into trouble.'

'Drink.'

'It doesn't seem right,' said Damon, 'with Osgar here not, well . . . not. Feels like we're celebrating.'

Tobrytan prodded him with the tip of his sword. 'Drink!'

Damon took the smallest sip imaginable. His throat contracted, refusing to let the wine down. He coughed, spraying drops of liquid everywhere.

'More.'

Damon drank some more. 'I want to see you swallow,' said Tobrytan.

Damon's mouth was too full to supply the obvious punchline. Fighting the gag reflex, he forced the wine down. Spasms gripped his stomach. His head swam. Quicker than expected. He wasn't going to have time to stick his fingers down his throat. At least it wasn't painful.

As Tobrytan looked on dispassionately, waiting for him to die, Damon realized he wasn't. His taste buds alerted him to what he had consumed along with the wine: basil, oregano and was that sage? The bloody apothecary had ripped him off.

He relaxed, had another drink. Thyme in there as well. Bit of a mismatched bag, culinary-wise. Still, non-lethal, which was the main thing.

He flashed Tobrytan a smile, hiding his relief in cockiness. 'You were expecting someone deader?'

Gwyneth summoned the captains to the throne room at dawn to hear the news. Despite being neither a captain nor ignorant of the news, Damon invited himself along. He wasn't the only hanger-on. Tobrytan and Sener had each brought with them a contingent of loyal lieutenants and sergeants who glared at each other from either side of the central aisle. Word had got out then. Maybe they'd kill each other in an orgy of violence. The thought cheered Damon immensely.

Gwyneth seemed in no hurry to start the meeting. She was curled up on the throne, looking up to the ceiling. Damon peered up to see what fascinated her. It was a window barely a foot in diameter, of glass so pure it was almost invisible.

'It's very small,' said Gwyneth.

Damon thought back to his history lessons. 'The sun shines down through it at noon on Saviours' Day.'

'Sounds very pagan,' said Gwyneth. 'Why noon?'

'That's the time the Saviours traditionally appeared to Edwyn,' said Damon. 'Just in time for lunch. I wonder who picked up the tab.'

'Is that important?'

'Have you ever eaten in Statham? The prices are astronomical.'

Gwyneth beckoned him closer. 'You did well,' she whispered, her breath tickling the fine hairs around his ear.

'It was nothing.'

'Come to my apartment tonight. I have a reward for you.'

Damon didn't like where this was going. 'That's really not necessary. I did it for the love of my fellow man. Well, not *all* my fellow men, obviously.'

Sener stepped forward. 'If we're disturbing you . . .'

Gwyneth gave him a wave that was half magnanimous, half shooing. She straightened up in the throne. 'I have some bad news,' she said. 'I'm sorry –' Damon coughed – 'to announce the general passed away in his sleep.' This was technically correct: smothering caused unconsciousness before death. She nodded at Sener. 'My condolences for your loss, captain.'

The throne room held its breath, wondering how Sener would react. That he'd suspect foul play in the death of his father was a given; whether he'd dare voice his suspicions was another matter. His jaw clenched; his hand drifted close to his sword. One of his lieutenants whispered in his ear. Sener took a breath and folded his arms.

'Thank you, Mother,' he said. 'During these difficult times I think it's important we respect my father's wishes, his decisions.' His words sounded stagy, rehearsed. He'd be all too aware of the danger facing him now his father and protector was gone. 'They were for the good of us all. We shouldn't think of rushing into something against his wise counsel.'

'That's for General Tobrytan to decide,' said Gwyneth. *'General?'*

'I have made my decision.'

'It is not your decision to make.'

'I am the Mother of the Saviour.'

'You're not the only one,' said Sener. 'And we don't take orders from *her*.'

'The Apostate will be dealt with very soon,' said Tobrytan. 'A crack force will march double time to Hil and retrieve the Saviour.'

'You will command it,' Gwyneth said to Sener.

'Me?'

'Mother,' said Tobrytan, 'I really think I should be the one who—'

Gwyneth dismissed him with an idle flick. 'I think we can trust Captain Sener, can't we?'

Sener's eyes darted around the throne room, their agitation betraying the calculation behind them. Gwyneth was forcing him to prove his loyalty, and by removing him from New Statham she was ensuring he couldn't act against her.

'What about the Hilites?'

'They will be no match for your guns. They'll hand the Saviour over at the first explosion.'

'Unlikely,' said Sener. 'They don't have a reputation for giving up.'

'I'm sure your men will fight bravely,' said Gwyneth. *And die bravely, diminishing what support you have.* 'The safety of the Saviours was your father's paramount concern.

I'm sure you'll give everything you have to continue his work.'

'I shall honour *my* family, Mother.'

Gwyneth pursed her lips but didn't rise to the bait. 'On the subject of family, I think it's best we bring my daughter to New Statham. We can protect her here better than . . . Where exactly is she, general?' Tobrytan whispered in her ear. 'Why on Werlavia . . . ?'

'Last place anyone would think to look for her.' Tobrytan looked apprehensive. 'I think it's best she remains there, Mother.'

'What?!'

'Until we have secured her sister,' said Tobrytan, taking a step back. Was he really that scared of her, wondered Damon, or was he just playing up for the audience? 'The city has too many people, too many possibilities for treachery.'

'I don't mind you thinning out the population,' said Gwyneth.

Tobrytan smiled thinly. 'Once we have both Saviours the people will understand. And then nothing will stop us.'

Damon had just enough time to take in the soldiers looming over his bed before the pillowcase was thrown over his head. He thrashed around in the blackness, trying to free himself. Spots danced in front of his eyes as he sucked in fabric. This was it. Gwyneth and Tobrytan were getting rid of the witnesses.

A knife pierced the linen and pricked his throat. 'Be still.'

Damon froze, though he could do nothing about his heart hammering away against his ribs. He could just about breathe through the pillowcase, though there was a strange taste to the air. Sweat and dandruff and night terrors.

'You're coming with us. Make a noise and you won't be.'

Strong hands hauled Damon out of the bed. He winced as his bare soles touched cold stone. Probably futile to ask if they'd brought slippers.

They marched him through the palace. At first, Damon tried to keep a mental map of where they were going, counting off steps and turns, but he soon lost track. Not that it mattered. This was a journey he'd be doing only once. He just hoped they wouldn't make him dig his own grave. Spadework always played havoc with his back.

Light breached the veil. Heat prickled his skin. There was a whiff of perfume in the air and other, more primal, odours. The pillowcase was ripped off his head. He was in a bedroom. A young woman was fastening up her gown. The brief glimpse of flesh under the silk gave Damon very inappropriate thoughts given the circumstances.

'That will be all, Taite.' A man's voice. Damon turned. Sener was by the window, pouring wine.

The woman curtsied. 'Yes, my captain.'

Damon couldn't help but watch as she left. 'Working out your grief?'

'Leave us,' said Sener. Damon made to leave. 'Not you, fool.'

Damon's escorts retreated. He shuffled awkwardly on the spot. This wasn't what he had been expecting. He supposed it was better than a night-time execution, though he conceded this was based more on optimism than evidence.

'My father . . .' said Sener.

'You don't know how sorry I was to hear his – hear about his death.'

Damon moved closer to the fire. When Sener didn't object, he warmed each of his feet in turn.

'What do you know about it?'

'Me?' Damon tensed and gauged the distance to the door. 'Nothing!'

'I meant death in general.'

'Well, I wouldn't recommend it as a lifestyle choice . . .'

'There are ways of testing if a death is natural or unnatural, correct?'

'You mean an autopsy?'

'Is that what it's called?' said Sener. 'Do you know someone in New Statham who can do one?'

136

'You think your father's death was unnatural? That he was . . . ?'

Sener stalked close to Damon, so close he could practically see the alcohol seeping out of the captain's pores. 'Do you know someone?'

'I did . . .'

'What's that supposed to mean?'

'Let's just say we don't need an autopsy to know how *they* died,' said Damon. Sener's brow creased. 'Who controls the learning in the Realm?'

'The prie— ah.'

'You should really learn to think before you slaughter.'

'There is no one else?'

Damon shook his head. 'Anyone with that degree of medical knowledge would have been conscripted into the army of the Faith.'

'How about you?'

'Me?'

'You received a priest's training, I hear.'

'That was . . . I was strictly history and languages, not the gooier subjects. Do you *know* what they do to frogs in—?'

'How about books?' said Sener. 'Priests like writing things down. There must be some treatise somewhere with instructions.'

'Possibly,' said Damon, 'but by the time we've educated ourselves in post-mortem investigation your dad's going to be a bit . . . squishy. Look —' he plucked Sener's goblet out of his hand and went to refill it, pouring himself one at the same time — 'even if you do find out something was a bit dodgy with the general's . . . you know . . . what can you do about it?'

'Kill the bitch.'

Not jumping to any conclusions then? 'And what'll happen then? You'll be cut down faster than you can say, "Argh!"'

'I'm not without support.'

'You will be once they dismember you.'

'My men . . .'

'. . . might or might not volunteer to get hacked down in sympathy. You never know how these things are going to turn out.'

Sener downed his wine and stared into the fire. 'We shouldn't have come here.'

'New Statham's hell this time of year. You'd think a city this rich'd pave its streets. I heard the cobblers' guild kept blocking the proposals.'

'We should never have crossed the Savage Ocean. We should have stayed in the empire. What did we come to Werlavia for? A mad woman's fantasy, and to avenge crimes few of us can even remember.'

'It's not too late,' said Damon. 'You could always go back.'

'No. We've started the war; we must end it. I must march north and claim the "Saviour".'

Damon grimaced, thoughts going to places he'd prefer they'd leave well abandoned. 'I'd pack warm if I were you,' he said with a flippancy he didn't feel.

'She won't surrender the child without a fight, will she?'

'No . . .'

'I'll have to kill her,' said Sener.

'Good luck with that.'

'You don't care?'

'Many people have tried to kill Megan. No one's managed it.' Damon grimaced. He could have said that about Eleanor.

eleven

Over the next few days, the first of the refugees trickled into Hil. Fordel tried to monopolize the organization of how they were settled and Megan had to stop herself from letting him. She couldn't afford to be seen as some vassal of the Hilites and made a point of being involved in every decision. Unfortunately Fordel took this rather too literally and flooded her with paperwork covering the entire minutiae of life in the city. Megan retreated to her room – the best to keep an eye on Cate – and spread the scrolls and parchments and sheaves of paper all over her bed to wade through them there, with only Father Galan and Ími, Hil's official mathematician and Fordel's boyfriend, to stop her drowning.

Megan grabbed a parchment at random and held it up to Ími. 'What's this one about?'

Ími leaned forward and squinted. He was a wiry man of about thirty with jet-black hair and beard cropped so short they looked painted on. 'Latrines,' he translated.

'Latrines?' said Megan. 'Fordel thinks worrying about latrines is the best use of my time?'

Father Galan grimaced and poured himself some more wine. 'Feeding all these extra people is going to lead to . . . certain results.'

'No shit.'

'That would be the ideal solution if you could arrange it,' said Ími.

Afreyda hovered by the door. 'May I speak with you, Your Majesty?'

'Your Majesty?' said Megan. 'Afreyda, it's me.'

'You are queen. You must be addressed correctly.'

'I guess . . .' Megan looked to Ími and Father Galan. 'Gentlemen, if you could . . . ?'

The two men took their leave, Father Galan taking the wine's leave too. Afreyda went over to the cot and stroked the cheek of the sleeping Cate. The monotonous droning of the bureaucrats, which had made Megan's eyelids heavy, had had a wonderful effect on her daughter. She'd slept solidly for hours.

'I have been thinking,' said Afreyda. 'I should move back here.'

Megan's heart started to race. 'If . . . if you think that's best.'

'It would be best for Cate.'

'Cate, yes, sure.' Megan shuffled papers to distract herself.

'If you disagree, I will stay in the barracks.'

'No, no, you should come back. She's missed you.'

'How can you tell?' said Afreyda. 'She is a baby.'

'A mother knows these things.'

'You are making it up.'

'Maybe.' Megan grinned. She'd take Afreyda's return no matter the excuse. 'We'd better go get your stuff.'

'There is no stuff to get. My bag has gone.'

'Gone?' said Megan. 'Why would . . . ?' She remembered whose the bag had been originally, who had been so desperate to retrieve it. 'Aldred.'

'I do not understand.'

Given everything that had happened, Megan had forgotten to fill Afreyda in on a mere murder attempt. 'He was frantic to find it. We had an . . . altercation.' She felt his hands on her throat again, a phantom strangulation. There had been no sign of Aldred since the coup attempt. He must have holed up somewhere then lost himself among the refugees, settling in one of the other Snow Cities, maybe, or slipping through the Kartik tunnels back into the Realm. 'He blames me for what happened to Eleanor.'

'He should not.'

'Shouldn't he?' said Megan. 'Because no matter how much I claim to have been manipulated and forced by events, I still had a choice in everything. I could have forced Eleanor to come with us, we didn't have to march on Ainsworth with the army, and as much as I love her —'

she nodded at Cate's cot – 'I didn't have to let a boy who I never really liked talk me into . . . you know . . .'

Afreyda sat next to Megan and took her hand. 'Gwyneth would have made sure you got pregnant one way or another. If you had not come to Eastport, I would still be in her service. And Eleanor did what any mother would be glad to do. Aldred is trying to find someone to blame, someone to seek vengeance from.'

'Still doesn't explain what he wants with an old laundry bag,' said Megan. 'Maybe he has a sentimental attachment to his dirty underpants.'

'Maybe he has an attachment to *my* dirty underpants,' said Afreyda.

They looked at each, shuddered, then collapsed into giggles. Megan rested her head on Afreyda's shoulder, feeling the warmth of her body, the steady pulse of her blood. It felt so natural to be here like this, like she'd found the place where she fitted. She looked up and caught Afreyda looking down at her, her eyes a rich brown like varnished mahogany. Desire made her heart pound. She started to lean in, close the narrow gap that existed between them.

There was a cough at the door. 'I'm sorry, Your Majesty,' said Father Galan. 'We thought you'd finished.' Behind him, Ími gave an apologetic shrug. 'We do have work to be getting on with.'

Megan hurriedly broke away from Afreyda. 'Yes, of

course.' She started to pace the room, work off the nervous energy. 'I've been thinking. Father Galan, could you draw up a captain's commission for me?'

'Who are you commissioning?' asked the priest. His eyes were drawn to Afreyda. 'Her?'

'Me?'

'Interesting,' said Ími.

'We have hundreds of soldiers and no one to command them,' said Megan. 'Afreyda had six years at the Diannon Officers' Academy. Our own men were lucky to get two weeks of basic shouting.'

'But I am a woman,' said Afreyda. 'I am not of the Faith.' Concern etched itself on to her face. 'You do not expect me to convert, do you? I cannot betray—'

Megan shook her head. 'The men need someone to lead them, someone brave and loyal, who will never put her own needs above those of the greater good.'

'They will not accept me. I killed three of them.'

'They'll know not to mess with you, won't they?' Megan took Afreyda's hand and squeezed it. 'I need you to do this for me. There is no one else.'

'Do you really think I can?'

'I wouldn't ask otherwise,' said Megan.

'Then I will,' said Afreyda. 'By the time I have finished, your soldiers will be the fiercest fighting force this side of the Savage Ocean, or they will be dead.' She considered a moment. 'Dead is more likely.'

Rekka ostentatiously hobbled into the meeting room, supporting herself with an ornate walking stick. 'Don't mind me,' she said. 'Just the latest victim of religious intolerance.' She made a show of staring at Megan, looking for sympathy or an apology. Megan made a show of offering neither.

She took the seat to Vegar's right, opposite Fordel. From the head of the long table, Vegar continued to glower at Megan. He'd been in a bad mood since peace had been restored to the city. Megan wasn't sure what irked him most: the fact she'd brought it about or his being deprived of things to hit as a result.

'Are we all here?' asked Fordel.

'Not quite,' said Megan. She had the other end of the table, flanked by Afreyda and Father Galan. In between the two ends were the ambassadors from the other Snow Cities: three burly men who thought the council was a beer-and-beard party, and a middle-aged woman with a full figure and ash-blonde hair who watched proceedings with sharp eyes. None had said much to Megan, treating her like a child they'd unwittingly been left to attend while her mother ran an errand.

There was a gasp as the last attendee arrived: Father Broose. Rekka flushed. Vegar hauled a mace on to his hefty shoulders. Even Fordel raised a surprised eyebrow.

'And he's here because . . . ?'

To annoy you. 'The spirit of reconciliation,' said Megan. 'Plus he's one of the few of us who can remember fighting the witches the first time around.'

Vegar stalked around to Father Broose. He held out his hand. Father Broose gave it a suspicious look before he took it. Vegar yanked him close and drove his forehead into the priest's face. Father Broose staggered back, clasping his nose. Blood dribbled through his fingers. Vegar spat some words of Hilite at him and swaggered back to his seat.

'This your idea of reconciliation?' Father Broose asked Megan, his voice reedy.

'He could have killed you.'

'You think I fear death?'

No. It was a trait he shared with the witches. It made him dangerous, but Megan needed his support, however grudging, as a bulwark against Fordel. 'Why don't you take a seat?'

'There are chairs at the back, Brother Broose,' added Father Galan.

'*Brother?*'

'I'd roll with it if I was you,' said Megan.

Fordel stood and beckoned to Ími. He scurried forward and unrolled a map of Werlavia. Vegar slammed his mace on one end, weighing it down, and cast a challenging look down at Megan. She flicked out a couple of knives and pinned her end of the map to the table.

'Thank you, Ími,' said Fordel. He took a box of tin soldiers – tiny models of fearsome warriors, a disturbing number of which brandished the decapitated heads of their enemies – and spread them out on the map. 'The witches are marching.'

'Not away, I assume,' said Rekka.

'How many?' asked Megan.

'A thousand men, maybe two,' said Fordel. Megan grimaced. The witches had taken Eastport with less.

Fordel pushed some soldiers up the map, skirting the western shore of Lake Pullar and the edge of the Smallwood Marshes, and then up to the Kartiks. 'They're looking to hit us fast and hard.' His gaze flicked to Megan. 'I think we all know why. We have a few weeks at most.'

'How do we know they will not send their fleet around and attack us from the sea?' asked Afreyda.

Everyone looked at her as if she was a child who had asked why you couldn't see air. 'The small matter of rocks one side of Werlavia, and ice on the other,' said Fordel. 'But apart from that, it'd be a strategic masterstroke on their part.'

'I was just asking,' muttered Afreyda.

'When will the Kartik Mountains become impassable?' asked Megan.

'Not for a few weeks at least.'

'Can we hold them at the pass?' asked Father Galan.

'That's the interesting question,' said Fordel. 'No one's ever fought against guns in this situation.' He looked to Afreyda. 'Have they, captain?'

'We never got that far,' said Afreyda.

Megan wondered what it was like, that short desperate rebellion of Afreyda's family. If they hadn't lost, then Afreyda wouldn't have ended up here in Werlavia with Megan. But then there'd be no Emperor to arm the witches and they might never have had the strength to return. Megan might still have her home, her grandfather, her sister.

'Didn't you plan for it?' said Fordel. 'The Diannon capital is surrounded by mountains. You must have thought about retreating there.'

Afreyda thought for a moment, then repositioned a handful of soldiers. 'Spread the men out,' she said. 'Hide them high in the rocks. The witches will have nothing to target. They will have to push forward. Come in range of our archers. They will be faster, more accurate than the guns.'

'Pretty much what we agreed on, wasn't it, Ími?' said Fordel. He pointed at one of the repositioned pieces. 'And you just moved a navy across land.'

'That is a soldier.'

'Tóki smashed all his toy boats,' said Rekka. 'His teacher said he had "issues", whatever that means.'

'Did your commanders ever calculate the chances

of this strategy succeeding?' asked Ími. Afreyda nodded. 'And . . . ?'

'One chance in twenty.'

Megan would have hated for the situation to be *completely* hopeless.

twelve

Gunfire echoed around the mountains, the constant pounding slamming into Megan's brain like a migraine. The stench of sulphur floated up on the air, along with other odours: the metallic tang of blood, the ammoniac stink of fear. Smoke mixed with dust, billowing up from the ground in great clouds, making it impossible to see what was going on. Megan had climbed to this archery emplacement high up in the Kartiks to try to make sense of what was going on, but she was reduced to guessing, looking to the flash of firing weapons, listening for where the screams where loudest. What was going on? Was anyone winning, was anyone losing? Who was dead, who was alive? Would the battle ever end or were they condemned to fight forever?

The rocks under her feet shook as a projectile smacked into the mountainside closer to her than she would have liked. As a trio of Hilite archers rose and fired, she ducked behind a wall protecting the emplacement. Arrow after arrow arced into the sky then dived, disappearing into the fog of war. They seemed so inconsequential compared to the brute power inherent in the witches' guns.

The archers prepared to fire a fourth volley. The mountains trembled again, causing them to fall against each other. An arrow spiralled from a bowstring, bouncing off Megan's arm before clattering by her feet. That shot was closer. A lot closer.

Two of the archers disappeared into the access tunnel, ducking into the narrow opening one after the other. The second grabbed Megan and bundled her after them.

'*Dák!*'

No need for a translation: retreat. Or, more accurately, get the hell out of here. She scrambled down the tunnel, having to scurry on hands and knees and grope her way in the cramped blackness. There was a low rumble. Grit and stones rained down. Megan heard a scream behind her. Fighting instinct, she squeezed round in the narrow space and crawled back up.

'I'm coming!' she cried into the darkness.

Leather fingers brushed her face. She snatched the hand, squeezed it. 'What is it?'

Hilite jabbering answered her, the fear and pain clear in any language.

'We'll get you out of here,' she said. 'It's not far.' She pulled. The Hilite refused to shift. 'Come on, a little cooperation here.'

Megan heaved again. She flew backwards with nothing more of the archer than his glove. The world whirled as she slammed into the floor. Specks of light swam in her vision but refused to illuminate the way.

Megan forced down nausea and made her way back to the archer. She ran her hands over him, looking to grab him under the arms. That was when she hit rock. She felt around, praying her suspicions were wrong. No, that was the archer's waist. Beyond that, solid stone. The ceiling had collapsed on him.

Another roar. More stones rained on her, larger ones this time. She covered her head, trying to quell the panic rising inside her that the mountain would trap her forever.

'*Dák!*'

'I'm not—' Chunks of the ceiling dropped, unprovoked by gunfire this time. An ominous crack echoed around the tunnel. 'I'm sorry!'

Megan scrabbled backwards. There was a crash then a cloud of dust enveloped her, almost thick enough to suffocate her. Nothing more solid though. She whispered a prayer, twisted around and fled down the tunnel fast as its confines would let her.

She tumbled into the main passageway and was immediately pulled out of the way of a stretcher party bearing rather less of a soldier than should have been there. She turned away, only to find herself staring into the questioning eyes of one of the archers she had been with.

Megan shook her head. He nodded grimly and beckoned to his comrade. They moved on, heading for the next emplacement, to fire at the witches until the witches fired back. Who knew if either would make it out of that one.

She needed to get to Willas, find out what was happening. Megan hurried along, continually making way for men stampeding back and forth carrying orders, fresh arrows, the injured and the dead. She reached the gates, two slabs of stone-covered wood that opened up into a hidden passage on the south side of the Kartiks. The air was thick with the stench of sweat and grease and the metallic tang of congealing blood.

Willas was conducting operations, barking orders at the men who bustled around him, volume substituting for coherence. 'What the hell are you doing here?' he shouted at Megan. 'You should be back at the wall!'

The wall: a mile back up the pass and the last defensive position before Hil itself. Afreyda was stationed there with her men. Megan hoped they had nothing to do but stamp their feet against the cold.

She exercised royal prerogative and ignored Willas's question, asking her own instead. 'How are we doing?'

'We're holding on. Just.'

'For how long?'

'Depends how determined they are.'

They were witches; of course they were determined. 'What can I do?'

'If you could get me a thousand more men and some of those guns, that'd be a start.'

'I'll do my best,' said Megan. 'When do you need them by?'

'A couple of hours ago?' said Willas with a wry smile.

Megan stared at the gates. Beyond them was a narrow corridor through the mountains, defended on either side by hidden archery emplacements gouged out of the rock. 'Have the witches found the passage yet?'

Willas shook his head. 'They're still trying to push over the pass. I don't know what'll happen if they do find this way. The gates'll hold up for a while, but—'

'Open them,' said Megan.

'They work better closed.'

'I need to get past.'

'I don't understand.'

'You want guns, captain? I'm going to get them for you.'

She made for the gates. Stomping echoed around the cavern as Willas hurried after her. He placed his bulk in front of her. Megan tried to go around him. Willas sidestepped into her path.

He took her by the arm – gently, but firmly – and led her into a natural alcove in the rocks. The background noise lessened; the ambient smell didn't. Saviours knew what this cranny had been used for.

'I can't let you go out there,' said Willas.

154

'I don't need your permission,' said Megan.

'My mountains. What I say, goes.'

'I have to do something,' said Megan. 'Do you know how many deaths are already on my conscience?' In her dreams they were all there – Eleanor, her grandfather, Lynette, Silas, Clover, Odette, Brother Brogan, the families of Thicketford, the countless people whose names she never knew and whose anonymity amplified her guilt. 'I can't stand by doing nothing while people are fighting and dying.'

'Yes, you can. That's what being queen is about.'

'No one ever stopped Eleanor.'

'And look at how that worked out for her.'

The emotional wound that Willas's remark reopened was as raw as any of the physical ones suffered by the injured men sprawled around them. 'The witches have come for me,' said Megan. 'We can use that against them. They don't think straight where I'm concerned.'

'We can't risk you.'

Megan felt more like a young girl imploring her father to allow her to go to a party than a queen making a last, desperate gamble to avoid annihilation. 'Captain, if they break through, we're all dead or worse. Please, I can do this. And more to the point, I'm the only one who can, the only one they'll come after no matter what.'

Willas let out a sound that was half sigh, half growl,

and looked up to the rocky ceiling of the cavern. 'For both our sakes, don't tell Afreyda about this.'

Megan picked her way through the rocks, wincing every time an arrow flew over her head or gunfire echoed around the mountains. She wished just for once she could come up with a plan that didn't involve probable suicide. The grey furs the Hilites had provided were doing a good job of camouflaging her, but sooner or later one of the witches would spot her, fire, give chase. Knowing that's what she wanted didn't make it any less scary.

She made her way down the witches' left flank. They were arranged in tight ranks of slowly-but-inexorably advancing guns. Men were visible through the smoke; some flitting about as they fed the monsters; others protecting them, shields painted with the star-broken circle strapped to one arm, axes in the other. Corpses or soon-to-be corpses were scattered around the fighting force. A detached head stared at its body, eternally alarmed to see the rest of itself from such an unexpected angle.

Megan passed beyond the witches' rearguard. Down in the foothills she could just make out massed horses: the witches' cavalry waiting for the guns to clear them a path. Something to worry about later. She lowered her hood and shook out her hair. The icy wind blasted so hard against her skin it was painful, but the witches had to see it was her. She edged closer, hefting the crossbow in her hands. Willas had told her it had an effective range of three hundred yards, less if she wanted to be accurate. She didn't care about that: she just wanted to be noticed. Megan smiled to herself. Didn't every girl?

She broke cover and pulled the trigger. The weapon shuddered as it released its pent-up energy, flinging the bolt towards its target. Even above the cacophony, Megan heard the sharp chime of iron striking iron. She fought the urge to flee. They had to see her. A crossbow bolt whizzed past her head. That sorted out the being-seen bit. She abandoned her own crossbow and ran.

Lungs straining, muscles burning with acid, Megan pelted up the mountain path. Bolts and arrows continued to fly at her, making her nostalgic for the days when the witches had been terrified of hurting her. A projectile screeched overhead and smacked into the rocks. She lost her footing and tumbled to the ground. Witches approached, their shapes solidifying as they advanced through the fog. Megan scrambled to her feet and continued running.

She reached the passage. The high walls of the narrow corridor blocked out the sun and muffled the noise of the battle, reducing everything to a dreamlike state, and like in a dream Megan kept on running but didn't seem to advance. Her limbs grew heavier and heavier. The gates seemed as far away as ever, their presence not encouraging but taunting.

Something snapped under her foot. An arrow. She

glanced over her shoulder. A witch bowman was steadying himself, preparing to fire. Megan could expect no help, no rescuing arrow shooting out from one of the slits concealed in the rock. She threw herself to the ground, rolled in the shingle even as the arrow flew over her, and pushed herself up before her body could realize it liked the idea of staying down.

The gates were getting closer. She could see soldiers through the gap, torchlight flashing on their armour. Just a few more steps. Pain flashed through her shoulder. Megan didn't have the breath to cry out. Her legs started to give way. Her run became a fall. But exterior became interior. She tumbled to the floor. Hands grabbed her, dragged her away. The world darkened. A slam echoed around the chamber. She had made it.

Megan groped behind her to examine the source of the stinging in her shoulder. A throwing knife. She pulled it out, wincing as she did so. The tip glistened with blood. Her blood.

'You can actually hit people with these things?' she said, holding the knife up to Willas.

'Not very well,' he said. 'You're still alive.'

'Your men must adore your cheerfulness.'

Willas motioned at her furs. 'Let's see what the damage is.'

Megan peeled off her top layers. Some of the men

blushed and looked away. All this carnage and they were still agitated by a pair of breasts.

Willas called for more light and peered at the wound. 'It's not very deep,' he said. 'Won't need stitches.' He grabbed a bottle of spirits from an adjutant and splashed it over Megan's shoulder. The sudden burning prompted vehemence that made the men blush all over again.

'I'm not sure that was regal,' said Willas, tying a bandage around Megan's shoulder.

'Sod regal,' said Megan. 'Did they . . . ?'

Willas called out. A soldier scurried up to him and delivered a report. 'A detachment of guns has broken off,' Willas translated for Megan. 'Headed this way.'

'Don't dissuade them too hard.'

'We know.'

Soldiers started to stream past, heading for tunnels that stretched the length of the passage outside. As well as the archery emplacements concealed in the rock, there were hidden exits from which men could pour out and fall upon besiegers. Megan pulled her clothes back on and made to follow.

Willas pulled her back. 'You've done your bit,' he said. 'Let the men do theirs.'

Megan slipped on a puddle of puréed innards and almost went head first into the cavity that once contained them. Willas caught her at the last moment. She stabilized herself, tried not to gawp at the man a gun had pulverized. It was impossible to say whether he was a Hilite or a witch.

It was carnage all along the passage. Blood glistened scarlet against grey rock as if part of some psychotic attempt to add colour to the mountains. Corpses were strewn about, their wounds steaming in the icy air. Limbs lay separated from their owners, now nothing more than cooling meat. One man had had his helmet driven into his skull, his eyeballs bulging out from the pressure. And there, amidst the death, hunkered the objects of the exercise, three guns, smoke wafting out of their ugly iron mouths.

Megan picked her way over to one of them, her footsteps squelching more than she would have liked. It sat in a wheeled carriage, ropes protruding from its front like an insect's feelers.

'Doesn't look very impressive,' said Willas.

Impressive enough to conquer two continents. 'Stand in front of it and say that.'

'How does it work?'

Megan pointed at a cart at the far end of the passage, which contained the ammunition. 'Fill it with gunpowder and one of those iron balls. Light the fuse and stand well back.' She remembered the witches' invasion of Eastport, when an exploding gun had taken down one of their own warships. '*Well* well back.'

Willas shouted orders. Hilite soldiers began to drag

the guns around and back to the entrance to the passage. It wasn't much – three guns against Saviours knew how many the witches had – but it might be enough to turn the battle.

She was about to follow them when a soldier came dashing through the gates and up to them. He delivered a breathless message to Willas, who pulled a face and started issuing more orders.

'What is it?' said Megan.

'The witches' cavalry has broken through,' said Willas. 'They're headed for the wall.'

The wall – Afreyda. Megan's feet were already moving before her brain gave the order.

thirteen

Megan dashed through the mountains until she found the tunnel closest to the wall and scrambled along it. Winter light almost blinded her as she burst out on to the rocks, but she couldn't wait for her eyes to acclimatize. She kept on moving, kicking up shale and stones as she half ran, half fell down the mountains. She had to get to Afreyda, make sure she was safe.

The wall was less a wall and more a heap of rocks that stretched from one side of the pass to the other, held together by ice, obstinacy and its own weight. It ranged in height from something a child could peer over to a good ten feet tall. There was no gate, just a narrow gap at the centre that served as a chokepoint. Witch horsemen were attacking it, lobbing grapefruit-sized balls that fizzed and exploded, before wheeling around and racing away as bolts shot back in reply.

Afreyda was in the thick of it. Near her, jammed up against the wall, a dozen teenagers were rearming crossbows, arms whirling as they wound strings back. Occasionally a bolt would pop out and career to the ground, prompting jeers and cheers at the poor unfortunate who had almost speared themselves. They seemed awfully young to be in battle, but they weren't much younger than Megan; some looked older. If the witches reached Hil there wouldn't have been much point in sparing them the action, and didn't they deserve the chance to fight for their homes, their freedom, their way of life?

Afreyda scowled at Megan. 'What are you doing here?'

'I wondered if you were free for dinner.'

One of the witches' devices sailed over their heads and exploded a few yards away, knocking them off their feet. Megan lay there, ears ringing, coughs racking her lungs, before Afreyda hauled her to her feet.

'It is not safe.'

'I've been in worst places,' said Megan, patting herself down.

'That is no excuse.'

'Eleanor wouldn't have minded.'

Afreyda diverted a girl carrying a brace of crossbows and pointed to one of the ladders that led to the top of the wall. 'Yes, well, I would like a word with her.'

Wouldn't we all. 'Willas has guns,' Megan said, trying to change the subject.

'I am very pleased for him,' said Afreyda. 'Maybe

now he can give me my archers back.' Her eyes narrowed. 'How did he get guns?'

'Er . . . luck?'

'What did you——?'

There was a sequence of booms from the vicinity of the gap in the wall. Soldiers raced for cover. Megan grabbed Afreyda and pulled her to the ground, shielding her body with her own as dust rolled over them.

The booms faded. Afreyda disentangled herself from Megan and got to her feet, brushing down her uniform. 'They are trying to collapse the wall.'

No, that wasn't their plan. Horsemen burst out of the fog and raced up the pass. Afreyda snatched a crossbow from one of the reloaders and fired. The bolt buried itself in a witch's back. He toppled off his mount and hit the ground without offering any resistance.

A score of crossbows followed Afreyda's example, their strings thrumming like a badly tuned band. More witches fell: some instantly, some staggering on for a while with bolts sticking from their torsos, some thrown from wounded horses and set upon by vengeful infantry. Not all though. Some were streaking ahead.

Another horseman raced out of the smoke by the gate. There was an explosion – one of the witches' devices detonating late or early. The horse staggered, disorientated. Afreyda drew her sword and ran, up an outcropping that formed a makeshift ramp, and launched herself at the rider. Her blade arced. A string of blood flew through the air, the droplets as bright as rubies.

A free horse. Even as Afreyda was picking herself up, and its witch rider was facing the prospect of soon knowing if his cause was just, Megan hurried to the animal and grabbed its reins. She had no time to be scared, to dwell on the ease with which it could kick or trample her to death. The witches couldn't be allowed to get to Hil, to get to Cate.

Megan swung herself up into the saddle. Afreyda screamed her name.

'Get your own ride!' she shouted back, before kicking the horse into a gallop.

The cold wind blasting into her face made tears stream from her eyes. She blinked them away, counted the number of witches she was pursuing. Three of them. One of her. The rational part of her cleared its throat and offered up the polite suggestion she was perhaps outnumbered. Megan was well used to ignoring it by now.

The rear witch glanced back and saw her. He fumbled around his saddle, grabbed something, hurled it at Megan. She swayed to one side as an axe spun past, whistling as it cut the air.

From out of her belt Megan pulled the blade that had hit her in the shoulder. She recalled everything Eleanor had taught her about throwing knives and immediately discounted it. She urged the last drop of speed out of her horse, drew a little closer to her target, and threw.

The knife whizzed past the witch. The curse had barely escaped Megan's lips when the next horse along reared and threw its rider. The witch slammed into the ground head first and was still. As Megan shot past the now-meandering animal, she saw her blade sticking from its rump. A success of sorts. She shouted an apology at the animal and kept on going.

After the initial burst of speed, horses of both pursuer and pursued were slowing. They were getting higher. Snow blanked out patches of ground as if the world hadn't finished being painted. The air was getting thicker, condensing into a freezing mist. Megan wondered how long she could keep going, if she should keep going. How was she going to deal with the two remaining horsemen if she caught them?

Movement in the corner of her eye, hoof beats echoing her own. Afreyda had taken her order seriously and commandeered the mount of one of the fallen witches. She was soon riding beside her. Afreyda took the reins in one hand and drew her sword.

'Flank him!' she shouted at Megan, pointing her sword at the rear rider.

Megan kicked her horse back up to a gallop, praying it wouldn't rebel. The gap between her and her quarry narrowed, close enough to see the sweat frothing on horseflesh. A final push drew her level. The witch's head snapped around. He snatched up a battleaxe and swiped at Megan. She jerked out of the way, but stayed close enough to remain a target. The witch struck again. A scream bounced around the pass. Not Megan's – the witch's. Distracted, he'd failed to see Afreyda come up on his left, nor spotted her sword until it embedded itself in his arm.

He lurched round, swung his axe. Afreyda had already anticipated the attack and moved out of range. The witch's arm ended up wrapping around his own chest, almost knocking him out of his saddle. He tried to stabilize himself. His injured arm could barely grip the reins. Megan drew a dagger and moved in close. The witch raised his arm to strike. Megan lunged, burying her knife into his exposed armpit. The witch cried out. His axe clattered to the ground. He pressed his arm to his side, concentrating on remaining upright. Afreyda's sword broke his concentration, broke everything.

Just one witch left, but that last burst had pushed their horses too far. They dropped to nothing more than a canter and a reluctant one at that. The last witch pushed on further and further ahead. Then, just as he was about to disappear over a ridge, a figure stumbled out of the mist, heading straight for him.

The rider was going too fast to pull up. Horse met man with an inhuman shriek. They tumbled to the rock floor. Moments later Megan and Afreyda caught up. Afreyda dispatched the dazed rider with a quick thrust. Megan slid off her horse and examined the other man.

It was Aldred, head gashed from the horse's hoofs, fingers frozen around the straps of a bag.

Soldiers soon arrived, bringing news the witches' cavalry had pulled back, panicked by being fired upon by the captured guns. The men hauled Aldred, who was in a state of semi-conscious delirium, on to the back of one of their horses. One of the soldiers assured Megan he'd ministered to many battlefield injuries, but when she pressed him on how many he'd successfully treated he became vague and told them he'd see them back at the wall.

Afreyda and Megan followed at a more sedate pace. Not just to save the horses, Megan realized when Afreyda turned on her. A scowl clouded her face.

'You should not have gone after those riders.'

Megan reeled at the admonishment. 'If they'd got through—'

'They would have been dealt with in Hil,' said Afreyda. 'Do you think a few soldiers posed a threat? We did not leave the city undefended. You forced me to abandon my men to make sure you did not get killed.'

'I didn't force you to do anything.'

'You know I had to come after you.'

Their eyes locked and Megan understood why Afreyda had had to come after her. It was the same reason she had gone after Afreyda at the pier. And she still had no idea what to do about it.

Willas calling down from the wall broke the moment. 'I'm sorry,' mumbled Megan. 'It was instinct. I had to do something.'

'That is my job now.'

'It turned out all right, didn't it?'

'Only because I spend half my nights pleading with my ancestors to protect you.'

They kicked into a canter and joined Willas at the wall. 'The witches retreated,' he said. 'All the way back to the treeline.'

'Really?' said Megan.

'You think I came all this way to lie to you?'

'How do you know they're not trying to lure you into a trap?'

'If they are, I'm not biting,' said Willas. 'Not with arrows and swords against guns.'

'What about the guns I left you with?'

Willas looked sheepish. 'There was a small accident. The instructions you gave us were pretty basic.'

'Was anyone hurt?'

'We lost many eyebrows,' said Willas. 'Standing well back? Good advice.'

'How many men did we lose?' asked Afreyda.

'Not sure until we match up all the bits of corpses. That's the trouble with guns: they do leave you with a bit of a puzzle.' Willas grimaced. 'I'd say a few hundred. Some of the men might fight again.'

'And the witches?'

'The same, maybe.'

The bulk of both sides' forces was still intact. This was a skirmish, nothing more. 'They'll try again,' said Megan. 'Once they get over the shock of someone firing guns at them.'

'I wouldn't say that,' said Willas. He pointed up at the western sky, where black clouds were gathering on the horizon. The first snowstorm of the winter. 'Our reserves have arrived.'

Megan and Afreyda made their way along the wall to an outcropping, behind which a temporary infirmary had been set up. Aldred seemed quite peaceful, which was surprising considering he was now missing his left arm. The soldier Megan had left him with was by his side, wiping off the blood from a hacksaw with a dirty rag.

'What . . . ?'

'Had to amputate, Your Majesty,' said the soldier. 'Frostbite in his fingers. Very cold at the top of the pass, so I'm told.'

'You had to take his whole arm?'

'Can't do fingers. Tricky little blighters.'

'Where is the bag he was holding?' asked Afreyda. The soldier held it up. 'We do not need the arm as well.'

'Sorry, ma'am. He was holding on pretty tightly.'

He moved to break the fingers off. Megan held a hand up. 'Just cut the strap,' she snapped.

The soldier shrugged and did so. He handed the bag to Megan. Ripping it open, she pulled out clothes, remembering whose they were only when Afreyda scurried around after them.

'This is it?' she said, perplexed. 'He risked everything for this?'

Afreyda peered at the bag. 'It is not hanging right.'

She was right, it wasn't, and it felt heavier than it should. Megan rummaged around in the bottom. She felt something hard beneath the canvas. She pulled out a knife and slashed at the material. Jewels spilled out on the ground – diamonds, sapphires, emeralds, rubies.

'What . . . ?' said Afreyda.

'A king's ransom,' said Megan.

'Or a queen's,' said the soldier. Afreyda's hand moved to her sword. 'Just saying, ma'am.'

Megan scooped up some of the stones. Even in the dimming light, they glittered in her hands with ethereal brightness. 'Where did he . . . ?'

'The house in Kewley,' said Afreyda. 'Damon was not the looter. Aldred was.'

'Damon was innocent?'

'I would not go that far.'

No, Damon had gone to the jeweller's house for a

reason; it had been his own fault he'd missed the boats evacuating Kewley from the witches' attack. Still, that didn't stop Megan missing him, wondering if there was something she could do for him, the by-now-traditional badly planned rescue attempt. However, she didn't even know if he was still alive; she'd asked Fordel, but his spies weren't able to get any information out of New Statham. Whatever mess Damon was in, he'd have to get himself out of it.

Megan looked across to the sleeping lieutenant. *What did you do?* The question would have to wait until he recovered consciousness, if he ever did. Megan almost hoped he wouldn't. She didn't know if she could bear the truth, for Eleanor's sake more than her own.

fourteen

From a balcony high up in one of the palace towers, Damon stared down at the boats sneaking up the Rustway under cover of the night. It was too far away and too dark to tell for sure, but the robes swirling around in the black looked awfully suspicious.

'You're bringing in Sandstriders?' he called out over his shoulder.

'It'll remind the people *we're* really not that bad.'

'And here's me thinking summary executions and forced conversions were the way to everybody's heart.'

'We are not forcing anybody. We are liberating them from the tyranny of the priests.'

Damon wandered back inside. On a bed used by kings, queens and supreme priests, Gwyneth was stretched out. She'd arranged the bedclothes so the most private parts of her naked body were just about covered. Damon assumed she thought it was alluring.

He could stop coming here, face Gwyneth's wrath,

but girls didn't take rejection well at the best of times and certainly not when they commanded the most fearsome fighting force the continent had ever seen. Why did she want him? To play with him? To exercise power? To put one over on her sister?

Gwyneth patted the mattress. 'Come back to bed.'

'I'm not in the mood.'

'I am,' said Gwyneth, her voice sharp.

Damon rubbed wrists made raw by their last encounter. 'Can you give me a few minutes?'

'No.'

There was a soft rap at the door, the knock of someone not wanting to be noticed. He was out of luck. Damon shouted an order to enter before Gwyneth could object. She glared at him and pulled the sheets up.

A soldier pushed the door open and poked his head around the gap. He looked young, very young. The end of a very long chain of delegations.

'I have a message for you, Mother.'

'What?'

'It's from Hil.'

Gwyneth beckoned to the soldier. He scurried over, placed a scrap of parchment in her hand and then got the hell out of there before Gwyneth could exact retribution.

'Sometimes I think I have a reputation,' said Gwyneth, unrolling the parchment and squinting. She had self-

174

awareness? That made things worse somehow. 'Bring some light over.'

Damon took a candle to the bed. He watched Gwyneth's eyes flick as they read, her mood darkening with each word. She came to the end and screwed the parchment into a ball. It bounced off the crib her daughter had yet to sleep in and ended up in a dark corner of the room.

'She's declared herself queen!' screeched Gwyneth. 'Queen! Her! How can she? She's not True. She doesn't even believe in the prophecy.'

Damon retrieved the message, having to scrabble about in the blackness. 'I wouldn't think that's the basis of her claim.' He read the message.

'Well?' demanded Gwyneth.

'Father Galan does well to get so much text in so little space, doesn't he?'

'Why does she think she can be queen?'

'She says she's Countess of Ainsworth and the only known heir to the throne,' said Damon. He thought about the tangle of family trees and the pruning done by both the priests and the True. 'She's possibly right.'

'How can she be Countess of Ainsworth? Isn't it that –' Gwyneth waved, trying to think of something – 'woman?'

Damon's heart tore as he thought of Eleanor. 'She's –' he had to swallow before he could get the word out – 'dead. She must've named Megan her heir.'

'That's . . . silly.'

'That's the legal system.'

Gwyneth took back the message, read it again, screwed it up again. 'Who is this Father Galan anyway?'

'You had him imprisoned and tortured and nearly executed,' said Damon. Gwyneth looked blank. 'Sorry, that doesn't really narrow things down, does it? He's the High Priest of Eastport. More of a titular role these days, I guess.'

'Oh, him.' Gwyneth frowned. 'I don't remember torture.' She jumped out of bed and prowled the room. 'There should only be one queen in Werlavia –'

'It does save arguments over protocol, who's allowed the bigger hat and all that.'

'– and that queen should be me.'

That's when Damon knew he had to get out of there.

Tobrytan took the news as well as Damon expected. He glowered over the table, porridge sliding off his spoon. All around the vast dining hall – constructed to accommodate Edwyn the Third and a thousand of his closest friends – ranks of soldiers dutifully broke their fast. There were no Sandstriders among them. Were their newly arrived guests not housebroken?

'She wants *what*?'

'To be queen,' said Damon. 'Regnant not consort, I'm guessing.'

They were the only ones at the high table. No one else had seen fit to join Tobrytan. Damon couldn't think why. He was such an outgoing kind of guy.

'She can't be.'

'You're supporting *Megan's* claim?'

'The Apostate is mocking us.'

'Naughty Apostate.'

'Remind me why I haven't killed you again?'

'Your undying love of humanity?'

Tobrytan had another go at the porridge but gave up before the spoon reached his lips. He pushed the bowl aside. 'She has to understand the world doesn't revolve around her whim.'

Damon leaned in close and lowered his voice. 'Pity you removed the only person capable of controlling that whim.'

'I can control her.'

High up in the rafters, wings fluttered as two pigeons fought over a captured morsel. 'And if not? Which side is your army going to come down on? Yours or hers?'

'Being the Mother of the Saviour is a sacred duty, but it isn't absolutely sacred. There is a precedent for Mothers being . . . dealt with.'

Yes, thought Damon, *badly.* 'Why not let her be queen then? Would she be any less controllable?'

Tobrytan called for water. He didn't offer Damon any. 'Werlavia has no need of a queen.'

'Really? The Saviours did explicitly create a throne for Edwyn. To represent his secular authority as opposed to their spiritual one.'

'That's one interpretation.'

'The people love a good crowning,' said Damon. Tobrytan gave him a look that suggested 'the people' were the least of his concerns. 'Big party, cement your connection to the old regime. Most people still think you're – we're – demon-worshipping witches. Show them you're not. Rally them to your cause.'

'The truth will rally them to our cause.'

'But a piss-up doesn't hurt.'

Tobrytan ground his teeth. 'Did she send you to talk to me?'

'No,' said Damon, 'but I am the one who's going to get it in the neck if she doesn't get her way.'

'I thought you were getting it somewhere else?'

'She *is* very adventurous for one so young.'

'I'll talk to the captains,' said Tobrytan.

'Sener'll be overjoyed.'

'If he survives the Kartiks.'

'In the meantime,' said Damon, 'why don't I do some research into coronation rituals? You know, rites, oaths, who stands where, who does what with the sacramental oil . . .'

'I don't care what you do.'

What Damon really wanted to do was investigate the

secret tunnel out of New Statham Edwyn the Third was rumoured to have built. It stood to reason he would have done – the whole city was testament to his paranoia – but no one had ever found it, or no one had ever found it and lived to tell about it in a handy sequence of notes and diagrams. But if Damon was going to get out of the capital he was going to have to evade not only the witches but their Sandstrider allies. This might be his only chance.

He licked dry lips. 'I'll need access to the records, both here and in the temple. If you could sign this pass . . . ?'

He slid a piece of paper he'd prepared earlier across the table. Tobrytan glanced at it, his face showing little interest. Damon fished a quill and a bottle of ink from his pockets and pushed them in the pass's wake. Tobrytan shrugged. He dipped the quill in the ink and made to sign. Then he stopped and read what Damon had written.

'"I hereby command the bearer of this warrant access to all areas and all materials he sees fit." Seems a little . . . broad.'

'I don't want to keep disturbing you because some pig-headed guard wants to argue technicalities.'

Tobrytan considered, continuing to hold the quill in mid-air. A droplet of ink welled up on the nib and dropped to the paper below, blooming across the surface. Damon affected as much disinterest as he could manage while pleading inside, *Sign it, sign it!*

Tobrytan dropped the quill back into the ink. 'I'll do it later.'

'Sure, no problem,' said Damon. 'I'll just stick by your side, wait until you get a moment. It'll give us a chance to bond.'

Tobrytan grabbed the quill and scrawled a signature on the pass. Damon snatched it up before the general could change his mind.

The temple was eerily quiet, with only the odd creak of timbers settling in the winter sun breaking the silence. After the embarrassment in Kewley, when the True had inadvertently burned the only source of maps, they had spared the temples in New Statham the ritual arson, but they still barred access to all but the bell-ringers, who were needed to toll the hours. One didn't need temples and priests to communicate with God; one just needed to open one's heart to Him. If you got the message confused, the True were always willing to clarify.

Damon hurried along the circular concourse, his way illuminated by shafts of light penetrating the gaps in the stairs above his head, the delay in the echo of his footsteps making him suspect a stalker. He reached the offices, which he unlocked with keys the guards outside had surrendered. There was no point bothering with the junior priests' rooms: what he wanted was far more sensitive than that. He pushed on, through the senior priests' office – more a common room than anything else; the juniors did all the work – until he reached the Supreme Priest's office.

Damon set about searching. He went through every scroll, every sheaf of parchment, every sheet of crumpled paper. Personnel records, supply requisitions, dispatches from the first war against the witches – not going well, apparently – the odd bit of pornography. No, what he wanted would be under lock and key, but there were no safes, no lockboxes, no trunks. Maybe it was up in the temple library. Damon grimaced. That could take him weeks.

Exhausted, he sat down on a couch upholstered in a hideous green. It was harder than it looked, the cushion soon giving way to solid wood and jarring his spine. He guessed certain priestly leisure activities appreciated a firm surface. The thought of what might have happened on the seat made him squirm. The seat squirmed with him. Damon frowned, pushed forward. The seat moved with him a little, then jammed.

He scrambled off and with a little to-ing and fro-ing was able to slide the seat off. The entire bottom of the couch was a solid box, a single item breaking the expanse of oak: a lock. Damon grinned and tried each of his keys. One of them turned.

There was a satisfying creak as he lifted the lid of the couch-cum-strongbox and an even more satisfying sound of a booby trap not going off. He poked about inside. Pouches of coins, the kings' sovereigns noticeably heavier than those minted by the priests; relics of monarchs and holy men, body fragments swimming in jars of murky formaldehyde; and scrolls of paper and parchment, browning and brittle to the touch.

Damon pocketed some of the sovereigns for form's sake and carefully unrolled the scrolls. He found the one he was looking for – the plans of the palace – and laid it flat on the desk, weighing the corners down with three of the money pouches and a jar whose label claimed it contained the mummified testicle of Landon the Second. He pored over the plans for what seemed like hours but they didn't yield the secret he had hoped existed.

Not expecting much, he checked the remaining scrolls. One was another copy of the palace plans superimposed on a map of the city, drawn on paper so thin it was translucent. Another scroll of equally thin paper was marked merely by a pair of crooked lines and two crosses at opposite corners. Seemed a waste of expensive paper.

Damon gathered everything up and made to drop them back in the base of the couch, when a thought occurred to him. He unrolled the scroll that depicted the palace and the city. Two crosses at opposite corners. He unrolled the almost-blank scroll, positioned it over the first, pressed them up to the window. The light streaming in through the glass merged the two sheets. The crosses aligned. The crooked lines became routes through the palace and the city.

He had found it: Edwyn the Third's secret tunnel out of New Statham. It emerged by the Rustway beyond the south side of the outer wall, perfect for slipping away on a fast boat. Where did it start? Nowhere near the throne room or the royal apartments, which surprised Damon, but instead at the end of the east wing. That explained why no one had ever found it.

A banging echoed around the room. 'What're you doing in there?' a voice demanded from out in the corridor.

'Nothing, nothing!' Damon shouted back, hurriedly rolling the scrolls back up.

The click of the door opening made him jump. The plans slipped out of his hands and fluttered to the floor. He tried to grab them but they slipped out of his grasp as if playing with him.

A True soldier stood in the doorway. 'What're those?'

'What those?' said Damon.

'Those those,' said the soldier, pointing at the plans.

'Oh, *those*.'

The soldier crouched down. The plans had settled on the floor, one on top of the other, their ends curling around. He picked them up, his head cocking from side to side as he interpreted them. Damon inched towards the door. The soldier's eyes narrowed. Adrenalin spiked in Damon's veins. His nerves screamed for him to run.

'Lines?'

'Er . . . ?'

'That all it is?' said the soldier. 'Lines?'

Damon breathed deeply to calm himself. 'You know what it's like. You start a grand project in good faith and get disheartened within a few minutes.'

The soldier screwed the plans back into tubular form and held them out to Damon. Damon held back, fearful of some trap, that if he accepted them he'd be admitting some sort of guilt.

The soldier jabbed the plans at him. 'I don't know where the sodding things go, do I?' he said.

'Course not, course not.'

Damon took the plans and dropped them on the nearest shelf. He'd got what he'd come for. The tunnel would get him out of the city; the coronation would distract the True long enough for him to get far away. Now he just had to find somewhere to run to.

fifteen

Megan watched with fascination as the tattooist worked at Afreyda's bare back; his needle and ink in a slow dance, etching a whorl on her left shoulder. Desire pricked her own body, desire that made her want to reach out, feel the heat of the other woman's body beneath her fingers, the softness of the skin, the hardness of the muscles. Megan swallowed down the feelings. This wasn't the time or the place. A moan of desire came from an adjoining room. All right, maybe the tattooist's-cum-tavern-cum-brothel *was* the place, but it wasn't the time.

She cleared her throat. Afreyda and the tattooist looked round.

'For your parents?' said Megan, pointing to the half-formed tattoo. Diannons tattooed shapes on their body to commemorate the memories of their ancestors, a practice the witches had picked up during their stay in the empire, though Saviours knew what *they* commemorated.

'I have put it off too long,' said Afreyda. She bent her

head around so she could look Megan in the eye. 'Do not make me get one for you.'

'I promise.'

Megan looked to the tattooist. 'Could you give us a minute?'

He looked back blankly. Afreyda said something to him in Hilite. He shrugged and sloped off.

'Picked up the local lingo?' said Megan, settling herself on his abandoned stool.

'A few phrases. Go away, come here, put it there, faster, slower.'

'What more does a girl need?'

They exchanged awkward grins. Megan shuffled on her stool. 'We heard back from Janik,' she said.

'The priests?' said Afreyda. 'What did they say? Do they recognize you as queen?'

'Not exactly,' said Megan. She had hoped the first victory over the witches, or at least stopping their advance for the first time, might concentrate minds, show the Faithful what could be done if they forgot about their own ambition and united. 'They offered to set up a committee to examine my claim, which I understand is bureaucratese for "sod off". In the meantime, I'm to put myself and my troops under the command of the Supreme Priest.'

'There is no Supreme Priest.'

Not one that wasn't smeared over the remains of the Endalays' old palace in Eastport. 'They've called a

186

convocation to elect a new one,' said Megan. 'Father Galan reckons Father Kimball's going to get the job.'

'Who is he?'

'High Priest of Levenport.'

'Is he a good man?' asked Afreyda.

'According to Father Galan, his sole contribution in council was to demand tax breaks for aubergine farmers.'

'Aubergines will not win the war.'

'Not unless the witches have one hell of an allergy.'

Megan leaned in close to examine Afreyda's tattoo. Droplets of blood welled up as if the skin was weeping. 'Doesn't that hurt?'

'That is the point,' said Afreyda. 'But the hurt goes away and you are left with the beauty and the memories.' She pointed at a bottle of spirits. 'But in the meantime, if you could . . . ?'

After confirming Afreyda didn't want to drink this one, Megan soaked a cloth in the spirits and dabbed. Afreyda winced at the contact. Without thinking, Megan bent forward and placed a comforting kiss on Afreyda's shoulder. Afreyda let out a soft whimper. Megan swallowed hard. All-too-conscious of what she was doing, she kissed Afreyda again, a little harder, a little closer to the base of her neck.

Boots stomped at the door. Megan jerked away. 'Busy?' asked Willas.

'Not particularly,' said Megan, heart fluttering. She

really was going to have to start locking doors behind her.

She re-soaked the cloth and applied it to Afreyda's shoulder. A little too hard. Afreyda shrieked and swore at her. 'Sorry.'

'Fordel would like to see you both,' said Willas.

'Now?'

'You said you weren't busy.'

'Afreyda's having . . .'

'It is all right, Megan. I can come back another time.'

Afreyda swung off the couch and began to dress, making no attempt to hide her breasts from Willas. He in turn paid her half-naked body no heed. The familiarity of barracks-life, or had he already seen it in a different context? Despite – or because of – what had just happened, jealousy stirred within Megan. It was silly, she tried to tell herself, but the two captains did spend a lot of time together and, as much as Megan wished otherwise, it wasn't as if either was tied to anyone.

Instead of heading to the mansion, Willas led them towards the docks.

'Where're we going?' asked Megan.

'Out of the city,' said Willas. He looked apprehensive. 'There's something you should know. Aldred's dead.'

'What? How?'

'The shock of sudden weight loss.'

'That's not funny,' snapped Megan.

188

'Didn't he try to kill you?'

Megan shot Afreyda a look. She shrugged. 'I did not realize it was meant to be a secret.'

Megan's anger at the pair wasn't entirely due to their glibness at Aldred's demise. *Get a grip*, she told herself. *You're meant to be a queen. Eleanor wouldn't've behaved like this.*

'How did he really die, captain?'

'He was a walking corpse when you found him,' said Willas. 'No one survives the mountains, not this time of year. Surprised he got as far as he did.' He looked up to the brooding Kartiks. 'Strong bastard.'

'Did he say anything before he . . . ?'

'Afraid not.'

That was that. With Aldred gone and Damon who knew where, Megan would never know the truth about what had happened that day in Kewley. Maybe Aldred had had noble reasons for doing what he'd done; maybe Damon had; maybe neither had. It was in God's hands now.

Willas and one of Fordel's clerks – Flóki, Megan thought his name was – helped Megan and Afreyda into a rowing boat. They cast off and headed down the still waters of the inlet. They skimmed past fishing vessels lumbering out to sea; raced the packs of seals who would occasionally break the surface to bark a challenge or a greeting; ducked as seabird swooped over their heads and dived into the water, emerging with a silver fish wriggling in its beak.

The inlet meandered left then right, hiding the city

behind hills and trees. Megan wondered if they were going to hit the open sea, but they docked at a ramshackle jetty. From there they trekked through a patch of pines, frost crunching beneath their boots. Their destination was a long, low hut that stood by itself among the trees and whistling wind. It was brighter inside than Megan expected. Dozens of lanterns hung from the ceiling, quiet creaks escaping their chains as draughts rocked them. Jars filled with powders and crystals and liquids of every conceivable colour lined the shelves. Workbenches had been shoved against the walls to accommodate a trio of iron torsos. Guns.

Megan looked to Willas. 'You said . . .'

'I said there was a little accident.' Willas indicated one of the guns. Looking closer, Megan could see it had ruptured, like a snake that has eaten too big a meal.

'Why didn't you tell me?'

Fordel stepped forward. 'The fewer people who know we have them the better.'

'Why?'

'The fewer people who know anything the better.' Fordel shrugged. 'Plus, it's better the witches think we no longer have them.'

Megan swallowed her annoyance. She cleared a sheaf of papers covered with calculations from a bench and sat down, huddling into her furs. It was chilly in the hut. The fireplace contained nothing but ashes.

Ími flitted around the guns like a child on Saviours' Day. 'These are fascinating,' he said. He looked to Afreyda. 'How long have your people had them?'

'A few years.'

'And do you know anything about the construction?'

'Apart from the fact it's lousy,' said Willas.

'It is a very brittle iron,' said Ími. 'Most unsuitable for the —' he twirled his fingers, looking for the word — 'pressures it must go under.'

'Just like your swords,' Willas said to Afreyda. Her Diannon blade had been shattered by a Sandstrider during their escape from Ainsworth. 'You might as well make your weapons out of cheese. At least you'd get a snack out of it.'

Afreyda scowled. 'What is it you want?'

Ími prised open a barrel and scooped up a handful of gunpowder, which he let drain through his fingers. 'I've been trying to figure out what's in this?' he said, looking at Afreyda. 'Sulphur, obviously, from the smell. Charcoal. But there's something else. Something that makes it go bang.'

'I do not know,' said Afreyda. 'It is the Emperor's secret.'

'You didn't try to find out when you had your little rebellion?' asked Fordel.

'Please think,' said Ími. 'Do you remember any rumours, overhear any speculation what was in it?

191

Any kind of clue. Something I can start experimenting with.'

'Always with the experiments,' said Fordel, the ghost of a smile playing on his lips.

Afreyda shook her head. 'I am sorry. I know nothing.'

'Hmm.' Ími pursed his lips. 'What about something your Emperor was very keen to keep to himself?'

'I do not know what you mean.'

'Well, obviously he wanted gold and silver and iron and farmland, but what about something that made you go, "What does he want with *that*?"'

'No,' said Afreyda, frowning. She gave an apologetic shrug. 'I cannot . . . Wait . . . during the rebellion, we heard he had ordered a regiment to secure the *p'ta* caves.'

'*P'ta?*'

'I do not know the Stathian word,' said Afreyda. 'It's what comes out of bats.'

'Bats . . . ?'

Afreyda let out a sequence of screeches and flapped her hands. 'Bats.'

'Yes, I know what bats are. But, please, do that again. It was funny.'

Ími browsed the jars lining the walls. 'Aha!' He pulled down a jar filled with a salt-like substance and unscrewed the lid. 'This the stuff?'

Afreyda peered into the jar. 'It could be. What do you call it?'

'*Sápet*. I don't know what the Stathian is either.'

'Saltpetre,' said Fordel. 'The Hálforans used it for fertilizing crops and curing sausage.'

'And now we can use it for explosions,' said Ími. 'It does explain why Hálforan sausage always gives me heartburn.'

Willas coughed loudly. Fordel gave him a warning look. 'If it is the right thing,' he said to Ími.

'There's only one way we'll find out. Of course, we'll have to find the correct proportions. The correct way of mixing it. Stuff that goes bang might go bang at exactly the wrong time.'

'I'm not going to see you for the next few days, am I?' said Fordel.

'You wouldn't want me any other way, *vulfi*.'

Willas sniggered. '*Vulfi?*' asked Megan.

'It means "adorable little wolf cub",' said Willas.

'Just "wolf cub",' said Fordel with a sigh.

'I think the "adorable" and "little" are implied.'

'Whichever,' said Megan, 'it's very sweet.'

Fordel rolled his eyes. 'This is all very well,' he said, flipping off the bench, 'but we've all got work to do.' He gave Ími a kiss. 'Try not to blow yourself up.'

'I'll take every precaution,' said Ími. He beckoned at Flóki, who had been observing proceedings quietly from the door. 'This is how I want you to start . . .'

*

When they docked back in Hil a servant was waiting to tell Megan Rekka was expecting her. Megan wondered if this was some power-play game cooked up by Rekka and Fordel, to have her scurrying this way and that, show her who was in charge. She thought of refusing the summons, but Afreyda and Willas had already presumed her acquiescence and after a brief goodbye had departed for the barracks in deep conversation.

Megan found Rekka in the Lord Defender's study along with the ash-blonde woman Megan recognized from the council table. Rekka smiled insincerely and hobbled to Megan. She was still using the stick, though the severity of her hobble depended on the number of people actively observing it.

'Your Majesty,' said Rekka, 'let me introduce Skúla, the ambassador from Trávi.' Trávi was the smallest of the Snow Cities, way off to the north-east of Werlavia.

'It is a pleasure to finally meet you, Majesty,' said Skúla, curtsying. Her Stathian was good but accented, with a slight slur around the *s*.

'Er, you too, Lady Skúla.'

Skúla stood there expectantly. Rekka's gaze flicked to the couch the ambassador had vacated. Megan realized what was required of her.

'Please, sit,' Megan said, wishing Eleanor had fitted some etiquette lessons in with all the knife fighting.

Skúla did as bid. Megan took the couch opposite.

Rekka made a great play of fetching wine. Megan waited until the glass was in her hand before affecting concern.

'Is your knee still playing up?' she said. 'You should have said something. I could have got the drinks.'

Rekka smiled sourly. Skúla took a sip from her glass. 'Percadian?'

'Make the most of it,' said Rekka, nodding. 'We only have a few barrels left.'

It just tasted wine-y to Megan.

'How did the archers we sent get on?' said Skúla.

'They . . . um . . . arrived,' said Megan. The Trávians had sent a single squad, which had impressed Willas and Afreyda no start. Megan didn't recall them making up in quality what they lacked in quantity.

'We would have liked to send more, but we needed to defend the Death Pass. Don't want the witches sneaking around the back way.'

Megan thought anywhere called the Death Pass could look after itself. She'd possibly pushed her lack of gratitude as far as diplomatically wise though. 'Every contribution is valued.'

'I understand the witches contributed to their own defeat.'

'Huh?'

'You captured some of their guns?'

Megan thought about what Fordel had said, about keeping the existence of the guns secret. She assumed that meant from their own allies. Especially from their own allies, knowing Fordel.

'Briefly,' she said. 'They blew themselves up.'

'Unfortunate.'

Rekka swung her injured leg on to the couch next to Megan. 'Do you mind?' she said. 'Bit of a twinge.'

Megan inched away from the invading leg as much as possible. Rekka leaned back and called out. A few moments later, one of her daughters scurried in. Vega, the oldest: a teenager who was all spindly limbs and copper tresses. She crouched by her mother and started to massage the back of her knee. Rekka let out a sigh of contentment. Perhaps her injury really was troubling her.

'Have you given any thought to your coronation?' Skúla asked Megan.

Coronation? That sounded a little premature, considering only a tiny fraction of the Realm recognized her claim and even then only as the least worst option.

'Been a bit busy,' said Megan. 'Besides, where does one pick up a crown these days?'

'Funny you should ask that. Yrsa, be a dear and get me that box over there.'

Yrsa – which one was Vega then? *was* there a Vega? – abandoned her mother and scuttled over to the desk. She retrieved a wooden box, so old dust was embedded in the grain, and placed it in front of the fire between Megan and Skúla.

196

Skúla gestured to Yrsa. 'If you would . . .' Yrsa struggled with the lid. It was jammed on tight. 'You need to give it a good yank.'

'Good lesson in many areas of life,' said Rekka.

Yrsa pulled hard, rocking backwards as the lid came off. Her eyes went wide as she peered inside. Her mouth dropped. The lid slipped out of her hand.

'Don't gawp, dear,' said Skúla. 'Show the queen.'

Yrsa reached into the box and pulled out a crown, a latticework of gold with six tines that arced over and met in a circle in the middle. Grime had settled in the ridges, but the bodywork still shone enough to reflect the fire, the images of flames giving an illusion of life.

'Is that . . . ?'

Skúla nodded.

The Unifier's crown. Legend had it the Saviours themselves had presented it to him; history told them his son, Edwyn the Second, had lost it in the Kartiks while trying to retake the Snow Cities.

'You kept it?' said Megan. 'You didn't melt it down?'

'Sentimental value.'

Megan bent forward for a closer look, semi-unintentionally dislodging Rekka's foot. There were holes stamped into the metal, where precious stones had once been set. Megan pointed at them.

'Where are the . . . ?'

'Bills to pay,' said Skúla. 'We're not *that* sentimental.'

197

She spread her palms like an obsequious merchant. 'Please consider this a gift, from the people of Trávi to the Queen of Werlavia. Might need a bit of a polish to really bring it up.'

Rekka smirked. 'And we're back to life's lessons.'

'You can't help yourself, can you, Rekka?'

'How else do you think I got five children?'

'Six, mama,' said Yrsa.

Rekka ticked off her fingers. 'Oh yes, you're right. I'm glad someone's keeping count.'

'Why don't you try it on, ma'am?' Skúla said to Megan.

Megan was afraid to touch the crown, afraid of everything it represented. It had been touched by the regal, by the divine, and she was neither, just a political pretext. On the other hand, it was a piece of metal that had languished in a box for three hundred years.

She accepted the crown from Yrsa and tentatively placed it on her head. It slipped down, only the top of her ears and the bridge of her nose preventing it becoming a necklace.

'Edwyn had a big head,' said Rekka. 'Who knew?'

Skúla lifted the crown off Megan's head. 'We can pad it.'

Maybe they could. But Megan felt it was going to take more than a few stuffed rags to make her queen.

sixteen

Afreyda was waiting for Megan outside the great hall after the morning's worship. 'Ími has something to show us.'

'I hope it's more impressive than last time,' said Megan. 'How is Flóki, by the way?'

'His hand has not yet grown back, if that is what you are asking.'

Brother Broose hurried after them, feet slipping on compacted snow. He reached out to steady himself on Megan. Afreyda caught his arm before he could make contact and threw him to the ground.

'I wasn't going to hurt her!' said Brother Broose, limbs flailing as he tried to get back up. 'I just wanted to talk.'

Afreyda pressed a boot to his chest and pinned him back to the ground. 'You can talk from down there.'

'It's cold!'

'It is hardly summer up here.'

'Let him up, captain.'

Afreyda reluctantly stepped back. Brother Broose

struggled to his feet, brushing ice from his shoulders as if it was dandruff. Afreyda placed herself between him and Megan. Megan was touched by the gesture but also a little annoyed. She could look after herself.

'What is it, Brother Broose?'

'We need a proper temple, Your –' he swallowed, struggling to complete the honorific – 'Your Majesty. We can't keep using the barbarians' drinking den. It stinks of beer.'

Megan was surprised a priest thought this objectionable. 'We've barely got enough roofs for everyone. We can't waste men and material building you a nice office.'

'The Faithful are willing to volunteer their time.'

'If they have time, I have a hundred jobs they could be doing.'

'If we do not celebrate the Faith, then what are we doing this for? To survive? The witches offered us that.'

'We can still worship, can't we?' said Megan. 'If you show me where in the Book of Faith it demands temples before shelter, I'll consider it.'

'Their own temple would give the people hope.'

'So will not freezing to death.'

Brother Broose scowled. Snot trickled down the channels of his lined skin. Megan squeezed his arm. 'We don't need a temple here, brother, because we're not stopping. We're going to go home, when this is over. Back to our own cities and lands, our own houses and temples.'

Brother Broose stepped back, doubt etched into his face. It was a look she had seen on many faces, sometimes subsumed immediately, other times held as if in defiance. Megan wished there was some way she could convince him, convince everyone else, convince herself.

'If you'll excuse me, Your Majesty, I have lessons to give.'

Megan gave him leave and followed Afreyda to the docks, where a boat was waiting for them. As they cut across the calm waters, into which snow gently sprinkled and melted, she brooded on what Brother Broose had said. Eleanor had once said survival was the first step, but what about the second step and the third and every step after that? It was easy to offer promises, no matter how sincerely meant; much harder to keep them.

Afreyda studied Megan with a soft but unflinching gaze. 'What is wrong?' she asked.

'Oh, you know.'

'The affairs of state?' said Afreyda. Megan nodded. 'You are very young to have such a burden.'

'No older than you, captain.'

'No, I think I am older.'

'Really?' said Megan. 'How old are you anyway?'

Afreyda thought for a moment. 'I think I turned nineteen a few weeks ago,' she said. Megan wouldn't be eighteen until the sixth day of midsummer, a date the witches considered oh so important.

'You should've told me,' said Megan. 'I would have got you a present.'

'I was not sure. It is hard to tell. You have no proper calendars over here.'

'I know, I know. Everything is better in the empire.'

'Apart from the head of state,' said Afreyda. As this was a man she had vowed to kill, Megan wasn't sure she could take it as much of a compliment.

They made landfall at the end of an expanse of snow-covered beach, whose purity was broken only by a trail of tiny paw prints that looped round in a confused trail before disappearing into the tundra of the bordering hills. There was a small crowd waiting for them: Ími, Fordel, Willas, Vegar, Rekka and one of Fordel's clerks. The last had a certain singed quality to him.

Megan tried to stamp some life into her chilled feet. 'What's this about?'

The crowd parted. Rekka swung her walking stick, causing a chime as it struck one of the witches' guns. It had a brother, or rather a distant cousin: a second gun, longer and broader, its body formed of shining steel that reflected the overhead clouds rather than dull pig iron. Both were mounted on wheeled carriages.

'You made that?' asked Megan, pointing at the shiny gun. Ími nodded. 'And the gunpowder?'

'We found the formula, Your Majesty,' said Ími. A strained look flashed across the clerk's face. 'Eventually.'

'And what is the formula?'

Ími's response was a smile and a sweep of his hand towards the hills that lay beyond the beach. 'If you like to come this way to the observation post . . .'

Rekka pouted. 'We have to walk?'

'If you want to volunteer to stay here and fire the guns,' said Ími, 'you're most welcome, my lady.' The clerk nodded enthusiastically. 'We are still in the . . . experimental stage though.'

'I've not fallen so low as to attempt science.'

Leaving the clerk behind, they made their way up the hill. Rekka insisted that not only should her husband support her, but Willas should too. Megan got the honour of carrying her walking stick. Only fears of causing a diplomatic incident prevented her from whacking her cousin with it.

Ími wove his way between the shrubs that poked through the snow as if they were an obstacle path, gabbling on like a used-carriage salesman. 'Because of our superior steel, we're able to pack more gunpowder in our gun than the witches can theirs. Withstands the forces better.'

'How d'you find that out?' asked Megan.

'Trial and error,' said Ími. He wrinkled his mouth. 'It was the error that did it.'

'What does more gunpowder mean?' asked Afreyda.

'Well, louder . . .'

They reached a bunker almost buried into the ground. Steep steps led down to a bare room that reeked of stale urine and rotten fish. That part of the wall facing the beach that was above ground was open, giving a clear view of the inlet beyond. Megan guessed it was used for reconnaissance in times of trouble, most likely by observers with no sense of smell.

'Make yourself comfortable,' said Ími, heading back for the stairs. 'I have to go direct things.'

'Is this where he brings all his dates?' Rekka asked Fordel, who answered with a sardonic smile.

Megan had to stand on tiptoes to see out, which soon put a strain on her calves. She gave up and followed Ími outside, pulling her hood up to protect her ears from the biting cold.

He frowned. 'I really think it's safer for you to be inside, ma'am.'

Megan pointed at the guns, which were aimed down the beach. 'They're not going to hit me from there. Are they?'

'It's not impossible.'

Megan shrugged. 'I'm here now.'

There was clomping behind them. Afreyda, Willas, Rekka and Fordel trooped up out of the bunker. 'Really!' said Ími, exasperated.

'It does pong a bit,' said Rekka.

'What about Vegar?' asked Megan.

'He quite likes it. Reminds him of his youth.'

'If you get your legs blown off, don't come running to me.' Ími waved them away. 'I'd advise you to stand a bit further back.'

The crowd shuffled back a foot. Afreyda took Megan's arm and pulled her further up the hill. Megan wondered if it was entirely a coincidence they ended up with Rekka between them and the guns.

Ími pulled two kerchiefs out of his pocket, one red, one blue. He held the red one above his head, waved it and dropped his arm. Down on the beach, the clerk lit the fuse of the witches' gun with a torch and raced to a safe distance. There was a boom. The gun recoiled as if disgusted at what it had spat out. A few hundred yards down the beach, a column of snow, sand and smoke was sent into the air.

'That's for reference,' said Ími. 'Now for the interesting part. Or for the spectacular failure. Given there are important people watching, I predict the latter.'

Ími raised the blue kerchief, waved it, let it drop. The clerk crept towards the Hilite gun as if it was a slumbering monster and gently touched the torch to the fuse snaking out of its back. Then, even faster than before, he dashed for cover.

Megan held her breath, waiting for the gun to fire. It was taking longer than the first – a longer fuse? She sought out Afreyda's hand, squeezed it. A squeeze came in response.

An explosion ripped around the inlet. Megan cringed and instinctively jerked her head away. When she looked back, there was a second crater smouldering away on the beach. This one was further away from the guns by half as much again.

Her brain whirled with the implications. 'We can outgun the witches,' she said, facing Afreyda.

'We can hit them before they could even get close enough to touch us.'

'We can defeat them.'

'We can win this war.'

'We can be free.'

The emotion overwhelmed Megan and burst out into a kiss she planted on Afreyda's mouth. Afreyda stepped back, looking a little shocked, her fingers going to her lips. Megan swallowed, realizing what she'd done, instantly regretting it.

'I'm sorry. I didn't mean . . .'

She stumbled away. Afreyda caught her before she'd managed more than a couple of steps and twisted her around. She stepped up close so their hoods merged and they were enveloped in their own pocket universe and Megan could feel Afreyda's elevated breathing play on her skin. Her heart raced until her body trembled. She had faced swords and guns, armies and navies, priests and witches, but this was more terrifying than anything else. She wanted to run away. She wanted to be here and nowhere else.

In the end, Megan couldn't say who kissed whom. All she knew was her lips were on Afreyda's, that their mouths were opening, that their tongues were intertwining. They were exploring one another, giving and accepting, declaring themselves.

A polite cough prompted them to break. 'We do have a war to plan,' said Fordel.

Megan looked into Afreyda's eyes, pulse raised, breath not quite filling her lungs. 'Get the witches to concentrate their forces,' she said. 'Give you a target to fire at.'

'Ships would be best,' said Afreyda.

'Lure their fleet up here.'

'How?' asked Rekka.

'I'm sure you'll figure out a way,' said Megan.

Right now, she had other things on her mind.

Megan couldn't remember the last time she had felt so serene – before the witches had come, at least; never, quite possibly. The cares of the world were reduced to background noise, every other person as real as a fading dream. She would have to face them sooner or later – all right, sooner – but for now all that mattered were the arms wrapped around her, the touch of Afreyda's body as they lay in bed.

'How long have you known?' asked Megan. 'That . . . you know?'

'I do not know. You could be talking about anything.'

'That you liked . . . ?'

'You? Girls? Tea?'

'All of them,' said Megan. 'Well, I possibly don't need the complete history of your relationship with tea.'

'It is a very strange drink.'

'There was someone else? Back in the empire?'

'Yes.'

Megan tensed. Afreyda shushed her and kissed her bare shoulder. A spark ran the length of Megan's body.

'It was a long time ago.'

'What happened to her?'

'Her father found out about us. He banished her.'

'They disapprove then, in the empire? Of two women . . . ?'

'Yes.'

'But you did it anyway?'

'Yes,' said Afreyda. 'They will disapprove here too? The priests?'

'Priests disapprove of everything other people do,' said Megan. 'Do you think about her? This girl?'

'Do you think about Cate's father?'

Wade. 'Not for a long time.'

'Did you lo— Did you like him?'

'I don't know,' said Megan. 'I thought I did at the

208

time, but I think that's how everyone expected me to feel. I convinced myself I cared for him, but I was just doing Gwyneth's job for her. It's what you're meant to do, right? Meet a boy, get married, have children. I almost got that right. All right, I cocked up the order . . .'

'And now?' said Afreyda. 'Are you going to do what you are meant to do?'

'No. I'm going to do what I want to do.'

'Because you are queen?'

'No,' said Megan, 'because I'm me.' She lifted Afreyda's hand to her lips and planted a soft kiss on each of her fingers. 'Priests, witches, they all want to tell people what to do, what to feel. Not me. Not any more. I don't care what they say; I don't care what they do. No one's going to stop me being with you. If they try, I'll have a blade waiting for them.'

seventeen

The throne room fell silent. Everyone got to their feet. Horns blew. A shiver rippled across Damon's skin. Gwyneth entered and paraded down the aisle, the True captains carrying her train like the world's grimmest bridesmaids. Her gown was a gorgeous concoction of white silk slashed at regular intervals to reveal the red velvet underneath – wounded innocence, how very like Gwyneth – bare at the shoulders to show off her perfect olive skin. She looked utterly beautiful. Then she smiled and Damon wanted to say a prayer for the whole world.

It was ludicrous, this elevation of a peasant girl to Queen of Werlavia, but then what did justify power? Bloodlines, money, popularity, the ability to kill a large number of people in a short amount of time? How long would they endure her? How long before distaste of her capriciousness outweighed the fear of splitting the True? How long before someone raised her daughter, and reminded the True she was the one they should be following, the one they had fought for?

Tobrytan was waiting by the throne. He bade Gwyneth sit. Gwyneth gave him the kind of look that suggested she needn't be bid to do anything then regarded the assembled throng. They stared back, unsure of the expected response. Gwyneth gave Tobrytan a regal wave. Tobrytan swallowed and started. Gwyneth had insisted on using Werlay in the ceremony – classier, she claimed – though she had at least agreed to spare Tobrytan and the audience the traditional recitation of *The Unification*, an epic poem telling the story of Edwyn's conquest, written by someone who thought the version in the Book of Faith neither long nor hagiographic enough.

Tobrytan's delivery was hesitant and monotone, as stiff as that of a schoolboy made to present his homework in front of class. Mispronunciations were rife; many words were omitted or replaced with 'um'; at one point he called Gwyneth the 'evil she-wolf from hell' instead of 'our glorious monarch' – Werlay was not a language that forgave sloppiness. A few merchants in the crowd sniggered. They looked rich enough to afford the kind of useless education that included dead languages.

Tobrytan declaimed each of the three coronation vows, Gwyneth answering each of them with a simple *Prana* – 'I pledge'. If she was being honest, which was probably asking too much, she would have answered

Mata, *Pōta*, *Diso Kătera* – 'I might', 'Possibly' and 'Not a chance'.

A lieutenant marched in from a back room, carrying the crown on a velvet cushion. They'd found the headpiece in the old royal vaults. Best guess was it had been made for Queen Alodie, who had abandoned the throne after internecine battles with the priests and founded the Sisters of the Faith, a career path Gwyneth was unlikely to follow. The crown had been reset with sapphires, with the star-broken circle picked out on its front in rubies. At its apex was a massive diamond.

Damon leaned forward. Was that . . . ? The guards yanked him back but not before he recognized the Endalay diamond, the ultimate reason for his capture by the True – that and a treacherous lieutenant, a violent fence and his own greed. How had they got hold of it? Damon suspected it didn't involve a mutually beneficial transaction.

'Is it time?' Gwyneth whispered to Tobrytan.

'Almost.'

She beckoned the lieutenant closer. Light reflected off the gold and shimmered across her face. The jewels caught in her eyes and sparkled. Tobrytan made to lift the crown. Gwyneth held up a warning finger. He backed off, frowning. Gwyneth took the crown herself. Before Tobrytan could intervene, she placed it on her head.

In the distance the temple bells struck noon. Damon realized what was going to happen, why the coronation had been this day, this time. The sun aligned with the window above Gwyneth's head and a column of light shone down upon her. It hit the diamond at the centre of her crown and split into a thousand beams, dazzling the hall. For a moment it was as if God himself had inaugurated her.

Damon tried to slip away after the ceremony, looking to take a flagon of wine to a dark corner of the palace, but Tobrytan collared him and marched him out of the throne room.

'You speak Trávian?' said the general.

'Sure,' said Damon. 'Once you speak one Snow City language you speak them all. They're all variants of Werlay with just the—'

'Do I look like I want a linguistics lesson?'

'Open-minded chap like you? Thought you'd be thrilled to acquire new knowledge.'

Tobrytan gave Damon the glare of one for whom open-minded meant someone with the top of their skull sliced off and bundled him into an antechamber. Gwyneth was there, the crown still glittering on her head. A dark-haired serving girl whose face Damon couldn't quite place was detaching the train from her gown. Sitting on the couch was another woman, with ash-blonde hair and a face that was attractive if weather-beaten. Two witches stood behind her, hands on their weapons, but if their presence made the woman nervous she didn't show it.

'Ask the ambassador what she wants,' said Gwyneth.

'Ambassador?' said Damon, putting two and two together. 'From Trávi? She didn't bring her own translator?'

Gwyneth gave a small shrug. 'There was an incident.'

Damon turned to the blonde woman and dredged up his memory of Trávian. It had been a while since he'd had cause to speak it. Well, yell it pleadingly. That fisherman had been *really* annoyed about his missing purse.

'Greetings, Lady . . . ?'

'Skúla.'

'Greetings, Lady Skúla.' Damon looked to Gwyneth. 'Lady Skúla,' he said, pointing at the ambassador.

Gwyneth rolled her eyes. 'Yes, we got that far.'

'What brings you to New Statham?' Damon asked Skúla. 'I have to warn you – the nightlife's gone really downhill these past few months.'

'I came to congratulate the queen on her accession.'

'She likes your hat,' Damon paraphrased for Gwyneth.

'And to discuss the military situation.'

'Ah,' said Damon. 'That's a bit of a sore point.'

Gwyneth had been furious at Sener's defeat at the hands of Megan and the Hilites, and even more so at his refusal to attack again because of the upcoming winter. If it wasn't for the continued sympathy for Sener and his late father among the True, she would have had him recalled to New Statham and executed. Instead the captain was skulking in the foothills of the Kartiks,

214

preventing the Snow Cities raiding the Realm for supplies.

'I have something that could help,' said Skúla.

'What kind of something?'

'A route into Hil.'

Damon translated for Gwyneth and Tobrytan.

'We've heard about the tunnels through the mountains,' said Tobrytan. 'The Hilites have them well defended. And with the guns the Apostate captured . . .'

'You don't have to worry about the guns,' said Skúla in response to Damon's translation. 'They blew themselves up. Prone to doing that, I hear.' She shrugged. 'Anyway, the route's not through the tunnels. It's by sea.'

'Really? One end's full of ice, the other end's full of rocks.'

'There's little I can do about the ice, but I can get you around the rocks.'

'You know a route through the Sarason Sea?'

'It is ours.'

Skúla held out a tightly rolled scroll.

Damon passed it to Tobrytan, who unrolled it and frowned. Damon and Gwyneth each peered over one of his shoulders. They were looking at the northern coastline of Werlavia, the far eastern end near Trávi. The Sarason Sea lay above it, its expanse pockmarked by numerous small islands. Those were only the large hazards: the Sarason was infamous for rocks, fierce winds and the occasional iceberg. Dashed lines appeared to show a way through.

'We can supply larger, more-detailed maps,' said Skúla.

Gwyneth turned to the serving girl. 'Taite, leave us.'

Taite: Damon recognized her now. Sener's — what? — girlfriend? She gathered Gwyneth's detached train in her arms and, barely able to see over the mound of fabric, tottered out of the room.

'Offer the ambassador some wine,' Gwyneth said to Damon before stepping aside to engage in a low conversation with Tobrytan.

'Percadian, if you have it,' Skúla said in reply to Damon's translation.

'An excellent choice,' said Damon. It wasn't. Percadian was what people asked for when they wanted to pretend they knew about wine. They also didn't have any: priests wouldn't lower themselves to drinking the anaemic dribble.

Skúla accepted the glass off Damon. '*Prita, taka.*' Her attention wasn't on him; it was on Gwyneth and Tobrytan. Damon recognized the expression: that of a pickpocket waiting for her opportunity. Or a professional eavesdropper.

Tobrytan and Gwyneth finished their conference. 'Why not simply let us over the Death Pass?' asked Tobrytan.

'Because then everyone will know what we did,' said Skúla. 'We'd prefer our cooperation to be kept private.'

'How modest,' said Damon. 'Won't the other cities get suspicious when they notice you're the only one left untouched?'

'Not if you leave them untouched too. Do what you like with Hil though.'

'All of Werlavia belongs to us,' said Gwyneth.

'Please, Your Majesty. The cities have no worth to the Realm. Take your Saviour, leave us in peace and we will do the same with you.'

'We can march over the Kartiks in spring without your help or paying your price,' said Tobrytan.

'Yes,' said Skúla, 'but you can sail to Hil much sooner. And it might be best if you do. The rumours from Janik are the priests are about to declare for Queen Megan.'

The sound of her sister's name made Gwyneth flush even before Damon had finished translating. 'She is no queen,' she snapped.

'I apologize, Your Majesty,' said Skúla, with an ingratiating smile that suggested she was only lying through half her teeth. 'But if the priests move their army to the Kartiks it may make it even harder for you to cross the mountains.'

Gwyneth stiffened and turned to Tobrytan. 'Prepare the fleet, general.'

'We should study this more—'

'You heard me. We have a Saviour to rescue. And a false queen to slaughter.'

By the time they joined it the party was in full swing, which as the True were involved meant everyone was drinking morosely and awaiting the next execution. Gwyneth, who had exchanged the crown for a simple tiara – if you could call a piece studded with enough diamonds to pay the entire army 'simple' – glided from room to room, accepting the feigned congratulations of her new subjects. There had only been one assassination attempt so far: an old man, possibly a priest, had lunged at her with a pâté-smeared knife. Gwyneth's bodyguards had cut him down with brutal efficiency, leaving his body on the floor where it fell as a warning to others, or possibly as a bench should they get short on chairs. Gwyneth herself had taken the assault with remarkable equanimity. Had she taken something to calm her nerves or was she convinced she had God's protection?

'You're really going to trust this Skúla?' Damon asked Tobrytan.

The general looked grim, eyes scanning the crowd as if on the hunt for people to stop from having a good time. 'If she has the means to deliver us the Saviour.'

'You know she speaks Stathian, don't you?' said Damon. 'I could tell by the way she was watching you and Gwyn— the queen.'

'What of it?'

'Maybe it's not the only thing she's keeping from you.'

'We'll send scout ships to test the route,' said Tobrytan. 'Sandstrider scout ships.' He beckoned a soldier. 'You, keep an eye on him. I've got an invasion to plan.'

'Sir.'

Tobrytan stalked off. The soldier took his place by Damon's side and stayed there, clinging to him like a child who had attached himself to the teacher on the first day of school.

'Why don't you go mingle?' said Damon.

'Mingle?'

'You know, talk to people, girls maybe? You can impress them with tales of bravery and brutality.'

'I don't want to impress girls.'

'Well, it's a cosmopolitan bunch. I'm sure we can find you a—'

'I have a wife. Back in the empire.'

Another one. Damon recalled Tobrytan also had a wife waiting for him. The Diannon Emperor liked to collect hostages, it would seem. 'Miss her?'

'No.'

Damon indicated a courtier whose corset and low-cut dress weaponized her cleavage. 'Then why not . . . ?'

'I made a vow before God and the Saviours.'

Damon beckoned the courtier over anyway. Her approach was reluctant at first, then more enthusiastic as she seemed to recognize him. 'You were at the coronation, right?' she said. 'Near the front?'

The springs in her laboriously curled hair were beginning to unravel. Cracks in her make-up revealed a woman at least ten years older than she was pretending to be. The former mistress of some priest, angling for a way into the new regime, working out who was whom, where the power resided. You don't want anything to do with this lot, Damon wanted to tell her; it'll only lead to misery and death.

He didn't though. He forced his mouth into a disarming smile and nodded. He had only been so prominent because Tobrytan wanted to keep an eye on him. 'I'm Damon. This is . . .'

'Cole.'

'And you are . . . ?'

'Eleanor.'

If his cup hadn't been pewter, it would have shattered in Damon's grip. The world blurred to grey. Conversation reduced to a ringing in his ears. His throat constricted, buffering his breath in his windpipe. The fatal leap played itself over in his mind again and again and again.

A slap between the shoulder blades snapped everything back in focus. He spluttered as respiration resumed, took a steadying drink. He coughed it back up again.

'Are you all right?' asked the courtier.

He looked at the woman. Eleanor. Not Eleanor. *Pull*

yourself together. It's just a name. There must be hundreds of Eleanors out there. 'Yes, yes. Probably just the sausages. Bad thing to eat in a war zone. You're never quite sure what's in them. Or who.'

'What are you on about?'

Damon wasn't sure. His mouth was running away of its own accord. 'Why don't you . . . ? Why don't you and Cole get better acquainted? I need to go find the . . . find the . . . privy.'

He staggered away, not really sure what he was doing. Only when someone gave him a shove backwards and he didn't collide with armour did he realize he'd shaken off his guard. He looked to the sky. *Still looking after me? I don't deserve it.* He could almost hear the countess's voice in reply, haughty but with a hint of suppressed humour. *I know.*

Damon composed himself, got his bearings. It wouldn't be long before Cole realized what had happened. He hurried through the palace, fast as he dared, keeping his head down and his senses alert. It was the getaway of a felon fleeing the scene of a yet-to-be-discovered crime: the thief who had helped himself to a purse, the conman who had palmed a loaded die, the forger who had passed a dud coin – and he had been them all. He considered offering repentance if God would grant him this last escape, but he knew he didn't mean it or, if he did, that he'd end up doing far worse in the future.

Worse than what happened to Eleanor?

After making his way through corridors littered with mats and blankets and strange utensils that looked like drunken exercises in pottery, he reached the east wing. There were no Sandstriders on duty this time: they were all at the party. For once a plan was coming together. He just hoped he had enough time to find the entrance to the tunnel.

Someone lurched at him. Damon skipped out of the way. The Sandstrider grabbed at fresh air and toppled over.

Damon bent over to examine him. 'Are you hurt?' he asked in Andaluvian. The Sandstrider gave him the vacant smile of the truly hammered. 'Guess not. If anyone asks, you didn't see me.'

'Which one?'

Damon patted the Sandstrider's shoulder and moved on.

There, beyond that door. There should be a small chamber with an alcove or a chimney place against the far wall, some out-of-place brick or ugly ornament waiting to trigger counterweights. It was locked. Of course. He put an experimental shoulder to it. Not for budging.

Damon searched the belongings of the absent Sandstriders. He turned up a knife whose tip had snapped off and a hooked spike whose purpose he felt better off not knowing and set about tackling the lock. Pins and tumblers appeared to succumb to his ministrations then snapped back, like a coquette teasing a potential seducer. He didn't allow himself to be discouraged but kept on probing away, learning every part of the lock, decoding its secret.

Shouting from the far end of the corridor. Approaching boots. Drawn weapons. Damon forced himself not to look back, to concentrate on his task at the same steady pace. Almost there. The final pin slipped into place. Adrenalin took over. He twisted the knife. Too hard. It jammed. He breathed in through his nose, exhaled through his mouth. The soldiers were close enough to make out their words. Not very nice words. He rotated the knife, slowly but firmly.

The lock gave way. The door swung inwards on rusty hinges. The room beyond was bare. Dust motes swam in the hazy light streaming through the windows, excited by the breeze he'd introduced. Damon pushed himself off his knees and took a step forward.

A boot connected with the back of his knees and sent him sprawling on to the floorboards. 'Going somewhere?' demanded Tobrytan.

'Me?' said Damon. 'No.'

'You are now.'

eighteen

Damon rubbed his forehead after he'd banged it on yet another low-hanging beam, this one in the ship's mess. Everything on board was cramped and half the size it should be. It was as if he had stumbled into a child's playroom, albeit a child with the kind of friends you didn't want to invite to tea.

He'd been condemned to be part of the witches' invasion fleet, ostensibly as a translator but in reality as a punishment. They had given him his own cabin, at least, instead of making him share a hammock-space with the rest of the crew, but it was a cabin that bolted on the outside.

The line behind Damon grumbled. The cook glowered, steam from his kitchen making sweat roll down his face and into the bubbling pot in front of him. In the best maritime tradition, he was covered in scabs that could be crumbled up and used as seasoning in emergencies.

'You want some?'

Head still throbbing, Damon held out his bowl. Unidentifiable stew splatted into it. This didn't bode well. First night out and they were already on the slop; what was it going to be like months from now when they were tracking Werlavia's desolate eastern coast? He began to miss the sausages from the coronation party.

Damon took his dinner over to the benches, where soldiers sat eating with little enthusiasm. They had ditched their armour and were dressed in a variety of shifts and tunics, yellowed from years of sweat. Bared arms displayed a variety of scars, tattoos and coiled muscles. There was history written there. A monotonous history dominated by violence, but a history nonetheless.

He shuffled to an empty space, keeping his head down like a wary tortoise. 'Mind if I . . . ?'

'Yes.'

'Someone's seat?'

'Not yours.'

Tough crowd. Remaining standing, Damon hunched over his bowl and tried some of the stew. It was enough to put anyone in a bad mood. He abandoned it on the bench behind him.

'I'm Damon, by the way.'

'We know.'

'Any of you fellows play dice?'

'Not with you.'

'That's a shame. Hoping someone could teach me. I know the basics, but I always seem to lose.'

'Go away.'

'Before I do, anyone got change for one of these?' Damon held up one of the sovereigns he'd lifted from the High Priest's office. Tobrytan hadn't bothered to search him before throwing him on board.

One of the soldiers made to grab the coin. Damon palmed it and showed an empty hand. The soldier rammed a fist in his stomach. Damon crumpled to the deck, gasping for breath. Gold flashed as the coin rolled across the planks and spun to a halt. The soldier pocketed it.

'Let's call that the——'

A boot smacked into Damon's chest. He curled up, wrapping his arms over his head. More boots joined in. Pain thudded the length of his body. There was a crack, then excruciating agony. One of his ribs breaking. He hardly felt any of the subsequent kicks.

The beating stopped. It didn't lessen the pain, merely transformed it into a constant throbbing complete with stabbing sensation in his chest every time he breathed. Damon peered around the arms he still had clasped around his head. His attackers had resumed their seats and were continuing with dinner. No one paid any notice to the bruised, bloodied lump of flesh coiled up on the floor.

He tried to get up. A dozen new torments assaulted him. He fell back, coughing. There was blood mixed with the sputum. Not a good sign. Holding one arm across his broken rib, he managed to pull himself along the deck. A few men watched him, their eyes devoid of emotion. He bumped into a pair of stout legs. Damon stared up into the glowering face of the ship's captain: a short, stocky man chosen for command for his lack of height as much as anything else. Damon managed a strangulated 'hello'. The captain ignored him and looked to his crew.

'What happened here?'

'He talked, sir.'

The captain looked down on Damon in every sense of the term. 'The general was very clear. You are not to talk unless ordered to.'

'I'm True,' protested Damon. 'Do I not—?'

A kick to his supporting arm sent him back to the deck. He lay there, the smell of blood and tarred timbers filling his nostrils, waiting for the follow-up blow. It didn't come.

'Because you are True, we will not kill you unless you force us to. But remember, you are here to do the work of God and the Saviours. Nothing more, nothing less. You do what you're told and nothing that you aren't. Fail, and you will be punished. Succeed, and you might not be punished.'

Ah, the old stick-and-stick routine. 'I understand, sir.'

Another kick. This one forced tears from Damon's eyes. 'I didn't ask if you understood. I will never ask if you understand. If you don't understand, you will fail. And if you fail . . .'

Damon crawled back to his cabin and lay on his bed, hugging himself, trying to squeeze away the pain. He didn't know how long he stayed there before hunger and other biological imperatives drove him out – days, probably. When he did surface, no one paid him any heed. He tried to catch the eye of one or two fellows, but they either stomped past or clenched a fist; even the cook snarled at him and his wasn't the complexion that could afford to turn away a friend. The captain was serious, it would seem.

He bound his ribs up as best he could – no one volunteered to help him – and settled in to a life of isolated monotony. The fleet ploughed on across the Great Inland Sea and through the Bardanian Straits that separated Percadia from the Niko peninsula, and then on to Eastport, now under Sandstrider control, where they stopped for supplies. Damon stared out at the city – he wasn't allowed ashore – thinking about all that had happened there, trying to work out what, if anything, he could have done differently.

The fleet hugged the coastline of Ainsworth as it journeyed south down the Harris Sea. More memories flooded back, far more painful than the physical assault he had endured. He wasn't the only one with bad memories of this part of the world. As soon as the first peaks of the Endalayan Mountains were sighted the fleet swung out into the open sea, out of sight of land. The True were avoiding Trafford's Haven, where so many of their forebears had met their end.

It got warmer as they tracked around the Andaluvian peninsula. Damon's bruises faded, his rib started to knit together. At the Andaluvian capital, Kil M'sta, they rendezvoused with the vessels the Sandstriders had promised: less like warships, more like troop barges. The True plan was clear. Their guns would provide cover while the Sandstriders landed and took Hil. Took Cate.

They plodded up Werlavia's east coast. It started getting colder again. The weather got worse and worse, until one night a storm hit them. Damon clung to his bed as the ship lurched up and down while thunder and lightning shook the boiling seas, wondering if God's wrath was finally upon them. The calm the next morning revealed they had lost a couple of Sandstrider ships and a handful of men dragged overboard. Merely a divine tantrum, it would seem.

The fleet passed the line of the Kartiks and left the waters of the Realm for the Sarason Sea. The water was continually agitated now. Despite the cold, Damon spent the days above decks, scanning the horizon and the passing coast for threats, although he couldn't comprehend what threat there could be. Even if the Hilites knew they were coming, and sent the combined naval forces of the Snow Cities against them, what could they do against the witches' guns? More ships just increased the chances of the witches hitting something.

They entered a channel between the northern coastline of Werlavia and a rocky island whose name Damon had forgotten. The Trávians had indicated this was the safest route through to Hil; swing north around the island and you'd run into rocks lurking beneath the surface, waiting to shred your hull to splinters. Cliffs loomed a few hundred yards either side of them. The fleet formed into a column: True warships to the front and rear; Sandstrider troop carriers protected in the middle. Damon huddled into the hodgepodge of fur, leather and fabric he'd been able to scavenge, swaying with the deck as it rocked from side to side. Rigging creaked. The occasional gull squawked a lament. The wind dropped, as if the weather was holding its breath.

'I don't like this,' said the captain, half to himself.

'There is a distinct lack of bunting,' said Damon. The captain was too distracted to enforce his no-speaking rule.

Was that movement among the rocks? Damon wasn't the only one who noticed it. The hands muttered among themselves. The channel narrowed. Despite the expanse of water, claustrophobia squeezed Damon. He recalled the fire arrows the Faith had used when the True had first tried to take New Statham. Were they coming in range? The True had taken steps to lessen their vulnerability – made sure all gunpowder was safely stashed below decks, stationed barrels of sand and water so fires could be tackled before they spread – but if fire rained from the sky, who knew if they could prevent panic. Plus Damon would prefer not to get skewered by flaming metal.

Shouts floated across the waters. Damon's head snapped around as he tried to identify the source. It sounded like it was coming not just from the coast, but *everywhere* on the coast. The words were indecipherable, but their intention wasn't. They were orders.

A series of sparks raced along the cliffs. Damon whirled about. Twin lines of fire that hemmed in the fleet on both sides. His stomach twisted. Was that what he thought it was? *Please God, no.*

Events tumbled on top of each other. Flashes, screeches, explosions. Men running around in fear and confusion. Something smacked into the water, sending spray sky high. It rained back down on Damon, soaking him. He looked for somewhere to run to, found none, tripped over his feet, slipped on the saturated deck.

Whistling overhead. The end of a yard arm snapped clear of the rest of the mast. It spiralled to the ground. Damon buried his head in his arms as the structure thudded on the deck beside him, the impact making his whole body shudder.

Flares of light illuminated the smoke-wreathed clifftops. A pounding filled the air like the hammer of a pagan god. Damon scrabbled to the stern. The fleet that lay in their wake was being pulverized. Projectiles smacked into ships, sending wood flying like injured flesh. Some listed, taking in water; others were already going under. Fire raged on one of the witches' vessels. Despite their precautions, its powder store had been hit. Damon cringed as an explosion took its bow clean off.

The captain yelled an order. The ship rocked as a sequence of booms ripped through it, throwing Damon across the deck. They were firing back. No good. Their shots dropped short of the coastline both sides of the channel, sending up a huge wall of water but nothing more damaging. They were too low, too far way.

He staggered over to the captain, struggling to keep upright. 'You can't fight!' he shouted over the din. 'Run!'

The captain stared back, his eyes wild, uncomprehending. *You never expected them to fight back, did you? Not like this. You thought guns were a sign of God's favour, and now she has them.* Damon shook him. 'Get us out of here!'

The captain came back to his senses. He hurled Damon out of the way. 'Full speed ahead!' he yelled. 'Signal the fleet!'

Men scrambled to obey, hoisting flags and crawling over rigging. The ship deployed its full complement of sails – those that remained, anyway. They lurched forward, like a runner getting a second wind. The thunder of guns dropped off. The smoke cleared. Open water to starboard. They had cleared the channel, escaped the death trap.

Escaped *one* death trap. Damon went cold as he saw what was in front of them. A wall of Hilite ships sitting low in the water, their broadsides presented to them. Tiny figures rushed about their decks, tending to the monsters they had brought into creation. Damon shouted a warning, but it was too late. The monsters spat out their rancour.

A projectile hit them amidships, punching a hole in the deck and sending men flying. The captain lunged at Damon.

'You did this!'

'Me? What? No!'

The captain grabbed Damon's throat with both hands and squeezed hard. The world went grey, amorphous. Damon tried to prise the captain's hands away. Conscious thought failed him. He was acting on instinct, kicking and slapping against leather and armour. Ineffectual, pointless. Only seconds left. Only seconds left on this world. Only seconds before he had to face Eleanor.

The ship was hit again, flinging Damon and the captain to the deck. Damon scrambled clear of his would-be murderer, spluttering, trying to focus. The world lurched as he slipped in a puddle – blood as well as water. He pushed himself up, looked for a way out. There was only one.

He stumbled over to a bulwark, the sound of guns and the captain's yells ringing in his ears. Damon hardly heard them now. In the chaos he had found serenity, understanding. He had chosen wrong and now he had to face his punishment, throw himself on the mercy of God and the Saviours.

Damon took one final step and dropped off the ship.

nineteen

They tried to cremate the bodies of the witches and the Sandstriders that washed up, but they were too sodden to burn so they buried them in great pits dotted along the shoreline, occasionally hollering as one of the corpses started to writhe and cough up seawater. Megan joined in with the digging and the lugging even though Willas kept telling her she didn't have to. She'd been responsible for the massacre; it was only right she helped clean up the aftermath.

The witches had lost half their fleet, and of the ships limping home at least one-third were damaged. The Snow Cities had lost a couple of ships that had drifted within range of the witches' guns, and a couple more to the volatility of their own weaponry; their own guns had also accounted for a handful of men up on the cliff-top batteries. They had won what in strategic terms was a great victory, but Megan couldn't see it that way. It was too easy to picture the faces of those she had lost in those they covered with sand, to construct narratives of the dead men's lives. As cold winds and the spade handle turned her hands raw she tried to harden her heart, remember what these men had come for, but it was impossible to hate or fear the pale, bloated faces that stared at her, gazes forever fixed in terror.

A covered carriage rattled up to her, its wheels drawing elegant curves in the sand. Fordel opened the door and beckoned. Megan hesitated before hauling herself inside, grateful to escape the cold and the death.

Rekka was there, swathed in furs, her injured leg propped up on the seat opposite. Megan almost got back out again, but Fordel was already draping a blanket around her. He encased her hands in his. She wanted to pull away, but they were warm and comforting, like a father's.

There was a jerk as they set off. 'You're missing the party,' said Fordel.

'Not really in the mood.'

'Never mind,' said Rekka. 'It'll still be going on when we get back. We're going to have to invent a collective noun for hangovers.'

Megan ignored her. 'Any news on the witches?' she asked Fordel.

'They made Trávi, last thing I heard.'

'Any . . . repercussions?'

'They seem intent on getting away as fast as possible,' said Fordel. 'The ones camped at the Arrowstorm Pass are also retreating.'

'Where to?'

'All the way to New Statham, it would seem.' He wiped condensation from the window and looked out at the grey sea. 'We have to discuss what happens now.'

'Like . . . ?'

'Cate's betrothal, for one,' said Rekka. 'We need to seal the alliance between Hil and the Realm. Tighten the familial bonds. It's not as if you're going to have more children.'

'Betrothal?'

'It's never too early.'

'Too early?' said Megan. 'The highlights of her day are sleeping, sucking on breasts and peeing in her pants.'

'Those are Vegar's highlights too,' Rekka said brightly. She leaned forward and rubbed her knee. 'I was thinking of Tóki. I know he's got some disgusting habits, but he'll grow out of those. Unless he takes after his father, but what are the odds on that?'

'Evens.'

'Thank you, Fordel. Where would we be without your literalism?'

The sly looks on the faces of Rekka and Fordel tightened Megan's skin. They were trying to take Cate from her, with smiles and promises of friendship to be sure, but their aim was the same as the witches'. Cate was nothing more than a vessel to receive their overweening ambition. And what was worse, Megan had let them do it, had to let them keep on doing it, because without them the Realm was lost. It didn't stop her wishing she'd gone off with Afreyda, fled to the Diannon Empire, when they'd had the chance.

'Can we discuss this later?' she said. 'It's been a long day.'

'Of course,' said Fordel. 'You need to rest. Just the treaty to discuss before we can let you recuperate.'

Megan had learned the more casual Fordel sounded, the more serious he was. 'What treaty?'

'Just a bit of administrative tidying up.'

'What treaty?' repeated Megan, her voice hardening.

'The treaty that will bring Andaluvia and the Snow Cities back into the Realm,' said Fordel. 'Congratulations, Your Majesty. You'll be the first monarch in three hundred years to rule over a unified kingdom.'

The coach hit an outcropping, jolting Megan out of the stupor Fordel's words had induced. Andaluvia and the Snow Cities back in the Realm? The dream of every monarch and Supreme Priest since Aldwyn the First, and Fordel was treating it like paperwork?

'What the hell are you talking about?'

'We have to present a unified front if we're going to defeat the witches,' said Fordel. 'We'll have to lay siege to New Statham, and that isn't going to be pleasant. The witches will fight to the last man. We don't want anyone getting squeamish. We need a single leader to rally

238

behind.' He flashed a vulpine grin at Megan that made her shudder.

Oh, she thought, *they'll have a single leader all right, only it's not really going to be me, is it?* 'The other Snow Cities will never agree to this,' she said.

'You'll be surprised what monetary motivation can accomplish.'

'You're going to bribe them?'

'No,' said Fordel. 'You are. The Realm's far richer than Hil, and the witches can't have plundered all its treasures.'

'What about the Sandstriders? There's no way—'

'Their ambassador seems quite compliant.'

'What ambassador?' said Megan, feeling like a gambler whose elevens kept getting beaten by her opponent's perfect twelves.

'It was a kind of ad-hoc appointment,' said Fordel. 'Prince Y'donno, one of the Andaluvians we picked up after the fleet went . . . He's Prince Y'benne's son. Well, one of them anyway. I understand the randy old bastard does like to procreate.' Rekka blushed and looked away. 'He seems to think his father will cease hostilities and accept your suzerainty in exchange for . . .'

'. . . A fleet not being sent down to flatten Andaluvia?'

Fordel really was a clever bastard. He'd bought the other Snow Cities off with other people's money; the Sandstriders were in no position to refuse him, with most of their men washing up on the shores of the Sarason Sea or defending Gwyneth in New Statham; the Realm could present reunification as a victory for the Faith; and Megan needed him to defeat the witches and ensure Cate's safety. And all he wanted in return was a new dynasty, one that would control all of Werlavia, one he and Rekka would control. Megan and Cate would be nothing more than figureheads, and how long before Rekka's son or grandson replaced them on the throne?

It seemed the only thing worse than losing a war was winning one.

Night was well into maturity by the time they reached Hil, but that hadn't stopped the revellers. After checking on Cate, Megan went in search of Afreyda. She needed someone to talk to, someone to confide in, someone to make her forget, for a few hours at least.

She found her in a tavern colonized by soldiers of the Faith, drinking at a bottle-strewn table with her sergeants. Megan squeezed through the crowd, paused briefly to kick the legs out from under a man who made a drunken pass at her and squeezed in between the commanders of her forces.

'It's the queen!' cried one of the sergeants. 'Everyone stand!'

'Please,' said Megan. 'There's no need.' Someone tried anyway. He toppled backwards. A cheer went up.

It was that time of evening when any action was cause for celebration.

'You're a great queen,' continued the sergeant, swaying in his seat as if to an imaginary band, albeit one that lacked any sense of rhythm. 'In fact . . . in fact . . . I'd say you were the best queen . . . *ever*. Better than that last one. What was her name?'

Megan turned to Afreyda, who stared back through bloodshot eyes, a happy grin on her face. 'Good night?'

'We were playing this great game with Father Galan,' said Afreyda. She hiccupped. 'You have to have lots of beer and –' *hiccup* – 'not fall down.'

'You were playing drinking games with a *priest*?' said Megan. She looked around. 'Where is he anyway?'

Afreyda pointed downwards, a manoeuvre that took all her concentration. Megan leaned back and peered under the table. Father Galan was asleep on the floor, his jowls wobbling in time to his snoring.

'You literally . . . ?'

'Isn't she the best?' said the sergeant. 'We all love her.' *Of course you do; she's kept you well away from the action.* 'She's prettier than the last officer we had too. He was an ugly bastard. Had this hairy wart right –' he held a finger up in front of his face and tried to focus – 'here.' He jabbed himself.

'His eye?'

'That's why it went dark. No . . . here.' He poked

241

himself in the corner of his mouth, smearing his cheek with beery spittle.

'I am thinking of making him a lieutenant,' said Afreyda. 'Can I? Say yes. Please.'

'You don't think he's overqualified for the role?'

'He is not overqual . . . he is not overqual . . . he is not too good for anything.'

There was little chance of sensible discussion with Afreyda in this state. 'We need to get you home.'

Afreyda slammed the table and whooped. 'You will have to do without me, boys! I have pulled!' Raucous cheers filled the tavern.

'Not tonight you've not,' muttered Megan.

Afreyda frowned. 'It is a very strange expression, "pulled".'

'I'm sure you have a very precise phrase for it in Diannon,' said Megan, slipping an arm around Afreyda's waist and pulling them both along the bench.

'Of course. We would say . . . we would say . . .' Afreyda rested her head on Megan's shoulder. 'I have forgotten. Am I forgetting home? Who I am? Are they forgetting me? I have a brother, little . . . brother sons and brother daughters. Have I told you that? He stayed with the Emperor when we . . . when we . . . you know.' She looked up at Megan. 'He is a bastard. Why am I talking about him? I have you.'

Willas appeared in the crowd, his head jerking about

as if looking for someone. He spotted Megan and waved. She beckoned him over.

'Give me a hand with this one, will you?' said Megan, draping one of Afreyda's arms over his shoulder.

'What's she had to drink?' said Willas.

'Pretty much everything.'

'Where have you been, captain?' asked Afreyda. She beamed. 'Hey, "captain", that is my name! Are we related?'

Willas patted her shoulder then leaned around her to address Megan. 'I've been interrogating the prisoners,' he said. 'One of them asked after you.'

'I'm not interested in being berated for blasphemy.'

'He asked for you by name.'

Megan's skin tingled. 'What name? The queen? The Mother? The Apostate?'

'Megan.'

twenty

The prison was underground, a low-ceilinged warren with water seeping in through the pores in the rock. It was a dank cold, the kind you could never escape, no matter how many layers you wrapped yourself in. Megan had had some wine to warm herself up, but all it had done was screw her stomach into knots and engender a mugginess she couldn't quite shake off.

A single lantern her side of the rusting bars cast long shadows that danced constantly against the walls, as if searching for an escape route. On the other side, sprawled on the floor, was the prisoner; the chain joining the manacles clamped around his wrists looped through an iron ring hammered into the floor. He was barefooted, dirty, his clothes reduced to rags – but oh so recognizable.

'Where did you find him?' Megan asked Willas.

'On the beach.'

Megan grunted. 'It happens.'

'He was clinging on to a plank,' said Willas. 'Had a hard time prising it out of his hand.'

'I guess it saved his life.' Megan nodded at the captain. 'All right. Open it up.'

'You sure?'

'He's not dangerous.'

Willas selected a key from the ring he'd commandeered from the jailer. Neither the clunk of the lock snapping back nor the creak of the gate swinging open disturbed the prisoner. He remained slumped, his back to them. Really unconscious or faking it?

Megan stepped inside, picking her way carefully across the slippery stones and the drain – nothing more than a track gouged into the stone – that snaked out of the cell. Still the prisoner didn't react. Had the Hilites been a little too enthusiastic in their interrogation? The wine and the beer had been flowing freely, and restraint could be so terribly restraining.

Willas picked up on what she was thinking. 'He was alive the last time I saw him,' he said. 'I can kick him up if you like.'

'There's military thinking for you,' said the prisoner, at last breaking his silence.

Megan took a steadying breath. 'Never could resist an opportunity for sarcasm, could you?'

'That wasn't sarcasm, that was criticism.'

Damon sat up. Droplets ran down his face, tracing the

imprints the stone had left in his cheek. 'Are these really necessary?' he said, holding up his chained hands.

'They are if you want to wipe your own arse,' said Willas.

'I meant the manacles.'

'I don't know,' said Megan. 'Which I guess means they are necessary.'

'You were fighting for the witches,' said Willas.

'Me? Fighting?'

'Helping them then,' said Megan.

'Me? Helping?'

'Why are you being so evasive?' said Willas.

'Why are you asking so many stupid questions?' said Damon.

Megan sighed. They weren't going to get anywhere with Willas around. Some men showed off with muscles; Damon did it with his mouth. She asked the captain to leave. He did so reluctantly and only after pressing a knife into her hand. It was endearing he thought her innocent enough not to already have five blades strapped to various parts of her body.

Damon shifted position on the stone floor, trying to get comfortable. 'How's Afreyda?' he asked.

'She's fine.'

'I heard she found her way to you.'

'Isn't there someone else you should be asking about?' said Megan, her voice stiff.

'You look great,' said Damon. 'Queen, eh?'

'Not me.'

A haunted look passed over Damon's eyes. 'I . . . I . . .'

'Yes, Damon, what exactly did you do?'

'I . . . They gave me no choice.'

'You're not giving me the impression of someone who was brutally tortured to near death.'

'I'm a quick healer.'

Megan swallowed. 'You *were* tortured?' Awful as it was to think it, it would make things much easier to accept if he had been.

'Well, they were very mean.'

'Did they?'

Damon squirmed. 'Not exactly. But I don't think they'd have to clear it with the ethics committee if it came to it.'

'You know what happened, don't you?' said Megan. 'When you told the witches where Cate was. You know what Eleanor –' Damon looked away at the sound of her name – 'had to do to stop them.'

'Yes.'

'And?'

'And what?' said Damon. 'Oh, I'm sorry, I see from that look on your face you expect me to feel guilty about something.'

'You betrayed us.'

'And you sent her to her death.'

Megan dropped her head, fiddled with the knife Willas had given her while the guilt fed on Damon's words. 'It was her idea,' she said.

'And you couldn't talk her out of it?'

'You don't think I tried?' said Megan, anguish breaking her voice. 'We had no other choice. The witches were coming for Cate.'

'And?'

'And what?'

'And what would it matter?' asked Damon.

'They . . .'

'Yes, Megan, they what exactly? You think Cate was in any danger? As compared to being dragged across the mountains to this place with these people?'

'You know what the witches want with her.'

'And how's that going to change anything?' said Damon. 'I don't notice the witches holding back, do you? What do you think this is, the pre-war?' He gave his chain an angry wrench. 'You and Gwyneth are like toddlers arguing over a doll.'

'That's my daughter you're talking about.'

'And is she any more valuable than all the other people who have died for her? I mean, from their perspective, not yours.'

'You think I don't ask myself that every day?' said Megan.

'You might ask,' said Damon, 'but do you answer? You don't have to watch – do you? – because you're always miles away at that point. You don't have to look in their eyes and see the life slipping away. You don't have to feel their despair, their hate. You don't have to witness themselves throwing themselves off . . . off . . .'

Awareness enveloped Megan like dread. That look on Damon's face. He wasn't hypothesizing, he was talking from experience. 'You were there, weren't you? When Eleanor . . . ?'

Damon's eyes widened to that of a prey animal who had spotted a predator. He edged away, as far as the chain would allow him. 'I . . .'

'Weren't you?'

'Yes.'

'Then why the hell are you still alive?'

Megan snapped. She hurled the knife Willas had given her at him. It missed – just – and bounced across the stones, the clamour making them both wince.

Damon held up his hands in surrender. 'There was nothing I could have done.'

'There's always something you can do!' screamed Megan.

'It was hopeless.'

'It's never hopeless. Not if it's someone you love. Not while you're still capable of making a fist or kicking out or just holding on to them and telling them they're not alone, that whatever they're going through you'll share it.'

'You'd prefer us both to be dead?' asked Damon.

'At least then I'd know you cared.'

'I apologize for my continued existence.'

This was getting them nowhere, this sequence of accusation and counter-accusation. They were both responsible for what had happened to Eleanor; they were down to arguing who had the least amount of choice in the matter. And it wasn't only a matter of what choices they had made on the day of the countess's death either. Megan had dragged Damon and Eleanor down to Eastport, but they had let themselves be dragged. Eleanor had convinced Megan they couldn't go back for Damon, but she had let herself be convinced. The witches had caught Damon, but he had let himself be caught.

'What happened in Kewley?' asked Megan.

'What've you heard?'

'This is not about getting your story straight, it's about the truth.'

'Saviours,' said Damon, 'has it come to that?'

'You do realize I can stab you with impunity, don't you?'

'Because you were so concerned about the legal ramifications before.'

Megan turned her back on him and took a step towards the gate. 'Fine. Explain it to Willas.'

'Wait.' Damon made a play of pushing his manacles up his arms and rubbing his raw wrists. 'There was this guy. He owed me money.'

'Money?'

'Man cannot survive on homicidal rage alone.'

'Why did he owe you money?'

Damon gave her a sly grin. 'Do you really want to know?'

'I guess not,' said Megan. 'What happened with Aldred? What was he doing there?'

'He barged in with the local branch of the workers' collective and set about applying the principles of the distribution of wealth.'

'Huh?'

'He was on the rob.'

'Go on.'

'Things degenerated,' said Damon. 'It got all squelchy, and not in a good way. You would have enjoyed it.'

'Why did Aldred lock you up?'

'Getting rid of witnesses.'

'Why not kill you?'

'You could ask that of almost anyone,' said Damon. 'What did he tell you?'

'Not much,' said Megan.

Damon beamed, like a schoolboy who'd got his sums right. The smugness ignited the rage within Megan, making her muscles twitch and her fists clench. Everything was reduced to some smart-arse game with him, even the loss of someone who meant so much. She wanted to slap him and punch him and kick him, make him feel some of the pain she did, offload some of it. She restrained herself. Barely.

A wailing filled the air, dozens of voices combining into a harmony that prickled Megan's skin. 'What's that?'

'The Sandstriders,' said Damon. 'Pledging themselves to the arrival of the sun goddess.'

Sun goddess? Was it dawn already? How long had she been down here? 'Do they do that every morning?'

Damon nodded. 'And every evening, when they throw over the sun goddess and commit themselves to the moon god. Flexible people, the Andaluvians.'

Megan let out a long 'hmm'. The Sandstriders certainly had had no trouble switching their allegiance from neutrality to the witches then to the Realm and the Snow Cities.

'What happens now?' asked Damon.

'That's for the Hilites to decide.'

'I was thinking more of when I was getting fed.'

'I'll have chef prepare you something special,' said Megan. 'Maybe a little wine on the side.'

'You have wine this far north?'

'It's import— I was being sarcastic.'

'I suspected,' said Damon. 'Thought I'd roll with it anyway.'

'You'll get fed when the other prisoners are fed.'

'I'm still a prisoner?'

Megan rested her arm against the wall and watched the condensation darken her sleeve. 'We picked you up from an invading fleet,' she said. 'What else are you going to be?'

'It's not like I was there voluntarily,' said Damon, spreading his palms. 'They conscripted me. For the second time. I was just a translator.'

'They trusted you to translate?'

'They're a very trusting people,' said Damon. 'It's one of their few redeeming qualities.' He shrugged. 'I wasn't really needed. You know what foreigners are like. They all speak Stathian really.'

'So you weren't really working for the witches?' said Megan, trying to keep the hope from her voice.

'The bastards certainly never paid me.' His smile vanished at sight of Megan's look of exasperation. 'You do what you have to do to survive.'

'There are limits.'

'But they're always just that one step beyond the worst you ever have to resort to.'

Megan snorted. 'You can excuse anything if you put your mind to it. Is that what you're saying?'

'I guess.'

'What exactly are you looking to excuse, Damon? Tell me. Because to hear you speak, you're as innocent as a newborn kitten.'

'Are we going to do this again? Don't think I don't regret the things I was made to do. I did love Eleanor, and I'm sorry if my love doesn't live up to your suicidal standards. If all you're going to do is stand there and be morally superior at me, I'd prefer you to piss off and leave me to rot in peace.' He looked around. 'State of this place, I don't think it's going to be hard. Do the Hilites know they have a damp problem?'

Megan needed someone to talk to, but the person she needed most wasn't there, would never be there. It was at times like this she felt the truth of her adoption, that she was a little girl crying out for a mother. Only Eleanor could have understood. Her real parents, her grandfather, even Afreyda, they could offer her love but not guidance, not in a situation like this. Life hadn't prepared them for this, hadn't prepared *her* for this. She wanted to believe Damon. She wanted her friend back, her connection to Eleanor, but how could she trust him? He was telling her what she wanted to hear, or what she expected to hear; how could she know he wouldn't sell her out to the witches if it ever became the easiest option?

She found Cate and Synne beside the fire in the mansion kitchen, the former suckling contentedly at the latter's breast. At least there was one parent–child relationship not troubled by treachery and politics and the fate of the world. Megan pulled up a chair and warmed herself against the flames until the heat sent prickles rippling across her body.

Synne stroked Cate's head. 'She'll be weaning soon. You'll be able to feed her yourself. You won't need me any more.'

'We'll always need you,' said Megan. Concern flashed across Synne's face, a hint of 'but you said . . .' Megan leaned across and patted her knee. 'You should do what's best for you, but you'll always have a place with us if you want it, if you need it.'

Synne managed an embarrassed smile and looked down to Cate. 'Everyone's talking about going back home now the war's won,' she said, wiping away a dribble of milk with her thumb.

'The witches haven't been defeated yet.'

'I thought—'

'One battle, that's all we've won,' said Megan. 'There's many more to come, and we won't be so lucky next time. The witches'll know what to expect. They'll be waiting for us. They'll throw everything they have at us, they'll fight to the last bastard. Many of the people out there celebrating . . .' She shook her head. 'And even if we do win, who knows who our next foes will be.'

'Next foes?'

'Whoever controls the guns.'

Synne frowned. 'I thought we did.'

'Fordel does.'

255

'Isn't he our friend?'

'He's our ally,' said Megan.

'What's the difference?'

'Friends are with you because they like you; allies because they dislike someone else. And while they have the guns . . .'

twenty-one

Boots thundered, doors crashed, voices cried in alarm. Before Megan was aware of what was happening, she found herself hauled out of bed and marched through the mansion by a squad of soldiers.

'What's going on?' she said. A soldier barked back something in Hilite; it didn't sound good whatever it was.

Megan whirled round. Synne was behind her, hair in disarray. Megan rushed to her, throwing off the arm of the soldier who tried to restrain her.

'Where's Cate? Afreyda?'

Synne stared back, dazed. 'She's—'

Megan spotted her daughter cradled in the arms of one of the soldiers. She flew over.

'Give her to me!' she demanded, her voice cracking. The soldier twisted, putting Cate out of reach of Megan's outstretched hands. She battered his padded arm. 'Please!'

An order cracked down the corridor. Willas, with another contingent of soldiers, all with weapons drawn.

The soldier put Cate into Megan's eager arms. Her daughter immediately started crying. Megan rocked and shushed her. For once, Cate was content with the comfort.

'What's going on, captain?'

'Some of the witches have escaped,' said Willas. 'They'll be coming for you –' his gaze flicked to Cate – 'for her. We need to get you somewhere safe.'

'Where's Afreyda?'

'Organizing the search. This way.'

Willas led them down into the cellars. Rekka was already there, huddled in furs among the crates and the barrels, her children gathered around her. She called Willas over and squeezed his arm.

'You will stay with us, won't you?'

'Those were the Lord Defender's orders, my lady.'

'Wouldn't want to disobey orders,' said Rekka, her mouth wrinkling.

Willas dropped his voice. 'You know I'd be here whatever.'

Candles puttered and flickered in the draughts. The chill of the underground chamber made Megan shiver and goose pimples prickle her skin. She was wearing nothing more than a loose shift and she was completely unarmed. Megan didn't know which one made her feel more vulnerable.

Willas saw her discomfort and came over with a

blanket, which he draped over her shoulders. 'We'll have them rounded up before you know it.'

'I should be out there.'

'Best you stay here with this little one.'

He ran the finger of a gloved hand across Cate's cheek. She gurgled. There was something about the expression that reminded Megan so much of Gwyneth. If she thought about it rationally, it was just herself she was seeing, but she couldn't and it filled her with melancholy, a sadness for times long gone and never to be repeated.

Floorboards rattled above their heads. Cate started to grumble. Megan pulled her closer. Instinct caused her to sing, an old melody her grandfather had used to help her sleep. Cate stared up at her, fascinated.

A little girl was off to the fair
With rings on her fingers and golden hair
She met a boy upon the way
Hanging around, nothing to say
A man crept out from beyond the trees
Crooked his finger, said, 'Come with me, please' . . .

'You're really singing *that* to her?' said Rekka. 'A lullaby about execution and child abduction?'

'It's not about—' Megan thought about what she'd been singing. 'It's not the words that matter, it's hearing her mother's voice. It's bonding.'

'"Bonding". Of course.' Rekka screeched something at Tóki, who had been getting a little too interested in one of the tapped beer barrels. 'And a subconscious dread of nooses and forests.'

There was more scuffling above their heads. Everyone turned their faces up, trying to see through solid oak, then jumped as a loud thud echoed around the cellar.

'That was a body hitting the floor,' said Megan, wishing life hadn't taught her to make such an identification.

'You should make up a song about it,' said Rekka.

Slow, deliberate footsteps now. Megan tracked their route. Heading for the door. 'How many witches escaped?' she whispered to Willas.

'Not sure,' said Willas.

'Rough figure.'

'A few.'

'You didn't have to take *rough* so literally.'

Rekka summoned her children to her, then de-summoned Tóki after he wiped his snotty nose on her gown. Megan did a head count: six soldiers plus Willas and her unarmed self. The cramped close quarters would negate any numerical advantage. She had no idea what the witches were armed with but, if they'd got this far, it'd be enough.

A distant slam made them all start. It had come from the opposite direction to where they had been looking.

Megan remembered the night of Brother Broose's coup attempt, when she had broken into the mansion.

'Did anyone remember to lock that hidden trapdoor?' she asked.

'Forgot it was there,' said Willas. Megan flashed him a look. 'What? It *is* hidden.'

The slap of descending footsteps echoed around the cellar. 'They're flanking us,' she said. *Blocking off our escape route.*

'It's what I'd do,' said Willas, drawing his sword.

Tóki ran back to his mother. This time Rekka didn't shoo him away. Cate gurgled merrily and played with Megan's fingers. *I appreciate your lack of fear*, Megan thought. *I'm just not entirely sure it's appropriate.*

'Give me a knife,' she whispered to Willas.

He looked to Rekka, who shook her head. 'I don't think that's wise,' he whispered back. 'We don't need you getting into a fight.'

'I'm not looking to fight.'

Willas twisted round, glanced down at Cate. 'You wouldn't . . .'

Use her own child as a hostage? 'It might be our only chance of getting out of here.'

'And if they call your bluff?'

And if they did? How far would Megan go to stop the witches getting hold of Cate? She had a brief, horrible vision of plunging a knife into her daughter and felt as if she had stuck the blade into her own heart. 'I'm sorry, I'm sorry,' she whispered to Cate, holding her as close as possible.

Scuffling in the blackness: someone trying to soften their approach. The soldiers drew into a tight circle around mothers and children. Megan stroked Cate's hair, more to calm herself than her daughter. The witches wouldn't make it through the human shield. But if they did . . .

Candlelight flashed off something. A drawn blade. As one, the soldiers rushed forward. There was an indignant shriek. The soldiers froze, weapons in mid-air. They parted.

Afreyda stepped into the light, clutching her shin. 'Who left that barrel there?'

The terror that had been gripping Megan burst into relief. Nervous energy propelled her through the crowd.

'Are you all right?' she said, throwing her free arm around Afreyda. 'Why are you sneaking about?'

Afreyda returned the hug and kissed Cate. 'Fordel was worried some witches might have found this way in.' She looked to Willas. 'You should have bolted that trapdoor.'

'Don't you start. What's going on up there?'

'We have killed some of the witches, recaptured others. We are making sure there are no more hiding.'

'Is it safe?'

Afreyda shrugged. 'As safe as any place gets.' She licked her lips. 'Megan, Damon was one of those . . .'

'You killed?'

'Whom we captured. Fordel wants to execute him and the others right away.'

The prisoners had been assembled in the great hall. They were less men, more a collection of injuries. Damon stood at one end of the chained line, holding his side, following Megan's progress with the eye that hadn't swollen and coloured an ugly shade of puce. Blood had trickled and dried down both sides of his mouth, making it look like a child's attempt to draw a goatee.

Despite the lateness of the night or the earliness of the morning – Megan had lost track – the hall was packed with onlookers, both Hilites and Faithful. Many of them were drinking; none of them looked sympathetic. Father Galan was lurking in the shadows. Fordel was at the high table, engrossed in paperwork. Vegar was by his side, all beard and bad temper.

'I can explain,' said Damon as soon as Megan made the mistake of catching his eye.

'Really?'

'Given enough time.'

'I'm not in the mood, Damon. Why did you come after us?'

'What? Why would I—?'

'How did you escape?' snapped Fordel.

'One of the guards dropped a fork, and you have really rubbish locks. I know a great locksmith in New Statham, if you're interested.' He thought for a moment. 'Probably a bit dead by now.'

'You let everybody else out?' said Megan.

'Didn't really have a choice.'

'You were in a cell on your own.'

'We had to move him,' said Fordel. 'Space issues.'

A tankard flew out of the crowd. Damon ducked under the vessel but its contents splashed all over his neck and shoulder. 'Hey!' he called out in the direction of its source. 'If you're going to throw beer at me, at least aim for my mouth.'

There was a titter. Emboldened, Damon spread his hands as far as his manacles would let him and addressed the crowd. 'We weren't going to hurt anyone. We were just looking for warm clothes and supplies and a way out of here.'

'And then what?' said Megan. 'Make your way back to *her*?'

'Are you kidding?' Damon caught the glares the rest of the witches were giving him. 'Not that she's not . . . you know . . . In her own way.'

Fordel cleared his throat. 'Can we get this over with, please? It's been a long night.' He beckoned to Megan. 'If you could come and sign this, Your Majesty?'

'What is it?'

'A death warrant.'

Megan felt nauseous. 'I thought you didn't execute people.'

'These are difficult times. The Lord Defender isn't prepared to put his people at risk,' said Fordel. 'It might not be *your* child they come for next time.'

'You know that's—'

The crowd cut Megan short. There were cries of 'Kill the bastards!' and shouts in Hilite that probably amounted to the same thing. More missiles flew towards the prisoners.

An egg whizzing inches from her face forced Megan to back away. She could understand the fear, the fury. Given the number of witches they'd recaptured, it was likely one of them was directly responsible for the death of the loved ones of some of the people here, hell, even Megan's own loved ones – and she wasn't just thinking of whatever happened between Damon and Eleanor. But she couldn't condemn someone on the basis of probabilities, not like this, even after everything that had happened.

Fordel called for calm a little later than he could have. Megan rested her hands on the table opposite him.

'We should at least sleep on this,' she said. 'Consider it when everyone's nerves aren't so frazzled, when we're thinking straight.'

'We'd sleep better if we knew we weren't going to be murdered in our beds,' said Fordel.

Another round of protest from the crowd. Megan waited until the noise had died down to a murmur. 'They're chained and under heavy guard. What threat could they be, unless you get careless with the cutlery again?'

But accidentally careless or deliberately so? Had Fordel had a man who could pick a lock placed with the other witches and planted the instrument of his escape? Was he trying to scare her, panic her into compromising herself? But why? Fordel was more than capable of finding a route around any legal niceties. He wanted to prove his hold over her – and, by extension, the Realm – to have something to fling back in her face when the time came for him to do something unsavoury.

'We have to end this now,' said Fordel.

'No, we don't. I'll have Afreyda guard them if your own men are too scared.'

'It's not a question of being scared . . .'

'I thought that's why you wanted them executed?'

Fordel smiled sourly. Damon shuffled forward. 'May I suggest a compromise?'

'I don't think—'

'You don't kill us, we won't kill you,' said Damon. 'Not that we were going to,' he hurriedly added for Megan's benefit.

Megan shook her head. *The harmless idiot act's not going to work here*, she thought. *It's not about you, it's about me.*

'We'll give you our word,' continued Damon. 'One thing about the True: they always keep a vow.' He looked down the line of his fellow prisoners. 'What d'you say, boys?'

Damon's neighbour, a greying veteran who was cradling a broken arm, raised his head. 'We vowed to protect the Saviours and return Werlavia to their teachings. Those who are not True will face damnation in this world and the next.' He spat, then fixed his gaze on Megan. 'And you will suffer most for your crimes against us, Apostate. The Saviours will be anointed with the blood from your still-beating heart.'

Agitation exploded in the crowd. A man burst forward, his face contorted with rage. He smashed a mace into the back of the veteran's head. The witch toppled over, blood and brains oozing from the cracks in his skull. Fordel frowned, then scratched a name from his death warrant.

Megan looked over to Father Galan. The extent of his counsel was a shrug. She turned to face Fordel. He'd pushed the warrant towards her while she wasn't looking. An ink-stained quill rested above a blank line.

'At least have a proper trial, determine what they've actually done.'

Fordel regarded her, his face neutral. *Come on*, thought Megan, *you've had your little power play. Let's forget this and concentrate on the witches who are still a threat.*

Fordel slid the death warrant back towards himself. He gave Megan just enough time to offer up a prayer of thanks to God and the Saviours, before pushing it over to Vegar. The Lord Defender signed it without hesitation.

twenty-two

Megan got a few hours of fitful sleep before Rekka's braying dragged her somewhere towards the vicinity of consciousness. Her head felt muggy, her limbs as if lead weights had been sewn into them. She remembered the events of the night before, Damon's impending execution. She slumped back on to the bed.

Rekka clapped. She looked cheerful, which was never a good sign. 'What is it?' Megan said wearily.

'We need to discuss the details of your coronation.' Rekka bustled around the room – her leg seemed remarkably improved – and made a shooing motion at Afreyda, who was on the floor trying to interest Cate in some wooden blocks. 'We need the room.'

'I stay.'

'Oh, very well. If you could push into the corner then.'

Afreyda pulled Cate back a whole six inches. 'You could give us a bigger room.'

Rekka gave Afreyda the kind of smile that admitted

the possibility but denied the likelihood. She called out. A woman entered, a tape measure twisted around her hands like a garrotte.

'We've sent out invitations to all the important people. Your sister's probably a no-show but I guess we couldn't ignore her – family and all that. Fordel's sorting out all the vows and treaties and all the boring stuff. Which means we get to select your gown.'

As Megan struggled into a sitting position and poured herself some water, Rekka cast a disparaging eye over her. 'How do you feel about cutting back on the eating for the next couple of months?' Megan had spent too much time on the run and starving to treat that suggestion with anything other than the contempt it deserved. 'No? Never mind, Gulla can work miracles with pleats.'

Megan stood there, arms outstretched while the seamstress – Gulla, she assumed – flitted around her. 'Is this going to take long?'

'Prince Y'benne will no doubt propose to you –'

'Wait, what?'

'– but don't worry, the Andaluvians are like that. I've lost track of how many times he asked me to marry him.' Rekka fluffed Megan's hair. 'No, I think we can make you a much better match.'

Megan glanced at Afreyda. 'I'm kind of attached.'

'You can keep your concubine.'

'She is not my "concubine".'

'Actually,' said Afreyda, 'I think I am.'

'I was thinking of Nidár,' said Rekka. 'He's Vegar's younger brother. Smells of fish, but does spend most of his time out at sea.'

'I'm not interested in getting married. Afreyda is all I want. Besides, we wouldn't want to screw with the succession, would we?'

'Oh, Fordel's drafting a bill to smooth that out.'

'Fordel's making laws for the Realm now?'

'You don't have to pay him,' said Rekka with a dismissive wave. 'It's his hobby.'

Gulla moved to Megan's legs, her tape measure stretching to parts Megan wished she'd keep away from. She checked the measurements and shook her head at Rekka.

'We'll put her in heels,' Rekka said.

Megan swallowed a retort and changed the subject. 'How're the children?'

'The children?'

'After last night?'

'Oh, they're fine.' Rekka drifted off for a moment. 'You know what kids are like. Forgotten about it already. Apart from Tóki, but he's always been a bit of a weird boy. Perhaps a sailing trip to Hálfor would take his mind off it.'

'Where was Fordel while everything was going on?' asked Megan. 'I would have thought he'd be down the cellar with us. Never struck me as a combat type.'

'He was . . .' Rekka frowned. 'He was at Ími's.'

'Safe then? That's good.' Megan lifted a leg to allow Gulla to measure her feet.

'What are you getting at?'

Megan realized she'd been enjoying Rekka's discomfort a little too much. 'Nothing,' she mumbled. 'Nothing at all.'

Megan wished she could be like Fordel, wished she could solve her problems with a few words and someone else's signature, but she couldn't. She had to face up to what she'd done, what she'd allowed to happen. She had to see Damon again, look him in the eye. Maybe with the end so close, he would tell her the truth of what happened in Kewley and up in the Kartiks, if there was any more truth to tell.

The prison was crawling with soldiers, far more than were needed to guard a handful of battered witches; genuine paranoia, or an exaggeration of their threat to justify the death warrants? Willas was at a small desk, scratching away at a parchment, his penmanship laboured like a schoolboy trying to keep to the lines.

'Can I see him?' asked Megan.

'Fordel gave orders,' said Willas. 'No visitors.'

'*Fordel* gave orders?'

They exchanged knowing glances. 'Yeah, well . . .'

Willas whistled at one of his men, who lobbed over a key ring and beckoned Megan towards a trapdoor. He slid back heavy bolts and lifted it, releasing a belch of dank air. Megan peered down into the exposed void. It was pitch black.

'I don't see anything,' she said.

Willas grabbed a lantern. Its wan light splashed on to a winding stone staircase that descended into the blackness. 'We've got a bit of a walk, I'm afraid,' he said. 'Fordel wanted the witches somewhere a bit more secure. Haven't used these cells since, well, before my time.'

Megan followed him down, carefully selecting her steps, wary of touching the scarred walls, which were infested with algae and blooms of slimy fungi.

'Do you think Fordel set the witches up?' she said.

'What?'

'He does have form.'

A few feet below her, Megan caught a shifty look on Willas's face. 'We'd heard Broose was up to something back then,' he said, 'but last night? He wouldn't put the children at risk.'

'Perhaps he thought it a risk worth taking.'

'He'd better bloody not have,' muttered Willas darkly.

Megan remembered the family connection – Willas would be the children's uncle – and if Rekka had been feigning her fear in the cellar she was an awfully good actress. If Fordel had engineered the events, he'd kept it a secret from his usual partners. But what better way to convince Megan?

They reached the bottom of the staircase. How far had they descended? Two, three storeys at least. There was a single door, studded oak, locked and bolted. Willas handed Megan the lantern then set about opening it, the metallic clunks echoing around the staircase.

More blackness in the space beyond. The glow of Megan's lantern fell on two rows of cells, each containing a witch, kneeling in prayer. The men went silent, shrinking back at the unaccustomed light, then as they acclimatized they rose to their feet and advanced to the front of their cells. Grimy hands gripped iron bars. Eyes filled with cold hatred fixed on Megan. And then one of the witches hissed a mantra, words that were taken up by the other witches and repeated again and again.

'*I pledge obedience to God and His Saviours.*'

The chanting chilled Megan even more than the freezing air, but she wasn't going to let them know it. Fixing her gaze straight ahead, she stepped across the threshold into the cell block.

'*I pledge obedience to God and His Saviours.*'

The atmosphere was rank with the stench of human waste; Megan wanted to gag. She suppressed her reflexes, her urge to run away, and kept walking, trying to match Willas's purposeful stride.

'*I pledge obedience to God and His Saviours.*'

Where was Damon? Looking for him, Megan drifted too close to a cell. An arm shot out between the bars and made a grab for her. She yelped and jerked back, straight into the hands of the prisoner opposite. Nails dug into the flesh of her neck. She twisted out of the grip, at the same time whipping out a knife and slashing blindly. The blade caught flesh, slicing across the witch's forearm. He made no attempt to staunch the wound. He just stood there, arm stuck out, fist clenched, blood dripping in a continuous stream.

'*I pledge obedience to God and His Saviours.*'

Willas gave Megan a questioning look. She nodded and urged him on.

They reached the end of the aisle and yet another door, which Willas started unlocking. 'You're keeping him isolated?' said Megan.

'Wouldn't want them –' Willas jerked a thumb back at the witches – 'killing him before we do.' He craned his neck around. 'And will you shut the hell up!'

'*I pledge obedience to God and His Saviours.*'

Willas's hand dropped to his sword. Megan shook her head and placed a hand on his arm. He nodded in understanding and barged the door open.

Damon was in the room beyond, wrapped in so many chains it practically qualified as armour. Condensation collected on the ceiling above him and dripped on to his head. The drops that ran down his face gave the illusion of tears.

'Wish I hadn't complained about my last room now.'

Willas slammed the door shut, but the witches' incessant recitation still penetrated the wood, like the roar of the ocean. Megan hung the lantern on a hook and approached Damon.

'I'm sorry,' she said. 'There's nothing I could do.'

Damon made no attempt to accept or reject the apology. 'You know, I always thought I'd end up in a place like this. Some people know they're going to die in their beds, some on the battlefield, some condemned for a crime they didn't commit.'

'You didn't?'

'You really think I'd come after Cate?'

'It'd be one hell of a way to worm your way back into Gwyneth's favour.'

'You don't want to go on the run with a baby in tow,' said Damon. 'Why do you think Eleanor was so desperate to get rid of her?'

Megan flushed at the sound of Eleanor's name. 'Don't . . .'

'Sorry. Just pointing out it's not very practical to lug a baby from here to New Statham.'

'What about your friends?' said Megan. 'The witches are not noted for their practicality where the Saviour is concerned.'

'You'd be surprised.'

'What do you mean?'

Damon shifted a few inches to the right, trying to

avoid the drip, but another found him. 'There's a few – how shall I put this? – dissenters. Not all the True believe in Joanne's prophecy. You and Sener should have a chat sometime. You can both bitch about Gwyneth. I'd be willing to introduce you if . . .' He rattled his chains.

'Not possible,' said Willas. 'It's tonight. Midnight. When they . . .'

Damon nodded, trying to be casual, but Megan recognized the terror in his eyes. 'How?' he asked.

'Fordel's quite squeamish,' said Willas. 'He doesn't want a public execution. You're going to be thrown down *Kolida*.'

'*Kolida*?' said Damon. He cocked his head as he mentally translated. 'The Pit of Certain . . . ? Ah . . . That should do it.'

'I'm sorry,' said Megan. 'I really am.'

'I know, I know,' said Damon. 'There's only so much a good vassal can do.'

'I am not a vassal,' snapped Megan.

Oh, but she was, she really was. She was nothing more than Fordel's puppet, given an illusion of choice but always with the knowledge the Hilites had the guns to enforce their wishes. Everyone else knew it too – Fordel had gone out of his way to demonstrate it. Did Eleanor know what she was doing when she set these events in motion; had it been a price she'd been willing to pay?

twenty-three

Auroras washed across the night sky – blues and greens purer than any Megan had ever seen – and cast an eerie glow on the city. The Hilites believed they were the souls of the dead departing for the heavens. God knew there were plenty of those these days, and soon there'd be more joining them.

Megan had been unable to sleep so, with Afreyda out on patrol and Cate and Synne both dead to the world, she had slipped out of the mansion. She'd settled in the shadows of a side street, across from the prison, waiting for one last glimpse of the prisoners as they made their final walk, up to the tunnels and the chasm that awaited. The rest of the city was dark and silent, only the glow from the odd window betraying signs of life. Like Fordel, everyone preferred to feign ignorance of what was to happen.

Megan thought about hurtling through the void – everything being over in an instant. How long would it take? Seconds? Minutes? You wouldn't even be able to see the bottom rushing towards you. Would you be frightened or accepting, resisting even as you plummeted through the darkness? Or still in acceptance?

There was activity over at the prison. Soldiers filed out, silent apart from the beat of their footsteps, and then the witches, shuffling along, iron chains clamping them all together. They'd fought together, killed together, and now they were going to die together.

Megan bowed her head and began muttering. 'God, born of the eternal universe, ultimate arbiter of man, take these souls we deliver unto You. Show them Your mercy and love and the wonders of Your creation. Rejoice, for though life ends in death, out of . . .'

A second voice took up her prayer. '. . . out of death comes life.'

Megan whirled round. Damon was standing behind her. He grinned. She pointed at him then spun back round to gawp at the receding column of prisoners, needing confirmation he wasn't among them.

'What . . . ? How . . . ? I don't understand.'

A second figure stepped forward. Willas. 'One of the advantages of *Kolida* is no one'll be able to examine the bodies.' He handed a heavy cloak to Damon, who slipped it around his shoulders.

'You're letting him go?'

'Don't say it out loud,' said Damon. 'He might realize what he's doing and change his mind.'

'Why?'

'Because Fordel's a bastard and he doesn't realize there are people at the other end of his pen,' said Willas. 'It's always down to the likes of you and me to clean up the mess he doesn't think about.' He placed a hand on Megan's shoulder. 'And you've lost enough.'

'I don't know what to say.'

'Afreyda's organizing an escort to see him safely into the Realm. You'll have to lie low for a few hours. The tunnels are going to be . . . well . . .'

'Don't worry,' said Damon. 'Lying low's my speciality.'

'I have to go.' Willas pointed to the mountains. 'Good luck, Your Majesty.'

Megan was still trying to comprehend what was going on, still trying to comprehend if this was what she wanted. Damon alive? Did he deserve it? But after everything, he was still her friend; she cared about him. And Willas had risked so much to give her something back.

She flung her arms around the older man's shoulders. 'Thank you, captain. Thank you.'

'*Toca vela birá dubí*,' added Damon.

'Only one drink?' said Willas. 'Cheapskate.'

He gave Megan a fatherly kiss on the forehead and hurried off after the procession. Megan grabbed Damon's sleeve and pulled him further up into the darkness of the side street.

Awkwardness hung heavy in the air. 'So . . .' said Damon.

'So . . .'

'I didn't mean what I said.'

'About?'

'About you being a vassal.'

Of all the things to apologize for. 'The Snow Cities have the guns,' said Megan. 'But we need them to defeat the witches.'

'How *did* you get them?' said Damon.

'It was Ími. He's a Hilite scientist. He discovered the formula for making gunpowder.'

'And I take it he's not keen on sharing?'

'Not exactly.'

An idea began to formulate in Megan's mind, a dangerous idea, the kind that could get her killed or start a war. Or finish one. No time to think about it, to discuss it with cooler heads. She would need Damon for it to work, and he'd only be around a few hours more.

'Can you read Hilite as well as speak it?' she asked.

'Reading's easier,' said Damon. 'No accents, no slurring, no slang. Why?'

'Willas only told us to lie low. He didn't say *where*.'

Evading the patrols that mooched through the city, Megan led Damon to the docks. She scurried along one of the piers and down to a rowing boat bobbing on the gentle waves.

Damon held back. 'You never mentioned water,' he said.

'It's the fastest way,' said Megan.

'To where?' said Damon. 'I'd be happy with a long walk.'

Megan realized what was wrong. 'How long were you in for?'

'Long enough to appreciate the benefits of not drowning in freezing northern seas.'

'In better circumstances, I'd show sympathy.'

Damon took a breath and gripped the top of the ladder. 'I'll be fine,' he said. 'Well, manageably terrified.'

They cast off and made their way through the anchored fleet. The shimmering lights above their head lent the huge ships a spectral appearance. The sounds of the city faded until all that could be heard were their ragged breaths and the splash of oar dipping in and out of water.

'How much longer?' gasped Damon.

'A lot,' said Megan. 'Keep bloody rowing.'

'The quality of your motivational speaking leaves a little to be desired.'

'I'm sorry. Just a few more pulls. You can do it, you brave little sailor, you.'

The auroras dissipated, leaving the night pitch black apart from the moon, which occasionally peeked out from behind the clouds to see what was going on. Megan scanned the dark coastline, hoping she could recognize some contour from her previous trip, but nothing looked familiar or even definitely unfamiliar.

'What're you looking for?' asked Damon.

'The place to dock.'

'Move close to the shore.'

'Will that make things brighter?' asked Megan.

'No, but it will make them more bumpy-in-to.'

'You're advocating the crash method of navigation?'

They steered shoreward. The rocks seemed to lunge for them, but it was just a trick of the dark, Megan's nervousness manifesting itself. She concentrated on the rowing, the simple if tiring repetition. Her shoulders burned from the effort. This journey had definitely been easier when she wasn't the one doing the work.

'Tell me about this witch dissenter,' she said.

'Sener?' said Damon, amidst panting. 'What do you want to know about him for?'

'He a friend of yours?'

'He's a witch. They don't have friends, only people they've yet to decapitate.'

'Why do they tolerate his —' Megan searched for the word — 'unorthodoxy?'

'His dad was the commander of all True forces.'

'Was?' said Megan. 'What happened to him?'

'Your sister.'

Megan couldn't help but feel shame at the guilt-by-relation implicit in Damon's words. It made her wonder what would have happened had she been in Gwyneth's place, if she'd been taken by Brother Attor instead of Brother Brogan. Would divine power have seduced her as it had her twin? As much as she liked to claim not, hadn't she claimed a throne to less than universal acclamation and sent armies to fight her rival? Who was to say which sister had the more blood on her hands?

'Did you see her much?'

'Gwyneth?' said Damon. 'A bit. I think she's lonely.'

'Like I give a damn,' said Megan. She did though. It was hard not to empathize, not just because they were sisters, but because they were both queens with the crushing weight of expectation upon them. 'What do you think she'll do now?'

'Put an advert on the temple noticeboard? Friend sought for fun, frolics and flagellation?'

'About the war,' said Megan. 'I guess this Sener's done for.'

'Maybe,' said Damon. 'He's still got a number of supporters, and Gwyneth can't afford to lose the men after what you did to her fleet.' He craned his neck round to check their progress. 'Look –' they hit something and went spinning – 'out!'

They'd hit a jetty. After an argument, they regained control of the boat and moored it. This *looked* like the place; certainly Megan couldn't remember any other piers this far from the city. She had to assume it was, in which case they needed to go – she oriented herself – *that* way, perpendicular to the inlet. One way to find out.

They trudged through the forest, snow crunching underfoot. Chill air snuck in under Megan's hood, numbing her face and making the tips of her ears – or what tips she had left – burn with pain. Occasional moonlight flashed through the pines, catching a rabbit scurrying over the blanketed ground or a branch that had been swaying then froze when illuminated, as if scared it had been caught.

There was a thud and a cry of pain. 'You could have brought a light,' said Damon.

'What happened to the crash method of navigation?' Megan said over her shoulder.

'Not so good when it's you personally who's doing the crashing.'

'Here, take my hand.'

'It would help if I could see –' a slap echoed around the forest – 'it.' Damon peeled Megan's hand off his face and squeezed, his pulse just discernible under the layers of leather. 'My cheek's all warm now.'

'Want me to do the other?'

'Not that warm.' A pause, then, 'This is like that time we—'

'It can never be like that,' snapped Megan. 'There's one of us missing.'

They finally reached Ími's hut, its snow-covered roof sparkling like starlight. Megan struck her knife off a flint and lit the lantern hanging off the wall. A flickering yellow light promising, but not giving, warmth filled the clearing.

'Are you sure there's no one home?' asked Damon.

'I saw Ími getting drunk with Fordel at dinner,' said Megan. 'They're not shifting any time soon.'

She tried the door. Locked. 'Can you get us in?'

'I'll need tools.'

Megan handed him a hooked spike and a stiletto from her boot. Damon pulled off his gloves, blew on his fingers and set to work. Megan paced about, trying to keep warm, fretting and regretting. She was already committed, too late to go back.

A clunk made her start. It was Damon opening the lock. He grinned in triumph. 'Not very good with locks, are they?' he said. 'After this, fancy a trip to the city treasury, see what we can score?'

'We're not thieves.'

'Aren't we?'

'We're taking what we need,' said Megan.

'Most thieves do.'

She scooped the lantern off its hook and went inside. The smell of sulphur and other chemicals made her gag and her eyes water. Papers and parchments marked with indecipherable scribbling were strewn all over the benches lining the walls.

'Get searching,' she said to Damon as he crossed the threshold. 'No, leave the door open.'

'How do you know it's here?'

Megan didn't. 'Of course it's here.'

Damon started to root through the papers. Megan held up a parchment. 'What's this?'

Damon leaned in and squinted. 'Meatball recipe.'

'And this?' said Megan, grabbing another.

'Something about using an infinitely long strip of paper to do sums,' said Damon. 'Look, can you just let me get on with it?'

Megan bounced on her heels. 'I need to do something.'

'I don't know.' Damon frowned at a sheet of paper, nodded appreciatively and tucked it in his pocket. 'Go keep watch. You might get lucky. There might be someone to stab.'

'I'm not all about the stabbing, you know.'

'Sometimes you slash instead.' He motioned to the exit. 'Go. Guard.'

Megan propped herself against the door frame. The forest was silent bar the occasional rustle in the undergrowth as some animal braved the cold in search for food. The events of the past day – was it only a single day? – began to catch up with her. She dozed off, leaving the icy city for places that now existed only in her memories. She found herself back in the temple library in Eastport. She was searching for Eleanor, but every time she caught a glimpse of copper hair and chased after it, the countess flitted behind a bookcase and was gone.

A tap on her shoulder juddered her awake. 'This it?' asked Damon, holding a sheaf of scribbling in front of her face.

Megan rubbed her eyes. The writing didn't resolve itself into anything legible. 'You tell me.'

'Fifteen parts saltpetre, three parts charcoal, two parts sulphur.'

Gunpowder – this was it. The Diannon's secret, shared with the witches, discovered by the Hilites, and now stolen by her. Megan swallowed, chewed frozen lips. The parchment was as explosive as the mixture it described. If Fordel discovered she had it, she was done for. But it was the Realm's only defence against his ambition.

'There's a method for mixing it as well,' said Damon. 'More complicated than I would have thought. Apparently, you have to—'

'Can you copy it?'

'Sure.'

Nervous energy coursing through her, Megan paced outside while Damon set about his task. Round the back of the hut, she happened upon a freshly covered mound to which the snow refused to stick. She hoped it was some waste and not one of Ími's poor assistants. The mound looked a little small to hold a man, but gunpowder experiments did tend to compact a person somewhat.

She made it around to the front again. Scratching came from within the hut. She poked her head inside. 'Have you not finished yet?'

'Give me a little time,' said Damon. 'I've only just finished sketching out the drop cap.'

'You're doing *calligraphy*? This isn't the Book of Faith you're copying.'

'You've got to do it properly.' Damon looked around. 'Do you think there's any gold leaf in this place?'

'Damon . . .'

'Kidding, kidding. You're so easy to wind up. I've almost finished.'

A light caught the corner of Megan's eye, making her heart skip a few beats then thud frantically to make up. 'Someone's coming!'

'I thought you said . . . ?'

'One *tiny* thing didn't work out.'

Damon swore and blew frantically at the parchment in front of him to dry the ink. Megan urged him on. 'I don't think we care about smudges.'

'You say that,' said Damon, rolling up the parchment and tucking it inside his cloak, 'but fifteen becomes fifty and where will we be?'

Megan blew out the lantern and ushered Damon outside. The light was brighter now, an approaching lantern, she assumed. It was coming from the direction they had to go. She looked around. She could see no escape route, nor anything else for that matter. Only one thing for it. She jerked Damon off his feet and dragged him round to the back of the hut.

'Last time a girl did this to me, she—'

Megan shut him up with an elbow to the ribs. She could make out voices slurring in Hilite: Ími and Fordel's. 'What are they saying?' she whispered.

'Hard to make out,' Damon whispered back. 'They're very drunk.'

'Are they suspicious?'

'I don't know. Why don't you go ask them?'

Megan held back. She contemplated the distance to the forest. If Fordel and Ími had heard them, they could be around here before she and Damon reached the treeline. Best to wait, let the two Hilites disappear inside and get distracted by each other, then slip away.

There was a brief conversation, then the unmistakable sound of approaching footsteps, snow compacting in ever-increasing intensity. 'Hide!' hissed Megan. Damon moved. 'Not behind me.'

'There's nowhere else!'

'Round the other side.'

'This isn't turning into a farce,' muttered Damon.

They stumbled down the back of the hut. Megan looked back. They'd left footprints glittering in the moonlight. She made to go to kick snow over them. A figure loomed around the far corner. She threw herself around the wall.

Her foot slipped in the ice. The ground smacked into her before she could do anything about it.

Megan lay in the snow, her panting forming ephemeral clouds in front of her face. Distant words. She looked to Damon. He gave her a sarcastic thumbs-up. She jabbed a finger back in the direction they had come, flapped her hand like a mouth and shrugged. He screwed up his face, confused.

'What're they saying?' she whispered.

Damon made a show of listening. 'Something like, what the hell are those footpri— Oh . . .'

Instinct had Megan groping for a knife. She checked herself. Could she really attack Fordel? But if he discovered what she intended to do, she wouldn't be safe. He'd have her killed and Cate elevated in her place. She drew her weapon.

Snow scrunched underfoot, louder and louder. The blade peeked out from her glove like a predator's claw. Nothing she hadn't done before, more times than she cared to contemplate. Was this a step too far though, a shift from provoked defence to unprovoked attack?

There was a thud, a laugh, a second thud then silence. No, not quite silence. Was that . . . ? Megan exchanged quizzical looks with Damon. Yes, it was. Snoring.

She crawled through the snow and peered around the corner. Fordel and Ími were sprawled out on the ground, arms around each other, dead to the world. Megan got to her feet, brushed herself down, and inched closer to the two Hilites. The alcohol had caught up with them. They looked peaceful enough now, but come the morning . . .

'We should get them inside,' she whispered to Damon, who had snuck around and joined her.

'Why?'

'They'll freeze to death out here.'

'And?' said Damon. 'You were ready to stab them a minute ago.'

'I was not.'

'Oh, I'm sorry, you were offering a little light beard trimming, were you?'

Megan sheathed the evidence of her intent and grabbed Ími's arms. 'Yes, well . . .' The moment had passed and all she was left with was two drunk men exposed to the elements. 'Come on, give me a hand.'

Afreyda was waiting for them at the entrance to the Kartik tunnels, bouncing on her heels and slapping her arms to keep warm. Around her, soldiers of the Faith dozed, heads lolling or propped against the rocks. They snapped to attention at the sound of Megan and Damon's approach.

Afreyda held up a hand to put them at ease. 'What took you so long?' she asked Megan.

'Slight diversion.'

Afreyda glared at Damon, who spread his palms in innocence. 'Why do you automatically blame me?'

'It saves time.'

Megan nodded at Afreyda's men. 'Who did you pick to lead the mission?'

'Me,' said Afreyda.

'What? No!'

'I am the best person for the job.'

Megan pulled Afreyda aside. Damon made to follow. Megan shooed him away and dragged her further into the shadows cast by the rocks.

'You don't trust them?' she asked Afreyda in a low voice.

'I trust them if I am there,' said Afreyda. 'The men may not react well if they find out Damon was working for the witches. Or if he talks to them.'

'I can't lose you.'

'You will not lose me,' said Afreyda. 'The witches have retreated to New Statham. It will be a simple journey.'

'It's not just that.'

'It is not just what?'

Megan swallowed and looked away. She should tell Afreyda about her plan regarding the gunpowder, but she feared recrimination for the risks she'd taken and she didn't want to part on an argument.

'Damon'll explain on the way, once you're in the Realm.'

'What have you—?'

'Watch out for Hilites as well as witches,' said Megan.

If Fordel found out Damon had escaped, he might be prepared to ignore it to save the alliance, but if he found out they had stolen the gunpowder formula Megan didn't know how he'd react, how far he'd go to preserve his advantage. 'Get Damon to Janik, then come straight back.'

She drew Afreyda close, as much a parasitic need for warmth as a display of affection. They kissed, a little self-conscious at first, then forgetting the onlookers and acknowledging only each other and their mutual passion, their mutual need.

twenty-four

They were in the Realm, the free Realm, devoid of witches and Sandstriders and Hilites and anyone else who wanted to kill him. He was home. Damon would have got on the ground and kissed it had he not feared his lips would adhere to the icy rocks – the Snow Cities didn't have a monopoly on winter. Still, the cold was more welcoming here. It was *his* cold.

Afreyda sent their escorts on to scout the skeletal forest through which the road ahead passed, then brought her horse close to Damon's. 'What have you and Megan got planned?'

'We—'

'You stole the formula for gunpowder.'

'How did you . . . ?'

'It is the only thing that makes sense,' said Afreyda. 'Why did she not tell me?'

'No need to be jealous,' said Damon. 'Megan and I have been breaking into dangerous places since before you were . . . well, not born obviously. Not sure where I was going with that.'

'I am not jealous. I could have helped.'

'I'm sure Megan wanted to give you plausible deniability,' said Damon. 'In case things went the shape of the pear.'

'If Fordel finds out . . .'

'She wants him to find out. After we get to Janik, of course.' Instinct made Damon glance back, but the mountains were free of pursuing hordes. 'Once the Hilites find out the Realm has guns, they'll have to back down. There's no way even the priests could lose that war. The numerical advantage would be too great.'

'If the priests have guns, they will not allow Megan to stay on the throne.'

'I don't think that's her intention.'

'Then what is?'

'I don't know,' said Damon. 'You're her girlfriend and the captain of her guard.'

'But I am not Eleanor.'

That's where your jealousy lies, is it? 'Don't worry. There's a lot we didn't tell *her* either.'

They rode in silence until they crossed the treeline and entered what was less a forest and more an arboreal graveyard. Fossilized leaves crumbled under the hoofs of their mounts. A chill wind carrying the whispers of the dead made branches tremble. Hard to believe it would burst back into life here in a few short months.

Afreyda looked around, frowning. 'Something is not right.'

'Left?'

She put her fingers to her lips and whistled. The shrill note echoed around the trees and faded away unanswered.

'Your men aren't dogs,' said Damon. 'They don't come when you –' a trampling alerted them to an approaching horse – 'tell a lie.'

There was something about the rider, the way he sat slack in the saddle, the way the horse's canter buffeted his body with no attempt to counter it. He started to slip, tilting forward and then left, before tumbling to the ground. His foot stuck in the stirrup and the horse dragged him along for a few yards before dislodging him. The soldier made no protest. He was too busy being dead.

Horses burst through the forest, heading straight for them, their riders very much in control. 'Witches!' cried Afreyda. She wheeled her horse around. More witches came up from the rear, crashed through the undergrowth. 'We're trapped!'

'For Saviours' sake,' said Damon, tugging his horse to the left. 'And they made you a captain.'

He shot off, spurring his horse on as fast as he dared. Crossbow bolts flew at him. The forest whizzed past in a dangerous blur. Just in time he saw a branch speeding towards him and ducked.

The drumbeat of hoofs behind him let him know Afreyda had finally realized there was more than one dimension in the world. She quickly drew level.

'We need to get back to the mountains!' she shouted across to him.

'Too far!'

'Where then?'

'I don't know! Just keep riding!'

Afreyda pulled ahead of him. From both sides, witches galloped to intercept her. They were approaching fast. No time to reload their crossbows. They reached for their axes. Afreyda grabbed an overhanging branch and hauled herself up. Her legs windmilled, kicking her nearest pursuer in the head twice in quick succession.

Even as the witch was tumbling to the ground, Afreyda flipped herself over the branch. She dropped on to the horse of the second pursuer. Before he had time to register what was going on, she had a knife in his face and was throwing him to the forest floor. He hung on to her as he fell, dragging her with him.

Damon was thundering directly towards the pair. Afreyda's eyes widened. She cried out and threw herself to the side. The witch, blinded by blood, groped about, trying to feel where the danger was. Damon's horse whinnied in alarm and reared. The world lurched.

Damon lost his grip then his seating. He flew through the air.

The blanket of dead leaves cushioned his fall, but the impact still felt as if someone had taken a sledgehammer to him. He lay there, groaning, body throbbing in time to his heartbeat. A sound penetrated the pain. Someone calling his name.

He pushed himself up, opened his eyes. The other witches had reached them and dismounted. They approached from all sides, weapons drawn. Afreyda had her sword raised, but there was no way she could take on all of them.

Only one thing to do. Damon scrabbled to the witch Afreyda had knifed and pulled the blade out of his face, wincing at the squelching and the blood that erupted from the de-impaled flesh. Afreyda sidestepped to his position, head jerking as she took in their advancing enemies.

'You take those two, I will deal with the other four.'

Damon admired her optimism, but it wouldn't get them out of this. 'Sorry, captain,' he said, pressing the knife to her back. 'Drop the sword.'

Afreyda let her weapon fall to the ground and raised her arms, all the while giving Damon a glare that promised dismemberment. 'I have a prisoner,' Damon called out to the advancing witches. 'Where's your commander?'

The witches halted, unsure what to make of the

situation. Their heads snapped around in unison. Someone was approaching from behind. Damon's skin tingled. He looked over his shoulder.

'You!' said Sener.

'You!' said Afreyda.

'You!' said Damon, not wishing to be left out.

Sener dismounted and drew his sword.

'Glad we all know each other,' said Damon. 'Introductions can be so awkward, can't they?'

Agony shot through his arm as Afreyda lunged round and twisted his wrist. He dropped the knife into her waiting hand. She spun, kicking his legs out from under him. Damon found himself on his knees, a bloody blade against his jugular.

'Come any closer and I'll cut his throat,' Afreyda warned Sener.

'Go ahead.'

'Hey!'

Sener halted anyway. 'What are you doing here?'

'I was with the fleet,' said Damon. He swallowed. The blade was close enough to his neck the action shaved off a patch of stubble. 'I was captured. They were taking me to Janik.'

'Why?'

'The Hilites don't allow torture in their own territories.'

Damon took in Sener's appearance. He had grown

a beard, his hair was unkempt and dried mud and blood encrusted his clothes and armour. 'What are you still doing up here?' Damon asked him. 'Hiding from Gwyneth?'

Sener twitched. 'I was waiting to see what crawled out of the Kartiks.'

'Of course.'

'Where are my men?' demanded Afreyda.

'They are no longer men,' said Sener.

He took a step towards them. Afreyda jerked Damon's head backwards, exposing his throat more. As if she needed it.

'Is it true what they say about you and the Apostate?' asked Sener.

'What of it?'

'It's a perversion forbidden by the Book of the True.'

Damon raised a tentative hand. 'Actually it isn't, unless you interpret chapter six, paragraph nine with a *very* dirty mind. Fornication on the other hand . . . How is that girl of yours? What was her name . . . ? Taite?'

'I choose whom I love and how I love them,' said Afreyda.

'That makes it right, does it?'

'That makes it I-do-not-give-a-damn-what-you-think.'

'Listen,' Damon said to Sener, 'I can see you're busy. I don't want to keep you. We'll agree to disagree and be on our way.'

'On your way?'

'To Gwyneth. You don't think she'll want to question Afreyda about Megan's plans?'

'Wait until spring, then march on New Statham with her guns,' said Sener.

'It's not the most strategically complex of ideas, I guess. But there'll be other things to question her about.'

Sener's gaze flicked from Damon up to Afreyda. 'Aren't you neglecting something?'

'I'm sure Afreyda'll agree to a reversal of the captor–prisoner dynamic once she figures out the situation.'

Sener looked to Afreyda. 'Well?'

Her knife rocked across Damon's throat, making him shudder when part of the edge his body hadn't warmed caught his skin. He wondered how much it'd hurt if she pushed it in further, how aware he'd be of the life draining from his body.

The knife dropped to the ground. Afreyda released Damon and backed away. He struggled to his feet and massaged his aching muscles. A witch wrenched Afreyda's arms behind her back and bound her wrists.

'Thanks for this,' Damon said to Sener. 'I'll buy you a drink sometime.'

'I'm sure we'll come across an inn on the way to New Statham.'

'What?'

'We're coming with you.'

*

A witch stirred from his sleep. Damon froze mid-step, held his breath, willed his heart to stop beating so hard. There was a moment of wordless muttering, then the witch settled back down. Damon eased his foot down and made another scan of the camp. Sener, eager to be as far from any Hilite patrols as possible, had pushed them hard all day, and what soldiers weren't patrolling the perimeter of the camp had dropped on the ground dead tired. Safe for the moment.

He crept over to Afreyda, who was trussed up and gagged like a rebellious roast, and eased the handkerchief out of her mouth.

'What the hell do you think you are doing?' she spat at him.

He eased the handkerchief back in. 'Ask yourself how we're best going to get out of this,' he whispered. 'With us both captured or dead, or with one of us free to help the other?' The fury in Afreyda's eyes suggested her choice didn't necessarily correspond with Damon's. 'Look, if I hadn't disarmed you, they would have killed you.'

Afreyda squealed. Damon put a finger to his lips. Afreyda glared then gave him a reluctant nod. He loosened the gag again.

'I would rather be dead than . . . this,' she hissed, struggling against her bonds. 'And I definitely would rather you be dead.'

'No, you wouldn't, or you would have killed me and let them cut you down.'

'And what is your great plan?'

'I notice you don't deny it.'

'And I notice you have not come up with anything.'

'Be a good little captive,' said Damon. 'Don't annoy them.'

'That is you. Pander to everyone.'

It's kept me alive. 'They'll gradually drop their guard. Our chance will come. It's a long way from here to New Statham.'

twenty-five

The coronation procession wound its way from the Lord Defender's mansion. Synne carried Cate, who was wrapped in so much fur she looked like a bear cub. Megan buried her face in there and was rewarded with a delighted giggle from her daughter. She wished she could stay in there. The crowds lining the route were polite but standoffish, like someone invited to their sister's husband's cousin's best friend's wedding, maintaining a dignified air until the beer barrels were opened. Megan couldn't blame them. It was their lives she and Fordel and Gwyneth were squabbling over, with little regard to what they thought, what they wanted.

A flicker of motion in the sky caught Megan's eye. Birds wheeling out of the pigeon tower, carrying the highlights of her coronation address to all the major cities of the Realm. No sign of one coming in the opposite direction. Afreyda should have been back from Janik by now. Megan hoped it was nothing more than Fordel having her held up on the Kartiks in an act of petty spite.

Father Galan watched with her as the birds disappeared against the grey of the mountains. 'Are you sure about this, Your Majesty?'

'It's the only way we're ever going to get out of this mess,' said Megan. 'Did you dispatch the riders?'

'They should be entering the Realm as we speak.'

'And they understand what to do with my address?' The full text, in this case.

'Hammer it to the doors of the temples where everyone can see it,' said Father Galan. 'A touch sacrilegious, don't you think?'

'Are temples actually mentioned in the Book of Faith, father?'

They proceeded to the main square, which was festooned with flags and banners and strings threaded with coloured glass that glittered in the wintry sun. The crowd – refugees from the Realm for the most part, but there were plenty of Hilite citizens – flowed into every available gap, hung out of windows, braved steep, icy roofs. A few even cheered her. Megan offered them bashful smiles.

Through the flung-open doors of the great hall, she could see the dignitaries awaiting her: Fordel and the other leaders of the Snow Cities; the senior soldiers of her own army plus the more self-important of the refugees;

even the Sandstriders, who were both Fordel's guests and his hostages. Megan knew how the last felt.

Father Galan placed a hand on her shoulder. 'They're waiting for you, Your Majesty.'

They were, weren't they? Waiting for their puppet, the doll they'd dressed up and decorated and proclaimed majestic. But there wasn't anything special about Megan. She hadn't been appointed by God. Any one of the crowd could substitute for her – as long as you could find enough people with swords and guns to agree.

'We'll do it out here,' she said to Father Galan.

'But—'

'It's bigger, more people can see.'

'But not the people who . . .'

'Count?' Megan swept her hand. 'I think these people count.' *I'm their queen, not Fordel's.* 'You did bring the crown, didn't you?'

Father Galan nodded and beckoned. A soldier hurried forward, bringing the box Skúla had presented Megan with. Father Galan opened it. The Unifier's crown sat inside, its gold gleaming. *What were you, Edwyn: believer, madman or cynic? What were you thinking when they first placed this on your head? Did you believe it was God's will or did you know damned well it wasn't?*

'Go on then,' Megan urged Father Galan.

'You mean right here, right now?'

306

'If we leave it any longer there's a danger someone's going to start up a folk song.'

Father Galan straightened his robes. 'Very well.' He leaned in. 'Do you think we should do *The Unification*?'

'Best not,' she said. 'We don't want a riot. Skip straight to the vows.'

Father Galan held up a hand, calling for quiet from the crowd. In the corner of her eye, Megan could see movement from the great hall. Fordel and the other luminaries were starting to realize what was going on.

'*Pranadi*—' started Father Galan.

Megan cut him off. 'In Stathian,' she hissed. 'They should know what I'm pledging.' *So should I.*

'Do you pledge to uphold the laws of the Realm?'

'I pledge.'

'Do you pledge to follow the teachings of the Saviours?'

Fordel tried to push his way through the crowd. The Faithful, for whom the unofficial seventh Pledge of Faith was 'I pledge to uphold the sanctity of the Queue', were having none of it.

'I pledge.'

'Do you pledge to give all that you are in service of the Faithful?'

'I pledge.'

Father Galan lifted the crown from its box and held it up in display. A gasp rippled through the crowd as they realized what it was, to whom it had belonged. *They seem much more excited about that than they do me*, thought Megan. Maybe they were right to be.

Rekka barged her way to the front, displacing a little girl who staggered into the circle around Megan, limbs flailing as she tried to prevent herself slipping on the icy flagstones. Megan darted forward and caught her before she hit the ground.

'I'm . . . I'm sorry, y'reyeness,' said the girl as Megan set her on her feet.

'That's all right,' said Megan, flashing a dirty look at Rekka, who affected disinterest. 'What's your name?'

'Jetta, y'reyeness.'

'Can you do me a favour, Jetta?'

The girl looked back to the crowd, no doubt searching for her parents. 'S'pose . . .'

'See that crown Father Galan is holding? Can you put it on my head?'

Jetta nodded solemnly. Rekka rolled her eyes. Megan jerked her head, indicating to Father Galan he should hand the crown over. He sighed and did so. Jetta almost dropped it, the heaviness of the gold surprising her.

Megan knelt in front of her and bowed her head. Jetta held off, shivering from cold or nerves or both. Megan gave her a quick nod. Jetta plonked the crown on Megan's head and fled back to the safety of her family.

Megan adjusted the crown the best she could – the promised padding hadn't materialized – and rose. A cheer of acclamation went up. It was prompted by Father Galan, but Megan could live with that.

She took the now-empty box her crown had been in and stood on it, giving herself a few extra inches of height. The crowd hushed and looked at her, expectant. Megan remembered the first time she'd had to speak in public, when she'd been a scared girl desperate to find her sister. How things had changed since then, and how they hadn't. This was still a battle between her and witches, which everyone was looking to exploit or escape. Time to start repairing the damage.

Megan cleared her throat and addressed the crowd. 'This shouldn't have happened. I shouldn't be queen, we shouldn't be refugees in a foreign land, we shouldn't have lost the people we love. We were let down by our leaders, who put more worth in power itself than what to do with it, who thought others' obedience to God more important than their own. We were driven here by monsters we created ourselves, but we were helped by friends we long ago rejected. I'm not sure we deserved either, but what's done is done, and I can do nothing more than offer my heartfelt thanks to the people of the Snow Cities for all you have done for us.'

A murmur of assent went through the assembled masses, embarrassed nods of appreciation offered to the Hilites. 'The Snow Cities have taught us much,' Megan continued, noticing Fordel squeezing his way through the crowd. 'I want the Realm to be a land not just for the Faithful but welcoming to all no matter what their beliefs. And it is you –' she pointed to random members of the crowd – 'who should make the decisions that affect your lives.'

Fordel had reached Rekka's side. There was a suspicious look on his face. Megan caught his gaze. 'When we have defeated the witches – and we will, though I can't promise it'll be easy – I'm going to abdicate. No successor will follow me. I will be the last queen. The priests will return to teaching us the mysteries of the Faith. Let the counties and cities of the Realm elect their own leaders and keep them accountable. And by God, keep them accountable.'

Megan tried to avoid Rekka and Fordel during the celebrations that followed the coronation, but from the way they kept glaring at her she knew a confrontation was coming. Might as well get it over with. She took Cate from Synne, giving the latter instructions to enjoy herself, and left for the mansion. Sure enough, her antagonists followed.

'You really think you can walk away?' said Fordel.

'I can and I will,' said Megan, putting Cate down and offering her daughter her fingers to play with. 'All I ever wanted was to make the world safe for this one. And all *you* ever wanted was to be left alone.' She looked Fordel directly in the eye, daring him to contradict her. 'Or have I misunderstood three hundred years of history?'

He glanced to Cate. 'If you abdicate . . .'

'She can't be queen. She's illegitimate.'

'There are ways around that.'

Megan leaned into the cot and kissed her daughter's cheek. Keeping her voice soft, almost baby-talk-ish, she said, 'If you're thinking of taking Cate away from me, I'll stick every knife I have in you. And believe me, I have a lot.'

She stole a glance over to Fordel and was pleased to see him blanch at the threat. 'You weren't the only one with a claim, you know,' he said.

'Her?' said Megan, pointing at Rekka, who affected affront at the insult implied in the pronoun. 'You can try. But everyone'll know what you're doing. The priests and the Faithful won't support you.'

'We don't need their support,' said Fordel. 'We have the guns. You need them to defeat the witches, and once we enter the Realm we might just stay there. Or we can stay behind the Kartiks and let you take on the witches yourself. Remind me how that was going for you.'

Megan allowed Fordel a few moments of triumph, before saying quietly, 'The Faith has guns too.'

Fordel lost his composure. He exchanged wild, confused looks with Rekka. 'What the . . . ?'

'How did you . . . ?' said Rekka.

'You think Ími is the only scientist in Werlavia?' said Megan. 'The Faithfu—'

'No, no.' Fordel advanced on Megan, jabbing his finger. 'You, you stole the knowledge.'

Megan held her ground. He wouldn't be stupid enough to attack her, would he? She could drop him without even thinking about it. The knowledge gave her no comfort, reminded her why she had to leave all this behind.

'I don't know what you're talking about.'

There was a polite cough at the door: Willas. He held out a scrap of parchment to them and made to say something. Fordel waved him quiet.

'That night at Ími's hut . . .' Fordel rubbed his forehead, as if trying to tease the alcohol-drowned memories back to life. 'I thought that was a dream, but it was you. And that boy – the one who broke out the witches – he was with you, wasn't he? You needed him to break in. And . . . and . . .' He took a deep breath and looked to the ceiling. 'The interrogation reports said he spoke Hilite. He'd be able to find the formula among Ími's notes. Tell me, captain –' he twisted his head around to address Willas – 'were all the prisoners executed?'

Willas didn't take his gaze off Megan. He looked stern, angry even, like a father disappointed by a wayward child. Megan's head drooped, guilt making her heart heavy. After everything he'd done for her, she'd gone behind his back, betrayed his trust.

'All the prisoners were taken to *Kolida*,' Willas said stiffly. This was technically true: Damon would have to pass by it on his journey to the Realm.

Rekka dropped on to the bed and massaged her leg. 'It doesn't matter how she did it,' she said. 'All that matters is the priests have guns and it's going to be the end of us.'

'It won't,' said Megan. 'It's going to be diff—'

'You think everything's going to be peace and love and happiness in the Realm because of one speech?' snapped Rekka. 'Have you learned anything?'

'I couldn't let you take over the Realm. And not just the Realm. The Snow Cities and Andaluvia too.' Megan looked to Willas. 'Did you know that, captain? They want to reunify Werlavia, with Rekka's descendants on the throne and Fordel controlling everything behind the scenes. You were worried about the priests stealing your independence? You might want to worry about your childhood friends first.'

Willas flushed. His jaw clenched. 'Is this true?' he said, looking to Rekka and Fordel in turn. 'It sounds awfully like treason.'

'I decide what's treason,' said Fordel.

'No, you don't,' said Willas. 'The electors of Hil do.'

'And they would have been consulted. Now it looks as if reunification is going to happen without our consent.'

'Do you think the Realm wants another war?' said Megan. 'We'll draw up a treaty, confirming—'

'Ooh, a treaty,' said Rekka, her voice smothered in sarcasm.

'How long do you think you could've kept guns to yourself?' asked Megan 'How long did the witches? The Faithful would've got them sooner or later, and better we do while we're friends rather than enemies.'

She gave the Hilite trio imploring looks. They had to accept this otherwise there'd be another war and it would start here, on this day. Hil would be a battleground. The idea of cutting her way through friends and allies to protect herself and Cate made her sick, but she knew she'd be able to do it.

Fordel held a hand out for Rekka and helped her off the bed. 'I'll meet with Father Galan,' he said coldly. 'Draw up terms of this treaty.'

Megan swallowed, relief flooding through her. 'I'm sure we can reach an agreement.'

Fordel gave a non-committal grunt and led Rekka out of the room.

Now it was Megan's turn to collapse on to the bed. 'Thank the Saviours,' she sighed. 'I thought I was—'

'Why didn't you tell me?' demanded Willas.

'I'm sorry,' said Megan. 'I—'

'You didn't trust me? Or you thought I'd stop you?'

Megan prickled at the admonishment. 'It all worked out, didn't it? We've kept the peace between us, our independence.'

'Have we?' said Willas. He held out the parchment. 'This came for you.'

'From Afreyda?' said Megan, a thrill going through her as she anticipated reading her girlfriend's words, her imminent return. 'Is she on her way back from Janik?'

Willas shook his head. 'It is about Afreyda,' he said, 'but this didn't come from Janik. It came from New Statham . . .'

Terror gripped Megan, blocking Willas's subsequent words. She didn't need to hear them. Gwyneth had Afreyda and Damon. And Megan's plan to neutralize Fordel was a giant bluff.

twenty-six

Megan flew around the room throwing stuff together, giving little thought to what she was grabbing, whether it would be of use or actively hinder her. All she knew was she had to be out of here, Afreyda needed her.

'You're not . . .' said Willas.

'I'll need a horse,' said Megan. 'A fast one. Can you arrange it?'

'You can't take on all the witches by yourself.'

'I've done it before,' she muttered, weighing the practicality of a silver candlestick. Maybe not. She didn't foresee too many fancy dinners on the road. 'On the way back from Ími's, Damon told me about a secret way into the palace.' Well, *out* of, but she assumed it worked in both directions. 'I'll sneak in, free them both and sneak out again.'

'When you put it like that . . .'

'The witches aren't expecting an inside attack. They'll be preparing for a siege.'

'Why do you think Gwyneth sent that message?'

'She wants to gloat,' said Megan. 'Show me she's got hostages.'

'Hostages? She didn't even make any demands. If she wanted to gloat she could have executed them and sent you their heads. She's keeping them alive for one reason.' Willas pointed at Megan.

'You think this is a trap? For me?'

'You do have a history of recklessness.'

Megan shook her head. 'No, the witches aren't interested in me. It's Cate they want.' She looked down at her daughter, sleeping peacefully despite the agitation in the room. 'Will she be safe here? With Rekka and Fordel?'

Willas looked slightly disgusted. 'Are you really saying they'd hurt a child?'

'I don't know. Fordel—'

'Is a devious bastard, but he plays at politics, not murder. I grew up with him and Rekka, remember. I know what they're like.'

And I grew up with Gwyneth. 'What about what he was going to do with Damon?'

'Damon was an enemy of the state, not an innocent baby,' said Willas. 'Did you care if the other witches lived or died?'

'They were coming to kill me and steal my daughter.'

'And they'd leave *us* alone, would they?'

Megan had no answer to this. She reached for her

317

jerkin, which the draughts through the window had been airing.

Willas caught her arm. 'If we're going to do this, we're going to do it properly.'

'We?'

'I can't let you go after Afreyda on your own,' said Willas. 'She'd kill me if she found out.'

It was a long way to New Statham, but only half-chances to get away presented themselves, half-chances that Damon could never quite bring himself to take. Failed escapes – trying to flee Tobrytan when they were going after Cate; breaking out of the Hilite cell – played on his mind. If they failed to get away, well, Afreyda was a valuable hostage; Damon was a waste of rations.

The horizon shimmered – water. They were approaching Lake Pullar. The reality of the situation hit Damon. They'd soon be in New Statham. He'd allowed the drudgery of the march and Sener's not-entirely-hostile attitude to blind him to the peril. He had to get them out of there before Gwyneth took her frustration out on him and Afreyda. But maybe he didn't have to flee without Sener's consent.

A brief trot brought him level with the witch captain. 'You know Megan's won, don't you? She outguns you and she outmans you. This is just an extended final day with a rather grim last meal.'

Sener gave him a tired look. 'She has to take New Statham first.'

'Like you found it so hard to do.'

'She won't find anyone so venal among the True. We will fight to the last for every street, every building, every paving stone.'

'You want to turn New Statham into a second Trafford's Haven?' said Damon. He guessed Sener had been a child when the firestorm had engulfed the city, maybe even old enough to remember it. 'A population of your corpses?'

'And theirs,' said Sener. 'Many more of theirs.'

'You make it sound inevitable.'

'It is.'

'Then why are you so desperate to become one of the corpses?' asked Damon. 'As ambitions go, it's a bit of a dead end. Or lots of little dead ends depending on how you get killed.'

They descended a shallow valley and stopped at a brook to give their horses a drink and to stretch their legs. After dismounting, Sener strode a little way upstream. He beckoned Damon to follow him. Damon did so, his boots crunching the frost that dusted the hard ground.

'What would you suggest I do?' asked Sener.

What you've already thought about. 'Throw away your armour and turn your horses around. You could go to anywhere in Werlavia, start a new life.'

'And abandon the True?'

'More pre-empting their discontinuation.'

'I will not hide in the Realm,' said Sener, 'pretend to be one of them, allow the priests to dictate my beliefs.'

'There's always the empire,' said Damon. 'I'm sure Afreyda'll put in a word for you.'

'A disgraced princess?'

'There is that . . .'

'No,' said Sener, shaking his head. 'I pledged to protect the True, and protect them I will.'

'You've already said you can't,' said Damon. 'And do you think Gwyneth'll give you the opportunity to fight? You failed to get Cate, and you let your guns fall into Megan's hands. She's not the forgiving type.'

'You think I fear her?'

'You were being a bit skulk-y back at the Kartiks. Not the action of a man with nothing to fear.'

'She wouldn't dare move against me,' said Sener.

'You don't have daddy to protect you any more.'

'My family still commands great respect among the True.'

'Enough to save you?' asked Damon. The look on Sener's face answered that question. 'Better hope Afreyda's capture is enough to get you off the hook.'

Sener dipped a skin in the brook and took a heavy draught from it, letting his beard soak up the dribbles. Damon could guess what was going on inside his mind. Sener's whole life had been defined by belief, following it and drawing comfort from it and fighting for it. Belief was a powerful force, capable of giving you the courage to do the right thing, but it could also blind you into doing the wrong thing. Sener was trying to find some way of reconciling it with self-preservation, to convince himself he was doing the right thing and not just the right thing for him personally. Damon should know. How many times had he done it himself?

'You might be—'

The rumble of hoofs cut Sener off before he could announce his decision to Damon. He threw down his skin and pulled out his sword. Downstream, the rest of the witches mounted their horses and drew their weapons. Horsemen appeared on the ridge: witches. They made their way down the hill. Sener and his men lowered – but didn't sheathe – their weapons. Their commander made his way towards Sener and Damon.

'Sir.'

Sener gave the man the briefest of nods. 'Lieutenant.'

'The Mother got your message,' said the officer. 'There's a ship waiting for us at Aedran.'

Damon's heart sank. From Aedran they could sail all the way down Lake Pullar and the Rustway to New Statham. There would be no chance of escape.

It was time to take leave of Cate. Megan took her daughter out into the garden and tried to interest her in the snowflakes, in a small bird that flitted from branch to branch looking for a stray berry that had survived the winter, in the fish that waited under the cracked ice of an ornamental pond. Nothing appealed. It was as if Cate knew she was being abandoned, again.

'I'm sorry I have to do this, sweetheart,' she said. 'I won't be long and then it'll be over. Really over. There'll be no one after us any more, no one wanting to use us. I'll be a proper mother, I promise. We'll be a family: you, me and Afreyda. I'll take you home to Thicketford. You'll like it there. The river, the fields, the warm sun, the smell of fresh bread every morning.' Cate looked up, uncomprehending. 'I'll teach you how to make it, like my grandfather taught me and . . . well, let's not mention *her*, shall we?'

'They're waiting, Your Majesty.'

Megan looked up to see Synne standing in the garden, snow dusting her shoulders. With a heavy heart, Megan went over to her and slipped Cate into her arms.

'You will look after her, won't you?'

'Always, ma'am.'

They circled the mansion to where Willas was waiting for her. He had arranged a company of around a hundred men – half Hilite, half soldiers of the Realm – small enough to move fast, large enough to cope with most foreseeable threats on the road to New Statham. Once they reached the capital, the company would distract the witches while

Megan and Willas sneaked into the city. A city filled with Gwyneth and Tobrytan and thousands of witches. Megan's hands trembled as she mounted her horse. Just the cold, she told the watching Synne, nothing to worry about.

Synne moved Cate's arm in a likeness of a wave. Tears pricked Megan's eyes. That was just the cold too. *What if I don't make it back?* she asked herself. *Will she blame me, condemn me for abandoning her?* Megan had lost a mother twice now. She knew the suffering, the loss, the sense of crushing solitude it engendered.

She wiped her eyes and turned to Father Galan. 'You'll act as Secretary of the Realm in my absence,' she told him. 'I want you to work with Brother Broose, find out how we're going to give power to the people, how elections are going to work, things like that.'

'A . . . *constitution?*'

'It's not like I'm asking you to drink water.'

Megan blew Cate a kiss and spurred her horse into motion. They filed through the city in a long column, their progress rousing brief curiosity but little more. People had their own lives to lead: food had to be gathered, clothes had to be washed, lessons had to be learned. There was something reassuring about this normality. Megan had saved something at least.

They wound their way up the foothills of the Kartiks. Megan huddled into her furs, letting her horse find its own

323

way. How was Afreyda holding up? What was Gwyneth doing to her? Megan tried to put such thoughts out of mind, but she couldn't help imagining Afreyda's screams of agony, Gwyneth's leer of triumph.

Willas's 'uh-oh' snapped her back to the present. Fordel was waiting for them at the entrance to the tunnel. A detachment of soldiers flanked him. A large detachment of soldiers.

Fordel snapped something in Hilite. Willas shrugged. 'Just patrolling the border,' he replied in Stathian. 'It *is* my job.'

'I don't recall giving such an order.'

The company became agitated: mutterings and nervous whinnies. Megan glanced around. More Hilite soldiers were advancing on their rear. One or two of the Faithful started playing with their weapons in a non-playful way.

'You don't have the authority to give me *any* orders, Fordel,' said Willas. 'Only the Lord Defender does.'

'How hard do you think it'll be to get that particular signature?'

'I don't know. Have you managed to teach Vegar how to spell his name yet?'

Megan glanced up. There were men up in the rocks, their furs camouflaging them against the ice-smeared stones. Archers – loyal to Willas or Fordel? It didn't matter: at these close quarters you were as liable to hit your own men as the enemy.

She nudged her horse forward. 'You might be able to stop Willas, but you can't stop me.'

'Really?'

'You want to start a fight over what? Because we didn't fill in the right forms?'

'It's a little more than that.'

Megan chose her next words carefully. 'If the priests had provided Afreyda with a proper escort on her way back from Janik, we wouldn't be in this mess. But they didn't, so we are.'

'*Back* from Janik?' said Fordel. 'I thought they were taken going.'

Megan shook her head, as if the difference was of no consequence. 'That's what the reports indicated,' said Willas, giving Megan a look that said, 'The things I do for you.'

Fordel paced while he considered – if Afreyda and Damon had been captured by the witches on the way back from Janik, they'd have delivered the formula to the priests and there'd be no reason to hold Megan. Soldiers on both sides looked on uneasily. The tight confines of the path promised a massacre everyone could get to enjoy. Was Megan prepared to order her men to draw their weapons on their friends, countrymen and allies? Were they prepared to obey? Would it be a sacrifice too far?

Fordel beckoned to a soldier, who scurried forward. Steel rasped against leather somewhere behind Megan.

'Put that sword back where it belongs,' Willas said through gritted teeth. There was an apology and the hiss of a blade being slid back into its scabbard.

The soldier handed Fordel a large sealskin pouch. 'What's in there?' asked Megan. 'Death warrants?'

'Not technically . . .' Fordel threw the pouch up to Megan. 'You might want those if you insist on this suicide mission of yours.'

'What are they?'

'Maps of New Statham, plans of the royal palace, oh, and directions for that tunnel Edwyn the Third thought he'd kept secret from everybody.'

'You knew about that?'

'Who do you think dug it for him?' said Fordel. 'Always check up on your subcontractors. They might just be the people you built your fortress to protect yourself from.'

'Thank you,' said Megan.

Willas barked orders. Their company dismounted and led their horses into the tunnel, a column disappearing into the black and heading for Saviours knew what. Megan had talked them out of one fight, but she suspected the witches wouldn't be so cooperative.

She made to follow them. Fordel called her back.

'What is it?' she asked.

'Do look after Willas. I'm very fond of him.'

'And you look after Cate. Even I don't make it back, I'll be one sodding vengeful ghost.'

twenty-seven

Damon sidled up to Sener as their ship creaked into New Statham. The witch captain was observing the wharfs, a thoughtful look on his face. Sandstriders darted on and off docked vessels. They were loading them up, preparing to depart. Further down the Rustway, Damon could make out ships that had already started the long crawl home.

'Someone called the Andaluvians "Sandstriders" to their faces, didn't they?' he said. 'And they've gone off in a huff. You know they like it no more than you like being called "witches".'

'Shut up,' said Sener. He stroked his chin: the beard had gone the night before, as had most of the straggly hair. 'She's never going to be able to hold the city. Not with so few men. Not once they know *she's* on her way.'

'The occasional proper noun won't hurt, you know.'

'Didn't I tell you to shut up?'

'Next time specify a time limit,' said Damon. He lowered his voice. 'It's not too late, you know. We could keep going. No one's going to notice us with all the Sandstriders about.' Sener raised a questioning eyebrow. 'You're allowed to call 'em that behind their back. We can drift down the river, find somewhere warm, safe.'

Sener looked around the deck, taking in each of the bustling witches. Damon saw the calculation in his eyes, the formation of a plan of attack. He'd lost track of which were Sener's men and which Gwyneth had sent. They were outnumbered, he knew that much, but they'd have the benefit of surprise.

There was a hollering from the piers: stevedores calling them into dock. Sener shrugged, mentally casting his plan into the murky waters of the Rustway. Damon was going to have to find another way out of this mess.

Gwyneth and Tobrytan were waiting for them as they disembarked, a sizeable detachment of guards by their side. Neither looked impressed by the sight of Damon. He was used to it by now.

'How the hell are you still alive?' said Tobrytan.

'Most people settle for "hello".' He made a show of looking around. 'So . . . anything interesting happen in my absence?'

Gwyneth rolled her eyes at him and turned to Sener. She'd put on a little weight, and her cheeks were flushed in the winter air. *Better lay off the wine*, thought Damon.

'You were ordered back months ago.'

'I thought I'd best—'

'I don't remember ordering you to think,' snapped Gwyneth. 'Where's the prisoner?'

Sener called out. Two witches appeared from below decks with a sullen Afreyda. She gave Damon a look that condemned him for broken promises.

'When I told you to go after my sister,' Gwyneth said to Afreyda, 'I didn't mean *quite* like that.' Afreyda said nothing. 'I'd say "no harm done", but there was plenty of harm done. How many True have you killed for her? There'll be a lash for each one, three if you lie.'

'A dozen,' said Afreyda. 'A hundred. A thousand. You think I care what you do to me?'

Gwyneth pulled her cloak tight, battling the winds that whipped down the Rustway. 'Brave girl. I have to warn you, Trymian doesn't hold the whip back.'

'You killed my parents.'

'I was doing a favour for your emperor,' said Gwyneth. 'He liked you though, and . . . what was her name . . . ?' The tendons on Afreyda's neck bulged as she clenched her teeth. 'He asked me to keep you alive, if possible.' She shook her head. 'It's not possible.'

'Tobrytan,' said Sener. The general looked unimpressed by the breach of military protocol. 'Sir. We can't hold the city. We should evacuate before the blasphemers get here.'

'To where?'

'Andaluvia,' said Sener.

'Not entirely possible,' said Gwyneth. 'They're going

to be a bit annoyed with us.' She looked to Tobrytan. 'Are the guns in place?'

'Yes, Mother.'

'And Jolecia?'

'We got word to her ship,' said Tobrytan. 'They're holding at Samsun until it's over.'

Damon looked at Gwyneth, then at the departing Sandstrider ships. Gwyneth was going to blow them out of the water. She was following her sister's lead, but instead of firing on an invading enemy she was attacking a retreating ally.

'We don't need to evacuate,' Gwyneth said to Sener, 'or flee or hide. You need to place your trust in Joanne's prophecy, captain.'

'Because it's guided us so well this far,' said Sener, his face straight enough to give his sarcasm plausible deniability.

'We may have been guilty of . . . hasty interpretation. But God has spoken to me and shown me the way. This is a test, a trial we must overcome if we are all to know the glory of the Saviours.'

Gwyneth turned to Afreyda. 'When I say "all", there are one or two exceptions of course.'

After racing across Werlavia and down the western shore of Lake Pullar, Megan and Willas took a platoon and parted from the bulk of their company. While the remaining men were to approach New Statham from the north, with orders to get the hell out of there once the witches spotted them, Megan and the others wheeled around through the forest that covered the left bank of the Rustway. The aim was to cross the river at Samsun, a hamlet a few miles south of the capital if Fordel's map was correct, then hope they could find the entrance to Edwyn's tunnel.

'Why do you think he helped us?' Megan asked as their horses trudged through the undergrowth.

'Who?' said Willas. 'Fordel?'

'Is he still in love with you?'

Willas laughed. 'That was a long time ago,' he said. 'Fordel doesn't like to play a losing hand, especially not to destruction. He'll bide his time, wait for his opportunity. I'd be careful of him.'

'I'm hoping by the time we meet again, he'll be somebody else's problem.'

'You're serious about that? Abdicating?'

'Why does everyone sound so shocked?' asked Megan. 'All I want is to take Afreyda and Cate back home and lead a normal life without plots or politics or people trying to kill me.' *If Afreyda is still alive.* 'Anyway, it's you who has to worry. He's going to be annoyed at your near mutiny.'

'That's going to be somebody else's problem too.'

'I don't understand.'

'I'm thinking of leaving Hil,' said Willas. 'Too many memories there, too many desires that'll never be fulfilled.'

'Vegar might drink himself into an early grave.'

'With his constitution? And even if he did, I don't think she'd . . .' He shook his head. 'Does your Realm of the people have space for one more?'

'I'm sure we can find—'

A distant boom made everyone's heads snap round. The horses shifted nervously beneath them. 'That was gunfire,' said Megan. 'You don't think . . . ?'

Willas shook his head. 'Too close. Our men are on the other side of the city. Target practice, maybe?'

'They've had plenty of that, and why waste the ammunition?'

More booms. 'That's coming from the river,' said Willas. 'Who the hell are they shooting at?'

Megan felt a sickening in her stomach as she worked out the timelines, realized who on the Rustway the witches might be firing at, who had just agreed to a treaty with the Hilites. 'It's the Sandstriders. Gwyneth's attacking them.'

'Surely they wouldn't have told her *why* they were leaving New Statham until they were safely away.'

'My sister likes to get her revenge in first.'

They trudged on in silence. Gwyneth's actions against her former friends only emphasized how dangerous things were for New Statham, how quickly she could turn against them. And not just her: Tobrytan had been keen to destroy Eastport in revenge for the priests' burning of Trafford's

Haven. Now he was in charge of the witches' forces, there was no one to stop him completing his vengeance. Megan needed a way to end this war as quickly and bloodlessly as possible. She remembered talking to Damon about the witch captain, Sener. It was a shame *he* hadn't taken command of the True. Given his scepticism regarding Joanne's prophecy, Megan might have been able to reach an accord with him.

The return of a scout they'd sent on ahead interrupted her thoughts. Megan shifted anxiously in the saddle while the scout conversed in low voices and extravagant gestures with Willas, the latter's expression becoming ever more concerned.

She could wait no longer. 'What is it?'

'The bridge,' said Willas. 'It isn't.'

'What?'

'Looks like the witches blew it up. Guess they wanted to hinder any attacking army.'

Or hinder anyone trying to flee, knowing the witches. 'No way of crossing the Rustway then?'

'There are a few boats . . .'

'Any big enough to take the horses?'

'Should think so,' said Willas. 'One of them's a witch warship.'

'Saviours,' muttered Megan.

She pulled out the map, looking for the next crossing point. This was the last one between them and Statham, at the mouth of the river. It looked as if they were going to have to knock up rafts or swim. On the other hand . . .

'How many men would the witches have on this ship?' she asked.

Willas translated the question and the subsequent answer. 'About fifteen or twenty.'

'Not *im*possible odds.'

'And we do have the benefit of surprise.'

'Shall we go take a look?'

Megan and Willas dismounted and crept down to the treeline. The town of Samsun lay a hundred yards below, a smattering of houses, none occupied if the lack of chimney trails on a winter's day was anything to go by. The bridge was reduced to two stumps on each bank. Barges bobbed on the sluggish river, making half-hearted attempts to escape their moorings. And there, docked beside the solitary pier, was the witches' ship.

'Why've they stopped here?' asked Megan. 'New Statham's only a few miles upriver.'

'They're avoiding the guns,' said Willas. He pointed to a horse and cart that was rattling down the packed-mud road. Witches moved out to meet it. 'And taking on supplies.'

Not just any supplies. Megan recognized the design of the barrels in the cart: gunpowder. The witches were arming the ship, preparing for any Sandstrider vessels that broke free of Gwyneth's bombardment. But until they got the gunpowder on the ship . . .

'Captain, how good are your archers?'

As the trio of fire arrows arced towards the cart, Megan thought they weren't going to make it, that they'd drop short or putter out or the witches would have time to throw up their shields to protect their cargo. And even as they hit – two arrows directly thudding into barrels – she thought the witches would have time to grab the gunpowder and throw it in the river. And when the explosion ripped through Samsun with a ferocity that sent shrapnel flying all the way to the trees, she thought it would be mere moments before the witches dusted themselves down and came charging after them.

But nothing emerged from the clouds bar a couple of figures, the grey dust that engulfed them giving them the impression of walking – or, rather, staggering – statues. More-conventional arrows took them out.

The platoon tied scarves over their mouths and noses and advanced, leaving the archers behind them to cover their approach. They reached the buildings. Megan could hear the crackling of a fire: the product of a shattered lantern or a candle sent flying. She recalled blowing up the ships on the Speed, the ignition of the Smallwood Marshes, the destruction of the witches' fleet in the Sarason Sea. No matter how much she professed to hate death and destruction, she kept on doing it. It was another reason she had to step down when all this was over, to stop herself. Because she'd always find enemies to fight if she was prepared to look.

The archers ceased their arrows. Willas sent his men into the mist. Megan crouched, knives gripped tight in her hands, waiting for any witches who might decide to make a break for it, praying none would. The clang of metal on metal sounded from within the clouds, followed by hollers. Wordless cries of confusion and terror, then barked orders as the surviving witches tried to organize themselves. Megan caught snatches of phrases: 'fall back', 'the ship', 'the Saviour'. Her mind whirled with fear at the last. They had Cate? How? Fordel: had he bought them off? No, she realized. It wasn't *her* daughter they were talking about.

Flames flickered in the corner of her eye. The fire archers advancing down the hill, getting in position to fire on the ship. If they hit its gunpowder store . . .

Megan raced to intercept them. 'Stop!' she shouted, waving her arms frantically.

The archers paused, looking at each other confused. Their flaming arrows licked at the air, dashes of colour in the grey that smothered the environment, their heat prickling Megan's skin.

Boots pounded behind her. 'What the hell?' said Willas.

'The ship! Gwyneth's baby's on it!'

'Huh? How do you . . . ?' Willas looked to the river. 'Even more reason to take it out. The witches would have nothing to fight for.'

'She's my niece! An innocent baby!'

Megan couldn't let them do this. It was impossible to think of Gwyneth's child and not see her own. She couldn't sacrifice her.

Willas pointed to the ship. 'Target the—'

Light flashed through the clouds. A boom thundered. Everyone instinctively threw themselves to the ground and covered their head. Another boom. The ship was firing its guns.

'Hit that thing before it hits us!' yelled Willas.

One of the archers struggled back to his feet. He grabbed his dropped fire arrow and re-notched his bow, his glove smouldering as the flames licked it. He drew, aimed, released. The arrow leaped into the air and hung there, a miniature sun in the void. Then it dropped, gaining speed, heading for the ship's position.

Its former position. It had cast off and started crawling upriver. Willas jabbed a finger at one of the other archers. 'You!'

'No!' shouted Megan.

'I don't have time to argue!'

'We need to get out of here!'

Willas spun around. The hulk of the witches' ship was inching up the Rustway, approaching them.

337

'Run!'

They scattered just as the ship fired again, all of its guns this time in a single deafening volley that tore up the ground and sent everyone flying.

twenty-eight

Afreyda was stripped and marched out to Saviours' Square where a crude cross had been erected. Two witches tied her to it, each wrist bound to an arm of the 'X' with rough hemp. They left her there for hours, exposed to the world. The world preferred to look away. Citizens averted their gaze, as if making eye contact would mark them out as a sympathizer, next in line to share her fate. Afreyda bore it stoically. Perhaps this would be all she had to endure, perhaps Gwyneth would decide the humiliation was enough.

Gwyneth led Damon out to the balcony at the front of the palace, where her rather more legitimate predecessors would wave to the crowds gathered in the square in lieu of actually meeting them. Tobrytan was off debriefing Sener, leaving Damon to act as Gwyneth's audience. He tried not to look at Afreyda down below them, but there was something about the macabre scene that drew his eye.

'People underestimate whipping,' said Gwyneth.

'They think it's like the quick licks of the belt your father used to give you for being naughty, but it's much, much worse than that. It'll flay the skin, reduce you to nothing more than painful meat. I've heard it said a hundred lashes will kill you.' *There's witch small-talk for you*, thought Damon. 'How many did we settle on in the end, Trymian?'

'A thousand,' said Trymian, stroking the tails of his whip. He had the kind of body that looked as if it had been stitched together from spare parts. He was the witches' torturer, executioner and all-round last guy you wanted to see.

'A thousand. There won't be much left of her by then. Still, it'll make it easier to pack her up and send back to Megan.'

Damon shifted his weight to his other leg. 'What good's this going to do?' he asked.

'She betrayed me for her.'

'Shouldn't you be above this petty jealousy? As queen, I mean. And Mother of the Saviour. God is merciful, or so the rumour goes.'

'Alas, I can only aspire to God's perfection,' said Gwyneth. 'Why do you care?'

'I don't like seeing people's backs being flayed. I'm weird like that.'

'Perhaps you would like to take her place? You can't see your *own* back being flayed.'

'Er . . .'

340

Gwyneth's expression hardened. 'I'm serious. I'm offering you the chance to take Afreyda's place out there. I'll even drop the sentence to five hundred lashes. For old times' sake.'

Damon swallowed. He felt the overwhelming urge to run, only Trymian's lumpy bulk preventing him. God knew he deserved Afreyda's fate. He thought of Eleanor, out there in the icy wastes of the Kartik Mountains. Would he have accepted death if she could have lived? The situation was the same here, wasn't it? He might not love Afreyda like he had Eleanor, but if anyone was innocent in all this, she was.

Gwyneth crooked a finger in beckoning. A servant girl hurried out on to the balcony bearing a goblet of wine. It took a moment for Damon to recognize her: Taite, Sener's former paramour. She had dyed her hair so it was as black as Gwyneth's and arranged it in the same style. Gwyneth had reached the everyone-must-look-like-me stage of tyranny. Ironic, considering what she'd done to the person who looked like her naturally.

Gwyneth patted the empty space on the bench next to her. Taite obediently sat down. 'This brave soldier is about to sacrifice himself for a damsel in distress,' Gwyneth said to her. 'Or not.'

Taite peered over the balustrade, down at the spreadeagled Afreyda. 'She must be very cold.'

'Don't worry. Trymian will soon take her mind off it.

Or maybe we'll bring her inside, sit her in front of the fire with some warm clothes and a hot tea.' Gwyneth looked up to Damon. 'Your choice.'

Damon prevaricated. Sweat rolled down his brow despite the temperature. Any escape relied on him being able to get Afreyda out and not reduced to a set of extremities. But escape would be pointless if she was dead. But the thought of the lash stripping off his skin turned his insides to ice. But he owed her for saving him from the Hilites. But he couldn't conquer his fear.

'No?' said Gwyneth. Damon didn't react, unwilling to commit himself either way, still hoping a few seconds more would present him with an alternative. 'Very well. Trymian, you may begin.'

Trymian lumbered away. Damon knew what he should do. He should run after him, rip off his tunic, offer himself up. But he remained rooted to the spot, unable to muster up even a token objection.

Down below, a detachment of witches escorted Trymian across the square to Afreyda. A crowd gathered around them: a few passers-by who stopped to watch at first, then an ever-thickening circle as the contagion of morbid curiosity spread. Trymian ran a finger down Afreyda's naked back. She winced. He leaned in closer – was he sniffing her, trying to smell her fear? She jerked her head back, catching Trymian on what could be called his nose only by a process of elimination. He staggered back.

342

The crowd held its breath, as they waited for his reaction. He dabbed a finger on the stream of blood trickling down his chin, grinning as he tasted it.

The whip cracked against the blameless air. A test. The crowd took a collective step backwards; Afreyda's muscles tensed as she clenched her fists. Trymian circled the whip above his head. The square was so silent Damon could make out the *whoosh* as it ripped through the atmosphere.

A thought suddenly came to him. The formula – he still had the copied gunpowder formula hidden in his boot. Damon had a duty to get it to Janik. The Realm needed it to defend itself from the witches, the Snow Cities and God knew who else. Even Megan would have to accept Afreyda's sacrifice for the millions of the Faithful.

But as the leather tails sped towards Afreyda he knew it was an excuse not a reason, that he'd made his mind up long before he remembered the formula. And as the crack of the whip was obliterated by Afreyda's scream of agony he knew he'd only ever admit it to himself.

Spitting dirt from her mouth, Megan pushed herself up. She tapped her temple with the heel of her hand, hoping to dislodge the bells ringing in there. She succeeded only in aggravating the throbbing behind her eyes.

'Everyone all right?' she called out. Her voice sounded wrong and distant, as if she was listening to someone fifty yards away doing an impression of her.

Willas struggled to his feet and said something Megan couldn't understand. Had the bombardment scrambled her brains? Willas repeated himself, this time in a language Megan could decipher.

'Better go check.'

The final count was one man dead, three with injuries that needed tending. In purely numerical terms a victory, but Megan couldn't stop the guilt gnawing away at her. Were Afreyda and Damon worth the lives she was spending? Was the gunpowder formula? Why not let Fordel and his puppets rule over a unified Werlavia: couldn't she find justification for that in the Book of Faith?

No, it would lead to resentment and dissent and rebellion and tyranny and civil war. Only freedom could ensure peace, freedom for the Realm, the Snow Cities, Andaluvia, maybe even the witches. But you could never have freedom as long as one side had the means to destroy the others with ease.

Megan picked her way through the stripped bodies of the witches. She reached the group of injured men, where Willas was stitching up a gash in a man's arm. She stared upriver. The ship could just be made out in the haze. How long before it reached New Statham?

Willas looked up from his needlework. 'We could go after it.'

'So we could kill an innocent child?'

'You've never thought of it?'

344

Megan's instinct was to deny the accusation. She stopped herself. 'I had this dream once. We were out on the Speed, Gwyneth and me. She had her baby with her and I was trying to ram her boat with mine. I thought if I could sink them, it'd be all over. I'd be safe. Cate'd be safe.'

'What happened?'

'I fell in the river, then woke up to find it was raining.' She let out a hollow laugh. 'I told Eleanor we should've camped somewhere with better cover.'

Megan turned away from the ship. 'I don't think it would have made any difference if I had killed her. The witches would fight no matter what, Saviours or no. There's too much anger, too much bitterness, too many souls crying out for vengeance. On both sides. We either wipe each other out or learn to live with each other.'

Willas's needle slipped, prompting a howl from his patient. Willas snapped something, the Hilite equivalent of 'don't be such a baby', Megan assumed.

'You want to make peace?'

'It might be the only way. If we have to lay siege to New Statham, Saviours know how many will die.'

'After everything they've done?'

'What about the Snow Cities?' said Megan. 'Our fight with you lasted a couple of centuries longer than our war with the witches. And here we are, allies.'

'The witches would never agree.'

'Some might.'

'And the rest?' asked Willas.

Before Megan could answer that, there was a call down from the waterline. One of the barges they'd commandeered to ferry the company across the Rustway had returned and was waiting for them. Time to resume their journey. And hope it wasn't in vain.

twenty-nine

Trymian was on his fifth – or was it his sixth? – lash when Tobrytan hurried on to the balcony and whispered something in Gwyneth's ear. Her pose snapped from languid to upright. There was a touch of alarm in her eyes.

'Are you sure?'

'Yes, Mother.'

Gwyneth signalled to Trymian and shook her head. He froze. Blood oozed down the tails of his whip and collected at the tips. Afreyda slumped against the cross, her back lacerated, only her bindings keeping her upright.

'Bring the guns round,' said Gwyneth.

'They're on the other side of the city dealing with the Sandstriders,' said Tobrytan. 'It'll take time.'

'Better start immediately then.'

Gwyneth rose and headed inside. She stopped at the threshold and turned to Damon. 'See to her,' she said to Damon, pointing down at the square below. 'Don't let her die.'

'Me?'

'Didn't you once claim to have medical training?'

It took a moment for Damon to get his calcified legs moving. He dashed through the palace, almost tripping over his own feet, and out into Saviours' Square. The crowd, sensing the entertainment was over, was beginning to disperse. He reached Afreyda and called out her name. She lifted a weary head. Tears soaked her face. Her eyes were empty, as if Trymian had driven out her soul.

'Are you all right?'

It was the stupidest question in the history of stupid questions. Still, it prompted Afreyda's lips to twitch. 'Itchy back.'

'Hang in there.'

'That is not funny.'

Damon pointed to a couple of witches. 'You two, cut her down.' They hesitated. 'The Mother commanded it.'

The witches produced serrated daggers and sawed away at the ropes holding Afreyda up. She fell into Damon's arms, shrieking as he inadvertently touched her back. He whispered a volley of apologies and shrugged off his cloak, which he carefully draped over her shoulders. Even that soft touch was enough to make Afreyda grimace and bring a fresh round of tears to her eyes.

'We need to get you inside,' said Damon. 'Can you walk?'

Afreyda nodded. She placed a hand on Damon's

shoulder – he was too scared of hurting her to reciprocate the touch – and hoisted herself up. The two of them stumbled into the palace: Afreyda's steps slow and shaky; Damon's not much better.

Trymian was hulking in the atrium. He smiled. Or at least half his mouth moved in an approximately upwards direction.

'Nine hundred and ninety-five to go.'

'Are you sure?' said Afreyda. 'I do not think the third one counted.'

'Bravado, eh? Never lasts.'

Damon helped Afreyda into an antechamber and laid her face down on a couch. He lit all the candles he could find, then knelt down in front of her.

'I'm going to see what the damage is, all right?'

'Yes.'

He placed a tentative hand on the cloak covering Afreyda. 'This might hurt a bit,' he said.

'Just do it.'

Clenching his teeth as if he was the one with his skin ripped off, Damon peeled the cloak off Afreyda, hating the excess force he had to use, the tearing sounds that scraped his nerves, the fresh streams of blood that welled up. Afreyda screamed and gripped the side of the couch.

Damon folded the cloak over her legs. Her back was lacerated, bloody muscle exposed, skin hanging off in tattered strips.

'What *is* the damage?' asked Afreyda, her voice quivering.

'I need to get you cleaned up.'

'That bad?'

Damon called for servants. One he dispatched for soap and hot water, one for bandages, another for pen and ink. They obeyed without question, whether out of sympathy for Afreyda or because Gwyneth's order had percolated down, he didn't know.

The pen and ink arrived first. Damon scribbled a list on a scrap of parchment and handed it to the servant who had brought the pen. 'You know the apothecary by the statue of Aldwyn the Unfortunate?' he said. The servant nodded. 'Tell him I want everything on here. As much as you can carry.'

The servant's eyes widened as he read. 'Some of these are . . .'

'. . . a tiny bit forbidden, yes.'

'How do you know he'll have them?'

'Trust me, the bastard'll have them. Take a couple of soldiers with you, under the Mother's orders. They should make sure he gives you the real stuff.'

Damon turned back to Afreyda. It was impossible to apply any kind of pressure to her back, so he had to settle for dribbling water on to her wounds. Even that was enough to make her gasp.

'Talk to me,' she said.

'You normally tell me to do the opposite.'

'I need a distraction,' said Afreyda. 'Why did they stop?'

Damon trickled some more water on her. It left the sponge clear, ran off her pink. 'I don't know,' he said. 'Tobrytan brought a message for Gwyneth. They looked worried.'

'Megan is here.'

'You can't know that.'

'I can,' said Afreyda, 'because she loves me like I love her and it is what *I* would do.' She wriggled on the couch, trying to find a more comfortable position. From the pained look in her eyes, she didn't succeed. 'They will want to use me as a hostage. Maybe even you.'

'Me?'

'No, you are right, that is a stupid idea.'

By the time Damon had finished cleaning Afreyda's wounds, the servant had returned from the apothecary. Damon rummaged about in the sack he dumped on the floor. 'I'm going to have to put some ointments on your cuts.'

Afreyda looked wary. 'You are going to touch me?'

'Afraid so,' said Damon. 'That's why I got you this.'

He offered Afreyda a phial. Her eyes narrowed as she read the label. 'If this is what I think it is,' she said, 'it is banned in the empire.'

'Banned pretty much everywhere. Drink up.'

Afreyda tilted her head back and poured the contents

of the phial down her throat. She shuddered. An icy energy filled her eyes.

'Why is this stuff banned?' she gasped.

'Ask me again in a few hours.'

Damon treated and bandaged an increasingly excited Afreyda and got her into the only clothes he could find: a servant girl's gown. 'It's weird seeing you in a dress,' he said.

'I *know*,' said Afreyda. 'Do you want me to give you a twirl?'

She leaped to her feet and spun, the fabric of her gown circling around her. 'It is so light!' She accelerated, lost control of her feet, tumbled to the floor with an anguished yelp.

Damon picked her to her feet. 'Deep breaths. The rush'll wear off soon. Here.' He poured some water and made her drink. 'We need to get out of here before Gwyneth decides what to do with us.'

'How?' Afreyda beamed. 'Do you want me to kill everybody?'

'I was thinking of something a little less doomed to failure within the first minute. Edwyn the Third built an escape tunnel out of here.'

'From his own city?'

'He foresaw an occasion when that ownership might be contested,' said Damon.

'You talk funny.'

'The entrance is in the east wing of the palace.'

'Where is that?'

'East.'

Afreyda bounced on her feet. 'Do you want to race?'

'Probably best to act inconspicuous,' said Damon. 'Act like we're going exactly where we should be going. Do you think you can manage that?'

'If anyone asks, I will tell them we are not escaping.'

The main doors of the palace had been sealed. Witches were everywhere, weapons drawn, an eagerness to use them etched on their faces. Were they really this scared of Megan? Had they worked themselves up over a self-created adversary, like a child imagining monsters under the bed, or was there something outside the city he wasn't going to like?

Damon led Afreyda out of the antechamber and across the vast atrium, painfully aware of how much noise their footsteps were making. Dozens of gazes followed them. Powerful hands twisted axe shafts as if they were strangling chickens.

Afreyda leaned in to Damon. 'Are you sure you don't want me to kill them all?' she asked, her whisper a tad too loud for his liking.

'Yes,' he hissed back.

An officer stepped forward. 'Where're you going?'

'We are not escaping,' said Afreyda, beaming.

'The Mother wants to see her,' said Damon.

'What's with the bag?' asked the officer.

'That's no way to talk about . . . oh . . .' Damon lifted the sack from the apothecary. 'Medical supplies. The Mother wants her alive.' Afreyda patted her chest proudly. 'But she said nothing about sane . . .'

'I'll have to confirm it with——'

Without warning, the doors of the palace crashed open and a squad of heavily armed witches marched in. Huddled in their midst Damon could make out a woman in a white gown, her arms clasping a bundle to her chest. There was a wail. Not a bundle. A baby.

He looked to the officer. 'Is that . . . ?'

The rapt expression on the officer's face confirmed Damon's unfinished question. The baby was Jolecia, Gwyneth's daughter, Megan's niece, would-be princess of the Realm and Saviour of the True.

The squad swept past, heading for the interior of the palace. Damon pointed at their receding numbers. 'We'll just be . . .'

The officer nodded, distracted. Damon nudged Afreyda forward.

'Hey!'

Damon froze. The officer beckoned to two soldiers. 'Escort these two to the Mother.'

'She told us to meet her in the east wing,' said Damon.

The officer's brow furrowed. 'She's in the royal apartments with the general.'

'I'm just going where she told me to. If you want me to take a detour, I'll let her know it was your suggestion, Lieutenant . . . ?'

The officer was in no rush to supply Damon with his name. 'Escort them to the east wing. If they try anything funny –' he gave Damon a knowing look – 'keep them alive.'

They wound their way through the twisting corridors of the palace, which could have been a physical manifestation of Edwyn the Third's state of mind or an attempt to confuse the hell out of invaders. The passing traffic faded out until it was just Damon and Afreyda and the two witches, the stomp of their boots remorseless. Damon's heart was beating fast enough to smash its way through his ribs. He had to think of some way to get rid of their escorts, and soon. Escape attempts went so much smoother when you didn't bring your jailers for the ride.

'What is it with you and Gwyneth?' asked Afreyda.

'She likes me.'

'Really?'

'In the way you like Megan.'

Afreyda slammed to a halt. Their escorts almost collided with them. 'You and she . . . ?'

'It's not like I had a choice in the matter.'

She turned on Damon, anger so intense her eyes

flicked in every direction. 'How could you betray Megan like this? I should kill you for this!'

'Did you not hear——?'

Afreyda shoved Damon, hard. He went flying into one of the witches. Out of the corner of his eye he saw Afreyda spin fast, her leg snap out, catch the other witch full in the face. Damon realized what she was doing. He grabbed the witch he'd slammed into, as if trying to steady himself, and let his weight drop. It was enough to drag the witch to the ground.

He heard the crack of further blows, the ugly snap of bones breaking, the thud of a deadweight hitting hard tiles. A grunt and the jabbing of elbows into his flesh brought Damon's attention to his own immediate situation, the witch on top of him struggling to get up. A fist rushed towards him. Damon jerked his head aside. Not enough. The punch caught him on the ear, making him howl and the world break into a myriad of colours.

Metal scraped against stone: the witch reaching for his dropped axe. Damon screamed, tried to wriggle free. There was a *whoosh* as the axe split the air. Blood gushed over him. The witch toppled over, his head only half attached to his shoulders.

Dripping axe in one hand, Afreyda helped Damon out from under the corpse. 'You could've warned me,' he said, trying to wipe the worst of the gore away.

'There was no time.'

'Are you going to tell Megan about me and Gwyneth?'

Afreyda regarded him for a moment. 'Not if you do not want me to.' She looked down at the witches. 'We should hide the bodies.'

The witch Afreyda had tackled was stirring. 'I'm not sure he's technically a body,' said Damon. An axe swished. 'My mistake.'

Afreyda tossed the axe aside. 'Come on, help me.'

Damon's attention had been distracted by movement at the end of the corridor. 'We might want to leave the tidying up until later.'

A witch patrol was thundering towards them.

They raced through the palace, lungs burning, legs forever threatening to collapse from under them. Witches chased after them, hollering orders to surrender and loosing the occasional crossbow bolt to reinforce their point. Damon was lost, the sudden dives down side corridors and emergency dashes up winding staircases scrambling his sense of direction. They had to stop navigating by reaction, make at least a nominal attempt to reach the east wing.

The stairs terminated in an oak door. No other way apart from back. Damon opened it and they dived through into a bedchamber beyond and slammed the door shut. Damon rammed the bolt home. Wood shuddered beneath their hands as witches tried to charge their way in. The door was solid, but the bolt was more a polite hint than an absolute barrier. It wouldn't hold for long.

'The bed!' yelled Afreyda.

'You're eager.'

'A barricade!'

Damon dashed around to the bed and shoved it, inch by heavy inch, across the floor while Afreyda continued to hold the door against the pounding witches. She waited until the last second, then rolled across the bed and helped him shove it into place.

The door continued to shake. 'How long do you think we have got?'

'Depends if they've got axes,' said Damon.

On cue, the head of an axe crashed through the door.

'They are witches,' snapped Afreyda. 'Of course they have axes.'

Damon looked around. An archway led out to a balcony. He pulled Afreyda out on to it. The wind tugged at them, making Afreyda's gown ripple like the sea before an oncoming storm. They were six storeys up. Below them stretched the palace complex, larger than many a village. From this height you could see it wasn't a single building but many, jammed together to form a network of streets and courtyards.

'We need to get down,' said Afreyda.

Damon peered over the edge of the balcony. A witch

peered up from the level below. Damon pulled his head back before a crossbow bolt skewered him.

'We will have to go up,' said Afreyda.

'Are you serious?' said Damon.

'It is only one storey to the roof.'

'It's the storeys below us that worry me.'

Inside the bedchamber, splinters showered the air. 'You can stay here and reassure the witches I am not escaping,' said Afreyda.

She hauled herself up. Damon tucked the sack into his belt and clambered up on to the railings, hoping the witch below hadn't had time to reload. He examined the walls. Thick ridges between the stones; enough for a handhold. He stretched and wedged his boot into a gap. *Don't think about what you're doing*, he told himself. *Just do it.* He pushed up, leaving solidity behind. The strain on his fingers and toes was almost unbearable. The wind was sharp enough to make his eyes water. Not being able to see wasn't necessarily a bad thing.

Damon groped for the next handhold, the next foothold, swallowed down the panic of lessening his already tenuous grip. He heaved himself up a couple of feet. How many more times would he have to do this? Ten, twenty, a hundred? A crash of wood, not as distant as he would have liked. Whatever the number was, he had to reduce it to zero.

Muscles screaming in agony, stone scraping the skin

from his fingertips, Damon pulled himself up the wall. He reached for a handhold. Stone crumbled beneath his grip. His pulse raced. He scrabbled along for another hold, found it, hoisted himself up another step before he could realize how close he had come to falling.

His hand hit air. He'd reached the top. 'Here!' Afreyda grabbed his arm. Damon scrambled over the low wall surrounding the roof and rolled on to his back, clinging on to blessed levelness.

'We need another way down,' said Afreyda.

'We only just got here!'

Damon pushed himself up and squeezed his stinging hands in his armpits. They were on the roof of a tower. It was barren apart from a flagpole from which ropes spun out, each one carrying flags bearing the star-broken circle down to the ground.

'There has to be some way,' Afreyda continued. 'A ladder or trapdoor or something.'

'Why?'

'I do not know.' Afreyda pointed at the flagpole. 'The witches have to come up here and change the flags. They will get dirty.'

'Flag cleaners? Your plan relies on *flag cleaners*? Is that even a thing?'

Afreyda tugged one of the ropes stretching off the flags. It was taut, like a giant fiddle string. She eyed the path of its descent, down to an irregular-shaped courtyard that seemed awfully far away, where it was tied to a pole.

'We couldn't cut enough off to get to the bottom,' said Damon.

'Why cut it?' said Afreyda. 'It is already going to the bottom. And eastwards.'

Where they needed to be. That didn't stop apprehension gripping Damon. 'But . . .'

Afreyda jumped up and ripped one of the flags down. She tore it into two and offered one of the halves to Damon. He reluctantly accepted it.

'I don't think you're taking my "but" seriously.'

'We will slide down,' said Afreyda, twisting her half of the flag into a cord.

'Yeah, I got that,' said Damon. 'You done this before?'

'No. That is why you are going first.'

Damon didn't think he had the moral superiority to argue. He sat on the wall surrounding the tower and swung his legs over the edge. The wind whipped up in intensity, trying to push him over. He felt a little dizzy. He clenched his fists. The pressure on his abused fingers sharpened his senses.

Leaning forward, he looped his twisted flag over the rope. 'Are you sure about this?' he asked Afreyda.

'What is the worst that could happen?'

'I fall and shatter every bone in my body,' said Damon.

'Do not be so pessimistic.'

'You asked what was the worst that could happen!'

There was a commotion below. Witches on the balcony. One fired a crossbow. The bolt smacked into the wall a few inches below Damon's feet. The witch's compatriot raised his own weapon. Damon couldn't let him take advantage of the first's sighter. He dropped off the roof.

The jolt as the looped flag halted his descent wrenched his shoulders half out of his sockets. He dangled there, vulnerable, like a carcass in a butcher's shop. The gold light of the setting sun flashed on a crossbow bolt as it whizzed past his head. *Come on*, he urged gravity.

Damon started to pick up speed. Flags batted him as he zipped past them. 'Not quick enough' became 'dangerously fast' without staying anywhere near long enough in 'pleasantly brisk'. Friction was scraping up loose strands of hemp, sand, and was that smoke? The flag split, unravelled a fraction. Severed fibres fluttered in the breeze. *Hold together a few more seconds.*

The courtyard raced towards him, but before that there was another building to zip over. His legs weren't going to clear its roof. Damon pulled them up at the last second before the crenellations would have smashed into his shins. He whizzed past, reached the courtyard. The flag split. The world lurched. Flagstones slammed into his back like a giant fist. But he had made it.

Damon lay there, staring at the sky, waiting for the

throbbing to subside. No sharper pain. Nothing broken. Still, a few minutes' more rest wouldn't hurt. A chance to catch his breath, gather his thoughts—

A figure flashed above his head. Afreyda dropped from the rope and rolled across the courtyard, absorbing the force of the impact. She lay still, curled up. Too still. Blood was creeping across the back of her gown.

Damon crawled over to her. 'Are you all right?'

'Just give me . . . give me . . .'

'We have to get moving,' said Damon. 'It won't take the witches long to get over here.'

He helped Afreyda up. Anguish had replaced her earlier exuberance. 'Have you got any more of that . . . ?'

'Yes,' said Damon. 'And no. Second dose so soon'll blow your head off.'

He tried to get his bearings. There seemed to be no way out of the courtyard, no way back into the palace. They were going to have to break a window. No, wait. An expected corner wasn't there – there was an alleyway leading off. He led Afreyda to it. The world went dark as something clammy smacked into Damon. He peeled fabric from his face. It was a flag. Afreyda gave him a knowing look.

They slalomed around the drying laundry. There was a door at the end of the alley. It was unlocked. Damon eased it open and peered up and down the gloomy corridor beyond. Deserted. Probably not for long.

He recognized where he was: the Sandstriders' block. Not far from the tunnel. The witches hadn't reclaimed this wing of the palace since the Sandstriders had left. Evidence of a hasty retreat was everywhere: spoiling food; wine souring to vinegar; tipped-over mattresses; stray boots; an abandoned ear, welded to a windowsill by a smear of dried blood, as if someone had set it aside, meaning to come back for it. Had its owner survived the witches' bombardment? Had any of the Sandstriders?

Damon led Afreyda to the room where he hoped Edwyn's tunnel started. The knife and spike he had used to pick the lock were still on the floor where he had abandoned them all those months ago. Damon slipped them into his boot and pushed the door open, revealing a bare chamber, chilly with disuse. Undisturbed dust lined the floor tiles like soft carpet. The witches hadn't bothered to check here since he'd tried to escape the day of Gwyneth's coronation. The fanatical mind made little allowance for curiosity.

'Where is this tunnel?' asked Afreyda.

Only one place it could be. 'Fireplace.'

'Are you sure?'

'No ash in the grate. There's never been a fire there.' He poked his head in and looked up the chimney. It was bricked up. Edwyn hadn't been taking any chances.

Damon started to grope about. 'There'll be a lever or a switch or something that'll open a secret door.'

'Where?'

'In a small haberdashery in Eastport. Where do you think it'll bloody be? Start feeling for knobs.'

'You are asking the wrong girl.' Afreyda patted the wall, leaning against it for support. 'How long since this tunnel was last used?'

'Don't think it's ever been used.'

'So it might not be here or it might be blocked up or there could be undead monsters waiting to feast on our brains!'

'Deep breaths,' said Damon.

Afreyda obeyed the command. 'I feel funny.'

'I'm sure you do,' said Damon, continuing to push at bricks and pull on protrusions.

'I hear this strange stomping.'

The noise wasn't a drug-induced hallucination – soldiers were coming. Damon's search picked up pace until he was practically punching the chimney walls. It had to be here, it had to be. Because if it wasn't, they would soon be dead.

'Stand back,' said Afreyda.

'What? Whoa!'

She yanked him away from the fireplace, closed her eyes and marched in. Her hand flicked out, caught something. There was a squeal as hidden gears bit into each other. Stone ground against stone. A slab of stone at the back of the chimney swung open, releasing a blast of dead air.

'How . . . ?'

'I guessed where I would want it if I was a fleeing king.'

The witches were almost on them, their boots an approaching storm. Afreyda squeezed through the gap, squealing as the wall scraped her back. She urged Damon through. He didn't need urging. He forced himself through. They shoved the slab back in place – expelling the last sliver of light – just as the witches crashed into the room.

'Do you think . . . ?' Afreyda whispered.

Damon shushed her and listened. Nobody had seen them come in here, but they'd left footprints in the dust. The sound of the witches was muffled by the thick walls. Impossible to tell what they were doing. But then the unmistakable sound of retreat and silence. They were gone.

Damon and Afreyda let out simultaneous sighs of relief. 'It is very dark in here.'

'That's what that is.'

'Sarcasm will not help us find a way out.'

'You think? Hang on, I brought something for such an occasion.'

Damon unhitched the apothecary's sack and rummaged around in it, trying to remember the shape of the flask he was looking for. Ah, that was it. He searched his tunic pockets. He found one glove but its twin was long lost. It'd do. He pulled it on and uncorked the flask. After a moment, an eerie white glow filled the tunnel.

'What is *that*?' asked Afreyda, her voice hushed.

'Essence of piss,' said Damon. 'You think the empire is the only place with magical chemicals? I thought it'd be a bit suspicious if I asked the servant to bring back a torch from the apothecary.'

He held the flask up to illuminate a tunnel that gently sloped away. It was wide enough to accommodate him and Afreyda walking abreast; tall enough they wouldn't have to duck. Thick wooden struts supported the ceiling at regular intervals, giving the appearance they were in the ribcage of a giant snake. Duckboards, now rotting and smeared green with mould, protected the floor from the water seeping through the mud and rock.

'How long is this tunnel?' asked Afreyda.

'Few miles,' said Damon. 'It looked quite direct on the plan. Quicker than going over ground. Do you know what the traffic's like this time of day?'

They descended slowly, the only sounds their ragged breaths, the *plink* of dripping water and the squelch of mud underfoot. Damon tried not to stare at the ceiling, searching for telltale cracks. Two hundred years of construction work in the city above their heads could have easily weakened the tunnel so it would need only a small push to collapse.

They came to a door. 'We're there already?' said Afreyda.

Damon shook his head. 'I don't think so,' he said.

'Maybe this king of yours had some doors he needed using up.'

'Ah, the third-century door glut. No one saw that coming.'

Afreyda gripped the door handle and took a deep breath. 'If anything goes wrong . . .'

'Scream and run like hell,' said Damon. 'I know the drill.'

Slowly as she could, Afreyda eased the door open. Or at least tried to. It stuck no sooner than it left the frame. She pulled harder. Ancient planks gave way. She lurched backwards, smack into Damon. They tumbled to the ground, light fighting with the shadows as the torch fell from his grasp.

'Pity the door glut didn't make it to the empire,' said Damon. 'You could've got some practice in.'

He got to his feet. A constant plinking was coming from the space Afreyda had exposed, like the aftermath of a rainstorm. He crept forward. A draught raised goose pimples on his neck. A draught? Where was that coming from?

They emerged near the ceiling of a cavernous chamber. A forest of columns rose up from a gently rippling underground lake, calcified trees supporting an impenetrable sky. Stone walkways sprouted from the top of each trunk, branches intermingling among the heavens. Damon walked out on to one and peered down. Reflections from his glowing flask swam in the water far below. Condensation dripped on to his neck, making him shiver.

'What is this place?' asked Afreyda

'Cistern of Aldwynson the Drowned.'

'Who is he?'

'Who *was* he,' said Damon. 'The "drowned" appellation is kind of revealing. Your usual tale of stupidity treated as piety.' He looked around. 'This place provides fresh water for the inner and middle cities. Should have realized we'd have to cross it.'

'How do we get out of here?'

'You're the one with the insight into a fleeing king's mind.'

'We follow the walkways with the railings?'

'Uh-huh,' said Damon. Safety was very important to Edwyn, albeit only his own.

They made their way along the labyrinthine path marked out for them. Stone occasionally crumbled underfoot and pattered down to the reservoir below, and when it did Damon would extend a foot and test the walkway ahead and wish he'd manoeuvred Afreyda into taking the lead.

He could see their destination now: a door set into the

far wall, the companion of the one Afreyda had struggled with. Damon began to formulate wind-ups, then jumped back as the door crashed open and soldiers spilled through.

Soldiers wearing the star-broken circle.

thirty

'Who goes there?' Willas shouted into the cavern.

'Ah, traditionalists, I see.'

Megan didn't need to recognize the voice to identify the flippancy. She pushed her way through the soldiers, almost burning herself on one of their torches. Damon and Afreyda stepped out of the shadows and advanced along the stone walkways. Megan rushed forward and threw herself into Afreyda's arms. Relief flooded through her, and gratitude, and a fear it might be nothing more than a dream.

'I thought . . . I was scared I'd . . .'

Afreyda's tears wetted Megan's cheek. 'I do not want to let you go,' she said, 'but you are really hurting me.'

Megan released her hold and took a step back. 'Why? What is it?'

'Gwyneth,' said Damon. 'Hello, by the way.'

Megan checked her hands. There was a hint of blood on her fingers. 'What did she do to you?' Anger overtook her, followed by guilt. Gwyneth wouldn't have harmed Afreyda if it hadn't been for Megan. 'I'll kill her.'

'It could be worse,' said Afreyda. She looked to Willas. 'You shouldn't have let her come after me.'

'You think I could stop her?' said Willas. 'It's good to see you, captain.'

'And you.' Afreyda managed a smile. 'Captain.'

Damon indicated the soldiers. 'What's with the uniforms?' he asked. 'You scared the hell out of us.'

'We borrowed them from some witches,' said Megan. 'Thought it might give us an edge in the palace.' None of the Faithful had been prepared to don the star-broken circle: old fears died hard. Fortunately the Hilites didn't share such superstitions. 'Gwyneth's still there, I take it?'

'There and panicking about your imminent arrival,' said Damon. 'She's even had her daughter brought back from Andaluvia. Mind you, asking the Sandstriders to continue to babysit would probably have been pushing it a bit.'

Leaving Afreyda in Willas's care, Megan took Damon and led him down the walkway, deeper into the cavern until they were lit not by the warmth of the Hilite torches but the spectral light of Damon's flask.

'Have you still got the formula?' she asked.

Damon pulled a tightly rolled parchment from his boot and handed it over. 'Can we go now?' he asked.

Megan followed the direction of his finger, back the way they had come. It was the right thing to do, get away while she could, while everyone was safe. The right thing for her, but not for the Realm.

'I've been thinking,' she said.

'That's never a good sign.'

'That witch captain. Sener,' said Megan. 'Is he still alive? Is he in New Statham?'

'He was the one who took Afreyda and me prisoners,' said Damon. 'Quite agreeable as captors go. Very rarely hit me.'

'How are things with him and Gwyneth?' asked Megan.

'I don't think they're going to be spending Saviours' Day with each other.'

'And his supporters? How many are there in the city?'

'I have no idea,' said Damon. 'He's not dead yet, so "some" obviously. What are you getting at?'

Footsteps behind them – Afreyda. 'What is . . . ?'

Megan held up a silencing finger. 'Would he move against Gwyneth?' she asked Damon.

'They are True,' said Afreyda. 'They do not betray one another.'

'You'd be surprised,' muttered Damon.

'They're more pragmatic than they let on,' said Megan. 'They escaped from Trafford's Haven, they fought for the Diannon Emperor, they abandoned Eastport, they held New Statham when they could have thrown every last man at us at the Arrowstorm Pass. They're interested in staying alive.'

'Not as your prisoner,' said Afreyda.

'That's not what I'm offering them.'

'Then what?' asked Damon.

'What the priests wouldn't,' said Megan. 'Freedom. The right to live in peace, practise their religion any damned way they please.'

'After what they've done?' said Damon.

'How do you know they would not come after Cate?' asked Afreyda.

'Because I'm only offering it to those witches who don't believe she's the Saviour,' said Megan.

'And the rest?' asked Damon. 'Gwyneth?' Megan gave him a meaningful look. 'Oh, and I thought she was the cold-hearted one.'

'I need you to arrange a meeting between Sener and me.'

The blood drained from Damon's face. 'You don't . . .'

'I need you to go back to the palace.'

'There's no way in hell I'm going back there,' said Damon. 'The witches'll kill me on sight.'

'You know how to stop them seeing you.'

'No, Megan.' Damon pushed past them and headed for the tunnel. 'I got you the formula, I got Afreyda out, and now I'm done. I'm done with risking my life on your whim. I'm walking away now like I should have done a long time ago.'

Megan looked to Afreyda, who shrugged. She dithered for a moment then ran after Damon. She caught up and grabbed his shoulder. He spun around, knocking her off.

'You come to make not entirely humorous threats against me if I don't do what you want?'

'No,' said Megan. 'I've come to offer you forgiveness for what happened to Eleanor if you do.'

The retort died on his lips. He stared at Megan, throat bobbing, hands clenching. Megan stared back, grief and anger and self-loathing mixing like poison in her veins.

'What makes you think I need forgiveness?' said Damon.

'The look on your face every time you hear her name,' said Megan. 'I don't know what you really did up in the mountains, why you did it, how willingly, and I'm not sure if I want to. But I do know what Eleanor would have wanted, what she fought for. Do you think she would have condemned hundreds of thousands of people to die if there was a chance she could prevent it? You always wanted to prove yourself worthy of her. Now's your chance.'

'You manipulative bi—' Damon sighed and leaned on the railing that protected the walkway. Rust flaked off and floated down to the lake below. 'I'm sorry. I didn't . . .'

'No, you're right,' said Megan. 'I am my mother's daughter. For better and for worse. But I meant what I said. Show me you care about something more than your own skin. *Please.*'

'Why do you care about turning Sener? You have an army.'

'Because I'm not prepared to see hundreds of thousands die in a siege. Because I don't want to give Fordel the excuse to march his guns into the Realm. Because I want to right a decades-old wrong.'

Damon snorted. 'You want to piss off the witches, the priests *and* the Snow Cities?'

'What do you say?'

'Can I at least wait until nightfall?'

thirty-one

Damon slipped back into the palace and considered his options. He could give it an hour then turn back, tell Megan he couldn't find Sener – how likely was he to agree to talk to Megan, anyway, never mind to her request? He was on a fool's errand, all to assuage Megan's conscience. It was an errand to assuage his own conscience too, though he doubted risking his life would gain him absolution from what he had done – or not done – up in the Kartiks.

A barked order echoing off the stone walls made his testicles retreat into his body with an implicit cry of 'Nice knowing you'.

'You! Stop!'

'Me?'

'See anyone else skulking around in the shadows?'

'No,' said Damon, 'but they might be really good at it.'

The soldier approached. Steel armour. Not good. He was one of the original True, not a convert they had press-ganged. The original followers tended to be a little less flexible.

'What're you doing?'

'Skulking,' said Damon. 'I thought we'd already established that.'

'Why?'

'Are we talking philosophically, theologically or ontologically?'

The soldier looked him up and down. One of the Hilites had given up his True uniform. Damon was hoping most of the witches wouldn't recognize him, and it wasn't as if they would be expecting him to return.

'I have a message for Captain Sener,' said Damon. 'From the Mother.' He didn't specify which one.

'The Mother wants to speak to Sener?'

Damon nodded. 'She said it's urgent.'

'And she sent you?' said the soldier.

Damon nodded.

The soldier considered for a moment, then beckoned to Damon. Damon grabbed a torch from its sconce and followed. Through darkened corridors they marched, running into only one other soldier, who had a whispered conversation with Damon's escort before rushing off. Most of the troops must be manning the walls, guarding Gwyneth, or out in the city, indulging in the odd spot of miscellaneous oppression.

They descended into the basement. Stone walls

became iron bars. The air became thicker, not altogether pleasant to breathe. The hairs on Damon's neck rose. They were in the dungeons: row upon row of cells, fetid black holes gouged out of the ground beneath the palace. Most were empty, home only to obese rats who screeched defiantly at them as they marched past, all except one. A man in the scraps of a uniform hunched on the floor. Sener.

'Saviours . . .' whispered Damon.

A woman's voice made him whirl round. 'Hello, lover.'

'This is not what it looks like,' said Damon.

'What does it look like?' asked Gwyneth. Tobrytan and a squad of soldiers were at her side.

The torch burning close to his head was making Damon's temple sweat. 'I'm not sure. It just seemed the right thing to say.'

'You had a message for Sener? A message from me?'

Gwyneth took a step forward. The soldiers moved up with her. Damon would have been impressed with the synchronization had it not brought the witches' axes a yard closer. He looked around, calculating escape routes, wondering if throwing his torch at Gwyneth would give him enough of a head start. No chance.

'I appreciate you taking the time out for a bit of melodramatic intimidation,' he said, 'but shouldn't you be doing something more practical? Like getting the hell out of New Statham or negotiating the terms of your surrender?'

'Why would we surrender?' asked Gwyneth.

'You've only got a couple of months before a besieging army turns up,' said Damon. 'An army with bigger guns than yours.'

'We can hold out. We have God on our side.'

'Without the Saviours?'

'Who says we don't have them?'

Damon was thrown. There was a satisfied smirk on Gwyneth's face. This wasn't a bluff. There was reality behind her words. A horrible reality.

'We allowed our enthusiasm, our hubris, to get the better of us,' continued Gwyneth. 'We should not have shown ourselves before we had secured the Saviours. We tried to reunify the Realm before we were ready. God gave us a glimpse of what we could achieve, then allowed the Apostate to destroy it.'

She moved in closer, close enough Damon could catch her rosewater scent above the stench of body odours permeating the cells, close enough he could see the rise and fall of her breathing underneath the white silk of her gown, close enough to dread the fanaticism burning in her eyes.

'We did not fulfil Joanne's prophecy – I might have known Megan would let me down – that is why we failed. I've taken steps to correct that.'

'What . . . what kind of steps?'

Gwyneth took Damon's free hand and placed it on her stomach. 'Congratulations,' she whispered into his ear.

The torch fell from Damon's grasp and sputtered away on the damp flagstones. He stumbled backwards, trying to put whatever distance he could between Gwyneth, her revelation, and himself. Witches grabbed him, held him still.

Gwyneth smiled and nodded. 'You're going to be a daddy.'

'Posthumously of course,' added Tobrytan.

Born to a dead father. 'You can't . . .' stammered Damon. 'You can't be . . .'

The witches seemed to be mocking Damon's distress. Gwyneth had used him and she was going to kill him and his child would be one of them – cruel and heartless, hated and feared. Not because of their own choice or own mistakes, but because their father had condemned them to be so.

'Wait . . . wait. There's two Saviours. What're you going to do about the other one? There's no way you're getting Megan pregnant again.'

Gwyneth pouted. 'You think I don't learn from my mistakes?' She motioned to the soldiers, who parted to form a corridor through their ranks. 'I'd like you to meet my sister.'

Damon was confused. The witches had captured Megan? No, the young woman who stepped forward was

Taite, Sener's paramour. Former paramour, it was safe to say, judging from the look on the captain's face.

'When is your birthday, sister?'

'The sixth day of midsummer, Your Majesty. Three hundred and thirty-seven years after Unification.' The same day as Gwyneth and Megan. And four score years after the parents of Jolecia and Ahebban.

'Attor took Joanne's prophecy too literally,' said Gwyneth. 'Taite and I were born under the same stars. We're astrological sisters. God guided me to her.'

The words of the prophecy played themselves out in Damon's mind. '"*And in their sixteenth year,*"' he found himself muttering, '"*a Saviour each will bear.*" Aren't you seventeen? And you'll be eighteen by the time—'

'Joanne was wrong,' snapped Gwyneth. She recovered her demeanour. 'A minor mistake. She could not see the future perfectly.'

'She does keep making minor mistakes, doesn't she?' said Damon. 'She can't get the ages right, the sexes of the Saviours. What next? Maybe it wasn't four score years, maybe it was five.'

He anticipated the blow and was rolling with it even as the axe shaft smashed into his shoulder blades. It didn't stop it hurting like mad, didn't stop the nausea clamping his stomach from erupting into acidic mush that burned his throat.

The witches holding Damon wrenched his arms so

382

hard he wondered if their planned method of execution was dismemberment. 'I know things,' he said, squirming in a vain effort to relieve the pressure. 'Useful things. About Megan and the Hilites and their plans. You don't have to kill me.'

Gwyneth stroked his cheek. 'We're not going to kill you.'

'You aren't?'

'Not until dawn anyway. The hour mandated by the Book of the True for executions.'

Damon slumped on the stone block and stared up at the rancid ceiling of the cell, the throbbing in his arms and shoulders nothing compared to what tormented his thoughts. A baby; his baby; Gwyneth's baby. He'd had little choice in the matter, but that didn't exempt him from fatherhood. Now his child was about to suffer the same fate the witches had had lined up for Megan's.

Megan. He still had a mission to complete for her, for Eleanor. He waited until the receding footsteps indicated the retreat of the last of the guards, before scurrying across the cell to Sener. The captain had resumed his maudlin hunch, contemplating the wet stones under his knees. Gwyneth had used him like she'd used Damon and Megan and the poor saps she'd got to father the first pair of babies. Damon had met one of them once – Wade, he thought his name was – a frightened boy who'd realized too late what

Gwyneth had in store for him. He'd run away. It hadn't saved him.

Damon shook Sener. The captain raised his head and regarded him with a weary expression. 'What?'

'I can get us out of here,' said Damon, pulling out the knife and spike he had concealed in his boot.

'And then what?'

'And then there's someone who wants to talk to you,' said Damon.

Sener's mouth started forming a 'who' before he answered his own question. '*Her?*'

'You want to live? End the war? Talk to Megan. Listen to her.'

'What can she offer?'

'She's Queen of Werlavia. She has every force on the continent aligned against you,' said Damon. 'She can offer you anything she damn well pleases.'

'At what price?'

'Well . . .'

'I will not turn against the True,' said Sener. 'It would be a betrayal of God and the Saviours.'

Damon had been expecting this. Honour before sense: it was practically the witches' motto. He had one final roll to him, but was it worth the price he'd pay for it? This time he couldn't load the die, this time he was at the mercy of fate and a large man who could get very angry very quickly.

'How about turning against the people who killed your father?'

'What?'

'Tobrytan killed the general. Smothered him.'

'How do . . . ? How do you know?'

Damon edged out of Sener's reach. 'I was there.'

'Why?' asked Sener, his voice low and dangerous.

'Because –' bars banged into Damon's back – 'because Gwyneth sent me there. To . . . to kill him.'

The air between Damon and Sener crystallized into ice. 'You were going to kill my father?'

'You're over-focusing on side issues.'

Sener uncurled himself and stalked towards Damon. Damon fumbled with the knife, held it between them. Sener slapped it away without breaking stride.

'It was Gwyneth and Tobrytan who wanted him dead, not me,' gabbled Damon as Sener reached for him. 'I didn't even touch him. I was just trying to stay alive.' Fingers wrapped around his throat. 'Kill me, what do you gain? Who avenges your father?'

'God will avenge him.'

Damon's vision blurred. 'Are you not –' he gasped for a scrap of breath – 'the instrument of God's vengeance?'

Sener paused his squeezing. Damon sucked in air while he had the chance. 'And I suppose He sent you as His messenger?'

'Was my arrival at this time a coincidence?' said Damon. 'Think about it.'

He reached up and plucked Sener's hands from his neck. The captain didn't resist. Damon crouched down, retrieved the knife and sidled over to the cell gate.

'Keep a look out while I attack this lock.'

'Are you one of us? Or one of them?'

'I'm one of me.'

Damon slipped his tools into the lock. It was old and basic. 'I didn't want to come here. I'd be happy to see you all starve or burn or die in a hail of gunfire.' *And I could really have done without knowing about a child who's doomed no matter who out of Megan or Gwyneth wins this bloody war.*

The lock clicked open. Damon eased the gate open as gently as he could, wincing as the rusty iron shrieked as if the souls of the desperate were trapped in the metal.

'Give me the knife,' said Sener.

'Can I trust you?'

'As much as I can trust you.'

'In that case . . .' Damon pulled the knife away from Sener's outstretched hand. 'Only kidding.' He handed the blade over. 'Happy stabbing.'

He turned his back as Sener crept down the dungeon, tried to ignore the sounds of metal ripping through flesh, of bones crunching against stone, pleas for mercy cut brutally short. Damon hadn't killed the guards directly or forced them to fight for Gwyneth or to believe in the witches' cause, but he shared responsibility for their deaths. He could see why Megan was so desperate to avoid a siege. Having that many deaths on your conscience would be unbearable.

thirty-two

Megan took Afreyda down to the bottom of the cistern and washed her wounds in its icy waters. Gently as she could, she applied the ointment as Damon had instructed and re-bandaged her. Each time Afreyda whimpered or grabbed Megan to distract herself, Megan felt a lash almost as bad as the ones Afreyda had suffered.

'I'm sorry,' she whispered.

'It was my decision to go,' said Afreyda.

'I could have ordered you not to,' said Megan. 'I *should* have ordered you not to. I am queen.'

'And if you had, what would have happened? We might be safe in Hil, but Damon could have been killed, we would have lost the formula –' Afreyda gave Megan a knowing look that made her wince – 'and there would be nothing to stop Fordel. We can speculate on what we should have done or not done but we cannot know. We can only deal with the things we *did* do.'

Megan helped Afreyda into a spare Hilite uniform.

'Do you think I'm doing the right thing? Trying to reach a deal with the witches.'

'You are the queen,' said Afreyda. 'It is not for me to say.'

'You could just say no, you know,' said Megan. Afreyda stayed silent. 'It'll probably come to nothing. Damon probably won't find this Sener, and even if he does he probably won't agree.'

'But whatever happens, we are leaving, right?'

'I guess . . .'

'What?' said Afreyda, her voice sharpening.

'It's just that . . . my niece is in there . . . What's going to happen to her?'

'I am sure she will be fine.'

'Really?' said Megan. 'She's my family –' she looked Afreyda in the eye – '*our* family. I can't let her—'

Afreyda's head snapped up. A white glow dancing about up among the stone treetops: Damon's strange chemical. A soldier called out a command to halt. The echoes repeated his order like a childish ghost.

'They are back,' said Afreyda. 'We should . . .'

'I suppose,' said Megan. 'You OK to climb?'

They hauled themselves up a ladder and on to the network of walkways that criss-crossed the heights of the cistern. Damon had a companion, a bulky man in the remnants of a witch's uniform. He was carrying an axe that didn't look a stranger to decapitation.

'Are you Sener?' Megan asked.

The man nodded. 'And you're . . . What do I call you exactly?'

'I'm not fussed.'

'You don't look like her.'

'I'm a little lesser in the ear department,' said Megan.

'It's not that . . .' Sener shook his head. 'This waste of space –' he half indicated, half swiped in Damon's direction – 'tells me you want to talk.'

'This waste of space broke you out of prison.'

'Joanne's prophecy,' said Megan. 'What do you think of it?'

'About the same as you, I imagine.'

'You have no interest in my daughter.'

'I couldn't care less about the brat.'

Megan flinched but swallowed her reaction. 'And there are others who think like you do?'

'Possibly . . .'

This time anger did get the better of her. 'Don't be bloody coy,' she snapped. 'I didn't come here for some diplomatic flirtation. How many are there of you, and are you prepared to take up arms against your fellow wi— your fellow True?'

'Some of the original True are still loyal to me and my father,' said Sener, 'and the conversion of some of the auxiliaries was less than –' he glanced at Damon – 'sincere. What do we get in return?'

'Your lives. Your freedom.'

'Your forgiveness?'

'You have got to be—'

Sener gave her a humourless smile. 'Just seeing how far you're willing to go.'

'Even I have my limits.'

'We are not converting to the Faith,' said Sener. 'No priest will tell us what to believe.'

'I'm not asking you to convert,' said Megan. 'People can worship whom they want, how they want, where they want, when they want. It's no damned business of mine.' She looked him in the eye. 'But I don't want anyone left who could be a threat to my daughter.'

Sener bowed to Megan, possibly only half mockingly. 'And so begins the glorious reign of Megan . . . Megan the what? The Reunifier?'

'Megan the Abdicating-As-Soon-As-All-This-Is-Bloody-Over.'

'You're handing power back to the priests?'

'No.'

'Then who?'

'Thought I'd let the people rule themselves,' said Megan.

'You were among the barbarians in the Snow Cities too long,' said Sener.

Willas reached for his sword. 'Watch what you're saying.'

'You taught it to speak?'

Steel rasped on leather. 'All right, all right,' said Megan, stepping between them. 'Can we leave the laceration to a more appropriate time?'

'You mean when there *isn't* a war on?' said Damon.

Megan silenced him with a filthy look and turned back to Sener. 'You'll be the people too.'

'A very distinct minority of the people.'

'Not my fault you haven't made many friends,' said Megan. 'Are you with us or not?'

'We won't surrender our weapons,' said Sener.

The demand rankled with Megan. Her plan relied on every side being too well armed to risk fighting any of the others, but to leave the witches in a position where they could do this all again? 'You can keep your blades,' she said. 'The guns you leave.'

'And where do we go?'

'Wherever you want. The Realm's a big place. You might find somewhere the people don't want to take revenge. But keep out of Ainsworth.'

Sener gave her a curt nod. 'I wonder what would have happened if we'd had you instead of Gwyneth. Maybe I could have believed you were the Mother of the Saviours.'

'I would have fought you whatever my circumstances,' said Megan. 'I pledge every day of my life to defend God's people, not rule them. Perhaps it's time you start considering what the Pledges really mean, not how you can twist them.'

Sener made to leave. Megan called out to him. 'One more thing.'

'What?' said Sener, unimpressed.

'Gwyneth's daughter. What's going to happen to her?'

'Nothing good, I should imagine.'

Megan's skin crawled at the implication of Sener's words, imagining Cate in her cousin's place, every horrible thing that could befall her. 'I can't . . .'

'You can't what?' said Sener. 'This is what we agreed.'

'She's a baby.'

'No chance of her putting up a fight then.'

Rage surged within Megan. For one murderous moment she thought of killing Sener where he stood; leaving all the witches to the mercy of Fordel's guns. Sener caught the look in her eye and backed off, raising his palms.

'I'll give orders she's not to be harmed,' he said, 'but I can't promise anything.'

No, he couldn't. In a battle, anything could happen. Too much scope for accidents, especially intentional ones.

Megan watched Sener leave, his torch flitting between the columns like a will-o'-the-wisp until there was nothing left of him bar a thin halo edging the pillars, then turned to Damon. 'Where will they be keeping Gwyneth's daughter?'

'Jolecia?' said Damon. Megan flinched at the name. One of the founders of the True. 'Royal apartments, I guess. Gwyneth has a crib in her room.'

'You know the way?'

'You're not thinking . . .'

'You don't have to come,' said Megan. 'You can give me instructions, draw me a map.'

'You'll get lost,' said Damon. 'You'll need a guide, someone to give you a potted history of the palace, point out interesting architectural details, show you the spot where Aldwyn the Third voided his bowels, that kind of thing.'

'You've done everything I've asked of you,' said Megan. 'You don't have to do this.'

'It's what Eleanor would have wanted.'

Was it? It was all too easy to ascribe her own desires to the absent, the dead, the supernatural. But doing this with someone was better than doing it on her own, even if Damon's presence emphasized the countess's absence.

Afreyda looked to Willas. 'Do you have a spare sword?'

'You're not coming with me,' said Megan. 'Not in your condition.'

'I cannot let you do this alone.'

'I have Damon.'

'As I said, I cannot let you do this alone.'

Damon spread his palms, his outrage only half feigned.

'What does a guy have to do to get any appreciation round here?'

'I'll go with them,' Willas said to Afreyda.

He motioned to two of the soldiers and barked an order. They shuffled on the spot and exchanged the sideways glances of the reluctantly volunteered.

'No,' said Megan. 'Just me and Damon. We'll be fast, stealthy, slip in among the chaos.'

'Do not take any unnecessary risks,' said Afreyda. 'If there is too much danger, get out of there. I need you to come back.'

'Don't worry.'

Megan pulled Afreyda close, pressed their cheeks together, felt the heat of her body, the vitality flowing beneath the smooth skin. Their lips found each other. Passion and fear and love and longing poured into one last kiss Megan wished would never end.

'I will be back,' said Megan, 'because I want to spend the rest of my life with you and I want it to be a long life and I want us to be old and wrinkly and lying in the warm sun while grandchildren and great-grandchildren and great-great-grandchildren skip around us, and I want to say, "Whatever happened to Damon?" and for both of us to have absolutely no idea.'

'Hey!'

'I love you,' said Afreyda.

'I love you too,' said Megan. 'But I have to do this.'

thirty-three

Megan didn't as much hear the explosion as feel it in the pit of her stomach. Dust trickled from the ceiling. Ripples disturbed the surface of the underground lake, dispersing the reflections of their candles. She hoped civilians hadn't been caught up in the blast. Megan snorted to herself. This was the witches they were talking about. The best she could hope for was that not too many civilians had been caught up in the blast.

She nudged the dozing Damon. 'Time to go.' He looked back with sleepy eyes. 'You need a few minutes to wake up?'

'I think it's best if I'm not conscious enough to think properly about what I'm doing.'

They trudged in silence through the tunnel that led back to the palace. *You can turn round*, a voice whispered inside Megan's head. *Why risk yourself again? Go catch up with Afreyda and get the hell out of here. Why put yourself through any more?* But she had to at least try.

Her blood was pumping by the time she passed through a fireplace into a dingy chamber. Confused footsteps and blood spatters marred a dusty floor. Despite her experiences below stairs in the High Priest's palace at Eastport, Megan had been expecting the royal palace to be more impressive. The bigger the house, the more rooms to neglect.

Damon corked his flask, killing its glow. They crept out into the corridor. The first hint of dawn broke through grimy windows. Megan strained her ears. She thought she heard the distant sounds of fighting, the clang of blade hitting armour. At least the witches would be distracted. She looked back, at the escape route dug for a monarch. One last chance to use it for its intended purpose.

'What do you want to do?' asked Damon. 'Sneak about or pretend we own the place?'

Megan was jolted from her thoughts. 'I think I *do* own the place.'

'Bring the title deeds?'

'Not exactly.'

'Sneaking it is then.'

Damon's idea of sneaking proved to be nothing more than sticking close to the wall and hoping no one came past. There was a cracking sound, not as distant as she would have liked. Gunfire this time rather than gunpowder exploding. Who was firing on whom? Did she care? If Sener didn't make it back, she wouldn't have to face the possibility of breaking her promise: who knew if the Faithful would agree to the deal she'd brokered? Of course, if she didn't make it back, Sener was on his own. She looked over her shoulder the way they had come. Maybe turning back was the responsible thing.

Damon stuck a hand out and waved her into a crouch. A squad of witches stampeded across the corridor fifty yards ahead of them. Megan could do nothing about the fear she tasted, the accelerated rhythms that racked her heart. The witches had been doing this to her since she had first seen them. They had invaded her home and her nightmares, dominated her life before she even knew they existed. And she wanted to make peace with them? She gritted her teeth. *Yes*, she told herself. The priests had tried to destroy them and failed; the deal would neutralize them, remove their threat.

The last of the witches disappeared from view. None had been interested in an abandoned wing of the palace. Megan and Damon tiptoed up to the junction they had crossed. There were no more of them, which was just as well as they couldn't have failed to notice the two heads peering around the corner.

'Where now?' whispered Megan.

'Up here,' Damon whispered back. 'There's a servants' staircase.'

'Gwyneth had you using the back way?'

'I wish.'

They started up the corridor. Shadows spread fast on

the far wall. More witches approaching. They dived for the staircase, pushed themselves hard against the wall as a trio of men marched past.

'That was close,' whispered Damon. Not quite whispered enough. The receding footsteps stopped. A single pair started back, leather slapping against stone like whip cracks. Megan silently admonished Damon, who silently protested his innocence, and readied a knife.

A soldier rounded the corner. Megan slashed out. Blood sprayed the walls. 'Go!' she shouted to Damon. She struck again. This time her blade raked across the leather gauntlets the soldier held up in front of his bleeding face. Megan didn't wait to find another angle of attack. She hurtled up the stairs after the rapidly disappearing Damon.

They reached the top. Shouts and stomping came from below. A bench was shoved up against the wall. Megan made for it.

'You can't stop for a sit-down while running away,' gasped Damon.

'Help me,' said Megan, dragging it to the top of the stairs.

Damon got what she intended. He grabbed the other end. Together they heaved it down the steps. There were alarmed yells, a metallic clatter, an ugly snapping. Megan spun and bolted down the corridor. Damon yelled after her. She skidded to a halt.

'What?'

'This way.' He pointed in the opposite direction.

Megan dashed after him. He pulled her up a second staircase just as a witch staggered up from the first. His face glistened scarlet. Had he seen them? Curses, charging. That was a yes. Megan scrambled up the steep steps almost on all fours.

A grunt of exertion from behind told her what was coming. She cleared the stairs and rolled away as the witch brought his axe down. Splinters flew as it bit deep into the floorboards. The witch tried to pull the axe out. Megan kicked out, connecting with his wrist. A snort of pain, then he grabbed her ankle. Megan tried to drag herself away. The witch was too strong. He started to pull her towards him. She looked for a handhold, something to anchor herself. Nothing but bare boards. She called out to Damon, who pivoted and started to run back. The witch leered, reached for the knife stuck in his belt. Megan stopped resisting, threw herself in the witch's direction. She whipped a knife out of her sleeve as she arced around and buried it in the man's neck.

They left the witch flapping on the top of the stairs like a stranded fish and covered the rest of the way in silence, padding down the corridor and up a staircase that coiled around the tower, at the peak of which lay the royal apartments. There was a single guard on duty, his body trembling with nervous energy. He frowned when he saw Megan.

'Your Maj—?'

The momentary confusion was all Megan needed. Without breaking stride, she punched him in the face with the underside of her fist. The knife she had concealed there went straight through the man's eyeball. She pulled it out and looked away as the witch slithered to the floor.

Damon grabbed the door to Gwyneth's chamber, looked expectantly at Megan. Megan gripped her knife so hard her hand went numb. She took a couple of deep breaths and offered a prayer up to God and the Saviours. What was she asking for? Courage? Luck? Forgiveness?

She nodded at Damon. He eased the door open. Megan inched forward. Shafts of pale dawn light streamed into the room through the gaps between billowing curtains. The bed was unoccupied, the sheets a crumpled heap at its foot. Next to it was the crib Damon had mentioned. Plain wood, its varnish scratched and flaking, a cot in which had slept more than a few generations. A curiously humble choice for Gwyneth.

Megan sheathed her knife and edged across the room. Flapping and chirruping caused her to tense. Just birds on the balcony outside, fighting over early-morning spoils. The sounds of a bigger fight drifted in: men shouting, blades striking, guns rumbling. It all seemed so far away, so irrelevant, so inconsequential.

She reached the cot. There was a lump there, wrapped in blankets. Megan touched it. There was a *chink*. She froze, hand still outstretched, not quite accepting the implications of the sound, then a compulsion seized her. She ripped the blankets apart. They had covered nothing more than bottles and goblets.

A decoy for a baby. The memories, the implications, punched Megan in the heart. 'Is this some . . . ? Is this some sick joke?' she stammered, continuing to stare at the remnants of Gwyneth's last drinking session.

'What are you talking about?' said Damon. He sounded bewildered. Or like someone feigning bewilderment.

'Did you lure me here? Because of what I let Eleanor do?'

'No, Apostate,' said a new voice. A man's. 'I did.'

Despite every instinct telling her to run, Megan made herself turn round in a slow and controlled manner. Tobrytan was stood by the doorway. He drew his sword. It was sharp and heavy, the kind of weapon designed to take off limbs, wielded by the kind of person who liked to take off limbs. Megan slid out a knife. It seemed so small – she seemed so small – in comparison.

'I knew you'd come for the child,' said Tobrytan. His face hardened, if that was possible. 'What happened to my daughter?'

'Your *what*?'

'My daughter,' said Tobrytan. 'You took her prisoner. Her name's Clover.'

Megan swallowed. He was Clover's father? 'She's . . . She's dead,' she said. 'I'm sorry.'

Tobrytan looked incredulous at the apology. 'Was it you who killed her?'

'Me? No. She . . .' Megan tried to reconcile parent and child. They shared a tenacious loyalty, an arrogance born of absolute belief. 'She died helping me save Cate.'

'My daughter died for yours?'

'It was her choice.'

Damon slunk back, putting the door between him and Tobrytan. The witch general didn't spare him a second glance. Megan shifted into a fighting stance, more to give her legs something to do than any hope it'd be effective.

'You killed Eleanor, didn't you?' she said.

'The countess? It was her choice.' Tobrytan leaned forward. 'Or was it yours?'

Megan's cheeks burned. 'You don't know what you're talking about.'

'Don't I?'

'You want to avenge your daughter, I want to avenge my mother.' Megan adjusted her stance. 'Why don't we do this?'

Tobrytan took a step forward. Megan nodded at Damon, who barged the door. It smacked hard into Tobrytan who, caught off guard, stumbled and dropped his sword. Megan dived for the exit. She got within a couple of strides of freedom. The world reeled as Tobrytan charged her. She fell sprawling on to a rug. Her momentum dragged it across the floor.

Tobrytan made for his sword. Damon made a grab for him. Tobrytan threw him into the wall. Dazed, Damon staggered forward and attempted a counter-blow. Tobrytan caught the weak punch, forced Damon to his knees and slammed a knee into his chin. Damon's eyes rolled upwards. He tumbled over, hitting the floor with a sickening thud that made Tobrytan's sword jump on the floorboards.

As he bent to retrieve it Megan rolled across and slashed at his hamstrings. Blood sprayed out in a fine mist. Tobrytan grunted, kicked out blind. Megan tried to sway out of the way, but his boot still caught the side of her face, scraping her cheek and making her head spin.

The blade rushing towards her gave Megan no time to indulge her wooziness. She threw herself out of the sword's path, but she was throwing herself further into the room. Tobrytan thrust again. Megan instinctively batted the blade out of the way with her knife and scrambled backwards. She hit the bed, flipped herself over it, put its bulk between her and the witch general.

Megan caught her breath and considered her options. She had to get close to Tobrytan to deliver a fatal blow, but he knew that and had shifted to a defensive stance. He could afford to wait for her attack. Megan feinted towards the door, testing him. He shifted to block her. Pain flashed across his face as he moved. She'd hurt him more than she'd thought.

Tobrytan lunged at her. Megan whipped off the bedclothes and threw them at him. He stumbled, blinded by the sheets in his face. She leaped across the bed, aiming her knife at his head. His fist wheeled around and caught her in the temple. She went flying, careering off the bed and smacking into the floor.

The impact jolted the knife from her hand, sending it skittering across the boards. Megan scrambled for it. Tobrytan stomped behind her. She changed tack and reached for the stiletto in her boot. Tobrytan stamped on her wrist. Blinding pain flashed up her arm.

Tobrytan kicked her on to her back. He loomed over her. Megan attempted to scrabble away. He pressed a boot in her stomach, pinioning her, squeezing the breath from her body. She tried to batter his leg off her, but it was solid as a tree trunk.

Tobrytan raised his sword and prepared to bring it down. Megan tried to shield her head with her arms. She whispered apologies to Afreyda and Cate, hoped it would be quick.

Blade sliced into flesh. Blood gushed. Searing pain given voice by ear-splitting screams.

thirty-four

The sight of Tobrytan toppling towards her jolted Megan out of her shock. She rolled out of the way as his body slammed into the floor. Tobrytan continued to jerk, as if Death was playing with his victim. Blood pumped out of the gash in his neck, flowing across the boards and soaking the fringes of a nearby rug. Megan scrambled to her feet before it could touch her.

Afreyda was wiping her sword with a rag. 'What . . . ?' said Megan, trying to comprehend the situation. 'What are you doing here?'

'Wishing I had Damon's gift for sarcasm.'

Behind her, Willas and a soldier of the Faith were hauling Damon to his feet and over the bed. He shrugged. 'I've given up trying to control either of you,' he said.

'How did you find me?' asked Megan.

'We followed the bodies,' said Willas.

'I could not stand by, knowing you were in danger,' said Afreyda.

'And I couldn't stand by if she wasn't.'

'I wasn't in danger,' said Megan. Afreyda pointed her sword at Tobrytan's body, which convulsed in its death throes. 'All right, maybe a bit of danger . . .'

Afreyda swayed on her feet. Megan caught her before she could fall and led her to the bed. They sat for a moment while Afreyda gathered herself, foreheads pressed together, fingers interlocking, listening to each other's ragged breaths. If only it could always be like this, just the two of them. No pain, no fear, no war.

Willas checked the still-unconscious Damon. 'How is he?' asked Megan.

'Still breathing.'

'Anything broken?'

'His jaw, hopefully,' muttered Afreyda.

'Hard to tell,' said Willas, 'what with him not being awake to shriek in pain when we prod him.'

'Leave him there for the moment,' said Megan. She looked to Afreyda. 'He came through this time.'

'Really?'

'He tried. Which is the important thing.'

Willas wandered over to the crib. He picked up a goblet, let the sunlight glitter off the silver, and chucked it back in. 'No baby?'

Megan shook her head. 'She could be anywhere in the palace, anywhere in the—'

A sound cut her off. It was faint, but it was a sound

that made every parent anxious, that made them want to rush to its source, offer comfort and protection. As one, everyone leaned forward and stared at the floorboards.

'On the other hand,' said Megan. 'Gwyneth could just have her in the room beneath her own.'

Willas clattered down the stairs and returned a minute later. 'Definitely a baby in there,' he said. 'Door's locked though.' He pointed at a soldier. 'Grab an axe. Start breaking it down.'

'Axe, sir?'

'They come attached to a dead witch.'

Megan regarded the door of Gwyneth's chamber, which made the average city gate look like a gossamer curtain. No one could accuse Edwyn the Third of being inconsistent in his paranoia. If the door to the room below was anything like it, it would take forever to get through.

'There's got to be another way,' she said.

'Damon could pick the lock,' said Afreyda.

Damon wasn't capable of doing anything at that moment. Megan looked around Gwyneth's room, searching for inspiration. The curtains billowing in from the open windows gave her an idea. She went over to them. There was a balcony, littered with the fragments of a broken bottle, dark red staining the stone. *An angry drunk are you, Gwyneth?* Megan stepped out and leaned over the edge, getting a little dizzy from the height. She straightened back up, took a breath to steady herself and leaned over again. There was another balcony directly below.

'What is it?' said Willas, hurrying over.

Megan didn't have time for the inevitable argument. She swung over the edge of the balcony, dangled for a moment, and jumped.

The drop was further than she'd estimated. The impact jarred her ankles and knees like a volley of hammers. She lay on the stone, waiting for the throbbing to subside, ignoring the cursing aimed in her direction from the balcony above. Movement in the chamber beyond interrupted her recovery. Someone was rushing for the windows. A woman in white. *Is it you?*

Megan snapped a hand out, flinging the windows into the face of the woman. The woman staggered backwards, arms flailing. Megan scrambled to her feet and stumbled across the threshold. It was gloomy inside. Her eyes took a moment to adjust. When they did, she could see the woman wasn't Gwyneth, but someone older – thirty, perhaps – in a loose gown and with a face that might be considered homely if Megan hadn't smashed a window frame into it.

Squalling from the bed grabbed Megan's attention. A baby in distress, limbs lashing out as if fighting some unseen monster. Megan took a step towards her. The woman dashed to block her way.

'You're her nurse?' said Megan. The woman wiped blood from her nose and nodded. 'You know who I am?'

'The Apostate. The fake queen. The denier of the Saviours. The one for whom God is preparing a special place in hell.'

'I'll take that as a yes.' Megan looked across to the baby, who looked so much like Cate it made her heart ache. Their fathers had been siblings as well as their mothers. 'She's my family. She's coming with me.'

'You will not take her.'

'There's nothing you ca—'

The vase smashed into Megan's temple before she had a chance to react. She staggered back, head spinning, blood streaming down her face from a dozen cuts. How could she have been so stupid as to underestimate the woman after everything she had been through?

Floorboards rattled as the nurse ran across the room. Megan groped for a knife to defend herself with, but there was no attack. She tried to blink the tears away, regain her vision.

'You can't escape,' she said between winces, everything still a blur. 'I have soldiers stationed outside.'

There was a hiss. A pungent smell filled the air. Escape wasn't the plan either. That was gunpowder. Saviours, the nurse was going to blow them all to God.

Still half blind, Megan dashed across the room. She could make out the nurse kneeling, powder spilling out of a barrel and on to her gown, sparks as she struck a knife against flint. Megan dived at her. The nurse cried out as their bodies collided. She lashed out. More blood spurted down the side of Megan's head. She groped behind, caught the woman's knife hand, smashed it against the floor until she released the weapon.

The woman wheeled her other arm around, smashing the flint into Megan's cheek. The flat side fortunately. It was still enough to send stars exploding in front of Megan's eyes, to make her want to vomit.

'You will not take the Saviour,' the woman spat in her face.

Megan thrust her forehead into the woman's nose. Cartilage crumpled under the force.

The woman dropped the flint and staggered backwards, clutching her bleeding nose. Megan made to snatch the flint. Too fast. Dizziness overwhelmed her. She lost her footing, hit the floor with a thud that knocked the energy out of her.

The woman was crawling by her side, scrabbling for the flint. Megan flung her arm around, sweeping the woman's supporting arm from under her. The woman dropped. For a moment the two of them lay there, looking across the floor at each other like post-coital lovers, then the woman lunged at Megan.

Nails slashed at her face like claws. Megan tried to smack her hands away with one hand while the other fumbled for a knife. She found an empty scabbard. The woman dug into her cheek and tore. Four lines of pain seared into Megan. She stretched down to her boot. Fingers wrapped around polished wood warmed by body heat. She yanked the stiletto out, whipped her arm around, buried the blade deep into the woman's side. There was a shocked gasp, then the woman went limp.

Thumping at the door. With the last of her strength Megan crawled over to it, turned the key in the lock, slid back the heavy bolts. Willas and Afreyda burst in.

'What the . . . ?'

'Staff problems,' gasped Megan.

Afreyda didn't look impressed by Megan's attempt to downplay what had just happened. She knelt down in front of Megan and examined her with not quite the tenderness she had hoped for.

'Just cuts,' Afreyda said stiffly. 'They will need washing, but you will live. Sometimes I am not sure you deserve it.'

'She was going to blow us up,' said Megan, pointing at the heap of gunpowder.

'You knew that when you jumped out the window?'

'Not exactly . . .'

They retreated to a room without its own corpse,

not a requirement as easy to satisfy as it should have been. Afreyda checked Megan's injuries while Willas took charge of the wailing baby, scooping her up into his bear-like embrace and rocking her. She settled down. He cooed at her, as delighted as if she was his own.

Willas caught Megan and Afreyda's bemused glances. 'I look after Rekka's children sometimes,' he said. 'What are you naming this one?'

Megan winced as Afreyda picked a shard of pottery from her cheek. 'Naming? I . . . I hadn't thought about it.' She supposed she couldn't keep calling her 'Gwyneth's baby', and Jolecia was out of the question for obvious reasons.

'Eleanor,' said Afreyda. She looked up at Megan. 'Unless you . . .'

Megan's throat tightened. She remembered that last desperate day in Staziker, the crushing despair as Eleanor had left for the last time, but then she remembered all the times the countess had been there for her, all the way back to that day in a Thicketford field when she had rescued Megan from the witches, and her heart swelled.

'No,' she said. 'It's perfect.'

There was a commotion out in the corridor: shouts, arguing, the drawing of weapons. Willas twisted, putting his bulk between baby Eleanor and the door, and felt for his sword. Afreyda unsheathed her own weapon and hurried out into the corridor. Megan slipped out a knife and dithered, torn between backing up Afreyda and staying to defend her niece.

'It is fine,' said Afreyda. 'Let him in.' Clomping. '*Just* him.'

Sener marched into the room, bruised, battered and bloodied. What looked to be bits of people were smeared across his armour. The witches were as committed to betrayal as everything else, it would seem.

'Well?' said Megan.

'It's done,' said Sener. 'Apart from Tobrytan. We can't find him.'

Megan jerked a thumb at Afreyda. 'Dealt with,' she said. 'What about . . . ?'

'The bitch –' even after everything, Megan flinched at the denigration of her sister – 'has retreated to the throne room with the last of those loyal to her.' Sener sneered. 'And there weren't many to start with. We'll soon have her.'

Gwyneth was still here, so close, and soon she'd be butchered by her own men. She deserved it oh so much, but that didn't stop the ache in Megan's soul, the wish the two of them could be sisters again.

'Not yet,' said Megan. 'I need to talk to her.'

Afreyda gave her a despairing look. 'Megan . . .'

'I need to see her, I need to ask why, I need to hear an honest answer, I need to hear her beg for forgiveness;

I might even need to grant it. There's no danger; it'll just be me and her.'

'And me.'

'You still need time to recover.'

Afreyda brushed Megan's cut cheek, making her wince. 'And you don't?'

thirty-five

They needed gunpowder to deal with the doors of the throne room and a short but bloody fight in the dust clouds to deal with the last of Gwyneth's men. Megan held back on Willas's orders, squeezing Afreyda's hand, wanting this to be all over but also reluctant to let go. The fight against Gwyneth and the witches had defined her for so long. Would she be able to adjust once it was ended?

Finally Willas beckoned Megan and Afreyda forward. They stepped into the throne room. Megan thought she'd be more impressed. This was the place her predecessors had been crowned, but it was just ridiculously oversized, the walls of marble and glass and now-flaking gilt nothing more than an ostentatious reminder of how much wealth the monarchs had sequestered and wasted. And here she was, the last of those monarchs who had basked in the reflected glory of the Unifier, the reflection dimmer in each successive generation. She felt no connection to those who had once ruled from here: no pride in their deeds, no shame in their sins. It wasn't her adoption – blood was as artificial a bond as the law – it was the centuries that divided them. She was not them and they were not her. They didn't confer legitimacy, nor did they deny it. Only the personal mattered, her own actions. Megan had fought for her position; she could be proud of Afreyda and Eleanor and the others who had been with her; she had to be ashamed of what her sister had done.

Soldiers from all ranks – witches, Hilites, the Faith – lined the walls. Rather less attentive, a similar mix lined the floors, blood oozing from their bodies and colouring the tiles. And there, sat on the steps in front of the throne, her legs tucked underneath her, was Gwyneth. Megan shivered. The chill of the early morning, she told herself, but she knew it was so much more.

Another girl – their age – was knelt behind Gwyneth, braiding her hair. Trembling fingers let strands escape and settle back on to Gwyneth's neck. Tears had smudged the girl's make-up and left dirty black smears under her eyes. Gwyneth herself, however, was perfectly serene. It could be a couple of years ago; the girl doing her hair could be Megan; the preparation for nothing more than a party in the village.

'You're meant to curtsy,' said Gwyneth.

'I was about to say the same to you,' said Megan. 'Accept it, Gwyn, you've lost. I have guns, your allies, even some of your own men. I have your daughter.' Gwyneth flushed at the last; there was some emotion then. 'It's time to surrender.'

'That's it, is it, Meg? You've come to gloat?' Gwyneth craned her neck around. 'She was like this when we played games as a kid, Taite. A terrible winner.'

'And you were always a terrible loser. You can't escape what you've done.'

'What I've done?'

'All the people you have killed,' said Megan. 'They deserve justice.'

'*They* deserve justice?' said Gwyneth. She threw her hands in the air so violently Taite had to duck to avoid being hit. 'What about the tens of thousands of True the priests slaughtered? What about all those who burned in Trafford's Haven? A whole city. Do they not deserve justice? That's what I was bringing to Werlavia. That and peace and faith and truth and God's love. And what do you do? Betray the teachings of the Saviours and sell us out to the barbarians.'

Megan endured the dramatics with a stony face. 'Nice speech. I assume you had a team of writers prepare it for you.'

'Nice sneering. I assume you had a team of priests school you in the art.'

Gwyneth wasn't entirely wrong – if she had been, Megan could hardly have come to a deal with Sener – and doubt scraped Megan's soul. It was all too easy to wrap base desires in abstract concepts, claim what you did was

418

for justice or God or the people. In the end, only history and your own conscience could judge.

'Take the men, captain,' she said to Willas. 'Secure the city before they can start rioting. Signal the rest of the company. Dispatch messengers to Janik and Hil.'

'You know she's armed, right?'

'It doesn't matter,' said Megan. She had seen the knife by Gwyneth's side – all gold-plating and diamond-encrusted hilt – and already dismissed it. Form over function, little threat. 'Go on, captain.' She pointed at Gwyneth's companion. 'And take her with you.'

'She stays,' said Gwyneth. 'My hair – still not right.'

Willas cocked his head. Megan nodded. He signalled to the men. They marched out of the throne room, the clomp of their boots echoing around the vast chamber. Then they were gone and there was silence.

Keeping her eyes on Gwyneth, Megan stretched down and slid a stiletto from her boot. Sharp, slender. If it came to it – *If? Who was she kidding?* – it would be quick, clean. Gwyneth would hardly feel it. The wound would leave but a small stain on her gown.

She took a single step towards her sister. Fear, reluctance, childhood memories made her stop. Afreyda drew her sword and advanced with her. Taite let out a sob and fumbled Gwyneth's hair. The braid unravelled.

'Oh, for Saviours' sake,' muttered Gwyneth. She batted Taite away. 'Meg, would you?'

'Do you regret anything you've done?'

'How can you regret following God's commands?'

'Not even Grandfather?'

Gwyneth looked away. 'He was an old man . . .'

Another hint of feeling, a hint of wistfulness, the tiniest sliver of humanity. 'Give up, Gwyn, please. Renounce the claim our children are the Saviours.'

'Or what?' demanded Gwyneth. Megan's gaze flicked down to the knife in her hand. 'You expect me to be scared of that? I am the Mother of the Saviour. God will protect me.'

'He's been strangely absent so far,' said Megan. The palace shuddered. Gwyneth looked smug. 'That was gunfire.'

Gwyneth shook her hair out. 'You don't understand the nature of God, Meg. He does not communicate via floods or bolts of lightning or plagues of locusts. He acts through His chosen ones, instructs them, guides them. He formed our nature to best do His work. He sent the Saviours back as children because He knew nothing would better protect them than a mother's love.' She jabbed a finger down the aisle. 'Or a father's.'

Megan turned. Damon was stood by the remains of the battered doors. He was pale and woozy, unsteady on his feet.

And he was aiming a crossbow at Megan.

*

'Damon? What the hell?'

'I can't let you kill her, Megan.'

'At the risk of repeating myself, what the hell?'

Megan looked back to Gwyneth, at the nascent smirk tugging the corners of her mouth. *Father . . . ?* No. Not that. Anything but that. The thought made her dizzy, nauseated, violated.

'She's carrying my child,' said Damon. 'I can't let you harm it.'

'How could . . . how could . . . ? I trusted you.'

'Did you?'

'Not to do that anyway. Not with *her*.'

Damon's aim wavered. He kicked some splinters of the battered door out of the way and steadied himself. 'I didn't have much of a choice. Like now.'

Afreyda raised her sword and advanced on Damon, her path putting her in between his crossbow and Megan. 'You will have to go through me.'

'Do you think that bothers me?'

'It will when Megan slits your throat while you are busy reloading.'

A voice echoed through the ages. *Who threatens two people with a one-shot weapon?* 'Step out of the way, Afreyda. If he wants to shoot me, he can try. It won't make any difference. What has to be done will be done, whether you do it or I do it.' Afreyda shuffled out of the way a fraction.

'She's using you like she used me,' Megan said to

421

Damon. 'Like she uses everyone. What do you think's going to happen? You're going to retire to Percadia and play unhinged families? You don't have to do this. You don't have to prove anything to me. Or Eleanor.'

'This isn't about her.'

'No. *She* was worth it.'

There was a tutting behind Megan. Gwyneth glided down the aisle, arms tucked in her sleeves like a bride. Taite remained on the bare steps, head swinging round, looking for a way out. Megan jerked her head. Taite took the hint and fled, disappearing into an antechamber.

'Let me take her, Megan,' said Damon. 'At least until the baby's born. After that . . .'

'Is that all I am to you?' said Gwyneth. 'A walking womb?'

'You really have no concept of hypocrisy do you, Gwyn?'

'We can be together,' Damon said to Gwyneth. He looked to Megan. 'If you'll let us.'

'You really do want to . . . ? After everything she . . . ?'

'I'm not saying it's going to be the perfect marriage . . .'

'Ma——?' Megan choked on the word.

'Child needs its parents,' said Gwyneth.

'No,' said Megan. 'You have to pay for what you did.'

'Isn't a lifetime with me punishment enough?' said Damon.

She looked to Afreyda who, after a pause, gave a

reluctant nod. Gwyneth leaned into Megan and pressed their cheeks together. The contact both repulsed and comforted Megan. When was the last time she had touched her sister? That terrible night in Eastport? Megan could only remember pain and confusion and panic.

'Accept it,' whispered Gwyneth, 'you've lost. You can't take everything from me.'

Megan bowed her head, trying to work out what to do, whether surrendering Gwyneth to Damon was the right thing to do or an abnegation of her responsibilities. How many enemies had she pardoned and accepted? Couldn't she manage one final one? But could she risk leaving Gwyneth alive and unrepentant, able to recruit followers?

A trickle of dark liquid ran along the edge of Megan's sole. She crouched down for a closer look. Was that . . . ? She stretched out and dabbed it with the tip of her finger. It was. She turned to Gwyneth, meaning to look her in the eye, but her gaze got no further than the spots of scarlet blossoming beneath the waist of her sister's gown.

The others had seen it, too. There was a crash as the crossbow slipped from Damon's fingers. Gwyneth backed off, her eyes wide with shock, leaving a thin trail of blood in her wake.

'I'm losing it?' she cried.

'Was there anything to lose?' said Megan, rising to

her feet. 'You sure you're not just getting your period, Gwyn?'

'This is all your fault!'

Megan had been expecting the strike ever since she'd noticed the knife missing from the steps in front of the throne and Gwyneth's clumsy attempts to keep her hands hidden, but she hadn't been expecting the sheer hatred in her sister's eyes. Sunlight glazed off polished steel as the blade hurtled towards her. There was no finesse to the lunge, but it had all of Gwyneth's fury behind it.

Instinct took over, instinct created and honed by the ordeals Megan had endured at her sister's hands. She sidestepped the blow and thrust forward with her own knife. The slender blade pierced flesh oh-so-easily, before Megan had conscious thought of what she was doing.

Gwyneth staggered backwards, clutching her stomach. She grabbed the knife, made to pull it out. Someone warned her not to – Damon, Afreyda, maybe even Megan herself. Gwyneth ignored them. The blade came out with a wet smack and a spurt of blood. More blood followed. Gwyneth tried to stem the flow, but it forced its way through her fingers and dripped to the floor.

Megan knew she should do something: staunch the wound, finish Gwyneth off, comfort her in her last moments. She could do nothing but remain rooted to the spot. Emptiness numbed her. She felt neither satisfaction nor grief, just an ill-defined nothingness.

Gwyneth was pale now. Her legs gave way. Her gasp as she hit the floor jolted Megan into movement. Gwyneth held out a hand. Dismissing not beckoning. Megan froze. Gwyneth raised her head, stared at Megan through the bedraggled curtain of her hair.

'My sisters will be born again.'

With that, Gwyneth crumpled. Nothing to stop her, Megan ran to her, the tears filling her eyes for the girl she had once been if not the woman she had become.

thirty-six

A knock prompted Megan to look up from changing Cate. 'Come in.'

Father Galan eased his bulk into the room. Access to unrationed food these past few weeks had allowed him to fill out again. 'They're ready for you, Your Majesty.' He nodded at Synne, who was sat on the couch bouncing baby Eleanor on her knee, then cocked his head and regarded Cate. 'Is that really the best use for the Supreme Priest's desk?'

Megan thought it best not to tell him what she'd scrubbed off it an hour earlier. 'I'm sure she's not the first girl who's been laid on it.'

'Quite.'

Megan had commandeered the Supreme Priest's quarters in the temple as it was the only place in New Statham she could be sure hadn't been tainted by the witches. She thought being close to God might help her find forgiveness, but whether she was praying with five thousand others, or alone at night when she had the temple steps to herself and stared up at the stars in vain search of a divine presence, she found herself no closer to knowing His will. She would have to find peace within herself, and deal with God in the afterlife.

She finished tying up Cate's nappy and sat her on the couch next to Synne. 'I'll be back soon. Are we all packed?'

'Yes, ma'am.'

'I think you can stop calling me that now.'

Father Galan led Megan through the temple, his sandals slapping against the dusty stone. 'Are you sure about this?' he said. 'It's not too late.'

'I'm sure,' said Megan. 'Did you sort out a constitution?'

'We have the basis for one.'

'And . . . ?'

'Every man who has reached his majority –' Megan glared at Father Galan – 'and every woman, will elect town elders who in turn will elect county governors who in their turn will elect a Secretary of the Realm.'

'And the priests?'

'We will be available as . . . advisors.'

And in control of the bureaucracy. Megan knew from dealing with Fordel how much power that conveyed, but she didn't have a choice: the priests were the only ones capable of administering the Realm. At least the people now had *some* say, something to build on.

'Do you think I'm doing the right thing, father?'

'I think you're creating a system perfect for bribery, back-stabbing and bickering.'

'Is that a yes?'

Father Galan stopped, took Megan by the shoulders. 'My child, we will be at the mercy of scores of petty princes each of whom will think they have the greatest legitimacy, the very thing the Unifier fought to protect us from. The Realm will not stand the pressure. It will fracture within decades.'

'You don't know that,' said Megan. 'The Snow Cities have been allied for centuries.'

'Because they had a greater enemy to defend themselves against.'

'If the Realm fractures, so be it. Does it really matter if people are governed from New Statham or Eastport or Thicketford?'

'If we had a strong monarch . . .'

'No,' said Megan. 'People rebel even against strong monarchs and I will not start a war to preserve my own power.'

'And what about the Diannon Emperor?' said Father Galan. 'The witches were only his first move. He will come again.'

'And we'll be ready for him, whether the Realm is in one piece or a dozen. Have faith in the people, father. Don't fear the worst all the time. Allow yourself to hope for the best once in a while.'

It was a speech aimed more at herself than the priest. Megan couldn't help fearing she was abandoning the people, destroying the legacy of the Unifier, but she couldn't let herself become a tyrant. It was presumptuous to believe she was the only one who could protect the Realm. There were millions out there as good as her – time for a few to stand up. And time for her to go home.

Megan and Father Galan stepped out of the temple and into the glare of the afternoon sun. A squad of soldiers was waiting for her, their captain resplendent in her new uniform. Megan smiled at the woman she'd fallen in love with, resisted the urge to kiss her. She was slave to protocol for a little while longer.

The squad fell in behind them as they set off across Saviours' Square, through the corridor in the crowd formed by a column of city guards. Faces turned to follow Megan's progress, neighbours barged out of the way, children held up above the forest of heads, all wanting to get a glimpse of the last queen. What did they think of what had happened, what did they think of her? Did they think she was deserting them or were they glad to be rid of her and her whole damned family?

'Any sign of . . . ?' she asked Afreyda, who shook her head.

'I can ask my successor to step up the search.'

'No point.' In a city packed with thieves and conmen, there was little chance of finding Damon if he didn't want to be found. And given the numbers streaming in and out of the capital in recent weeks, it would have been easy for him to slip away if he'd wanted to.

Trestle tables protected by a flapping canopy had been erected outside the doors of the palace. The original plan had been to hold the ceremony in the throne room, but there was no way Megan wanted to step in there again, so instead they were to do it outside, where everyone could see. The great and the good and the pushy were mingling about: the new Supreme Priest, Grandfather Kimball, Brother Broose almost literally chewing his ear; Fordel and Rekka to represent the Snow Cities, with Willas in close attendance; Prince Y'donno, officially instated as the Andaluvians' ambassador to the Realm, his robes occasionally catching the wind and smacking the other guests in the face; Sener, fresh bruises and a limp indicating the witches hadn't been entirely forgiven yet; and numerous other priests and self-important citizens whose involvement in the war had been very behind the scenes.

Pleasantries were exchanged, greetings murmured, small talk offered up about the weather and the New Statham traffic. Fordel tried to catch Megan's eye. Megan tried to pretend she hadn't seen him, but he approached anyway, grabbing a pair of drinks on the way. He handed one to Megan, clinking her glass before she had any opportunity to reject the toast.

'Looks like you won, Your Majesty.'

'The Faith's scientists report good progress making gunpowder.'

'I heard the explosions,' said Fordel. 'I hope no one was hurt.'

'Nothing that can't be sewn back on.'

Fordel took a deep draught of wine and swept his hand around the square. 'This could have been ours,' he said.

'I was never interested in having it,' said Megan. 'Admit it, it's better this way. You'd only be fighting insurrections and rebellions for the rest of your life.'

'Maybe.'

Megan's gaze fell on Rekka and Willas. He was stroking Rekka's cheek. She took his hand and pressed it against her face, leaning into it like it was a pillow.

'I never thanked you for looking after him, did I?' said Fordel.

'Think it was the other way round.'

'And now you're taking him away.'

Willas had stuck to his plan and decided to settle in the Realm. 'He's a grown man,' she said. 'It's his choice.' She took a sip of wine – Saviours, it was strong. She felt light-headed. 'You should retire too. Settle down with Ími and his experiments.'

Fordel gave her a smile that wasn't totally devoid of humour. 'One day maybe.'

Grandfather Kimball finally broke free of Brother Broose and bustled over. He was carrying a wicker basket filled with purple lumps, which he presented to Megan with obvious pride.

'A gift from the people of Levenport, Your Majesty.'

Megan wondered what she'd done to offend them. 'Er, thanks,' she said. 'I'm sure the kids'll find some use for them.'

'They're aubergines, ma'am,' said Grandfather Kimball. He caught Megan's blank expression. 'You eat them.'

'Willingly?'

Grandfather Kimball looked indignant. 'Just kidding,' said Megan. She handed the basket to Afreyda, whose look didn't exactly shout joy, then clapped her hands. 'Right, let's get on with this. Where are these papers I have to sign?'

Grandfather Kimball led her to the table. Three parchments were laid out there, their ends weighed down with stones. They each said the same thing:

I, Megan of the house of Endalay, Queen of the Realm, Countess of Ainsworth, Baroness of Laxton and Herth, First Lady of Kirkland, Overlord of the Spice Isles and Defender of the Southern Lands, do hereby declare My irrevocable determination to renounce the Throne and all Titles for Myself and for My descendants, and My desire that effect should be given to this Instrument of Abdication immediately.

'Sign anywhere, ma'am,' said Grandfather Kimball. 'An "X" will do if you can't write.'

Megan flashed him a dirty look and scratched her name underneath the text. Grandfather Kimball added his own signature then passed it down to Father Galan for him to witness. The process was repeated twice more. At the end of it Megan felt no different. There was no let-up in the pressure on her soldiers, no relief in her sorrow. It would take more than a few scrawls to accomplish that.

'Anything else?'

'No,' said Grandfather Kimball. He then pointedly added, 'Megan.'

That was it then. Megan might need time to adjust, but others were more flexible. She waved a finger back towards the temple. 'I'll just be heading—'

Afreyda barked out an order. To a man, their escort swivelled towards Megan and saluted. Then Afreyda did the same, and then Willas, and then Father Galan, then before Megan knew it everyone in the vast crowd was saluting her, the action forming huge waves in the crowds, and she could do nothing more than clasp her hands to her face and let the tears flow.

epilogue

Megan was wiping dough from the girls' hands when the figures darkened her doorway, silhouettes picked out by a fiery halo. For a moment she thought they were the Saviours, come to admonish her for her actions. Then they stepped inside the mill and she recognized Willas and someone she thought she'd never see again.

'Found this lurking in the village,' said Willas, dragging his companion forward.

'I wasn't lurking, I was looking for somewhere to tie up my horse. A quarter-shilling they were charging at the inn.'

'Rebuilding levy. He says he wants to speak to you. Want me to stick around?'

'No, that's fine, cap—' old habits died hard – 'that's fine, Willas.'

The former soldier nodded. He knotted his fingers, looking apprehensive. 'Was there something else?' asked Megan.

'Synne wants to know if you and Afreyda'll come to dinner sometime. She – we – have something to tell you.'

'We'd love to,' said Megan. 'Once I've dealt with . . .'

Willas nodded again and left, leaving behind an awkwardness that was almost palpable. Megan gave her visitor an awkward smile and turned her attention back to Cate and Eleanor, attacking their encrusted skin with renewed vigour.

'Bit young for baking, aren't they?'

'They like to "help",' said Megan. 'What're you doing here?'

'Came to see how you were doing.'

'Really?'

'Yes, really,' said Damon. He picked up a scrap of dough and rolled it between his finger and thumb. 'So . . . how are you doing?'

'Good.'

There was an awkward silence. 'This is the bit where you ask how I am.'

'I know.'

'So . . . ?'

Afreyda stalked into the kitchen. A tool belt hung where a sword belt once had, though the hammer she grasped was in no way an ineffective weapon. Damon gave her a wave; in return she scowled at him.

'What is he doing here?'

'It's all right, Afreyda,' said Megan.

435

'Have you forgotten that the last time you saw him he was aiming a crossbow at you?'

Megan sighed. 'No, but we agreed to leave everything behind. And that means everything.'

She wiped her hands clean of the dough the girls had transferred to her. 'Can you look after Cate and Eleanor for a bit?'

'Of course,' said Afreyda.

'Thanks.' Megan motioned to Damon. 'We'll go for a walk.'

She led him out of the mill and down the path that led to Thicketford, a path that took them past the graves of her grandfather and the girls' fathers. Megan hardly noticed them any more, but Damon made the sign of the circle. *Bit late for respect*, thought Megan, but she said nothing.

'What are you going to tell the girls about them?' asked Damon, indicating the graves.

'The truth,' said Megan. 'We both know the trouble the alternative causes, however well intentioned.'

'And Gwyneth's daughter?' said Damon. 'You're going to tell her you . . . ?'

'Killed her mother?' Megan hung her head, Gwyneth's last moments playing in her mind. She wondered if she'd ever be rid of the memory, or the guilt. 'Yes, I'll tell Eleanor. And she might hate me for it. But better to be hated for the truth than loved for a lie.'

They reached the ford. There had been little need for

it since the bridge had been reconstructed but something made Megan edge down the bank to the river. Damon hung back.

'Looks wet,' he said, screwing up his face. 'And muddy.'

'Scared you'll get your fancy new clothes dirty?' said Megan. Damon was wearing the kinds of fine silks and soft leathers normally found on rich merchants. 'I'm sure you'll be able to steal some more.'

'Hey, I bought these. I'm a legitimate businessman now.'

'Really?'

Damon nodded. 'Andaluvian spice trade,' he said. 'We're breaking the monopoly of the Spice Islands.'

'You're growing spices?'

'Not exactly,' said Damon. 'I suppose you'd say I'm a facilitator between producer and consumer.'

'You skim off both sides, in other words.'

'Legitimate commissions.'

'The more you use the word "legitimate",' said Megan, 'the more I suspect it's code for something else. Take your boots off. No one's going to steal them.'

Damon looked around, then did as she suggested, tucking the footwear in the undergrowth. They waded across. The icy waters of the Heledor were refreshing against Megan's sunburned legs; she had yet to adjust to summer in her homeland after her time in wintry lands.

She looked across the wheat fields. Banging sounded from the village, houses being repaired and rebuilt. Willas and Synne weren't the only ones who had returned with them. Other refugees had been drawn to Thicketford, attracted either by her mystique or the availability of free land. They had felt like intruders at first, but Megan had grown to accept them, appreciate the life they brought back to the village.

Damon stood a few feet off, seemingly reluctant to get closer. 'Do you think she really was pregnant?'

'Does it matter?' said Megan. 'Either way, that child wasn't meant to be.'

'God's will, huh?'

'People are too keen to see God's will in things. It helps them abdicate responsibility.'

'Do you blame me for what I did?' said Damon. 'What I tried to do, anyway?'

'I don't know,' said Megan. 'I probably would have done the same thing. Probably did do the same thing, somewhere along the line.' She sighed. 'What're your plans now?'

'Head down to Trafford's Haven. The Sandstriders have set up a staging post there. Get a boat there to Andaluvia.'

'Long way to Trafford's Haven.'

'According to my guidebook, there's an inn on the road south,' said Damon. 'I'll stop there for the night.'

'I really wouldn't recommend it,' said Megan. 'Stop with us.'

'You sure?'

'No, but . . . You can tell Eleanor about her namesake.'

'Is she old enough to understand?'

No, but I am.

Megan held out a hand. After a moment's hesitation, Damon took it.

the end

acknowledgements

It's almost four years since I started sketching out the notes for what became *True Fire*; it's been an odd time since. Now we're at the end, I have a few people to thank: my agent, Claire Wilson, who has provided much-needed guidance over the course of the trilogy; my editor Rachel Faulkner, who probably had no idea what she was getting into; editor in abstentia Sarah Lambert; Talya Baker, for much wise copy-editing; the Coven for their continued support, especially Alexia Casale, Alice Oseman and Mel Salisbury; Sarah Sky, for putting up with my moaning and bad jokes; various Wikipedia contributors without whom I would have had to do proper research; and my family – Tom, Mum, Dad, Lyndsay, Peter, Gary, Natalie, Abigail and Cody – for being there.

about the author

Gary Meehan was born in Bolton in Lancashire and was educated at Lincoln College, Oxford, the University of Aberdeen and the University of Warwick. When he's not writing, he works as a software engineer in Derby, where he lives with his son.